# "I'm here for you, Charly. Tell me how to help."

"Who the hell are you?"

"It's me, Will Chase. Were you expecting someone else?"

Yeah, she was expecting one of the bad guys. She still expected one or all of them to burst out of the night and attack. "You're working for them."

"Absolutely not. I'm on your side. You have to believe that."

She did. On instinct, she did believe him. Though she didn't understand how it was possible for him to be here.

"Charly, sit down here beside me."

"We're not safe here."

"Sure we are."

She shook her head, wobbling a bit. Shivering, she didn't protest when he put her back into her polar-fleece coat and wrapped an arm around her waist. She felt the weight of her revolver in her pocket. If he was with the bad guys, he wouldn't let her keep her weapons. He gui͏͏ ͏͏ ͏͏ ͏͏ ͏͏ ͏͏ ͏͏ ͏͏ ͏͏ ͏͏ ͏͏ ͏͏ ͏͏ ͏͏ lter of an overhang and helped

Her body recognize

obstinately. Relaxir

head drop to his sho

D0813924

# HEART OF
# A HERO

BY
DEBRA WEBB
& REGAN BLACK

Published in Great Britain 2015
by Mills & Boon, an imprint of Harlequin (UK) Limited,
Eton House, 18-24 Paradise Road, Richmond, Surrey, TW9 1SR

© 2015 Debra Webb

ISBN: 978-0-263-25295-8

46-0215

Harlequin (UK) Limited's policy is to use papers that are natural, renewable and recyclable products and made from wood grown in sustainable forests. The logging and manufacturing processes conform to the legal environmental regulations of the country of origin.

Printed and bound in Spain
by CPI, Barcelona

**Debra Webb,** born in Alabama, wrote her first story at age nine and her first romance at thirteen. It wasn't until she spent three years working for the military behind the Iron Curtain—and a five-year stint with NASA—that she realized her true calling. Since then the *USA TODAY* bestselling author has penned more than one hundred novels, including her internationally bestselling Colby Agency series.

**Regan Black**, a *USA TODAY* bestselling author, writes award-winning, action-packed novels featuring kick-butt heroines and the sexy heroes who fall in love with them. Raised in the Midwest and California, she and her family, along with their adopted greyhound, two arrogant cats and a quirky finch, reside in the South Carolina Lowcountry, where the rich blend of legend, romance and history fuels her imagination.

From Regan: To Jordan, for being my brilliant, beautiful star. Your wisdom and compassion are as wide as the sky and your future as limitless.

# Chapter One

*Washington, DC*
*Tuesday, February 3, 2:50 p.m.*

"I'm in. But I'm not wearing the shorts."

Director Thomas Casey eyed William Chase, one of the newest recruits to his team known as the Specialists. He respected independent thinkers. Went out of his way to select highly skilled individuals who knew how to solve problems quickly and creatively. Still, it was rare when anyone on his handpicked team showed this kind of attitude. Maybe he'd made a mistake with this cocky young guy fresh from an elite Navy SEAL team.

"A uniform is a uniform," Thomas said, keeping his voice even.

"That's true, sir," Will agreed. "And it should convey authority."

Thomas couldn't believe he was having this discussion with so many bigger issues at play. "You'll have time to come to terms with how the US Postal Service conveys authority in Colorado before the weather warms up out there." He wanted someone on his new task force planted in the middle of the country. Someone who could respond effectively to a variety of situations.

"Shorts are for kids and physical training. Are you going to pull me off this operation if I don't wear the shorts?"

Thomas reached out and closed the plain manila file outlining Will's assignment. *Potential assignment.* It could've been worse, Thomas supposed. He could be having this conversation in a public setting rather than the absolute privacy of his office. He couldn't get a read on whether or not Will was kidding around. The uncertainty and unease set off warning bells in his head. He considered asking why the shorts were such a big deal and decided it didn't matter. Through the years, he'd worked with so many men and women, those who did the impossible tasks in the field and those who worked right here supporting them. Eventually his luck with recruiting was bound to run out. One more sign that it was time to retire and put his personal life, his hopes for a family, ahead of the nation's problems. But his nation needed him, had demanded his expertise one last time. If he assembled the right team, he could walk away with confidence.

"I've changed my mind, Will. You're not the right man for this job after all."

"Because I won't deliver mail in those ridiculous shorts?"

Thomas drummed his fingers on the file, met Will's stony gaze. This recruit might be a bit too independent. "Because you're agitated over a small conformity issue and that makes me question what you'll do when the stakes are higher."

"Agitated is a bit of a stretch." The smile on Will's face didn't reach his serious eyes. "You have to agree every postman who complies with that dress code is nothing more than a sheep."

"Thank you for your time," Thomas said, determined to go with a different Specialist for this post.

Will didn't budge. "Forget the shorts. Forget agitated. You saw this one—" he pointed to the folder "—whatever it is, and chose me because I succeed, *always*, when the stakes are highest."

"I was wrong," Thomas said with a casual hitch of his shoulders. "It happens. Close the door on your way out."

"No, sir. I want this assignment."

Thomas laughed. Couldn't stop it. *No one* gave him this much trouble, other than his wife, and that had been long before they married. He shouldn't find it refreshing. "You think you know how far you can push me?"

"No, sir. I know how far I can push myself."

"From my perspective you can't push yourself far enough to comply with the basic standards of your operation."

"The shorts are irrelevant, in any circumstance. You need someone willing to dig in for the long haul. Colorado was built by rugged individuals who don't see conformity as strength. They value independence and wide-open spaces and they respect people with conviction."

"So this conversation was your attempt at an audition?" Thomas wasn't laughing now. "That's not how we do things here."

"It's how they do things there." Will's eyes, intent and serious, underscored his point.

Thomas turned to his computer monitor and adjusted his glasses, going over Will's service record one more time. "Tell me what happened at Christmas."

Will didn't evade or protest, didn't get defensive or make excuses. No sign of agitation or argument now.

Easing back into the chair, he smoothed his relaxed hands over his thighs. "Not much typically happens in the way of celebrating Christmas in Afghanistan unless you're on a military installation."

Thomas still had the formal report up on his computer; he'd reviewed it one last time before Will had walked into the office. Officially, Will had been in the nosebleed section of the mountains tracking down a terrorist cell that had gone inactive due to the harsh winter weather.

"And I wasn't on base over the holiday."

"You didn't have a chance to go home?" Thomas was impressed with the way Will maintained his composure. Maybe this was the real man, the real professional he'd been looking for since the meeting began.

"Didn't take it," Will replied with a dismissive twitch of his shoulders. "The other guys had family missing them. My parents were doing fine."

"I'm sure they missed you."

Will leaned forward. "If you're worried I'll crack or break cover, that's not a problem," he said. "I've been away from home a long time, sir. The scarcity works for my family."

"All right." Thomas rolled his hand. "Go on."

"As you know, recon and surveillance is long, quiet work, and I'm good at it. You get a sense of people when you're watching them day and night."

Thomas agreed, glancing away from the computer and giving Will another long study. Everything but today's meeting told him this was the right man for the Colorado job. Maybe the former SEAL was dealing with a postdeployment conflict with authority or some personality clash. But this new task force was too important. Thomas had to be sure Will could handle the emotional pressure of deep undercover work as well as the physical strain.

"I'd been keeping an eye on the family for days. The middle daughter hauled water every day. I knew her routine. The target had been spotted to the south and then I went days with no sign of him. On December 25, I noticed the water girl's routine changed. She made one extra trip, using a different footpath."

"You followed her."

"Right to the target, yes, sir." Will dipped his chin. Eyes calm and steady. "I made the report. It felt like the perfect gift at the time."

Thomas waited, but Will didn't seem inclined to share the rest of the story. "It took you two days to get your target out of that cave and into custody."

Will dipped his chin. "That's what the report says."

Thomas leaned forward. "Do you want the post in Colorado?"

"Yes, sir. Delivering mail and chatting up locals beats the hell out of crawling through caves on the other side of the world."

"Then tell me what really happened."

"I suppose you have the clearance," Will said on a heavy sigh.

Thomas managed to stifle his laughter this time.

"I refused to move in immediately," Will began. "On the twenty-fifth."

"You didn't want to make an arrest on Christmas Day?" Thomas asked, pushing harder than he wanted to. This interview was like pulling teeth.

"Everyone acts like I was sitting around waiting for Santa Claus," Will snapped, lurching up and out of the chair. "I didn't want the water girl to *die* on Christmas. Is that so damned terrible?" He stalked over to the window, hands braced on his hips. "If I'd gone in right after her they would've known. If somehow I couldn't take them all, if I missed just *one* man, she would've been killed for sure. I have enough blood on my hands."

He turned away, but Thomas didn't need the eye contact to know Will was thinking of his brother. The Chase family had buried their younger son after a training accident. Somehow, the grief had twisted, and Will carried guilt and blame because his brother had been inspired by Will's military service.

"So, yes," Will continued, turning back. "I waited. I came at them from a different direction. I practically laid a trail for them to find me in the secondary post."

"But they didn't."

"No." His wide shoulders rolled back. "And I took them all, starting with the weakest link in their watch rotation, until it was just a matter of escorting the target to the extraction point."

Thomas knew the target remained in custody, the terrorist cell out of commission, the attack they'd planned for spring thwarted. "You saved her."

"Hard to say." Will pressed his lips together. He walked behind the chair, his fingers digging into the upholstery. "She didn't die on Christmas because of me. That's all I know for sure."

Here were the character and integrity Thomas had sensed when evaluating Will as a potential recruit. Internal fortitude and an undefinable X factor that couldn't always be measured by personnel records and reports were essential for this new task force. He nodded, calmer now that his instincts had finally been confirmed. "Pick up your travel documents and postal service new-hire information from my receptionist.

What you make of the rest of your new life out there is up to you."

Will's face brightened with enthusiasm. "Thank you, sir."

"Despite your cover, you'll find a way to stay in contact with this office and stay in combat shape. There's no way to tell when we'll call you into action."

"You won't be sorry."

Thomas leaned back into his chair after Will walked out, more than a little relieved. If the current rumors could be trusted, they might be calling on Will sooner than anyone expected.

# Chapter Two

Charlotte Binali, Charly to everyone who knew her, muttered encouragement to her computer screen. The spreadsheet was almost complete, and she didn't want to offend the technology gremlins by looking away at a crucial moment.

Her coworkers teased her mercilessly about her tenuous relationship with technology. Give her a mountain and a footprint and she could hike any terrain to find anything or anyone, but computers and the entire mess inside them made her want to cry like a baby.

She really needed to hand more of the tech over to someone else on staff, but Binali Backcountry was hers now, and as the sixth generation, she was determined to bring the business into the twenty-first century.

"Charly?" Tammy, the newest employee, whom Charly had hired to greet customers and maintain the storefront, leaned into the office doorway. "Better break out the lip gloss. Your boyfriend's almost here."

Charly refused to take the bait, determined to finish the spreadsheet. Besides, her requisite lip balm had protective sunscreen, not shine.

"Lip gloss, stat!" Tammy urged before she disappeared from view.

The door chimed, and when Charly heard the smooth rumble of his voice, it was more of a challenge to keep herself on task. Just a few more clicks and she could give in to the distraction of the new mailman.

Tammy reappeared, a dazzled smile on her face. "He wants to know if you have a minute," she said in a whisper loud enough to be heard for miles.

Charly saved the changes to the schedule and pushed back from the desk. "Thanks," she replied, mimicking Tammy's loud whisper as she left the office to greet Will Chase, the hot new mail carrier working Durango's business district.

Hot *is a significant understatement*, she thought when he smiled at her. The strong, square jaw might have been carved from granite, and the wide shoulders, trim hips and strong hands had been starring in her dreams recently. Not that she'd admit that to anyone.

"Hey, Will."

"Hi," he replied, removing his sunglasses. "Am I interrupting?"

"No." She hoped her smile didn't look as starstruck as Tammy's. "Just finished." They'd only been out on two occasions—she couldn't bring herself to call them dates—but she melted a little every time he looked at her with those vivid eyes as deep and blue as a high mountain lake. It still startled her the way he could turn the pale, watered-down blue of the official postal service shirt and dark jeans into raw sex appeal. "Excel didn't implode on me this time."

"Glad to hear it."

Last week, when she'd been ready to smash the computer to bits one afternoon, he'd arrived with the mail, caught her midrant and given her a quick lesson on the program. Later, during what should have been movie night, he'd spent hours showing her where to find more video tutorials, which had saved her computer from going out the window more than once in the days since.

"Are we still on for a movie tonight?"

"Sure." She accepted the stack of mail, thick with outdoor-gear catalogs. "The schedule's set for next week and this time it doesn't even need to be labeled as 'The Spreadsheet that Conquered Charly.'"

He laughed, the sound as clear and fresh to her ears as a brimming creek on a hot day. "That might be the one title I don't have. I've got plenty of beer. You bring the pizza." He put his sunglasses in place and backed toward the door, graceful as a cat. "Say, seven?"

She nodded, her mouth going dry as he turned to make his exit.

Beside her, Tammy sighed. The girl liked nothing better than a clear view of an excellent male backside. Charly still didn't know which view she preferred. Will walking in was just as appealing to her as when he was walking away.

"He didn't kiss you goodbye," Tammy said.

"Why would he?" Charly made herself laugh off the image. She couldn't indulge in that little fantasy at work. "We're just friends. And this is a workplace."

"Not from where I'm standing, and so what?" Tammy flung a hand toward the spot where Will had been moments ago. "That man wants to sleep with you."

"Whatever." Charly refused to get her hopes up. So far they'd gone out for beer and pool at the pub up the street and gone bowling once, but she knew how this story ended before she turned the last page. The way it always ended—with one more tempting man in the friend column.

It had been that way her whole life. Part of it was being built more like a boy than a woman, but her business played a part, too. Binali Backcountry, her life's passion, took up the majority of her energy and time. She enjoyed the mountains, the risk and reward she could find there, and she rose every morning eager to share her passion and knowledge with others as the owner, as well as a guide. Her commitment and drive didn't leave much room for romance and relationships.

For as long as she could remember, she'd been drawn to the wild call of the mountains and canyons surrounding the Four Corners Monument. Born and raised just outside of Durango, she'd spent her life exploring until it all felt as personal as her own backyard. Her grandfather often boasted that you could drop her anywhere on the planet and she'd find her way home no matter the weather or resources. She could track and mimic any animal that called this area home and, more importantly, she could find lost people better than any bloodhound.

Typically, men looking for a good time didn't put those skills at the top of the list when they wanted a date. Or a girlfriend. It was too soon to tell if Will would be different. She returned to the office to print out the work schedule.

Looking it over as it came off the printer, she prepared for the inevitable complaints. She required all of her guides to spend a few hours in the shop each week. It wasn't a popular stance and she'd lost a few good guides to nearby competitors since she'd implemented the policy. No one loved getting out and guiding mountain and canyon tours more than she did. But it was important to her that everyone understood the gear they carried for customers and that selling tours was a group effort. It kept them all invested and focused on the overall success of Binali Backcountry. As she'd explained it—again—at last month's staff meeting, no one sold a tour better than the guide who loved to lead it.

The reverse was also true, and it was past time for Tammy to get out and away from the business district. "Have you decided which tour you'll join next week?"

Tammy cringed and busied herself with a sudden interest in the day's few credit card receipts. "I'm not sure my boots are broken in yet."

Charly glanced at Tammy's feet and noted the cute Western boots better suited for line dancing than hiking. "So start small. How about something down around Lake Nighthorse or along the river trail?" Those routes naturally had a slower pace, more photo opportunities and generally left people delighted rather than exhausted.

"Maybe." Tammy popped her gum while she flipped through the appointment book. "Clint only has openings on his two-night thing into the canyon."

Ah. Now Charly had the clear picture. Tammy was crushing on Clint. The girl had good taste, but Clint Roberts wasn't the one-woman kind of guy, and she didn't want Tammy's feelings getting hurt in the bargain.

"I know the tents are rated to thirty below or whatever," Tammy said, "but I can't believe that material is really effective."

"What you should believe," Charly said, her voice calm but stern, "is that your job here depends on you getting outside by next week."

Tammy's eyes went wide, shimmering with tears. "That's not fair."

This kind of thing was exactly why Charly preferred working with men. No emotional games, just the occasional posturing, and she knew how to shut that down. Charly took a calming breath, reminded herself the tears were an act, a tool Tammy had probably learned to wield early in life. "That was the deal when I hired you. Do I need to pull out the paperwork you signed?"

"No." Tammy's tears evaporated instantly. "I'll go with David on the river trail tomorrow. Unless…"

Charly was half-afraid to ask. "Unless what?"

"What if I took over the office stuff? All that computer crap you hate is a piece of cake for me."

"Really?"

Tammy nodded, hope clearly bubbling over as she laced her fingers and bounced a little.

Charly glared at her. "Why didn't you say something when I was ready to put a tent stake through the computer last week?"

"And miss a chance to stare at Will's ass?"

Valid point. The girl had priorities, even if they were different from Charly's. "You still have to take the tours." She held up a hand, cutting off Tammy's protest. "At least the ones close to town. It will help you sort out what treks appeal to what type of person."

"Okay, okay." Tammy shook back her cloud of perfect, bottle-blond hair. "But if I fall in the river you'll be on your own with the computer stuff."

"I'll tell David to be extra careful with you."

"Thank you." She tapped her fingernail on the counter. "You know, I could even put the tour schedules into a calendar app and then all of you would know what's what out on the trails."

She and her guides already knew that, but Charly appreciated the effort. "I'd go with that in a heartbeat if—"

"Right," Tammy interrupted. "Cell reception is crappy in the wild. One more reason to appreciate the city."

"Takes all kinds to keep the world turning." Charly flipped through the mail, finding an official envelope from the park service between the catalogs and handing the rest of the stack to Tammy. She ripped it open, pleased to find a check for her latest consulting work. "I'm going to run this over to the bank."

"I'll hold down the fort."

Charly breathed deep of the clear, crisp air as she strolled down the block. It always felt good when a consulting job had a happy ending. This time around it had been a weekend hiker who hadn't come back on schedule. At the twenty-four-hour mark, his wife had insisted the park service start a search and they in turn had called Charly. When they reached him, they'd found the poor guy had taken a tumble and lost his radio. Easy enough to do this time of year when the weather couldn't decide between winter and spring.

Up ahead, she saw Will on his route, but he was chatting with the owner of the pub where they had shared their first beer. The man was too easy on the eyes, and she purposely looked away, just to prove she could. It wouldn't do her any good to get attached to the idea that he would see her as more than a pal with breasts. She glanced down at her chest. Her barely B cups might not be big enough to meet the general definition. They certainly had never been big enough to change the way the local guys saw her.

Tammy might be right about the raw chemistry between Charly and Will, and Charly was definitely ready to see where pheromones and attraction could lead. How could she find out if Will was on the same page? She was darn sure ready for more than another buddy to talk beer, guns and trails.

She yanked open the bank door and stutter-stepped to avoid bumping into the police officer walking out. "Whoops. Sorry, Steve."

"No problem. How are things?"

"Can't complain," she replied. "How are the kids?"

"Good." He stepped back inside with her. "I'm thinking about taking my youngest down into the canyon when it warms up a bit."

Steve had worked part-time for her father during their senior year. They'd gone to the homecoming dance—as friends—because both of them had been too busy that season to find real dates. Suddenly she felt seventeen and awkward again, remembering the time they'd driven out to prep a campsite in the canyon and stayed long into the night, watching a meteor shower from the back of his pickup truck. She'd wished for a kiss as the stars fell, but Steve didn't oblige.

*Thank God*, she thought now. It would've been weird. More of an experiment than romance, even under that endless sky.

Steve waved his hand in front of her face. "Charly? You okay?"

With a little jump and a self-conscious smile, she apologized. "Just lost in thought." Steve's youngest daughter had recently discovered a new fascination with photography. "Take her into the canyons southeast of town and she can get some amazing sunset pictures."

"That's a great idea. She'll love that. I'm glad I bumped into you."

"Me, too. Have a great time."

They went their separate ways, leaving Charly feeling half a step out of sync with the rest of her world as she made the deposit. It irritated her. She had exactly what she wanted. More. With the business she had freedom and plenty of time in wide-open spaces, challenges of every variety. She had exactly what she needed, sharing the world she loved from mountaintop to river to canyon with new people every day.

"Living the dream," she reminded herself as she walked back up the block to the Binali Backcountry storefront. This was her heritage as well as her dream come true.

So why did it feel as though something was missing? Determined to adjust her attitude, she tipped her face to the snowcapped peaks kissing the horizon. This happened to her when she spent too much time in the office and not enough out in the field. Four days was about her tolerance for the city life, and she hadn't led a tour in over a week. Well, easy enough to fix that. She'd just make time for an early hike tomorrow morning since she had plans tonight. Plans with a man she definitely wanted to know better. In the biblical sense rather than strictly as a friend. Maybe she should ask Tammy for pointers on how to stage a seduction. Heck, she needed pointers in how to tell if a guy was open to being seduced.

She was laughing at herself, her balance somewhat restored, when she strolled back into the store.

"Must have been some check," Tammy said.

"Every little bit helps," she admitted.

"I opened the fan mail while you were gone."

"We got fan mail?"

"Sure." Tammy spun a handwritten note card around for Charly's inspection. "Take a look."

Charly read it aloud, happily recalling her time with the Ronkowski family. "'Thanks again for making our vacation something we'll remember forever. The kids are still talking about it with anyone who will stop long enough to listen. We've been camping and taken tours through all kinds of places, but Charly, your expertise and passion for the area made all the difference. We're already planning to return to Colorado and take another tour with you this summer.'"

The note went on, elevating Charly's mood with every word. She'd led the parents and their three kids on a camping excursion through the canyon she'd recommended to Steve earlier. "Wow. We can pull a few of these lines for the website," she said. In fact, she wanted to upload the new quotes right this second. "They were a fun family."

"They sure think the world of you."

"It's easy to share what you love best." An idea dawned, one she thought might be a good compromise for Tammy. "Want to go hiking with me tomorrow?"

"What? And close the store?"

"No. Before we open. Before breakfast."

Tammy's jaw dropped open. Then she snapped it shut and glared at Charly. "This is some kind of test."

"Not at all." Charly gathered up the mail as she rounded the counter, smiling again at the note from the Ronkowskis. "I just need to get outside."

Tammy pointed at the door with her perfectly manicured finger. "You just came in."

Charly laughed. "I meant the *big* outside, away from sidewalks and storefronts."

"You're a nature addict." Tammy shook her head, as if the diagnosis were fatal. "I have plans for tomorrow before breakfast."

"You do?"

"Yup." Tammy nodded emphatically. "Sleep."

"Fine." Unable to argue with a confirmed city girl, Charly ducked into the office to deal with a few remaining administrative details. If she lingered, she knew she'd ask Tammy for advice about men and that just felt too…needy, she decided.

She'd let the mysterious chemistry work, and whatever happened with Will happened.

WILL TOOK A final look around his apartment and decided he had everything set for his movie date with Charly. The clutter was gone, the kitchen and bathroom spotless. The beer was cold, he had microwave popcorn ready to go, and he'd bought a pack of cupcakes for dessert. Yeah, he had everything except the movie.

Binali Backcountry had quickly become the high point on his postal route each day. During his first week on the job, chatting up so many strangers all at once had left him drained and craving nothing more than hours of quiet at the end of the day. Then he'd met her. There was an ease about Charly that smoothed him out. He blamed it on the absolute confidence that hovered over her like a cloud. That particular trait wasn't something he saw in most civilians.

Casey expected Will to get involved here, so sticking to his hermit tendencies wasn't an option even for personal time. Following orders, Will had jumped in with both feet and asked her out, telling himself it was all part of burrowing deep into the cover story.

Being a mailman came easily enough. The tasks were so different from his military career, he appreciated having the mental space to assess the community. The people were nice and generally took pride in the area as a whole. He'd been right about the mile-wide streak of independence out here. While it had been hard work denying the part of him that needed solitude and quiet, he was making the adjustment.

*I'm dating*, he thought, checking his watch. Charly would be here in ten minutes. He picked up the remote and started scrolling through his extensive movie library. He'd picked up most of the titles during his time on bases where the troops had created dedicated servers packed with entertainment for relaxation between missions. Still, he couldn't make up his mind about what they should watch tonight.

This was the first time they were staying in, which felt like enough pressure, but he didn't know her tastes well enough to make a confident choice. Will decided to narrow the list to three and let her make the final call.

While he skimmed through the long list, his cell phone sounded with the old-school telephone ring he'd programmed for contact from Director Casey. The familiar anticipation of a mission shot through his system as he answered. "Chase here."

"This is a high-alert notification."

*Thank God, some action.* He was more than ready for a challenge bigger than movie selections.

"We have confirmed reports that a device known as a Blackout Key, a cutting-edge cyber weapon, has been stolen," Director Casey explained. "It's reverse-engineering software. I'm told the damn thing can breach everything from bank systems to nuclear weapon launch codes."

Will took a slow breath and waited for more details. Software could hide anywhere, on anyone.

It could be as sexy as a tube of lipstick or as unassuming as a car key. Hell, something like that could hover up in a technology cloud, just waiting for the right bad guy to access it. He fought the immediate disappointment. He couldn't hunt software. Not the way he hunted bad guys.

Still, he wondered how it tied in to Durango. Every business on his route relied on software security and the internet in some capacity. Thinking of the businesses on his route, he automatically prioritized them, starting with the prime targets. The two banks for sure, but he could see the value in targeting the investment group and a nationally recognized architectural firm, too.

"Three suspects were under surveillance," Casey continued, "but one suspect, a man we believe was instrumental in the key's development, has suddenly disappeared from the Los Angeles area. The files and everything related to the program have vanished from all databases in the DC lab."

"Am I being relocated?" The flicker of regret at leaving Durango—and Charly—surprised him. His SEAL training had made him innately qualified for action in this kind of rugged terrain.

"No. You sit tight. This is a nationwide alert. What we don't have yet is hard intel on the location of the key. Photos of the missing suspect and full details will be emailed to you. Keep the information secure and notify me at once if you spot anything that relates to this alert."

"Sit tight," Will echoed. "Does that mean you don't want me to act?"

Casey hesitated. "You are authorized to take whatever action is necessary to protect civilians or recover the Blackout Key. This breach cannot go public. We can't allow it to reach the black market, either."

"Copy that."

The line went dead, and a moment later a knock

sounded at the door. He set the phone to vibrate and pushed it into his back pocket. When he opened the door, the rich aroma of hot pizza spiced the air.

Charly smiled at him over the big square box. Her long hair, usually pulled back from her face in a braid or ponytail, was down tonight. It fell like a thick midnight curtain across her shoulders and lower, brushing the gentle curve of her breasts highlighted by the deep V of her light green sweater. His breath caught and his stomach growled.

"Sounds like I'm just in time." Her lips gleamed with a soft sheen, and she'd added some subtle touch that made her big brown eyes wider, more… It hit him suddenly—she'd applied makeup. For him. He liked it.

"You look great," he said, stepping back so she could come inside. She looked more delicious than any meal. He reminded himself they were friends. The smart play was to take it slow. His assignment was long-term and he didn't want to make the wrong move and alienate her—or anyone else.

While she settled the pizza in the kitchen, he pulled down plates and offered her a choice of the locally crafted beers he'd picked up.

His phone hummed, and he pulled it out. A quick check of the display confirmed it was the expected information from Casey.

"Problem?"

"Not tonight," he said, raising his glass to hers for a toast. "Let's eat."

## Chapter Three

The next morning, under a cloudless blue sky, Charly parked her truck behind the store and slid the key into the back door. Stepping inside, she silenced the alarm system and locked the door behind her. At just past seven, she still had two full hours before Tammy arrived.

She sighed happily. Two full hours to enjoy the sweet high resulting from the combination of an interesting evening with a sexy man and a perfect morning hike through crisp winter air.

It had been a bit more challenging than she'd anticipated getting out of bed after the impromptu double feature at Will's place. The beer and pizza had been impeccable accompaniment for the loud, over-the-top action flick they'd started with. But his unexpected admission that he had a weakness for Disney films had forced her to test his honesty. She'd woken up with random lyrics and lines from *The Little Mermaid* playing in her head.

Along with the memory of his face—so solemn—when he'd said the film had been required viewing during his navy training. She'd laughed in complete disbelief over both parts of his wild claim.

Oh, he undoubtedly had the well-honed body of a

warrior, but she couldn't fathom any reason a navy veteran would settle in Colorado. She'd blurted out the observation and listened, entertained by his colorful explanation of having had his fill of endless oceans and major waterways.

Whatever the reason, she was more than glad he was part of her landscape now. "You've got it bad," she scolded herself while she started a pot of coffee. A few dates was way too soon to be this enthralled over any man, but especially irresponsible when the man was new to town.

Still, she'd wanted to spin in a happy circle as she left his place last night, after he'd asked her for a pool game rematch at the pub tonight. This was almost like having a boyfriend, though they hadn't really discussed it in those terms.

She suffered another nearly deflating moment thinking the feelings were only on her side, but then she remembered the way he'd looked at her when she left last night. There'd been a certain chemistry—or at least something that felt distinctly warmer than friendship in his clear blue eyes.

Catching her reflection in the glass of the half door between the storefront and the back room, she wondered what Will saw when he looked at her. She paused, taking stock. With her hair pulled back from her face, a company ball cap on her head and only a sweep of mascara, she felt plain. Bland.

Not ugly, just…unfinished. *Unpolished* was the better word. But she had no intention of changing her habits. Makeup didn't go well with her career, though Will had seemed to approve of her effort in that area last night. She wasn't sugar and spice and everything curvy and nice like other women. A total tomboy, she'd spent her youth proving she could keep up with the nature-loving men in her life instead of embracing the critical differences that made her a woman, from chewing tobacco—once, on a dare—to splitting wood every winter. It was simply who she was. She wouldn't change for any man, no matter how hot and ripped or funny or intriguing. With an irritated huff for letting anything as silly as a reflection erode her good mood, she pushed through the door and into the storefront.

She hit the power button for the computers, then went out and took a quick stock of the displays. Tammy had everything neatly organized, and while she might not be a big fan of the great outdoors, she was an asset here in the shop.

"Here's hoping she's that efficient with spreadsheets, schedules and financials."

Charly filled a tall mug with coffee and returned to her desk, the same simple and scarred desk her father and grandfather had used. Now it was hers. Feeling connected to all they'd handed down to her, she started on the email.

She discarded the obvious spam and answered the easy ones before dealing with the rest of it. Inquiries ranged from advertising offers to shipping confirmations. A new shipment of ball caps was scheduled to arrive today, and she smiled when she saw they were coming by the US Postal Service. She'd make herself available to sign for that package when the hunky new mailman delivered it.

The time slipped away as she dealt with necessities and soon she heard the security system chiming as someone came in the back door. Her eyes went to the little monitor perched on the corner of her desk that kept an eye on the back entrance. Tammy and Clint.

*Well, that should keep spirits high around here today.* Charly stood up, stretching her arms and grabbing her empty coffee cup to go greet them.

After catching up and successfully dodging direct questions about her evening, she shared one of the more intriguing email messages with Clint.

"Take a look," she said, handing over the page she'd printed out. "It's a team-building thing. Sounds like we can name our price."

Clint gulped his coffee while he read the short message. One of her father's hires, Clint had joined Binali Backcountry almost on his first day in Durango. Blond, lean, with sun-kissed skin and deep dimples, Clint was a good-looking guy, and she understood Tammy's wistful crush on him.

But Clint had his own priorities. When he'd invited Charly to dinner, it had been for the sole purpose of learning all he could about the trails she'd been running tame on her whole life.

She valued his friendship, work ethic and love of the job. When Charly's father stepped back from the business, Clint stepped up, helping her maintain the reputation of excellence. And as each of her brothers followed their careers away from Durango, Clint had filled the void, becoming an important partner and friend.

"Says he'll be in this afternoon." Clint set the printed email aside in favor of a fast-food bag of breakfast. "Want me to be here?" He stuffed a big bite of a breakfast sandwich into his mouth.

Charly cut short the urge to tease and judge him. For a man comfortable eating off the land, he made up for it whenever he had the chance. "Something like this will take two guides for sure."

He nodded, chewing thoughtfully. "What are you thinking of charging?"

She tossed out a number. "Plus the rental gear."

Tammy whistled, but Clint's eyebrows dipped low. "For seven software geeks in this weather? Add in another grand for pain and suffering."

"You charge the *customer* for the chance to suffer?" Tammy was aghast.

"No, darlin'." Clint's dimples showed up. "That's for *our* pain and suffering. Desk jockeys tend to whine."

"I wouldn't whine," Tammy vowed.

"I'd never give you cause," Clint said, his voice oozing charm and innuendo.

Charly rolled her eyes. Tammy looked as though she might dissolve into a puddle. "Why don't you unlock the front door," she instructed Tammy. Clint had no idea the destruction his little flirtation could leave behind.

"Come on," she said to Clint. "Let's hammer out a few ideas and price points. We can give them options."

"You really don't want to risk losing them, I guess," he said, following her to the office. "But our books can't be that dire."

"They're not. We're doing great," she assured him.

Clint pushed aside some catalogs, making room for his coffee cup on a corner of her desk. Settling back in the only other chair, he finished off his breakfast while they came up with a few package ideas.

"Seems sudden," he said when she was printing out the varied proposals.

"What do you mean?" She shot him a look as he worked the wrapper of his meal into a ball between his palms. A sure sign he was thinking.

"Come on. You think this guy just plans to hand out

plane tickets when his crew comes in today or do you think they've been in on the planning process?"

"Does it matter? The email says they just wrapped a project. They want to cut loose and get out of the office."

"In their place I'd go to Vegas."

"Then be grateful they're coming here and want to give us their money."

"If you close the deal, I've got plenty of ways to spend my cut." Clint flipped through the pages once more. "Should we pad that pain-and-suffering number a little more?"

"There's padding and then there's outright greed."

His dimples flashed again. "True." He leaned forward, his eyes twinkling. "But if they go the mountain route, they'll be *cold*." He stood, pretending to shiver. "We could make a side bet that you'll cave to the inevitable whining before I do."

"No deal," she said on a chuckle. "I can be just as much a hard-ass as you when it's necessary."

Clint scoffed. "Then start practicing, sister, and get the payment up front." He clapped her on the shoulder. "I've got a feeling these soft, cube-withered geeks will have us earning every penny once they get a taste of nature up on the mountain at this time of year."

"You're a cynic." She shooed him out of the office with orders to make space in the back room for the delivery coming in. "And put some polish on your professional charm while you're at it."

A FEW HOURS LATER, as she listened to their potential new client, she realized both she and Clint were right. The job would be lucrative, but with every passing minute it was becoming more complicated.

"Let's do this," Charly suggested to the client.

"Which of the options presented comes closest to what you have in mind?"

Reed Lancaster had made it clear from the moment he'd walked in that money was no object. His precise though relaxed appearance gave her an impression of significant wealth to back up the statement. His cashmere sweater, perfectly creased and cuffed khaki slacks and stylish shoes told the story. She imagined he spent a small fortune to keep his hair trimmed, and the gray at his temples added distinction. It was pointless to guess how much he'd shelled out for the Rolex on his wrist. She hoped he had the sense to leave it in his hotel safe rather than wear it on the excursion they were planning. Now, if they could just agree on where he wanted to go and the top three objectives he wanted to get out of the hike.

"As I explained in the email, my team deserves a break. I want to build on our momentum and camaraderie. The three-day hike into the mountains sounds ideal."

"We'll make sure your team is bonding while they're having fun," Clint said.

Mr. Lancaster ignored him, focusing on the paperwork in front of Charly. "Ms. Binali, I've done the research, read the reviews and asked around since coming to town two days ago. Your company has a reputation as the best." He removed his reading glasses—no drugstore cheaters for Mr. Lancaster, these were designer frames.

"Your specific reputation—" he looked directly at Charly "—is what brought me here." He tapped the small table. "I've taught everyone who works for me that to settle—on anything—is equal to defeat. With every project, every day, we strive for excellence. We are the team that sets the bar others try to reach. I won't give them less than the best experience possible. That means I need you."

"I appreciate the vote of confidence." She gave him a smile and while she gathered the proposals into one stack, putting her favorite mountain hike option on top based on his decision, Mr. Lancaster reached into his coat and withdrew a long, slim wallet.

He'd said there were two hobby photographers on his team. While there wasn't a bad view on any of the routes she and Clint had chosen, Lancaster insisted on the mountain options despite the weather risks.

"The mountains will give you stunning views, crisp air and opportunities for teamwork from the campsites to the hike itself." She forced herself to keep talking as he counted out cash. "You're sure everyone on your team can handle the physical exertion?"

He added more bills, hundreds, she noticed, to the stack. "Fitness is another requirement to stay on my team, Ms. Binali."

"All right." The guy struck her as a tough boss. It would be interesting to meet the people who chose to work with him. "Clint and I will get things together."

Lancaster's gaze slid to Clint and back to hers. "You're sure two guides are necessary?"

She willed Clint to keep his mouth shut. "Two guides will guarantee you and your team get the most out of the excursion and the challenge course experiences we'll provide."

Lancaster dipped his chin in silent acknowledgment, though his lips were pressed into a thin line. "What needs to be signed?"

She offered the basic waiver and contract and explained the maps on the page, highlighting the parking and load-out areas. "We can meet at eight—"

"We'll start at seven o'clock. Tomorrow."

*The customer is always right.* It took a few repetitions to believe it. "Okay, we can do that," she agreed reluctantly. "This is the list of gear and waivers for each member of your team. I'll need them back by—"

"I have them here," he said, cutting her off again. He opened a leather portfolio and produced the documentation for each of the six people on his team. All men, she noticed, though he hadn't specified that detail. "I printed them from the website to save time. The photos were cropped from our company picnic last year."

She handed the pages to Clint, who skimmed them and gave her a small nod, confirming the required information and signatures were all in order.

"We won't need rental gear," Lancaster added. "Everyone has been outfitted according to the resources posted online."

*Efficiency must go along with being the best*, she thought. She couldn't fault him. Those lists covered the basics and were up-to-date. "Does that include tents and personal camping gear?"

"Yes."

"Great." She tried to show some excitement, but Lancaster's rigid determination to have everything his way got under her skin. The increasing profit margin should make Clint happy. "Does anyone on your team have food allergies?"

Mr. Lancaster shook his head.

"Then it seems we're set. Binali Backcountry will provide the necessary gear for the team challenges." She wanted to be absolutely clear on that point. It was standard procedure, for convenience as well as liability.

Relieved he didn't try to convince her he was bringing that along, too, she stood. Lancaster and Clint followed suit and they all shook hands. Since she hadn't been expecting to head out tomorrow, she'd need the rest of the evening for preparation.

"He's a tough bastard," Clint murmured, watching Lancaster climb into a glossy Mercedes crossover parked across the street. "You think that's a rental?"

Charly picked up the stack of cash and counted it. "For that guy? No way." She shook her head. "He probably bought it just for this trip."

"Is the money real?"

"Yes," she said with a tight laugh, retreating to her office. "Can you get started on the gear and packing?" Clint nodded, leaning against the doorjamb. "Great. Thanks." It was short notice, but just as Mr. Lancaster had said, Binali was the best. They could make this happen. "I'll send Tammy to make the deposit and pick up groceries."

"Sure thing. Just as soon as the mail comes," Tammy replied absently as she flipped through the waivers and photos, putting the information into the folder that indicated a booked excursion. "The best part of this job is getting a daily dose of superhunk."

Clint's face clouded over as he turned to face Tammy. "Lancaster? He's old enough to be your father."

"First, age is only a number," she scolded. "Second, ick," Tammy finished with a mock shudder. "I meant the mailman. The Lancaster dude is way too uptight for me. Good luck with him on the mountain."

"We'll be all right," Charly said. "He paid cash, all of it up front, and I know we'll surpass his expectations." She ignored the unanimous eye rolling. "Come on, both of you. Get busy. I have a schedule to adjust."

Clint disappeared into the back, and her butt had barely landed in her desk chair when she heard the chime on the front door. Judging by Tammy's warm greeting, Will had arrived with the day's mail.

Charly paused long enough to hit Print for the standard grocery list and then walked out to join the conversation. Tammy had signed for the box, her fingers tracing the corners while she flirted shamelessly with Will. Charly told herself it didn't matter. Tammy could enjoy the view of Will's body, but she sure as hell wasn't Will's type.

The catty assessment startled her as Charly watched them. What did she know of Will's type? Technically, she didn't have a claim on the man. They'd only been out on a few friendly dates. They hadn't even exchanged any romantic physical contact yet.

"Hey there, Charly." Will's smile lit up his silver-blue eyes.

"Hi." Her knees felt weak. How silly. "Having a good day?"

"Good enough." He nodded to the big box he'd set on the counter. "New gear?"

"Ball caps," she said. "We sell them—" she tipped her head toward the display in the front window "—but we give them to our guests. A gift-with-purchase kind of thing."

"The bright colors must make it easy to do a head count."

"You'd be right about that." She turned to Tammy. "I have the list and deposit ready to go."

"Cool." Tammy accepted the bank bag and the grocery list. "On account?"

"Please."

"You got it. I'll just take this back to Clint. Have a great day," Tammy said, aiming a wink at Will.

"She's got a little crush going on," Charly explained.

"On me?" Will's dark eyebrows winged up.

"On men in general, I think." She appreciated his quick laugh. "But I meant she has a crush on Clint. At least this week."

Will looked mildly relieved. "Hope that works for her. Are we still on for pool tonight?"

Charly winced. "Sorry. I have to take a rain check. We picked up a new client determined to squeeze every minute out of his tour, starting bright and early tomorrow morning." She tapped the stack of waivers on the counter. "Some bigwig software guy with more money than sense wants a team-building excursion. Clint and I need to prep."

Will glanced at the paperwork and then raised his gaze back to her. "No problem," he said easily. "We'll make up for it when you're back."

His smile looked sincere, but she wondered if she'd shown enough regret about canceling. She stopped before the analysis paralyzed her and turned her into a babbling dork. If she wanted something different with Will, she'd have to behave differently than she had with other guys. "Maybe you should practice your bank shots while I'm away," she said. Did that come out as a challenge or as the flirtation she'd meant it to be?

He rested his forearms on his side of the counter, bringing himself closer to eye level with her. "Maybe I threw the game last time we played."

She licked her lips, watched his eyes follow the move. "Maybe I don't believe you."

"Would you believe I was distracted by the view?"

*Oh, my.* Her throat went dry. She desperately wanted

that to be true. Just as she wanted to believe she could take some time to play a couple games of pool with him tonight and still get things ready on time, but she knew better. "I really hate that we'll have to wait to find out," she said at last, uncertain of the next step in the game.

He stood tall and gifted her with a smile guaranteed to keep her warm over the next three nights sleeping in a tent near the cold summit of the mountain. In that instant, she was determined to give him good reason to aim that sexy smile her way more often.

"I'll get back to my route and leave you to it."

"Okay." She did a mental eye roll at that profound comeback. "I'll see you as soon as I get home," she added as he reached the door.

"Can't wait." He pushed the door open and paused. "Be safe, Charly."

The gravity of his tone, the concern in his eyes, turned her mute. She stared as he left and passed the window. He looked back, caught her watching, and waved.

She managed to return the gesture before his long stride propelled him down the street.

"Whoa," Tammy said from behind her. "I thought the store might catch on fire from the sparks flying."

Not likely. But the comment made Charly feel better. She couldn't quite believe the attraction and chemistry went both ways. "I thought you were out on errands," she muttered, flipping through the stack of envelopes Will delivered.

"And miss that? No way."

Charly had to laugh it off, resisting the urge to ask Tammy for how-to advice on men. "We both need to get busy," she said and turned for her office. "We barely have enough time as it is." It would take a concentrated effort to keep her mind on the details. She promised herself the reward for her focus now meant she could daydream about Will on the hike tomorrow.

# Chapter Four

Will had spent the early-morning hours before his shift reviewing the full intel and reports from Director Casey. The capabilities of the Blackout Key Casey had outlined in the brief phone call were the tip of the iceberg.

The more he'd read and uncovered about Reed Lancaster, created a different kind of chill. If Lancaster had somehow pulled off this theft, if he had the key, this situation would get ugly in a hurry.

The man had an ax to grind with the top-level players in the technology and software development food chain. For years Lancaster had been outspoken, the proverbial squeaky wheel demanding justice from the companies he claimed had stolen his cutting-edge work and tossed him out without so much as a severance package. According to the file, Lancaster didn't just want the Blackout Key, the damned thing was his brainchild. Though it had gone through several development stages and was most recently funded by a government research group, the technology was his creation. While nothing proved he had it, a fully developed, working version of the key could help Lancaster strike back at his perceived enemies. If he did that—and succeeded—the security protocols that protected the nation would fall like dominoes.

As Will studied the file, Lancaster's outspoken threats didn't bother him nearly as much as the recent silence. Men didn't preach vengeance with such intense venom, only to walk away from it without any logical explanation. Not without a settlement or gag order. Will had combed the internet and the files and found no sign of either scenario involving Lancaster.

He'd had all of that rattling around in the back of his mind as he'd started his mail route, wondering what might bring a man like that to Durango. Nothing in the file suggested Lancaster could satisfy his revenge here, which made it more surprising when he'd spotted Lancaster's face on a picture attached to a Binali Backcountry liability waiver as he'd delivered Charly's mail.

The man hadn't bothered with an alias. Bold. In Will's experience that kind of bold meant all kinds of trouble. As he continued along his route, he prioritized the next steps: notify Casey, get a net over Lancaster. Good thing he knew where to find him. As long as Lancaster didn't get spooked before meeting Charly for the hike in the morning.

Hard to believe Lancaster suddenly wanted to commune with nature. It didn't make any sense. What was he after in the mountains? Nothing good, Will decided.

He stalked up the street, his nice-guy postman smile on his face, all the while knowing he couldn't let Charly just walk out into the wilderness with Lancaster. The man and the—missing—Blackout Key he'd envisioned were wanted by nearly every federal agency in the nation. He laughed at the irony. It was possible the postal service was the only agency that hadn't been alerted to the problem.

He spent the rest of his route brainstorming ideas to close in on the target. It would've been weird if he'd asked to go along. Charly would never let her new pal, the friendly mailman, tag along as an extra on what promised to be a tough three-day exercise. She had no way of knowing he could handle things as well as anyone on her staff. He needed more information about the client, the tour and who was going along, but she'd canceled their dinner and now he didn't have easy access.

Logistically, he couldn't tag along even if he wanted to. It wasn't an option to take time off from the day job. He hadn't accrued any personal days yet and maintaining cover and operation security protocol was essential to his long-term success here.

Instinct and responsibility battled inside his head as he chatted with people on his route. This new development had popped up sooner than he'd expected out of this current assignment. To be effective he had to do more than protect Charly from Lancaster. He had to approach this with a big-picture perspective. But she was leading a man wanted for questioning into the mountains and giving Lancaster too many options to avoid the authorities.

Casey would expect details, and Will wanted to give them to him. In between the stops on his route, Will sent a short text message up the line. The response was no surprise: he was tasked with observing Lancaster, but ordered not to interfere until he knew why the man was in Colorado.

Fine. Will understood how to follow orders during compartmentalized operations. It didn't take three guesses to know what the boss was thinking: Lancaster had come to Durango for the key. So why hire Charly? An exchange of some sort had to be involved. He slowed his pace and tried to look tired. Anything to make it more believable when his boss got the call tomorrow that Will was down with a late-season case of the flu.

HOURS LATER, AS the first evening stars lit the sky over the mountains, Will's new Jeep managed the rugged drive between the highway and the Binali property with no problem. When he'd bought the car, he'd told himself it was an investment, part of the cover for the job. And he'd been right, but soon discovered he enjoyed the rugged capability of this vehicle as much as he'd enjoyed the sleek, sexy speed of the Corvette he'd left in storage in DC.

She came around the far corner of her house as he parked next to her truck, stopping with her hands on her hips and her head tilted in a silent question.

"Hey," he called out, pushing open his door. "Am I intruding?"

"Not really." Her brow furrowed. "I thought we postponed."

"We did," he agreed with a smile. But he needed information and thought he could do something nice for her in the process. Two birds, one stone. "You have to eat, right?"

"Yeah. I can throw something together, I guess."

She didn't have to say it. He could see he'd made a mistake, thrown her off by showing up unannounced this way. Nothing to do but go big before she sent him home. "I brought burgers, fries and shakes."

Her face brightened with interest. "Chocolate?"

"Or strawberry. Your choice."

"Hedging your bets?"

"A little," he admitted. "I didn't even eat all the fries on the way over. Do you have time for a break?"

"Sure." She smiled and waved him closer. "Bring it on back."

He grabbed the takeout bags and drinks and followed her around to what appeared to be a small workshop set back from the house.

She cleared space on one end of a table loaded with all kinds of camping gear and then pulled over another stool for him.

Taking a seat, he placed a hot burger and scoop of fries in front of her and scattered a handful of ketchup, mustard and mayonnaise packets between them. "They're both loaded with everything."

"Sounds good. I didn't want to postpone tonight," she said after she'd unwrapped the burger and prepped it her way. "I was looking forward to beating you at pool again."

He laughed as he dragged a fry through the ketchup he'd puddled on a corner of the foil wrapper. "You said it's an early start tomorrow?"

"We're meeting at six thirty to load up. This guy's serious about getting the most of each and every day."

"Hope you charged him extra."

"Better believe it." She shot him a wink. "My family drummed business sense into me right along with camping and tracking."

He bit off more of the juicy burger, chewing as he looked around the workshop and up toward the mountain peaks before meeting her gaze again. "You've got a nice place out here."

Her lips curved with pride. "I've always thought so."

Stars came to light, more with each passing minute. He hadn't seen a night sky so full since those long nights alone in Afghanistan. "You don't mind being tied so closely to your family?"

"Tied?" She chuckled, brushing salt from her fingers. "It's an honor to carry on what my elders started. Is that why you went into the navy? To get untied?"

*Untied.* He'd never thought of it like that. "Maybe so." It hadn't started that way. His parents had been proud of him...before things fell apart.

"Hmm. You really should think before you gush on and on like that," she said with a wink.

The urge to explain his decisions surprised him. This was hardly the best time to confess his parents didn't speak to him because his brother had died while following in his military footsteps. There was never a good time for that story as far as Will was concerned. Besides, he had a job to do here, even if the company was beautiful and friendly. "Are you meeting this guy and his team at the main park entrance?"

She nodded. "Clint's meeting me at the shop, then we'll meet the clients at the parking lot." She balled up her burger wrapper and tossed it into the bag. "Clint's so excited about the extra team challenge stuff he probably won't sleep at all tonight."

Will knew the type. He only had to look in the mirror. "I competed in a few challenge course events during my navy days." He'd developed more than a few as a SEAL. He liked the way it felt when her dark eyes skated over his body. "Don't believe me?"

"I believe you," she said, her voice a little breathless. She cleared her throat and slid off the stool to consider the gear spread out on the other end of the long table. "We won't be doing static courses out there."

"Is that some sort of insult?"

"What?" She whipped around, color flooding her cheeks. "No. I would never—"

"Relax." He came to his feet, hands out, palms open.

"I was just messing with you. What kind of things does Clint have planned for the group?"

"Probably too many." She rubbed her arms through the thick fabric of the company sweatshirt she wore and sighed. "I didn't mean static courses were any less of a challenge than what we set up during an excursion."

"It's okay," he said, rubbing her shoulder. He was flattered by her concern about offending him. It made him think he had something to look forward to with her after the Lancaster operation was complete.

The powers that be wanted Will to report Lancaster's position, whom he met with and what items or information were exchanged. Apparently, those curious people at the top of the food chain didn't share Will's concern that in order for a man like Lancaster to feel safe about whatever he was up to, anyone who knew about his plans would have to be eliminated.

"I like you, Charly." He blurted it out, immediately wishing he could reel it back in. "I'm sure you've got this under control, but it all sounds sudden and risky."

She shrugged that off, clearly more comfortable with the camping prep than looking at him. "It's sudden, but not risky."

He listened, thinking it was too easy when she explained the route and the typical places where Clint set up various challenges and teamwork opportunities. "We're not even doing much of the heavy lifting."

"What does that mean?"

She rubbed at her temples, a frown marring her brow. "My client assured me his team is fit and up for anything."

"Is there some reason to doubt him?"

She spread her hands wide and then reached for a hiking pack, stuffing supplies into pockets with an efficiency he admired. "I hope not. For their sake. The route Clint and I are taking isn't for amateurs."

"I'm looking forward to getting out and doing some exploring myself soon." Right now he wished he'd done more than admire the mountains from the convenience of his route. Didn't matter. He'd always found his assigned quarry and survived no matter the odds or terrain.

"David does river hikes a couple of times a week," she said with a wince.

"What's wrong with that?"

"Two things." She balled up wool socks and tucked them into open spaces. "It's water, which you claim to be done with."

"And?" he prompted when she busied herself with the precise attachment of a canteen.

"Tammy is slated to go out on the next tour. She'd be ogling you the whole time, and I want her to pay attention to the tour."

He laughed. "She ogles me every day."

Charly giggled, then clapped a hand over her mouth. "You know?"

"I'm a mailman, not an idiot."

"Well, you'd be an idiot to invest so much time in your body and not expect some ogling."

"That's a fair point." He sent her a sideways look.

"You think I'm insulting you again."

"No." He stepped closer. "I say what I mean. You don't have to put words in my mouth."

"I'll remember that."

"Do." He kept looking for an opportunity to hide a GPS transmitter on her pack. Based on the route she'd described, she'd be out of cell range before noon tomorrow. "What can I do to help?"

"Dinner was plenty," she said with a shy smile.

He wanted to warn her, but if he said anything, she might telegraph her concerns to Lancaster. While she packed, he made a mental list of things to be aware of on the mountain. He was more than a little relieved when she unlocked a cabinet and pulled out a hefty .38 Special revolver along with ammunition and a flare gun. Not just because it gave him time to put the transmitter on her pack—he felt a little better that she was armed. "Expecting trouble?"

"*Expecting* is a strong word." Her wry smile told him she'd seen her share of the unexpected. "I was raised to be prepared for any emergency. I carry the revolver as a last resort in the case of a wildlife issue."

"Got a snakebite kit?"

"Already packed," she replied, distracted.

He'd been kidding about that. "Isn't it too cold for snakes to be a problem?"

She nodded. "But even when it's cold, snakes can wake up looking for water, so I take it anyway, every time." Her nearly black eyes met his with stark candor. "People do dumb things despite our best advice as guides."

He'd seen the same thing throughout his military career, in every part of the world. "Stupidity is a frequent problem with humans."

"Tell me about it," she said. She looked around the table, but everything was already in her pack. "Mr. Lancaster assures me his team is smart, but there's a big difference between being smart in the office and being smart in the wilderness."

"What's this?" He pointed to the knife she'd set apart from the other items. The dark, hand-tooled leather sheath was a work of art, and the hilt was inlaid with a stunning turquoise mosaic in the shape of a long, elegant feather. His fingers itched to pull it out, to confirm the blade matched the hilt and sheath.

Her face went soft. "A gift from my grandmother. She gave it to me before my first solo hike on Silver Mountain. I don't go anywhere without it." She slid it into her sleeping bag.

"You don't wear it?"

"Sometimes."

He considered pushing her but decided changing the subject was safer. There was more to the knife, more to her history, but she didn't seem inclined to share more right now. "How often do you need the revolver or the flare gun?"

Her sly grin, loaded with self-confidence, brought to mind too many inappropriate, off-topic images. Later, he reminded himself. There would be plenty of time to get to know Charly on a more intimate level later.

"I've only used the flare gun to signal rescuers," she said.

"When you've been lost?"

"No, I signal when I've found lost people." She laughed. "I don't ever recall being lost."

"You're kidding." He leaned back, startled by her claim. He'd been blessed with a perfect sense of direction, as well, which came in handy.

"My grandpa used to say I had a compass where my heart should be."

Will wasn't sure how to respond. It seemed like a backhanded compliment, but he didn't get the impression that Charly was the sort to put up with twisted family dynamics. He had a low threshold for drama, which was why he stayed out of his parents' way. Better for all concerned.

"You think that sounds cold."

"A little."

"He meant it as the highest compliment." She reached over and pulled apart hook-and-loop fasteners with a loud rip.

"I'm all ears."

"Hand me those tent poles."

He did as she asked, waiting patiently for the explanation. Instead, her phone rang, and she pulled it from her hip pocket.

It didn't take long to realize she was speaking with the guide who'd be her partner on tomorrow's hike. The story about her grandfather would have to wait. Will pointed from the tent to the pack, and she gave him a nod, so he finished putting her tent gear into the designated place while he listened to her end of the conversation.

Will didn't know much about Charly's employees, but he assumed she didn't waste time working with anyone subpar. He might've found that reassuring if the circumstances were normal. He made a decision right there. If Lancaster gave Charly and her partner more than they could handle, Will vowed he'd be close enough to clean up the mess.

When she wrapped up her call, he'd get out of her way. He had his own preparations to finish and if he kept asking questions, he was bound to raise her suspicions.

CHARLY WALKED WILL out to his truck, a small part of her wishing the evening didn't have to end so early. Who was she kidding? All of her wanted him to stay longer. "Thanks for bringing dinner by. That was a nice surprise."

"My pleasure." He pulled his keys from his jacket pocket. "I'm glad it worked out."

"Me, too." She nodded, unable to come up with any witty reply. No one but family had ever brought her dinner before a tour or kept her company during the packing. She should tell him that, let him know what it meant to her, but she knew it would come out as a lame thank-you for this or that. Why did she have to suck so badly at this kind of thing?

"Give me a call when you get back?" He opened his car door.

Grateful her lack of feminine wiles didn't seem to put him off, she grinned up at him. In the dark, under all the stars, she let herself fantasize about how it would feel if he kissed her good-night.

She couldn't imagine a better place for a first kiss than out here in the cold night air with the stars as silent, sparkling witnesses.

"Charly?"

"Mmm-hmm."

"You should go inside. Get some rest."

She felt the heat of his hand on her shoulder through the thick layers of her polar-fleece jacket and sweatshirt. The man was like a furnace and she wanted to burrow closer to all that warmth. "Right."

Neither of them moved.

"Drive safe."

His hand slipped away as he pulled out his keys, and she chided herself for missed opportunities. Until he caught her hand. Before she could decide what to do about that, he bent his head and brushed his lips against hers.

A fleeting kiss, over almost before it started, but it

rocked her world. "I'll call when I get back," she promised, knowing she was grinning like a fool.

He settled into the driver's seat, his lips tipped up on one side in a cocky smirk. She couldn't find a reason to be annoyed with the expression.

She stayed put, like any girl crushing hard on a boy, and watched until his taillights disappeared down the road. She wasn't sure how she'd get to sleep now, but if she did manage it, she knew she'd dream of Will.

# Chapter Five

Charly parked her truck next to Clint's behind the shop and had tossed her pack into the bed when he came out with two tall travel mugs of coffee. "I knew there was a reason I kept you on," she said as he set them in the cup holders.

"Next to you I'm the best guide in the galaxy," he said, boosting up into the driver's seat. "Let's roll."

"You're in a good mood."

"I'm all set." He bobbed his head and rubbed his hands together. "It's gonna be an outstanding day."

There was no reason to doubt him. They were prepared, the client had prepaid in full and when they reached the parking area, she saw Lancaster and his team were gathered around two vehicles, as eager to get started as Clint.

On first impression, Lancaster's team didn't fit her mental stereotype of software developers. She caught Clint's eye and exchanged raised eyebrows as Clint walked over to double-check their packs and gear. Lancaster hadn't been kidding about his employee standards. Each of the six men addressed Lancaster with quiet respect. She matched each man with the waivers as introductions were made with Bob, James, Scott, Rich, Max and Jeff. Without any protest, all seven guests donned the bright Binali Backcountry ball caps she handed out. The men weren't quite matching, but they'd certainly shopped from the same outdoor outfitter catalog. She counted it a good thing their boots looked broken in, though she'd packed the family remedy for blisters.

"You're all wearing layers as suggested?"

They nodded in unison.

"And you packed rain gear?"

Another nod multiplied seven times. "All right. Clint will give each of you the items you'll carry for the whole party." Next she gave a quick safety briefing. It was standard fare and Lancaster and his team were attentive, but she had the feeling they weren't really tuned in.

*Well, that's why I packed the snakebite kit*, she thought, leading the party out. Clint brought up the rear as they hiked into the state park along the main road.

Charly made small talk along the way, relieved when Lancaster and his men responded. Occasionally she walked backward to see how everyone was doing. No one seemed even winded, a good sign, but not typical along the first steep inclines. "Clint packed a thermos of coffee if anyone needs a boost."

"We're fine," Lancaster answered for all of them.

"Great." With a forced smile, she hiked on, pointing out various trees and bird calls. The men were polite, but not excited about any of it. "Clint, can you tell everyone what they can expect at our first stop?"

"Sure."

She listened while her friend explained the first team challenge. The rope bridge exercise sounded ominous, but no one usually suffered more than wet boots. With today's clear weather and a planned stop for a cookout at noon, she hoped the challenge and any possible mistakes loosened up this crew.

Lancaster pulled back his sleeve and checked his watch. "Can we up the pace?"

"Sure," Charly replied, shooting a look at Clint. "If we're all in agreement."

All six men agreed with monosyllabic replies, so she picked up the pace. It put them at the creek ahead of schedule, but maybe that was a good thing. At the wide creek, with the midmorning sunlight bouncing off the water, Clint laid out the supplies and explained the challenge once more.

Lancaster's crew looked at one another, then at the gear at Clint's feet, and finally to Lancaster.

"Make it quick," Lancaster said, checking his watch. He peered up at the cold blue sky while his men started on the exercise.

Clint came over to stand with Charly while the men worked out a solution to cross the water. "If these guys are software engineers, I'm a trained monkey," he muttered for her ears only.

"You brought coffee without a reminder," she pointed out. "I trained you well."

Clint snorted. "Your dad trained me."

She smiled and bumped his shoulder with hers, the easy exchange completely at odds with the tension twisting her stomach. "Family business. I get credit by default." She pulled her water bottle free and took a long drink. Judging by the progress the men were making, they'd be across the stream in less than fifteen minutes. And not one of them would have wet boots.

"What do you think really brought them here?"

*Something more than a team-building excursion*, she

thought, tipping her face to the sunlight. Her grandmother had taught her to pause, to reach out to the
world when she needed anything, from her next breath
to the answers for a geometry exam. Charly had learned
early how to listen to her surroundings. They had options: she could continue on, playing the happy nature
guide, or she could confront Lancaster about his real
intentions.

"Have I missed something crucial in the news
lately?" she asked Clint.

Clint shook his head. "Might be some kind of geo-
caching team."

That was possible. Except those types didn't usually hire expert guides and they got lost up here fre-
quently enough that Charly was often called in to help
find them. "When they complete this exercise, radio
back to the store and leave some happy message for
Tammy. Tell her to post our progress with this tour to
the website."

"She won't be there?"

"Not for another hour or so." Charly raised her phone
and snapped a picture of the bridge progress, quickly
sending it as a text message attachment before they
were out of cell range. Lancaster wouldn't know the
store schedule. It might be equivalent to baiting a bear,
but if he heard Clint tell someone where they were, it
might force him to expose his real plan earlier rather
than later.

The man made her nervous, though she couldn't pinpoint why. The sooner she understood what he was up
to, the better the odds she could keep everyone safe
up here. She watched, considering her options while
the team tested the new bridge. One by one, the group
crossed over, Charly last.

"That was fun," the man named Scott said, adjusting his pack to sit snug against his shoulders. "Do we take it down now?"

"No. We'll use it on our way back."

"The park service won't be irritated?"

She saw a new opportunity to push at Lancaster's real agenda. "No. They're used to us coming through. This is a standard route for Binali Backcountry."

Lancaster went still, and while she knew it was impossible, it felt as if the air temperature dropped a few degrees. "I requested a unique route."

"And you'll have it," she assured him, infusing her voice with all the patience she could muster. "But there are specific routes on the way in that allow us to get a feel for our clients on each tour."

"I assured you my team is at the peak of fitness."

"You did." She stood still as a tree, the picture of unflappable calm. "And now I know you didn't exaggerate. Thank you."

Lancaster's nostrils flared, his mouth set in a grim line. "I would like to head north, away from established trails so my team has the best experience possible."

She applied balm to her lips while she considered. "And we'll give you that." Capping the balm, she put it back into her jacket pocket. "Better if we stay westbound for a while."

"Why?"

"Heading north right now presents more terrain challenges." She decided not to outline the gulley or the snow-choked pass. She might need one or both of those surprises later, if the situation degraded.

"We can handle any terrain," Lancaster insisted. "I'd like to move north."

She bit back the waspish reply on the tip of her

tongue. It wasn't too late to turn this party around and refund his money. He could find another guide, one willing to cave to his impatience. "Mr. Lancaster, my brothers once goaded me into a race to the summit."

"So what?"

Only the memory kept her confident smile on her face. "Determined to win, I took the direct route and learned a hard lesson about variations in terrain."

"We can handle it."

She pulled her sunglasses from her face and planted her hands on her hips. "Mr. Lancaster, if you didn't want an expert guide up here with you, why did you hire me?"

He slid a glance to one of the men behind her. Whatever the response, Lancaster's shoulders relaxed a fraction. "You're right. We've heard so many good things and we all want as much time as possible on the peak itself. The views," he added.

She wasn't fooled. "You won't be disappointed, but questioning my route won't get us there any faster."

"Yes, ma'am." He swept an arm wide, inviting her to lead the way.

She looked at Clint. "Call the shop and let them know the first challenge is done. With flying colors."

"That's not necessary," Lancaster said.

"Of course it is." Charly replaced her sunglasses and set off while Clint obediently left the message they'd discussed. "All part of the service."

Lancaster caught her arm in a hard grip just above her elbow. "This excursion isn't about your publicity, Ms. Binali."

"Let go," she said quietly. When he did, she resisted the urge to rub at the sore spot. She'd have a bruise for sure by tomorrow. "I'm not about to jeopardize my licenses because you want a special, off-the-grid experience."

"But that is exactly what I paid for."

"You're in a national forest, Mr. Lancaster. The geography can't be avoided. There are regulations out here and I *will* stay in compliance for your safety as well as my long-term business interests."

He looked as if he'd argue, maybe grab her again, but one of his men held up a cell phone. "My trail app says snow is on the way tonight."

The announcement didn't make Lancaster happy. "How much?"

"We won't see more than a flurry where we'll be camping tonight," she assured them. "That report is for the upper elevations. We can't get that far today, even with a quick pace."

"Set a quicker pace anyway," Lancaster said.

"You got it." The customer was always right. The philosophy applied to the weird customers, too, as long as their demands didn't put anyone at risk. Charly dialed the pace right up to grueling. Maybe one of his supercapable not-engineers would snap.

Whatever Lancaster was up to, she led them away from easy emergency access and reliable communication. The tactic could backfire, but she trusted her abilities. In fact, with every step away from civilization, her confidence increased. Lancaster had hired the best, but he clearly hadn't considered how that could work against him if he was up to no good.

This part of the world had been her playground all her life. She'd explored it all, from the snowcapped peaks to the canyons to the pueblos farther south. Every step had made her stronger. Every season from birth to present had tied her closer to the land she loved, the land she'd inherited from her elders.

While it helped the business that she was one of the best guides in the area, what mattered more to Charly was sharing what she loved with others. Planting seeds of passion for nature in the hearts of tourists was her personal mission. When people cared about something, when they felt connected, they got involved to protect and preserve. At her grandfather's knee she'd listened to the stories and history of both nature and humans. Her family had taught her everything about the blessings and dangers of the plants and animals in these mountains.

As an adult, when people got lost in what she considered her oversized backyard, she looked at rescue operations as more than a service to one person. She never wanted anyone to hold a grudge against the power of Mother Nature.

Whatever Lancaster had planned—and her intuition was screaming it wasn't anything good—she wouldn't let him cause lasting problems out here. She'd never purposely led anyone astray on a job, but this might be the time.

The idea didn't sit well, especially since she couldn't be sure whom and what she was dealing with, but patience was another lesson she'd learned the hard way in the great outdoors.

The group was quiet behind her and the back of her neck prickled a warning of Lancaster's hard, unrelenting gaze watching her too closely. She turned often, doing an automatic head count as she kept up her litany about the surroundings, despite the hard pace. It was clear now none of the men were listening. Their loss.

Occasionally she caught a watch or compass check, but nothing was said. She thought maybe Lancaster was settling down until she suggested finding a scenic place to stop for lunch.

He shook his head. "Let's keep moving."

"All right." She carefully stepped around a rotting log. "If everyone agrees."

He dogged her heels. "My team follows my lead. You and your partner work for me now. We'll keep moving."

It had been too much to hope this jerk would give up on the power-play routine. He wasn't the first difficult customer she'd led around the mountain. She stopped short, letting him run into her pack. Her satisfaction didn't last as she did another head count and noticed one of Lancaster's men, Scott, wasn't in sight. Neither was Clint. She scanned the area down the slope, looking for a glimpse of the bright fabric of the company ball caps.

No sign of them. Dread pooled at the nape of her neck and dripped slowly down her spine.

She gripped her radio hard to still her shaking hands and called for Clint. The few seconds before his voice crackled from the speaker were a desperate eternity.

"Just explaining a deer trail," Clint said. "We're all good here."

"I've put you on edge," Lancaster said.

"Yes," she admitted. On edge or not, she was a professional. While Lancaster and his team might be comfortable out here, this wasn't their turf. To a person accustomed to city life, it might look as though she didn't have any recourse or resources out here. She was toying with busting that myth.

"My single-minded focus does that sometimes."

As apologies went, it wasn't good enough. "Putting me on edge isn't healthy for any of us out here." He muttered a better apology, but she wasn't buying it. The bruise on her arm told more truth than any of Lancaster's words. She mentally tossed around defense plans, unable to relax until she saw Clint wave as he and the other man came over the rise. "It might be best if we turn back and you find yourself another guide."

She should've suggested it the moment he'd grabbed her arm. To hell with the money; the business was flush and they were only out groceries and a little gas.

"That's extreme." His smile gave her the willies, made her think of a snake planning to strike. "And it can't really be necessary. My mind is already on our next project and I know our timetable out here isn't adjustable."

"That's easy enough. I'll radio a friend, have them meet us at the campsite tonight and take over from there."

"No. I want *your* guidance, Ms. Binali." He tipped his head toward his team. "We've all been enjoying your lessons today." Behind him six heads bobbed in silent accord. "We're all looking forward to the views from the summit."

Uh-huh. They were looking for something more than a good camera angle and she nearly said so when Clint gave her a hand signal to drop it. Fine. If he was comfortable, she would figure out a way to come to terms with the nerve-racking Mr. Lancaster.

"Considering our progress, I know just the spot to stop for lunch." She held up a hand when he started to protest. "We *are* stopping for thirty minutes to rest and refuel if you want to reach tonight's campsite safely."

She could tell by his sour expression he didn't agree. A small voice in her head begged him to protest, to push her, so she could leave him out here to manage on his own. That was the threshold, she promised herself. One more argument, one more improper exchange and she and Clint would leave them to find their own way. She'd have to answer for it, and as she trudged on, she imagined the fallout.

Lancaster would, at the very least, post a scathing review online. That kind of thing could be hard to overcome, but one negative review among literally thousands of positives? She refused to worry about that.

No, the fallout from her peers and park rangers concerned her more. While anyone who dealt with tourists understood the occasional desire to throttle someone, abandoning them to the elements was never acceptable. She didn't have anything other than a gut instinct that the men were up to something. While her instincts were respected, the authorities would need more than her hunch and general irritation to justify her leaving a client in the wilderness.

"Hey," Clint said, sidling up to her.

"Hey."

"You're thinking of tossing him into the gulley?"

"Rock slides can be a bitch," she confessed.

"So can gunfire," he whispered, putting an arm around her.

"I wouldn't—" She lost her voice, realizing what he meant. "They're armed."

"I'm betting on rifles instead of tents in the bedrolls. I smelled the gun oil and noticed one ankle holster."

"Damn."

"I agree. And that Max guy?"

"Yeah?" She resisted the urge to look back at the man Clint mentioned.

"He's got a major geek-factor electronic compass

disguised as some bogus camera accessory. He's sly about it, but I know what I saw."

Great. Based on Lancaster's insistence to head north, she assumed whatever they wanted was near the summit. Too bad that didn't narrow the possible destination. "What do you want to do?"

"We could ditch them at lunch."

"No." Too risky in broad daylight. "We'll do it tonight." They'd have a better chance of gaining a head start after dark. "We'll split up when they're asleep and you can head down and notify the authorities."

"What about you?"

"I'll circle back and tail them. Find out what they're up to."

"It's a date," Clint said, giving her shoulder a squeeze. Easing away from her, he raised his voice and announced that lunch would be coming up in about a half hour.

Hearing the enthusiastic replies, she wondered if Lancaster was issuing demerits for dissent among the ranks.

She racked her brain for the reason Lancaster and his armed escort wanted to reach the summit. Drugs? Weapons? It could be anything out here, away from prying eyes of civilization.

If Lancaster had come all this way for an illegal meeting or exchange, she didn't hold out much hope he'd leave her and Clint alive to talk about it. With Max's electronic compass and her advice on the best place to make the ascent, Lancaster wouldn't need a guide to get back down the mountain.

It would've been tempting to panic, but Charly wasn't built that way. She'd given him enough of an advantage admitting he made her nervous. That was water under the bridge. She'd use it, let him underestimate her again. It was her best play, because her revolver and a flare gun wouldn't make much of a dent against the arsenal Clint suspected their clients were packing.

## Chapter Six

Will had slipped out of his apartment in the middle of the night, geared up for tailing the hikers who were meeting at sunrise. In layers of muted black, the pockets of his cargo pants loaded with the few things he considered essential on an op, he was ready for anything.

The knife in his boot was an upgrade from standard-issue after his original had been used in self-defense during a hostage recovery operation. The modest nine-millimeter semiautomatic handgun in the holster at the small of his back was almost as comforting as having a buddy with him, and it gave give him ample defense— against wildlife or Lancaster.

He had food and ammunition in various pockets, along with gloves, a knit cap, a smaller knife, a flashlight, his cell phone, camouflage paint for his face and, with a nod to Charly's safety concerns, a roll of medical gauze and tape.

Will had done an assessment of the hotel, but Lancaster had booked rooms at a high-end chain and there hadn't been enough time or an easy way to search the rooms. Instead, he'd stationed himself near the park entrance Charly had mentioned and waited.

The cold didn't bother him; he'd learned to ignore natural circumstances during his SEAL training days.

Push-ups and sit-ups in the surf created a new definition for unpleasant. Training was a mind game, teaching the brain and body which details to ignore. Accepting that as fact was the first step to success. Some of the strangest things stuck with him, despite his best effort, and as he'd waited in the dark for Charly and her clients, the soundtrack from *The Little Mermaid* drifted through his head on a repeating loop.

No one seemed to have any good intel why Lancaster had left his California facility. Everyone with an opinion felt it was tied to the Blackout Key, but Casey reported that a search of Lancaster's Los Angeles office and residence hadn't revealed anything new.

There was plenty of proof Lancaster remained obsessed with taking out his industry enemies, but those enemies weren't in the San Juan National Forest. Will hoped being here early would give him a chance to overhear something helpful before Charly led these guys into an area where making an arrest—if necessary—would be next to impossible.

Lancaster had arrived well before Charly, right in line with the personality assessment Casey had provided. The software genius had a compulsive need to be first in all things. Will wondered if it had always been that way, or if that had stemmed from the man's fixation on revenge.

Observing both Lancaster and his team, Will hadn't felt any better about Charly guiding them into the wilderness with only Clint as backup.

This crew clearly had military training. The hair might be longer than regulation, and the clothing civilian, but the six men were hard-core efficient. No wasted motion, no mistakes, no visible distinguishing marks. While he didn't get eyes on any weapons, Will knew they were there. They used such common first names he nearly laughed as he noted them on his arm.

The only clue about their real purpose had been Lancaster's quiet question about the status of a beacon. The reply, from the one they called Max, had been an affirmative nod.

There were all kinds of things that could be attached to a beacon. Anything from software to equipment, even people. Not much to go on, but Will would pass it up the line before he followed them up the trail.

Charly and Clint had pulled into the parking area five minutes ahead of schedule. Smart, considering her client. She had moved with an efficient grace as she helped Clint unload and distribute supplies for the hikers. While she didn't address it, Will knew she caught the general apathy regarding her safety briefing. From his hiding place he grinned, thinking about the snakebite kit. The woman knew her business, even if she didn't know her clients as well as she should this time around.

Between her skill, Clint's assistance and Will trailing the party, he was confident they could manage the situation and prevent Lancaster from crippling national security.

As Charly led them out, Will lagged behind to search the cars. Peering through the window, he saw car rental paperwork tucked in the visors. No shock they were rentals, but this time Lancaster had used an alias. Will used his cell phone to take pictures of the rental agreement and the bar codes on the car windows and emailed the information to Casey's office. Completing all he could here, he hurried to catch up with the hikers.

NOT EVEN THE expertise of the men with Lancaster gave Will much of a challenge as he followed. Too complacent, they clearly didn't sense any threat, which gave him an advantage. He kept them in sight, waiting for some clue about their intentions out here.

Charly's smooth voice carried through the air periodically as she pointed out plants and bird calls, and the occasional track of an animal who'd crossed the trail. Will was sure her typical clients would love it, but Lancaster and his men weren't impressed.

Charly wasn't an idiot; she had to be picking up some vibe that these men weren't here for the scenery and team building. With every exchange—or lack thereof—he grew more concerned that she'd turn the party back before he could figure out what Lancaster wanted.

The pace was quick, but the brisk air felt good in his lungs and his muscles were warm from the exertion. He was starting to understand what Charly found so appealing up here.

Overhearing the disagreement about the route, Will waited until the group moved out of earshot before he called Director Casey. The cell service was sketchy, but he offered the few details he'd gained so far.

"A beacon?"

"That's what he said," Will confirmed. "But no mention of what kind or who or what they were tracking. They were too careful."

"I'll see what I can find out. We're deconstructing the alias."

"Any success?"

"A passport with that name was used four months ago traveling from LAX to France and back."

Will didn't know if that connected with this at all. "The men with him don't have any particular accents."

"He has men with him?"

"Yes. Six." He rattled off the names. "Flawless English, all of them."

"Accents could have been trained out of them."

"True." Will's instincts leaned more toward American mercenaries, carefully researched and quietly recruited to Lancaster's cause. He kept the opinion to himself. Either way, they were armed and dangerous. He was eager to catch up with Charly and keep her safe. "Any ties to Colorado?"

"Not that we've found. We're still looking."

Will understood how manpower and urgency shifted on a daily basis. Based on the file, someone had been dialed into Lancaster's public rhetoric and movements for years. "Any action in his offices?" Everything he'd learned about the reverse-engineering key in the past twenty-four hours made typical hackers look like social butterflies. The data on this sort of software development suggested the potential for abuse was astronomical.

"None. What about the guide?" There was static, and Casey had to try three more times to make the question clear to Will.

"She's solid," Will replied, shifting a bit to find a stronger signal. "The best guide out here."

"Could Lancaster turn her?"

"Into what?" The idea of Charly being influenced to do something illegal amused Will, though he knew everyone had a price. "She doesn't compromise." Especially not when it came to her beloved mountains.

"Good. Remember Lancaster's the priority. She's expendable."

The words, uttered between crackles and dead air, landed like rocks in his stomach. Will rallied against the reaction. Collateral damage had been part of every mission he'd accepted for his country. This wouldn't be any different.

Except he liked Charly and he wanted to know her better. Last night's dinner had started as a means to an end, but their previous dates had been a result of mutual attraction and friendship. And that kiss? He'd enjoyed it and, like any of his red-blooded male peers, it had left him working out how to get more.

More kisses and more of whatever she was willing to share beyond kisses.

"Lancaster is ruthless and…learned some things… he's out for blood," Casey said.

"Yes, sir." Will could fill in the missing words easily enough. "Let me know if you get anything on the beacon."

"It must…for the key…"

Will checked the display and moved again, hoping to hear a complete sentence this time. "…don't know how it got out there."

"I'll find it." He gave Casey the radio channels Binali Backcountry used and ended the call. Full of urgency, he navigated a route parallel to the track Charly was on and quickly closed the gap, catching up with them.

Despite the natural dangers, so far this assignment was a breeze. The mountain offered plenty of cover and resources. When he paused to listen or look around, the views were stunning.

But when he was in earshot of Lancaster again it was clear the older man wasn't as impressed with the environment. He became increasingly difficult for Charly as the day wore on, though she and Clint maintained their composure. Will watched the guides talk on two occasions, before and after lunch, and knew they were planning something. He didn't want to reveal himself or his purpose, but he couldn't let them jeopardize his mission, either. Casey and the authorities needed to know what had brought Lancaster out here, and Will couldn't let the guides jeopardize the primary objective.

As dinner wound down and Charly proposed setting up camp for the night, Lancaster protested again.

"There's plenty of light left," he shouted at her, sending birds that had roosted for the night winging into the air.

Will wasn't close enough to catch more than the sound of Charly's calm, quiet voice in reply. Taking a head count, grateful for the bright caps she gave to her guests, he planned his route and silently crept closer to the campsite.

"If we want to keep moving, you need to accommodate us," Lancaster said at a more reasonable volume. "Call the night hiking another team challenge," he added.

Clint spoke up. "That kind of challenge isn't worth the risk." He angled closer to Charly. "I have plenty of fun in store for tomorrow. It's better if we get some rest tonight."

"We're rested," Lancaster insisted.

The menacing tone, along with the eye contact between the others, had Will reaching for the knife in his boot. Could he break cover without causing more harm to people and the op? He wasn't sure he had the leverage to ensure Lancaster's honest cooperation.

"There's a meteor shower this week," Charly said. "Tonight's peak time is only a few hours away."

"Not one of us gives a damn about the stars!"

"I know you want to reach the summit, and we'll get there," Charly was saying. Will admired her ability to stay calm despite the evidence that Lancaster wasn't here for the nature high. "Patience is important in these mountains. Especially at night. We're farther along than I'd planned, which makes tomorrow a shorter day."

"We go north." Lancaster's gaze roamed over each of his men in turn, and then he faced Charly once more. "Now."

"No." Charly, only two or three inches shorter than Lancaster, stared him down. "Night falls faster than you think and I won't risk it."

"We packed lights."

"No." She crossed her arms, feet planted.

"By your own rules—" Lancaster circled his finger, indicating his team. "We're in agreement."

"High risks or impromptu changes require a unanimous decision or a life-threatening circumstance." She tapped her chest. "I'm not hiking any more tonight."

"You misunderstand who is in charge here, Ms. Binali."

Her thick braid rippled between her shoulders as she shook her head. "Nature is in charge here, Mr. Lancaster," she shot back. "You can get mad or you can accept the facts. Darkness means predators and makes natural obstacles impossible to see. Flashlights aren't enough. My responsibility is to show you the mountain without injury or worse. That's why you hired me."

"I hired you to get me to the summit." He pulled out a heavy black handgun and leveled it on Charly. "The sooner the better."

Will braced for panic, but in the waning twilight Charly didn't flinch. "We stay here tonight."

"Whatever you're after, we'll find it tomorrow," Clint said.

*Crap.* Big mistake. Will wished he could do something, but he had to let Charly defuse this situation. Lancaster was too sure his target was north of here. Will would head that way, despite Charly's warning, just as soon as the group decided to stay put for the night.

Lancaster slowly turned to Clint, giving a nod to one of his men. "What do you know about it?"

"About what?" Clint tugged the bill of his ball cap. "I saw Max tracking something, that's all. I—"

The violent crack of gunfire ripped through the air and the forest seemed to shiver as wildlife reacted, scurrying through the shadows around Will.

Clint dropped to his knees, his hand clutched over the chest wound, blood oozing through his fingers, spreading across his shirt. Charly rushed to his side, doing her best to contain the bleeding, but Will knew it was a lost cause. A shot like that would've been fatal if they'd been standing fifty paces from a trauma center. Up here, in the middle of nowhere, Clint didn't stand a chance. In silent fury, helpless to intervene, Will swore as he watched the macabre scene unfold.

"Take the radios."

One of the men came forward and took the devices right off Charly and Clint. She was too focused on helping Clint to protest. Will couldn't blame her. Damn it. She'd be dead by morning at this rate. Mission protocol or not, he couldn't accept that. There had to be a way to get her out of here.

"Search the packs for a phone or anything else she might use against us." Lancaster barked out more orders about breaking camp before aiming his gun at Charly once more.

Will watched as her revolver, ammunition and flare gun were confiscated. Their cover blown, it didn't surprise him to see the operatives making their own weapons more accessible. He counted three rifles and each man moved a handgun into view. Two of them were left-handed. Those were just the weapons he could see—he had to assume there were more out of sight and plenty of ammunition to spare. A pretty big arsenal for a team of software engineers, but about right for mercenaries looking for a big payday.

"Get up." Lancaster gestured with his gun.

"I'm not leaving him."

Lancaster dropped to one knee, his voice low, the threat unmistakable. "I'm tired of you hindering me. I want your full cooperation." He tugged at her arm, but she wrenched away. "Get up. We're moving out right now."

"Go ahead and kill yourselves. I won't stop you. I'm staying with Clint."

Lancaster pushed to his feet, stalked a few paces away to talk with his men. The argument was loud and heated and centered around the tracking device Max carried. Even highly trained mercenaries had to sleep sometime. When they did, Will would make his move.

He ached for Charly, understanding how she felt. He'd lost teammates on operations and while he hadn't been there when it happened, he carried the burden of his younger brother in what was left of his heart.

She had to know Clint wouldn't survive, but she refused to give up on her friend. He respected the emotion fueling her determination, but he worried how she would cope when the adrenaline wore off and the grief set in.

She started to sing, rocking gently with Clint in her arms, and the strange words raised goose bumps on his arms. Clearly a song from her Native American heritage, the cadence and tune, the rise and fall of her voice felt older than time and completely in tune with the wilderness. Lancaster and his men stopped and stared as her voice rose, powered by her sorrow.

Will could even the odds right now, maybe take them all, but any miscalculation would put Charly in the crossfire. He dragged his attention back to the real problem: Lancaster. Only one thing would push the man this close to madness: Lancaster's revenge. Will felt certain the Blackout Key was somewhere on this mountain. It didn't matter if it made sense; he had to follow the most logical lead. Will could bide his time, take out Max and the tracking device, but he couldn't bring himself to leave Charly alone with this deadly crew.

If there was one thing Will managed on every op, it was getting creative when it mattered.

# Chapter Seven

Clint was dying. In her arms. Charly felt him fading with every labored breath, every weak flutter of his heart. The copper scent of his blood choked the air.

A stronger woman would stand and fight, but that would leave Clint to die alone. She couldn't save him, but she wouldn't let him bleed out on the cold, unyielding mountain without any comfort.

Lancaster shouted at her, tugged at her, but she didn't listen. One of his men seized the radios and their packs. None of that mattered. Her hand pressed to her friend's wound, she tried desperately to slow the bleeding. Despite the losing battle, she put on a brave face. "It's not that bad," she murmured. "You'll make it."

"Right." He looked at her out of glassy eyes, his lips twitching in an effort to grin. "Could be worse."

She understood the sentiment even as her heart clutched with agony. In their line of work, accidents were inevitable, natural disasters a daily risk. Safety precautions failed. Between her friends and family, they often discussed there were worse ways to die than under a big sky in nature's embrace, doing what they loved.

"You'll make it," she repeated.

His head jerked to the side and his breath stuttered. "Get away."

"Together," she insisted. His eyelids drifted shut and she willed them to open one more time. It was too soon for goodbye. "Clint." She gave him a little shake with her trembling arms. "Hang on. We'll find help."

She rambled more nonsense as her elders' chants of sorrow whispered through her mind, echoed through the trees. Words and prayers that should be spoken for Clint, over him, and she was the only one to speak them. If she couldn't save her friend, at least she could honor him.

The words were soft at first, but her voice gained strength as Clint's life drained away. She let the songs and the spirit behind them flow over him like a gentle rain. Tipping her face to the clear night sky, the soft breeze dried her tears as she called on the heritage beating through her heart to guide and protect Clint on his next journey.

She finished the prayer, let the final note drift into the coming night. Opening her eyes, she looked down at her bloodstained hands, at Clint's lifeless body, and felt gravity dragging her down.

"Move out."

Lancaster's voice was hard and ugly and Charly ignored him. Her work wasn't done. She walked toward the shallow creek and knelt down, washing the blood from her hands.

"We're moving out." Lancaster hauled her to her feet.

"Good luck to you." She wouldn't waste energy hurling fury at him. She would not taint the grace of the moment or the task ahead by slinging insults and venom at the man who stole Clint's life. There would be time for that later. "I must bury my friend."

"A futile, sentimental gesture."

Her body coiled to strike, to lash out, but it would

be a useless gesture and prevent her from completing a necessary task. "Clint deserves better than to have animals tearing at his body." She picked up a stone only to have Lancaster knock it from her hands. She picked it up again, imagining herself in a Teflon bubble, his anger sliding off her as he followed her back to the body.

"Have you ever seen what scavengers can do?" she asked no one in particular. "You wouldn't wish it on your worst enemy." Back and forth, she hauled stones one by one to cover Clint.

"On top of that," she continued in her educational tone, "all the blood will attract predators. Are you prepared to outmaneuver them?"

Around her the men argued, uncertain how to proceed. Lancaster wanted to keep moving, others wanted to wait. All of them thought she'd lost her mind, but they were divided about the wisdom of leaving her behind. In a tiny corner of her mind Charly listened, amused, while her body kept on task.

"Pick up your pack or I'll shoot you, too," Lancaster threatened, his gun aimed at her face, when she'd placed yet another stone on Clint's incomplete grave.

"Go ahead." She turned her back on him, refusing to cow to his bluster and bullying. "You and your gadgets will have all kinds of fun up here without me."

More arguing was silenced by a wolf howl slicing through the night.

"Scavengers," she said.

"There are wolves out here?"

She didn't stop moving, but she slid a look at Jeff, the man who'd asked the question. "Didn't you listen at all? There are wolves, snakes, mountain lions, bears—"

"Shut up!" Lancaster bellowed.

With a shrug, she continued her work, not surprised Jeff joined her.

"What the hell are you doing?" Scott demanded, blocking Jeff's attempt to help her bury Clint.

"The sooner we get this done, the sooner we get out of here."

"Thank you," Charly said. "Clint wouldn't approve of being an easy meal."

Her back ached; her hands were cold and bleeding with fresh scrapes on her knuckles and palms. The sting felt good, reminding her she was alive and doing the right thing. Not just for Clint, but to defy Lancaster.

Knowing it made them uncomfortable, she started to sing again, the old creation story-song her grandmother had taught her. It had been one of Clint's favorites. Charly decided she would sing all of the songs of her childhood to honor Clint and keep Lancaster and his men on edge.

No one usually cared that she was part of the Ute nation. Her clients typically only asked about her Native American lineage when she led them down into the pueblos and canyons. Why couldn't Lancaster have headed that direction? The pueblos were riddled with places to lose these guys. Even better, that area was littered with ways to scare them to death and even up the long odds against her. That would've been fun.

It would take cleverness and a good share of luck to escape all seven men up here. On this part of the ridge, there were thick stands of trees, but also wide-open places. They were armed, but she had the real advantage. She knew her way over every inch of wild land east of the Four Corners Monument all the way to Telluride. She knew what the mountain offered by way of protection and danger. If she could be patient, she could clip them off one at a time, like a wolf culling a buffalo herd.

The image made her smile.

"What are you so happy about?" Lancaster had stepped into her path once more. "Your friend is dead and you'll join him when I'm done with you."

She looked straight into his eyes and thought she saw the glare of madness, something he'd hidden well when he hired her yesterday. "It would be an honor to join my friend. There are worse ways to die than out here under the big sky."

"You're crazy."

Possibly. Right now she didn't care if he shot her and she sure as hell didn't care about his opinion of her sanity. With a shrug, she stepped around him, determined to finish the burial. "Takes one to know one," she said, resuming her story-song.

Rich joined Jeff's efforts, and she couldn't get angry about their help. Soon Clint's body and the bloodstained earth around it were covered. The rocks glowed pale in the light of the rising moon.

One of Lancaster's men had started a fire, effectively ending the discussion of moving on tonight. If she'd known which man, she might've thanked him. Exhaustion crept up on her, and her limbs felt heavy as she rested near Clint's grave. But though her eyelids drooped, she listened to the talk of the men around her. They weren't careless enough to reveal the specifics, but whatever beacon they were following appeared to be on the other side of the peak.

She fought the urge to laugh. Assuming the beacon's signal wasn't distorted by the mountains, Lancaster and his men would soon discover just how much wide-open space they would have to cross to reach their goal.

She didn't argue when it was decided she'd spend the night tied to a tree away from the fire, away from Clint. She didn't care that Jeff would take the first watch as her guard.

Lancaster allowed her the use of her sleeping bag and a bottle of water only so she'd be more useful tomorrow. Jeff found the small knife she kept in her boot when he tethered her to the tree with nylon rope, but he didn't raise the alarm, merely pocketed it without a word.

In her anguished haze she felt some remorse that she'd have to hurt the one man in this crew with a shred of decency, but it had to be done. She would not be here when Lancaster woke in the morning.

WILL LISTENED TO the men argue as Charly slowly buried Clint. Unsure how much of the conversation she heard, he marveled at her unwavering behavior in the face of their cold discussion about killing her.

He'd certainly never seen anyone as resolute in a task as Charly hauling rocks to cover Clint's body. Hopefully it wasn't a sign that she'd snapped. Even if it was, he'd get her off this mountain in one piece so she could recover with people who loved her.

When Will was convinced Lancaster wouldn't shoot her out of temper or spite, he backed away from the camp, moving through the shadows until he couldn't hear her haunting voice any longer.

At the edge of a tree line, he paused and gathered himself before he even attempted to make the call to Casey. He'd seen men die. He'd been responsible for putting more than a few bad guys out of commission. But never had he witnessed anything as beautiful as the tribute Charly paid Clint.

The memory of his brother's funeral slammed to

the front of Will's mind. He didn't want to go there, had more than enough to deal with, yet he knew better than to fight the onslaught. When those memories were triggered, they faded faster if he simply let them flow.

The chapel had been standing room only, the casket closed. He'd walked forward to join the family—his parents—only to realize too late that there wasn't a seat for him. His mother had lifted her blotchy, tearstained face and stared at him with so much blame the words weren't necessary.

After so many times rehashing and reliving that terrible moment, Will expected the bitterness and ache to fade, but it remained fresh and raw.

He'd never heard anything as haunting as Charly's voice raised in that strange benediction. At first he'd thought it was grief, but he'd seen plenty of that along the way. Her song or prayer or whatever it was had clearly been offered as tribute for Clint.

He knew it was natural in the wake of death to think about his mortality. Will knew no one would ever grieve that way for him. He couldn't dwell on it because it was part of the job. As a SEAL he'd accepted the possibility of dying anonymously in the line of duty. He considered it an honor.

Pulling in a deep breath of the cold night air, he steeled himself for the work ahead. Nothing had changed except the number of innocents in the equation. He checked the signal on his phone and despite the miniscule single bar, he dialed Casey's office.

As the phone rang on the other end of the line, Will resolved that when they got off this mountain he would have Charly tell him about her song for Clint. It always helped him to have an end goal on a mission, especially a mission with long odds and high stakes. One against seven could almost be fun, as long as Charly came through unscathed.

The director answered, and Will snapped to full alert.

The signal was remarkably clear this time. "Lancaster shot one guide. The crew is camped for the night, but determined to reach the summit and points north ASAP."

"Still following a beacon?" Casey asked.

"Yes, sir. Could he have put it on the key somehow?"

"That's my fear. We've connected a few dots. Lancaster didn't disappear until a plane he was expecting to meet in Los Angeles never showed up. It's possible the software, or someone transporting it was on the plane, but I don't have any names to work with yet."

"I haven't heard any news of a plane crash around here," Will replied. Surely that kind of thing would've caught someone's attention.

"We know it was a small private charter. If it was off course or skirting radar systems, no one would know."

True. Calling in a helicopter to search for a missing plane was out of the question. Up here, in the thin air, there had to be a starting point and a reason to justify the risk. Neither was available with the limited intel. The altitude and terrain would cause all sorts of problems for both plane and helo pilots.

Will felt the weight of the world drop onto his shoulders. He and Charly—and a mountain—were the only things standing between Lancaster and whatever he had planned.

"Everything in the Los Angeles office and home point to a revenge strike against the big developers," Casey said. "After his long silence he wasn't even trying to hide his hate and vengeance anymore."

"Which means he's all or nothing out here." *Great.* Will sighed, rubbing the knots of tension at the base of his neck.

"Exactly," Casey agreed. "If the software was on that plane, he'll do anything to reach it."

"Could the key even survive the crash?"

"Lancaster must believe it has."

"He's a man with focus, that's for sure," Will allowed. Men like that were a crazy kind of dangerous.

"Can you get to the crash site before Lancaster's team?"

It didn't sound as though he had much of a choice. "Without set coordinates, I doubt it. But I can definitely keep them from leaving with the key if it's there."

"That's the objective. You're all that's standing between a madman and every locked door in the nation. Hell, the world. The intel coming in paints an ugly picture, Will."

Will thought it couldn't be much uglier than what he'd been watching unfold a few klicks away. "I can eliminate him and seize the tracker." It would be the clean, fast resolution. Then Casey could bring in experts to secure the plane and the key.

The silence stretched so long Will thought the call had dropped. "No," Casey said. "We need him alive. He's the only person who knows how to deconstruct the Blackout Key. He's likely the only one who can code a counter response if the key gets out into the world."

Will didn't offer his opinion that Lancaster wouldn't cooperate with authorities. Casey had to know that already and Will got paid for action, not opinions. If they needed Lancaster alive, Will would take him alive. It would be easier if he had a better read on the crew surrounding Lancaster. Would they bail if their boss fell apart, or were they dedicated to the madman's cause? "Do you have any intel on the mercenaries with him? Are they here for a big payout or something else?"

"No idea. We're combing his life for clues. What have you observed?"

*Nothing new*, Will thought. "Ruthless. Arms are US made." Which didn't clarify anything. American guns and ammunition remained a hot commodity and could be attained legally or otherwise from just about anywhere in the world. The men were also freaked out by Charly's behavior, but he didn't add that. "I'm fairly confident they're American."

"Stay on it. More information could lead to the second-tier targets after Lancaster's vendetta is satisfied."

"Stay tuned to the emergency radio channels." He'd said it before, but it bore repeating. Most people didn't understand the limited communication in these mountains. Worried about Charly, Will wanted to get back over to the camp. "Up here it may be my only way for me to get information out."

"All right."

Hearing Casey's frustration, Will sympathized. "Lancaster thinks he's close. I'll be there when he finds it."

"Good luck."

Will powered off the phone and returned it to his pocket. He wouldn't risk it again for hours and wanted to preserve the battery. While he had a solar-powered backup battery with him, he didn't anticipate having the luxury of recharging time.

His mind working, he carefully picked his way back toward the camp, slowing as he got closer and listening for sentries.

He heard the wilderness—the hoot of an owl and the

rustle of small prey in the underbrush—but he didn't hear any sound of humans. When he caught the smoky scent of the banked fire, he followed his instincts and crossed the stream.

It was unlikely anyone posted to keep watch would bother with more than a cursory glance in this direction. They'd consider the stream a natural barrier to predators of any variety. Lancaster's men weren't expecting any company out here anyway.

Will hunkered down at the base of a tree and waited for some sign of a sentry. He let half an hour tick by and with no sign or sound, he crept closer. The arrogance of men had made his job easier in the past and he never turned down a gimme when it fell into his lap.

Staying on the far side of the little stream, Will did a head count. Twice. Coming up one short, he circled the camp and counted again. Seven people. Six prone, resting close to the fire, and all of them a safe distance from Clint's rocky grave. All of them were breathing. One man sat apart from the others, leaning upright against a tree. Next to an empty sleeping bag.

Where had they put Charly?

His pulse raced and he felt the hot lick of panic for the first time since his early training days when the physical tests had pushed his body to the red zone. He forced himself away from illogical, unproven assumptions. Lancaster's men had refused to continue without her guidance. That ripple of dissent hadn't made Lancaster happy, but it was the reason Will had retreated to give his update.

Will counted one more time. Seven men. Zero women.

Charly wasn't in the camp.

Had Lancaster snapped and killed her anyway? No,

if Lancaster had done that the men would've moved on as he'd wanted all along. He moved closer to the seated man. Close enough to notice the man's hands were tied, to see the thin line of drying blood at his throat.

Will thought of the knife Charly had tucked into her sleeping bag and breathed a quiet sigh. The rush of relief was a palpable force.

Now he just had to find her. An expert tracker in a cold forest shrouded by night. He'd wanted a challenge.

# *Chapter Eight*

*An hour earlier*

Charly's heart pounded in her ribs as she shifted in her sleeping bag, trying to get comfortable while being tied to the tree behind Jeff. He'd done it up right, looping the rope around her ankle, then around the tree and pinning it with a tent stake. Leaning back against the tree trunk, he'd made a point of adding his key chain to the assembly, so even if he dozed off, he'd hear the rattle if she tried to escape.

Too bad for him that wasn't going to stop her. She stared sightlessly at Clint's grave, waiting for the other men to stop bickering and settle down. It took only a little less than an eternity. She rolled to her other side, kicking her legs a little and rattling the key against the tent stake. Jeff looked her way, but no one else said a word.

She needed to get out of here, and she would. But it would be foolish to bolt into the night with no plan. As she tossed and turned in her sleeping bag, she reviewed her choices and Lancaster's potential reactions to each.

Instinct warred with reality. Rushing straight back to Durango sounded ideal, but Lancaster could easily head off that kind of play. She knew the terrain, but he had the radios and rifles. If she aimed west for the nearest park ranger station, she had a better chance. While no one could track like her, she'd seen enough to know Lancaster's men weren't idiots. The crucial element, she decided, was getting away clean. Tonight was her best chance. Tomorrow he might kill her for any number of reasons.

She peered at her guard through slitted eyes and found him alert, scanning the area. So he took the watch responsibilities seriously. Sucker.

When she was a teenager, and even before that, when she'd started solo hikes, her family had taught her how to be safe up here. How to read animal tracks and watch for shifting weather. The wilderness was beauty and magnificence honed to a sharp and dangerous edge. She'd learned a little something from everyone in her family about protecting and defending herself from nature and man.

The sleeve sewn under the pillow of her sleeping bag had been a precaution against drunk or stupid hikers who might get the wrong idea about the services Binali Backcountry provided on overnight adventures. It was a rare thing, praise God, to fend off unwelcome advances, but it was better to be prepared than caught unawares. She counted it lucky that she'd chosen to tuck the knife from her grandmother into her sleeping bag this time out. It calmed her down and gave her a sense of empowerment as her fingers rubbed the familiar turquoise inlay.

Confident the other men were settled and asleep, she curled onto her side, jerking the tether on purpose again and adding a sniffle for effect.

"Go to sleep," Jeff said, keeping his voice low.

"I'm trying to get my boots off," she lied.

"Keep them on. Your feet will get cold."

"How nice of you to care," she muttered. "Feet and boots need to air out to stay healthy."

"Whatever." He shifted, adjusting his back against the tree. "Sleep."

"You know I'm right. I hope you packed lots of socks. For a guy with obvious field training, you're ignoring the basics."

"Quiet," he snapped. A moment later, she gave a mental cheer as he unlaced his boots.

It was a start. "You'll never get away with this," she said after a few more minutes.

"Our plans are not your problem, Ms. Binali."

She rattled the tether. "I beg to differ."

"Shut up."

She didn't stop rattling the key against the tent stake, even as the knife slid through the rope, freeing her. She wanted him to come at her, to give her a better reason than escape to sink her blade between his ribs.

Charly wouldn't relish killing a man, but she knew she could do it if necessary. Jeff might not have pulled the trigger, but he was part of something dark and evil by staying loyal to Lancaster.

Of course, Jeff had been the first to show compassion by helping her bury her friend. She preferred a solution for him that didn't involve death.

Survival was paramount. Her survival. Whatever these men were up to, when she escaped she trusted the mountain to keep them busy or kill them off until she could return with the authorities. Either by nature's law or man's law, one way or another Lancaster and his men would pay for murdering Clint.

"Stop screwing around," Jeff said, his impatience clear. "I can make this worse for you."

"I'd like to see you try," she dared. She'd considered the various ploys to get him to come closer. Seduction was out—even if she could stomach the idea long enough to get away, she didn't think Jeff or any of the others would fall for it.

She'd sensed a shift among them when she'd refused to quake and cower at the wrong end of Lancaster's gun. She'd sensed their fear. Not just of Lancaster's actions, but of her. On some level her reactions and her tribute to Clint scared them. With Jeff in particular, she would use that fear and spare his life. If possible.

She stared him down as she rolled over once more and rattled the key.

"Enough." He pushed to his feet, the scowl on his face twisting his features in the eerie glow from the fire.

She tucked the knife away and stood up as well, keeping her boots and the severed nylon rope covered by the folds of her sleeping bag. "Give me your hands," he ordered, pitching his voice low.

She held them out and used the distraction to block the knee she aimed at his groin. He buckled forward on a whimper and she drove her fist up deep into his diaphragm.

Pivoting him as he collapsed, she let him slide down the trunk of the tree until he was back where he started. He stared up at her with wide eyes full of shock and pain, unable to voice a protest as she retrieved her gun and ammunition. She tossed the radio out of reach.

She pressed her knife to Jeff's throat. "I could kill you."

He froze, his eyes locked with hers, though she could tell he wanted to keep rocking against the pain.

She drew the blade against his skin, just a scratch, but it raised a narrow line of blood. It distracted him from her real purpose, which was putting him into a deep sleep. When she found the pressure point in his neck, he went limp and she quickly tied his hands.

Unwilling to waste time and risk waking the others, Charly didn't take so much as a canteen as she darted, silent as an owl, into the dark. She knew how to survive off the mountain. Conveniently bottled water and packaged food would be more burden than help to her.

She started straight down the mountain, aiming for the nearest official trail, leaving a heavy boot print every few paces. She dropped her company ball cap at one point and veered sharply away, scuffing at the dirt as if she'd paused in the shelter of a tree to get her bearings. If she'd drawn a map for Lancaster it wouldn't have been as clear. If she was lucky, his arrogance and low opinion of her would be enough to follow this trail without question.

Right into her trap.

With no idea how much of a head start she had, she moved quickly, hoping the screen would hold up in the light of day. Maybe they'd search for her early and follow her tracks right over the edge of this rock slide and into the stream below. At least one of them would be injured, hopefully more, and that would start to even the odds.

As she finished, she willed her heart to be quiet so she could hear any pursuit. Hearing no sign of Lancaster's men, she moved on, this time without a trace. Every step of freedom was a pure joy, despite the heavy burden of Clint's death. The *should have done*s nipped at her conscience, telling her Clint might be alive if she'd handled things differently.

It was bull, she told herself, a natural result of being alive. Caving to guilt and fear and regret would only get her caught and killed. The best hope, the only real option, was to reach a ranger station and make a full report. Preferably by dawn.

Her mind set, she crept closer toward her real goal, picking her way through the fractured shadows of the forest. She'd only gone a few paces in that direction when she heard the distinct snap of a twig. She slowly turned toward the sound, straining to hear something that would give her a clue as to what was out there.

But the forest had gone still along with her. Not a good sign—that kind of stillness indicated something was out here that shouldn't be. Knowing exactly where she was, she knew she was too far from any real safety. Damn it. She'd never expected any of Lancaster's men to be this good.

They'd been heavy-footed and generally dismissive of their surroundings all day, making plenty of noise on the hike. Had it been an act?

Well, with any luck there'd be time and breath to berate herself later. Calculating the risk, she charged toward the break in the tree line. Her breath sawed in and out of her lungs as she pumped her arms and legs, plowing forward. Being exposed in the open space wouldn't be ideal, but she could minimize that in a race for the drop on the opposite side.

Almost there, close enough to see the moonlight on the high meadow, she went down hard under a heavy mass. She rolled with the tackle, kicking her legs out and pushing her assailant away.

On a grunted oath, she realized this wasn't something as simple as a confused bear or curious mountain lion. She wasn't that lucky. This was a man bent on subduing her. He lunged again, trapping her legs in a brutal grip against his chest.

Hell, no.

She wasn't going back to Lancaster, wasn't going down like this. Ignoring the bite of various bits of nature on the forest floor, she squirmed and rolled until he was on top of her. She drove her elbows into the sensitive points at the top of his shoulders, trying to get enough space to draw the gun or knife.

The reflexive release was short-lived. The grip loosened only enough so he could shift higher, wrapping her tightly and pinning her arms to her sides.

"It's me. Will."

The voice, hoarse in her ear, was foreign to her. She fought to get a leg free to strike, but his legs were stronger still.

"Relax, Charly."

As if. It had to be a trick. Will was in town. She let her body go limp, pretending to comply. When the man eased up, she scooped a handful of dirt and dried leaves into his face.

His muffled oath followed her across the moonlight-soaked meadow. She didn't look back—didn't have to, she could hear him closing in fast. His hands caught in her jacket, slowing her down. She shrugged out of it and shot ahead.

"Charly!"

Aiming straight for the drop-off, knowing the cost of her survival would involve plenty of pain, she kept going.

But he caught her again, slowing her just enough that they went over the edge together. As her body bounced down the rocky slope, knocking the air from her lungs, bright spots of light danced across her vision.

They skidded to a stop, and she willed herself to fight on, but her body wouldn't cooperate.

"Charly! Wake up. I'm here to help."

Hearing Will's voice she knew she was either dead or hallucinating. Will couldn't be here. He was down in Durango delivering mail. Waiting at the pub for another game of pool. She batted away the hands sweeping over her face, smoothing her hair.

"That's my girl. You're safe now."

It was a challenge to muster the energy to open her eyes. Her brain was playing tricks on her. Will couldn't be here. And she didn't care about cooperating in the slightest way with any of Lancaster's men.

"Just shoot me and call it done," she mumbled, feeling defeated. She couldn't beat them.

"No way. I'm not done with you."

The man who sounded like Will kissed her forehead. The touch was offensive and her melting reaction to it was worse. She rallied in outrage. Shoving the man off her, she scooted out of reach.

"Back off." She jerked the knife from her boot, holding it ready though she couldn't quite see her attacker in the weak light of the moon.

"Take it easy, Charly. Put that away."

She blinked several times to clear her vision. She must've taken a hard blow to the head. In the moonlight, this guy actually looked like Will. "This is a nightmare. You're a bad dream."

"It's good to see you, too," he said with a little laugh.

She knew that sound, that laugh. This was a serious hallucination. She rubbed her eyes with one hand, knife clutched in the other. "You can't be...can't be here." She pressed her fingers against the ache building in her temples. "You're in Durango."

"Not anymore. You're safe now. Put the knife away."

As her eyes adjusted and his features became clearer,

she did as he asked and sheathed the knife. "It's really you."

"Yes." His mouth tilted in that lopsided smile she liked. "I'm here to help."

"What?" What did that mean? This was a sick dream. She had to wake up, had to reach the ranger station. Determined, she tried to stand, called it a good start when she managed to stay upright a few seconds before slumping against the nearest boulder. Her ribs ached and her hands were stinging with fresh scrapes.

"Have some water."

She eyed the bottle he held out. "You first." He twisted off the top and tipped it back. "Fine," she said, accepting. She sniffed at it and then took a long drink, letting it slide down and soothe her dry throat.

"Believe it's me yet?"

"Maybe by daylight," she replied, shivering.

"I have a flashlight."

"I have a gun," she countered, wondering if it was still true. "Don't bother with the light." It could draw the others.

"You sound steadier."

"Yay," she said through chattering teeth.

"I'm here for you, Charly. Tell me how to help."

"Who the hell *are* you?"

"It's me, Will Chase. Were you expecting someone else?"

Yeah, she was expecting Jeff or one of the others. She still expected one or all of them to burst out of the night and attack. "You're working for them."

"Absolutely not. I'm on your side. You have to believe that."

She did. On instinct, she did believe him. Though she didn't understand how it was possible for him to be here. Maybe this was one of those spirit guide dreams. She nearly laughed, thinking how absurd it would be if her spirit guide was a white mailman from Illinois.

"Charly, sit down here beside me."

"We're not safe here."

"Sure we are."

She shook her head, wobbling a bit. "Did you drug me?"

"No, but my guess is you're a little dazed. Possibly dealing with mild shock."

"That's impossible." She couldn't be dazed or in shock. No time for that nonsense. Shivering, she didn't protest when he put her back into her polar fleece coat and wrapped an arm around her waist. She felt the weight of her revolver in her pocket. If he was with the bad guys, he wouldn't let her keep her weapons. He guided her under the shelter of an overhang and helped her sit down. "You've been through hell the past few hours," he said in that easy way he had.

It felt better to sit down, her legs outstretched, Will's hard body warm beside her. She didn't know how he'd found her and she needed a few answers, but she understood she was crashing from the stress of a sustained fight-or-flight response.

Her body recognized him even if her mind argued obstinately. Relaxing into his embrace, she let her head drop to his shoulder. "Clint is dead," she whispered into the night.

"I know, baby."

"He's dead." She looked down at her hands, muted smears against her khaki hiking pants. "He died in my arms."

"I know."

WILL BREATHED EASIER when Charly fell asleep. Giving her time to rest was the least he could do after the wicked fight she'd put up. If he'd known giving away his position would result in her rushing headlong off the mountainside, he would've come up with a better way to let her know he was there.

Her lean body was solid muscle under those subtle, feminine curves.

When he'd found the gun in her jacket, he counted himself lucky she hadn't shot him. He'd expected the knife—it only made sense—but she hadn't used either against him. He chalked it up to her being in full-flight mode. She'd done everything—including run off a small cliff—to get away from him.

It hadn't been easy to find her in the dark; if she hadn't left that bogus trail before doubling back, he might still be wandering around. The woman could move with the absolute silence and grace of a mountain lion when she chose. It had been more than a little spooky to watch her.

She didn't make a sound or leave a trace unless she wanted to, although their wrestling match on the other side of the meadow had left plenty of evidence that would gather unwelcome attention if Lancaster bothered to search this far.

It wouldn't matter. The only way Will could be sure what Reed Lancaster was up to was to stay on the man's tail. He smoothed a hand over the silk of Charly's midnight hair, hoping when she woke up she'd be willing to help him execute his plan. If they found the plane or key Lancaster was searching for, they could put this mission to bed and she could get back to her regularly scheduled life.

## Chapter Nine

Hours later, under the weak light of a dawn shrouded by misty rain, Charly planted her hands on her hips and glared daggers at Will. "We're not going back to where those devils are." She shook her head. "Absolutely not." Her muscles ached, her eyes felt gritty. Every time she looked at her hands she saw Clint's blood. She wasn't going to take any chances that Lancaster would escape justice. They needed the authorities up here. "We have to go for help."

"I am the help," Will said.

She wanted to believe it. Admittedly, he'd helped her last night, giving her shelter and security to recover a bit. "Why didn't you announce yourself rather than chase me?"

"I let you know I was there."

"Breaking a twig hardly counts." She needed to get over it, but it annoyed her that she hadn't even sensed him until he'd taken action. Mailmen weren't typically praised for stealth.

"You're pissed thinking I got the better of you, but really it was sheer luck I caught you before you disappeared from the false trail you laid."

She pushed her hands through her hair, combing out the tangles and wishing she hadn't ditched her ball cap in that effort. "How can we be sure you didn't leave signs out there showing them exactly where to find me?"

"They aren't here, are they?"

*Fair point.* She blew her hair away from her face.

"What do you need from me, Charly?"

His tone was as hard as the grim look on his face. She'd never seen him so serious. It scared her a little. Resigned, she pulled her hair forward over her shoulder and started weaving it into a braid. She didn't miss the way his eyes tracked the motions.

"Nothing," she insisted. "I'm going up to the ranger station to let them know Lancaster is a problem child. You go ahead and do whatever you have to do."

He'd told her he was on some kind of undercover assignment, but she couldn't quite wrap her head around that yet. Not that he hadn't proven himself capable—last night's fight was plenty of evidence. Could her mailman really be *this* guy?

They'd gone out a few times, but she wasn't naive enough to think he owed her anything. What irked her was how he'd given her a taste of the facts without telling her anything of real value. Navy was one thing. SEAL was completely different.

"I don't want you out here alone," he argued, not for the first time since he'd woken her.

"I can handle myself."

"In any other situation I'd agree."

Charly stamped her feet and blew into her cupped palms. It would be cold most of the day. The overhang offered a break from the worst bite of the wind, but a fire would've been nice. They just couldn't risk it.

"Aren't you going to say anything?"

Charly stared at Will. There was no mistaking the

honesty in his clear blue eyes. How could she have been so wrong about a person? Her mailman, her new friend, the guy she'd wanted to be more...well, based on the story he'd told her, he sure was more.

"Undercover?" She echoed the word he'd used when he'd tried to explain.

Will nodded. "I didn't expect anything to happen this soon. If ever."

"Unexpected is part of it, right?"

Again, the nod.

She couldn't figure out why her feelings were hurt. He hadn't led her on or used her, but she still felt cheated. Deceived. "Was I some kind of target?"

"No." He reached out, then let his hands drop. "Before Lancaster, no one in Durango was a target. You have a reputation for tracking, but that's not why I asked you out." His gaze roamed past her shoulder and over the horizon, then returned to her, but he didn't elaborate. "We don't really have time to do this now," he said flatly.

She supposed he would know more about the timeline for managing this problem than she did. "You're convinced Lancaster's trying to reach a crashed plane?"

According to Will, her deceptive client was out here trying to recover a bit of technology for his master plan. A plan that could break through any kind of security encryption. She thought about the vast size of the forest. The needle-in-a-haystack image didn't come close.

"That's how the intel is shaping up."

Undercover mailman. Government intel. A dead friend. She chewed on her lip. It was a lot to take in. He'd told her being a mailman in Durango went with the assignment. A *mailman*. She gave whoever had dreamed that up points for originality. Undercover explained the extreme fitness, and he'd certainly proved himself skilled and capable out here. It added up...but her *mailman*?

How had she let herself be so blinded? Tammy's voice popped into her head. Will had plenty of "blinding" features. The shoulders. The ass. Couldn't forget the eyes. Or the sexy scar on his chin.

"How'd you get the scar?"

He swiped at the thin white line with his fingers, then stuffed his hands into his pockets. "I'll tell you on the way back to Lancaster's camp."

Charly planted her hands on her hips and glared daggers at him. "Tell me on the way to the ranger station." She wasn't ready to go back. She might never be ready to face Lancaster again. The idea made her stomach clench. No matter how much she scrubbed, she knew she'd see Clint's blood on her hands for days. Longer. They were going back to Durango and alerting the authorities. She would not entertain any ideas that allowed Lancaster to escape justice.

"I have to stay on Lancaster," Will said softly.

She believed him, knew he'd probably spent more time than he should have caring for her overnight.

"I could use your expertise."

She didn't like that he knew just which buttons to push. She didn't want to part ways, didn't want to evaluate all of her reasons. "If you need to go back, fine. I'll get back to town and file a formal report against Lancaster for murder. That should make your job easier."

"That's not smart." His breath made soft clouds in the cold air. "We need to stick together on this."

She shook her head. Tracking was one thing. Tracking seven armed men, one of them too ready to kill—no. "We're both adults here. I can take care of myself.

"I don't want you out here alone," he said again. "He'll send someone for you."

"And I'll be ready." She patted the gun in her jacket pocket. "Don't worry about me. I'll be fine."

He grumbled something she couldn't quite make out. Wasn't sure she wanted to hear. She didn't ask because she was done wasting daylight. "Well." She knelt down to adjust the laces on her boots, struggling to keep herself together. "Thanks for the assist last night."

"What if we go straight for the plane?"

"I beg your pardon?" The idea was absurd.

He crouched beside her. "We know where he's going, so we beat him to the prize."

She stood up and paced away as Will kept talking.

"Sending men after you means better numbers for us. Two against six, then hopefully just five."

"If we take his prize, as you put it, he'll come after us."

"Exactly. Giving us the power to lead him wherever we want him to end up."

The idea had merit. It appealed to the voice in her heart clamoring to avenge Clint. But two against five, probably six? "One problem."

"Only one? That's doable."

She fought off her amusement at his bald confidence. "We don't know where the plane is."

"Sure we do."

"More intel?"

"Yes." He stepped close to her. "Your intel."

His fingertips brushed her temple, and she locked her knees to keep them steady. The heat of his body, so close, tempted her on a level that had nothing to do with national security. Different scenarios played through her head. Getting caught by Lancaster's men. Running off with Will. Lancaster getting away with murder. Will might only have one problem, but suddenly she felt inundated.

She focused on the biggest one first. Going after the plane was akin to snipe hunting. There were too many places it could be. Even more likely, pieces of wreckage could be scattered across miles. "Why do you think I have any information?"

"You're the best tracker in four states, Charly."

He delivered the statement with such sincerity. Not helpful. She gave a snort, tried to create a little distance, but he wouldn't give her an inch. "In order to track something, tracks are required."

His hands cruised gently over her shoulders. She wanted to lean in, to believe that something they'd shared in Durango had been more than his job. She resisted.

"He argued with you about the route, right?"

"Yes." She looked up into his eyes. "You were following us a long time." Close enough to listen in, and she hadn't known. She was glad Will played for America and not against.

He shrugged. "Off and on from the start." He stepped back, catching her hand with his, drawing her along with him.

*From the start.* She wrenched free of him. "You interrogated me last night."

He jerked back as if she'd hit him. "I did no such thing."

She waved her hands. "The night before. Over burgers and milkshakes, you interrogated me."

"That's stretching the definition."

"Is it? You asked me routes and times and—" She felt the heat flood her face with the embarrassment of it all. He'd kissed her goodbye. Their first real kiss hadn't been real at all. "You kissed me!"

"You didn't complain at the time."

She clamped her lips shut, covered them with a hand to keep from cursing him. Not that she really believed the wind would snatch him away on her command, but why take the chance? "You didn't give me so much as a warning!" She wanted to shout, but knew better than to indulge her temper that way. If by some horrible stroke of luck Lancaster's men were on the right trail, she wouldn't be responsible for making it easier for them.

"What was I supposed to tell you?" He leaned back against the rock wall, hands in his pockets, his dark blue gaze unrelenting. "Any warning I might have given you required a long explanation I wasn't cleared to give. There are restrictions that go along with my job."

No job was worth Clint's life. The fresh wave of sorrow stole her breath. "You thought it was better to send me up the mountain with a pack of wolves in engineers' clothing?"

"Yes." He tilted his head and cracked his neck.

"Clint died."

He didn't shy away from her blatant accusation. "You'd both be dead if I'd warned you."

She wanted to be angry; instead it seemed all she could muster was more misery and grief. She'd lost a friend. Two, counting Will.

"Warning you would've caused more problems," he contended.

"I wouldn't have brought him up here," she countered.

Will shook his head. "If you'd accepted my warning and *if* you'd believed my story, I think you would've gone ahead with this hike. But with my warning in your head, suspecting Lancaster was a problem waiting to happen would've made you nervous. He would've acted sooner and taken his chances on his own."

"You don't know that."

"He's desperate, Charly." His quiet voice, full of sympathy, pricked her conscience. "You've seen that for yourself."

Her arms were suddenly heavy as she remembered Clint's lifeless body. She wanted to look away from Will, wanted to deny the logic in his explanation. Instead, she faced him head-on. "Were you out there?"

"Yes."

She gave him points for not pretending to misunderstand the question. "You didn't do anything."

"I did what I thought best to protect you."

What did that mean? Her mind spun. She'd been a fool to think a man like her ripped, smart mailman could really be into her. "I thought you were interested in me."

"I am."

Unbelievable. In fact, she believed everything he said but that. She rolled her eyes. "God, I'm gullible. You—" she waved her hands, indicating his whole body "—interested in me," she repeated, incredulous. "I started to care."

There it was—her real sticking point. She'd started to care for him, *about* him. She'd started to let the romantic fantasy color her view, making her see his actions and reactions in ways he didn't intend. "Wow," she muttered, owning her weakness. "That must've put you in a tight spot."

"No." He took a step toward her. "Charly, hear me out."

She held up a hand, silencing him. She didn't want

to hear any more about how she'd developed a crush on the hot guy with the job to do. "Only if it's about the plane. If I can help you with that, fine, but please don't make me rehash the other stuff. I'm embarrassed enough as it is."

"Embarrassed?"

"I mean it, Will. We talk about the plane or Lancaster or I walk."

"Fine," he said through clenched teeth. "Ms. Binali, will you lend your skills to the United States government for the purpose of preventing a national security disaster?"

When he said it that way it made her want to help, despite the impossibility of it all. "Do you have any way to narrow the search field?"

Will took a sudden interest in his boots before he finally looked her in the eye. "Not according to my last communication."

She started to explain the futility of it when he cut her off. "But you know where it is. When did Lancaster protest about the route you were taking?"

"Almost as soon as we left the parking lot."

Will shook his head. "I'm betting there were specific moments."

"Sure. He wanted to go due north when we were near the first challenge course."

"Because he was tracking the beacon. We can head north on a line from those spots and find the plane first."

"I've heard amazing stories from navy SEALs, but I didn't know they could walk on air." She ignored the frustrated furrow between his eyebrows, ignored her silly, girl-crush urge to soothe him. "The reason I led them around is because at that point the land runs out in a hurry. Going due north would've been a dangerous scenic route that dead-ends in a steep canyon."

"Damn." Will paced the short expanse of their camp with long legs and a quick stride. He rubbed one thumb across the opposite palm as he digested her news. "Do you recall anything they said about the beacon last night?"

"Only that it was still sending a strong signal." She shook her head. "I was preoccupied."

"I know." His eyes were full of such a deep understanding she wanted to cry. "I know you don't want to go back to see any of them, but if you aren't confident about cutting them off, that's our only option."

She marveled at the emotions battling inside her. Never big on drama, it surprised her to swing from angry and empowered to sorrow and utter defeat in the span of a few seconds.

Giving up, she sat down at the edge of the slope and let her gaze roam.

Clearly, the job mattered to Will. He'd given her enough details that she understood the importance of his mission. Though she was angry with him, she recognized his determination to succeed against the steep odds.

"Charly?"

She felt him hovering behind her, smart enough not to touch. "I'm thinking."

He sat down close by, and she did her best to ignore the sound of his breathing.

"Splitting up—" she began.

"Not an option," he said.

"Makes sense," she countered. "More eyes covering more ground in the search for Lancaster's prize is sensib—"

"But—"

"Will, if you interrupt me again, our partnership is over and nothing you say or do will keep me from walking down this mountain." She waited, listening to her heartbeat and only her heartbeat for several long seconds. "I understand your concerns and the basic plan. Assuming you have the climbing skills, if we had the gear we could go due north and maybe with a lot of luck, find the plane."

She paused, gathering her thoughts, hating the words that had to be spoken. "If I'd taken a radio instead of a gun, things might be different. As it stands, you're right. We need to track Lancaster." It would be the greatest test of her self-control to watch and wait when she had Clint's murderer in her sights. "At least until we can narrow the search field."

Will remained silent.

"I'm done talking now," she declared.

"All right." His clothing rustled softly as he scooted up to sit beside her. "Before we even get started, I want to say thank-you." He bounced a fist on his thigh, then sighed. "It was my third op when it happened to me."

Sensing where this was going, Charly stiffened. She did not want to hear this. She didn't want to feel a connection. She needed her embarrassment over the lies he'd fed her in town, needed the anger to keep her steady.

"Just getting to graduation makes you feel immortal," he began, his voice barely a whisper. "We know in here—" he tapped his temple "—that certain actions are high risk. We know there are consequences when we go out."

She understood what he meant, though the context differed between civilian life and military action. There were risks when she helped on search and rescue, more risks when she helped track fugitives.

"Intel on the op was clear, complete as it gets. The plan was simple—get in, get our hostage, get out. But the bizarre happened in the form of an IED. We weren't even the target. Not really. We had the best training in the world, but I wasn't fully prepared for the weight of hauling my dying friend to the egress point."

Her mind drifted back to Clint's temporary grave.

"It's the strangest thing to see a man you've lived with, worked with, a man you consider a brother go down," Will continued. "It's worse when it feels sense-less. I know how that sticks with you, Charly. But even-tually you get through the grief and reach a point where you can recall the fullness of the life instead of the empty moment of death."

Steady? Her entire system was quaking like a leaf in a windstorm. She looked down at their joined hands. When had that happened? How was she supposed to maintain her composure after hearing a story like that? Feeling petty, she tugged her hand free. She wanted to call him a liar, to accuse him of manipulating her, but she couldn't get the mean words past the lump of tears lodged in her throat. Blinking rapidly, she pushed to her feet and buried the volatile mix of feelings whirl-ing inside her.

It would take huge doses of calm and focus to get them through this. By sheer will, her vision was clear when she looked at Will again. "Let's go."

He stood up and dusted off his dark pants. "You've got the lead."

She nodded, choosing the most direct path. When Lancaster was in custody, when Will's job was com-

plete and they were back in Durango, she'd take an entire day, maybe two, and wallow in her grief over Clint.

For now, they had work to do.

# Chapter Ten

Will knew he'd handled things poorly with Charly, and with every silent step carrying them closer to Lancaster, he vowed to make it up to her when this was over. That kind of decision came with a new risk factor he'd never considered before, but the woman pulled things out of him. Things he never discussed. Yet he'd sat there and held her hand and let it pour out. Telling himself it was for her benefit, to ease her grief, was complete bull.

This kind of sticky situation proved why he was better working the solo operations. Working alone, he couldn't embarrass himself by sharing pitiful memories of his failures. Alone, he couldn't cause others the embarrassment he'd caused Charly.

Her reaction to his purpose up here surprised him. He'd expected the anger, but he couldn't see any reason for her to feel foolish over their dates. He just didn't know how to explain it to her in a way she'd understand.

Thank God they were finally close enough to Lancaster's camp that talking wasn't safe. Too often since they'd set off he'd wanted to apologize, to make his feelings for her clear. She hadn't misunderstood his interest, but he figured he'd have a hell of a time convincing her of that anytime soon.

This wasn't the best time to get distracted by the

woman, so he gained a little detachment by focusing on her skills as a guide. Yesterday he'd discovered a serious appreciation for her endurance. Today, in closer proximity, he marveled at her commanding awareness of their surroundings—of all things nature.

As they'd become acquainted, she'd talked a little about her family and the traditions she carried forward with their business, but seeing her in action was nothing short of astounding. She moved swiftly, only occasionally glancing to the sky or pausing to listen to her surroundings. Granted, he knew she was familiar with the area, but watching her, he understood her grandfather's comment about her having a compass for a heart. Charly traveled with such confidence, without leaving a trace, that Will thought the military should hire her for training.

Without a word, she'd pointed out animal tracks as they appeared. Both prey and predator, from rabbits and deer to wolves. Thank God the bears and snakes were hibernating. He wasn't so ignorant about the area that he thought Lancaster's crew was the only threat on this mountain, but he was suddenly grateful he was navigating this wicked terrain with Charly.

He didn't give an opinion on their route, trusting her to find the most direct path to the campsite. He wondered what they'd find when they got there. He hoped the men had left behind a few provisions. His small pack wasn't going to carry them very far.

Much as he'd done last night, she crossed the stream and circled around, avoiding the trail she'd cleared with Lancaster. To his surprise, Will heard men shouting as they closed in on the campsite. He couldn't believe Lancaster hadn't set out already.

With no more than a look, he and Charly dropped flat, carefully creeping forward to watch and listen.

"We have a signal from that beacon to follow," Lancaster shouted. "Forget the bitch. We don't need her."

One of the men was down and one eye was swollen shut.

Charly tapped him. "Jeff," she mouthed, pointing to the ground.

Will nodded, understanding. The man who'd been charged with guarding her last night hadn't fared well in the hours since her escape.

"If she notifies the authorities," another man said, "we're all screwed."

"I say we leave Jeff to deal with any authorities while we go on to the plane."

Will noted Jeff kept his opinion on that plan to himself.

"Dumb move going without her. She can't be far."

"We're not incompetent," said Max. He held up the tracking gear. "We know where we're going."

"But you saw how well she knows the area."

"Enough!" Lancaster stopped the bickering. "This isn't a damned democracy. You work for me," he said, his face turning red. "All of you work for me."

Watching the body language, Will thought the men surrounding Lancaster disagreed. It seemed as though Scott was the man the others looked to time and again for guidance.

"You want to get paid, you follow *my* orders."

Will slid a look toward Charly while Lancaster ranted on. She met his gaze with a raised-eyebrow expression that told him they were on the same page. A madman running around on the mountain was going to be a particular kind of fun.

"We'll split up," Lancaster said, only slightly calmer. "Jeff and Bob will track down the guide and kill her. The rest of us will go to the plane."

"And how do we find you when we're done?" Bob asked.

"You have radios. I can't imagine she's gone far. She must be panicked, knowing we won't let her get away. Find her. Kill her. If you're closer to Durango when that's done, you'll wait for us in town."

Will took it as small comfort that the crew planned to return to Durango after retrieving the Blackout Key. He'd pass that intel to Casey. The director could have a reception waiting for Lancaster.

Will carefully watched the men tasked with killing Charly. It was clear they thought they'd be cut out of the profit. At worst, they'd be in place as the scapegoats if things went bad up here.

It wasn't any surprise, but the division of Lancaster's crew meant a new set of challenges. He and Charly couldn't follow both Lancaster and the other men. He had no intention of leaving Charly out here alone. Not just because he needed her expertise to get around faster. Not just because her need to avenge Clint rolled off her in perilous waves.

No, his need to keep her close went deeper than that. He told himself it was the mission, that he wouldn't leave a civilian out here, unarmed and underequipped, to bat cleanup for the United States. He wasn't believing it. Still, he couldn't risk letting his mind wander down that path littered with land mines. Better to keep it all business up here.

Charly was a civilian, and considering how angry she was at him, it was best not to bring his personal interest into the mix. Dating her was fun and exciting, but he'd known from the start it wouldn't turn into anything long-term. He wasn't built for the long haul. Didn't have the heart for it.

Beside him, Charly didn't even twitch as they watched Jeff and Bob gather gear, check weapons and head away from the campsite. Again he thought SEAL candidates could learn a few things from her. In a town like Durango it hadn't taken long to learn about Charly's stellar reputation for guiding and tracking, but she'd been so lively and animated when they played pool or talked over a meal. He'd had no idea she had this deep well of cool reserve.

It took a remarkable person to remain still and calm in the face of such a direct and deadly threat. It took something else—an undefinable quality—to do so this close to a friend's rough grave.

Will struggled against an inexplicable need to rush in and take down the five men distracted with their preparations to move out. For Charly. He could see the solution and call it a good day's work. They could take the beacon and find the damned key, and be done with it all.

Only Casey's desire to take Lancaster alive, along with Will's combat experience, kept him in place next to her.

She shifted closer, and her fingertips landed with a light flutter on his hand. He hadn't realized he'd reached down for the gun holstered to his thigh. He gave her a brief nod, and she seemed to understand he had himself under control again.

It felt like an eternity before he risked a cautious whisper. "We're not splitting up," he said, offering her a hand up.

She didn't accept his offer of help, but she deliberately turned her back to Clint's grave. "We can tail Lancaster," she said, surprising him. "He's your priority."

"You aren't worried about the other two men?"

She shook her head. "Are you? Unless they're blind, they'll pick up the trail I left for them."

Her easy dismissal of the pair caught his attention. "What did you do?"

"I led them toward a natural trap. If we're really lucky one of the men who feels like this mountain is his personal property will intercept them first."

"And if we're not really lucky?"

"They'll turn north and try to rejoin Lancaster, pinning us in the middle."

"Why didn't you go to a mountain man for help last night?"

"I didn't need help last night until you tackled me."

He figured it best if he didn't reply directly to that.

She cocked an eyebrow, clearly understanding his silence. "Besides, I'd talked myself into going to the authorities, thinking that was better than conducting my own manhunt."

"Come on," he said, crossing the creek to the campsite. "Maybe they left us something useful."

She surprised him again when she didn't even pause at her friend's grave. But he turned when she swore softly. "If it wasn't your job to secure Lancaster, I'd say let the mountain take care of these guys."

He walked over and knelt down as she gathered up an open pack of fresh food. "Did you expect them to be responsible campers?"

"A girl can dream," she muttered while she dealt with it. "But I'm not surprised."

Charly bit back the rant. It wouldn't help and it was only a diversion from the real problem. She might be out of her depth with national security and the mailman-turned-SEAL, but she recognized that truth. It felt as if her veins were trembling with grief, anger and fear. None of that would bring Clint back. None of those feelings would see justice done for him. Especially not the fear.

She found her pack and examined what Jeff and his pals hadn't taken. Her spare radio was missing, but they'd left her first-aid supplies and the meal bars.

She left the tent behind. It was too cumbersome for what Will had in mind. "Check Clint's pack for any rope or gear," she said to Will. Once they had a better idea of where the plane went down, she wanted every advantage to get Will to the objective first.

Hearing Lancaster order her death, hearing the others agree so easily to carry out the order, something had clicked into place. If Lancaster thought he'd hired the best, he was about to find out how right he'd been. She shrugged into the small backpack and cinched the straps so it wouldn't shift. Lancaster thought he could run roughshod over this forest, over land she considered as vital as her heart. She'd happily show him how wrong he was.

She spared a final glance for Clint's grave, making a silent promise to return and bury him honorably at her first opportunity. She promised herself that despite the sharp and lethal odds stacked against her, she'd survive both Lancaster and the perils north of the peak.

"Ready?"

She nodded, not quite prepared to test her voice or meet Will's gaze. Ready to do this was the only option, because she refused to give in.

"Lead the way."

It wasn't much of a test. Lancaster, feeling safe,

didn't care about hiding his trail. For the first hours, the real trick was holding back far enough that they didn't get caught.

There had been a call on the radio and another heated discussion about the route, forcing Charly and Will to fall back and discuss their options.

"Any ideas?"

"Might be entertaining when they try to walk on air."

"Entertaining," Will echoed, his eyebrows drawing close. "They must have some idea about the terrain."

"If so, they hid it well yesterday."

"They can check the area with their smartphones."

She shook her head. "Those are only expensive paperweights at this point."

"I'd think the beacon tracker would have some setting about terrain."

"Maybe." Charly swallowed the lump in her throat. "Clint got a look, said it was high-end. We didn't talk about it after that." Their time had run out. She felt Will's eyes on her, had just opened her mouth to fend off any sympathy when she caught the faint sound of voices.

Pressing her index finger to her lips, she drew them behind a screen of small trees. Rooted in place, absolutely still, she couldn't even hear Will's breathing.

Nearby, a radio crackled, but the disembodied voice on the other end was garbled. Beside her, she knew Will was straining for any clue about who was out there.

Bob's voice, slightly breathless, reached them just before he came into view.

Damn. She'd managed to get them pinned between Lancaster and the team he'd sent out to kill her. Why hadn't her trap worked? The strong and sudden urge to run surprised her. She had to smother it. Running wasn't an option. The men were too close.

Will touched her shoulder and the gentle contact grounded her. She scanned the area, looking for the best option for a fight or escape.

If they had any sense, the men should pass right by their hiding place.

"We should've gone back down," Bob said, stopping to catch his breath.

"I'm telling you she's out here somewhere," Jeff argued.

"You saw her hat. She's dead or long gone."

"I'm not staking my cut on your theory. That was a fake trail."

"No way. She was scared, is all. It was dark. She got lost." Bob swore. "And Scott knows better than to cut us out of the take. Besides, that mad bastard left too much behind in Durango. Let them freeze their asses off out here. It's easy enough to catch up with them when they're done."

She could see Jeff wasn't buying it. His eyes, one dark and bruised, scanned the forest floor, moving into the trees. Any second now and he'd spot them.

How had she missed his skills?

Because she hadn't been looking. Too busy operating on the assumption that she was leading curious software developers, she'd been focused on giving a good tour.

"She didn't get hurt, lost or dead," Jeff insisted. "It was a trap for whoever followed her."

*A trap that failed*, she thought with more than a little regret. Hopefully there'd be time to feel like an idiot about that later. Right now they had to start evening the odds.

She looked to Will, grateful one of them was dressed

for stealth. She pointed to herself, indicated her plan to stand up and draw their attention. He could circle around and they'd have them.

Will gave a nearly imperceptible shake of his head.

She sent him a defiant glare, motioning for him to circle around.

He reached for his gun and this time she shook her head. They needed to handle this quickly and silently, without allowing Jeff or Bob to notify Lancaster.

She thought that kind of tactic would be second nature to a man with Will's professional experience. Grabbing his jacket, she pressed her mouth close to his ear and outlined her plan.

He was already nodding as she eased back. Good. He needed to trust her ability to handle herself and drop this archaic need to protect her at every turn. She would not allow herself to be a liability for him. Shifting, she made just enough noise to draw Jeff's attention.

"What was that?"

"Nature," Bob replied, bored. "I want hot food and a soft bed."

"It could be her." Jeff peered into the trees.

She waited, holding her breath until Will made his move.

"You're obsessed," Bob accused. He reached for his radio. "Let's find out where the hell the mad bastard is and catch up with them."

With a sturdy stick in her hand, she launched from her hiding place. A moment early, yes, but she couldn't let Lancaster learn that she was out here alive. With an ally like Will.

Will moved in a black blur, tackling Bob at the waist and plowing the man into the dirt.

Jeff turned, facing her when she'd been counting on

taking him from behind. Didn't matter. Temper and fury simmered just under the surface of her skin, pushing her, making her strong. She saw the reaction in his eyes, the memory of what she'd done to him last night.

His hand slapped for his weapon holstered on his thigh and the hesitation made up for the ruined surprise attack.

Her heart sang with a warrior's pride as she slammed the stick she held against his jaw. The blow turned him, and she brought the stick hard across his throat and pulled back with both hands.

He clawed at her fingers, desperate to loosen her grip. She used her knee in his back as more leverage, willing him to go down before she crushed his windpipe.

Once more, thanks to her, he passed out. But this time when he came to, she wasn't giving him any good options.

"You okay?" Will asked, stalking over, his features clouded with temper.

"He didn't lay a finger on me."

"Good."

She looked past him to the prone form of the other man. "Did you kill him?"

"No." The single word carried a hefty dose of regret.

"But we should," he said. "It's the only way to be sure they won't escape and attack us again."

"I have a better idea. Take the radios and weapons. Search the packs. I'm sure there's something we can use to restrain them."

What their search of the packs revealed set her back, turning her blood to a cold sludge as she understood the implications. The pieces of menacing long-range rifles. The ammunition clips for the rifles and handguns. Explosives and detonators. They might have killed Clint early, but this trip would've definitely been her last.

"Mercenaries," Will said quietly. "They tend to have rough edges."

It made sense, but it didn't diminish the chill creeping along her skin.

"Want me to finish them?"

She shook her head, unwilling to leave that burden solely to him. "I'd rather they paid a harder price."

# Chapter Eleven

It wasn't easy hauling the two men upstream and more than once Will was sure he'd made the wrong choice letting Charly talk him into this, but when Jeff and Bob were secure, he had to admit the plan had merit.

"Last chance," Charly said. "Tell us where the plane is."

Both men stared past her with hard eyes, their features set in stone. Will didn't expect either of them to crack, but he hadn't expected Charly to come up with this crazy idea, either.

"All right." She dialed a radio to an emergency setting and used the carrying strap to loop it over a branch well out of reach of the men. "We're leaving now," she said, standing back from where they'd trapped the men near the base of a small waterfall.

Jeff bellowed for help.

"Shout all you want," she told them as they glared at her. "But I recommend you take the time to get your story straight before help arrives."

"Where did you come from?" Jeff glared at Will. "You're in over your head."

"Not the first time," Will said, walking away.

"We'll be on your tail by nightfall," Bob promised.

Will gawked at Charly's deadly smile as she leaned down close to Bob. "Best of luck with that."

Bob spat at her while Jeff swore. Will stepped up to defend her, but she didn't need his assistance.

She easily dodged Bob's assault and laughed at Jeff's threats. "Good luck, boys. And if you do break free, I recommend you follow the stream downhill and get yourself to safety. If you attack us again I'll help him—" she pointed over her shoulder at Will "—kill you both."

Sure-footed, she stalked back up the bank. Will tried to keep his mind away from her speech, but he couldn't quite keep his eyes off her shapely butt as it swayed from side to side in front of him.

When they were out of earshot, he laid a hand on her shoulder. "You meant it."

"About killing them if they attack again?"

He nodded.

"Better believe it."

"Then why not kill them now?" He knew he sounded bloodthirsty, but he was trying to figure out her thought process. He supposed he had the no-loose-ends philosophy in common with Lancaster. Not a comfortable thought, but reality was rarely comfortable.

"If they come after us again, it's on them," she replied. "Not orders, not financial reward, just them. Jeff showed a small measure of compassion last night. I returned the favor today."

"So the ball's in their court."

"That's how I see it."

Per his military training and absolute necessity, dead or alive, prisoners were contained. "You're sure they can't escape?" He didn't want to get pinched between Lancaster and these two again, regardless of her new-found willingness to end their lives.

"They can try."

The men were at a significant disadvantage. Will had their weapons and flashlight, and the one radio was well out of reach. They'd wasted enough time giving the pair a chance to live. He needed to drop the subject and resume his mission: getting to the plane.

"The park rangers should come through within a day."

"What? A day?" He'd thought a few hours at best. This was getting better all the time. "You're telling me they'll be out here all night?"

"Yes. And I wish we could watch them squirm in the cold and wet, but we need to catch up with Lancaster."

"Remind me never to cross you."

He caught her sideways look, the arched eyebrow and the little smirk on her lips.

"It wouldn't be in your best interest," she admitted, picking up the pace.

He wanted to revel in the moment, but another problem weighed on his mind. "What if those two convince the park rangers you're responsible for their condition?"

"I hope they try. That would only make the rangers more curious." Her shoulders jerked up and down. "A bizarre claim versus my reputation? Not a chance. The rangers know me. With you backing my story, the weapons we found and Clint?" Her voice cracked on her friend's name and she went quiet for a few minutes. "Those two can't say anything that will hurt me or the business. Even if they tried, one of my brothers is a lawyer."

"Good to know. I guess we'd better stick together then."

She stopped short. "You were right about that. I get it now."

"That's not why I said it," he said, striding up to join her.

"Relax, Will. I just thought you should know you won't get any further argument from me on that."

"Oh." He knew he should be happy about her cooperation. He should've noticed her attitude shifting to line up with Casey's agenda. Instead, he'd been distracted by the woman under the impressive, cool facade. So far the only thing to crack was her voice when she thought of her friend and trail partner.

They trekked on at a brisk pace and moved faster without the burden of two prisoners. He had the radio, but it remained silent. They weren't retracing their steps back to Lancaster's campsite; she was guiding them around it. Smart, he thought. A direct route was easy, but easy often led to more trouble. In this situation, he had to believe Lancaster and his men would stick with areas they knew.

"You would've been an asset to the navy SEAL program."

Her laughter bubbled around him. "That's ridiculous."

"Not so much," he replied. "You're unflappable."

"Out here, maybe." She stopped, frozen in place, and held out a hand so he would do the same.

He listened, unable to pin down anything other than the sounds of nature all around them. Though he wanted to ask, he kept his mouth shut, following her gaze in search of what had startled her. Sunlight lanced through the trees, the light and shadows dancing with the gentle breeze.

From his perspective, they had the advantage. Trees down the slope, a clear view across an open snowfield at their backs. He couldn't see anything, couldn't hear any trouble. But something had her spooked.

Suddenly bullets marched across the trees he thought were fair cover, tearing at bark and branches in vicious bites.

They both dropped to hands and knees behind the wide fanning branches of a spruce tree. He pushed her back and up, away from the shooter. The radio crackled and the man named Scott gave instructions to someone else. "Two targets. Two. Someone is with her."

"Two targets," one of the others confirmed.

Will exchanged another look with Charly. They didn't know if they were up against the whole party or a scouting team. No time to assess as more bullets came at them. Not a lucky volley in a random attack, he realized. He got up, setting off at a dead run and drawing the fire away from her.

It worked, but there wasn't much time to celebrate the success. He was running out of trees, being chased into the open of the high snow plain. If he gave in, made a dash for it, he had to assume there was a sniper in place to take him out. He hated admitting it, but somehow the enemy had gained an advantage.

Dirt and bark flew, following Charly as she came at him.

"What are you doing?"

"We stay together."

He shook his head. "Not this time."

"I saw Scott. Do you think they're all together?"

"Does it matter?" They had her revolver, his handgun and the weapons taken from Jeff and Bob. Will worried it wouldn't be enough.

"Guess not." She crouched, ducking for cover at another three-round burst. She inched close enough to whisper in his ear, "We have to cross that plain. Head over the ridge."

He frowned down at her and shook his head. It was a killing field for sure. There was too much space between them and the closest shelter. "We'll be sniper fodder," he said. It was too easy to picture the white snow splashed with blood. Her blood.

"We can't go forward."

"I can flank him."

"No."

She was going to run for it. He saw it in her eyes an instant before she made the first move. A certain death trap, he thought as he laid down cover fire in a last-ditch effort to protect her.

But the cover fire he directed at Scott did nothing to stop the sniper from taking aim at Charly. Worse, as he raced after her he realized their tracks through the snow left a clear trail for anyone to follow. Assuming either of them survived long enough to be hunted.

"Find cover!" he shouted at Charly. He skidded behind the shelter of a boulder, his eyes tracking the tree line, then higher, looking for the logical sniper's roost.

Too many options, he realized, as he tucked away his pistol and readied the rifle he'd taken off Bob. Will saw Scott strolling along the leading edge of the trees, but he wasn't about to waste another bullet. When he pulled the trigger next time, he wanted it to count for more than a diversion.

Waiting for his opening or the sniper's next bullet, he let his mind drift across his past. He'd been in worse situations. Probably. There had certainly been other instances when national security had been on the line. Other times when he'd worked solo to protect civilian interests.

"Take your time," he murmured, his cheek pressed to the stock. He drew in a long, slow breath, calming his heart rate. "I've got all day."

He couldn't fail. Not just because Casey was counting on him to stop Lancaster's deadly, self-centered quest for vengeance. Not just because he wanted to live past this particular mission. More than either of those salient points, he flat-out refused to fail Charly. She needed an ally to get off this mountain alive.

He should've let her go for help. He could've drawn them away from her. But his mission focus, colored by urgency and no small amount of pride, had kept them out here.

It was too late to send her back alone. Her skills were superb, but Lancaster's men were proving themselves more adept out here than Will had anticipated. The marksmanship didn't surprise him. Nor did the cold-blooded nature of the mercenaries Lancaster had hired. The tenacity…that was a bigger problem.

Lancaster didn't want loose ends. That much was clear. But Lancaster's team hadn't met Will's determination. He would do this job. He'd own it. Not just for Casey or the nation at large, but for Charly.

The awareness trickled into him like cool water sliding down his throat after a grueling week in the desert. He hadn't felt this type of personal connection with anyone since his brother died. He hadn't needed anything else. Hadn't been sure he was useful to anyone beyond the job anymore.

Charly was making him reevaluate.

As seconds ticked by, turning into several minutes without any gunfire, Will compared the few options available to both sides.

Based on previous behavior, Scott and whoever was

sniping for him wouldn't stray far from Lancaster. The Blackout Key was too valuable and from what he'd overheard so far, Lancaster needed the mercenaries to get away cleanly.

Through the rifle's scope, Will had a close-up view of Scott as he answered the radio. He couldn't hear the conversation, but the scowl gave him an idea of how well the exchange was going.

Scott grew more agitated and started to pace. Will squeezed off two shots, but didn't get to enjoy the reaction as the sniper got a bead on his position. Bullets ricocheted but didn't find their mark, and he heard Scott call out a retreat. Will watched for movement and cursed the well-trained team when he still couldn't spot the sniper.

Through the scope he saw Scott wrapping some kind of tape around his lower leg. A minor injury would have to be enough for today. Will turned away from the trees, eager to check on Charly. Noting the blood spattered across the snow, his heart lodged in his throat. Somehow he managed to call her name as he staggered to his feet.

Snow exploded to his right, and Charly's voice erupted from his left. "Get down!"

She leaped at him, grabbing his coat and hauling him down as they went sliding across a snow-covered slope. They gained speed on the incline like a runaway sled. Adjusting, Will turned so they were going feetfirst instead of sideways. One arm holding Charly, he tried to grasp for anything to slow them down with the other. He lost the rifle in the process, but was more concerned about losing her.

There was no cover, and he was sure the sniper would pick them off any second. Another rock speared up from the snow, and Will said a prayer it would stop them as he braced for the impact.

It held. Thank God.

"Are you hurt?"

"No," she said, breathless. "You?"

"There was blood back there. On the snow," he added, looking her over from head to toe. He couldn't see any wounds, though her clothing had taken a beating. "It isn't yours?"

"Unlucky rabbit, probably."

Her answer left him speechless and beyond grateful she was okay.

"Come on, we have to keep moving." She rolled to her feet, tugged on him to urge him along.

"Where are we?" The snow here was more like a thin, icy layer dusting rocks and stubborn plants.

"We slid into a dried-up creek bed. This way."

"They'll be on our trail fast."

"I know," she said, legs churning as she ran. "Hurry."

He grabbed his pistol as they moved, trying to keep up with her as she crossed the rocky ground with the confidence of a mountain goat. He heard the shouts of pursuit and glanced back, relieved the rocks disguised their trail. If they could just get out of sight, they had a chance.

He'd no more thought it than Charly disappeared behind an outcropping. Following, he squeezed between two boulders and into a shallow recess in the mountainside. Not enough space to qualify as a cave, there was barely room for their packs and bodies. She was pressed against him from shoulder to thigh, and he hoped like hell it was enough shelter to keep them hidden. Between the adrenaline and Charly, his system was completely revved. He tried to dial it down, but knew it wasn't working. "Best bet is to wait them out."

"We'll stay here until nightfall," she murmured. "Then we can move."

"Agreed." He could only be grateful the daylight hours were short this time of year.

She trembled, and it might have been his body shivering, they were so close. "Are you cold?"

"I'll be fine."

Her husky reply tested the thinning tether he had on the desire pumping through him. He only had to make it to nightfall.

Peering up at the sky, he told himself it was possible. Possible to ignore her soft curves pressed against him. Possible to forget the sweet taste of her lips. He had to find another line of thought.

He wanted to get up, to shake his head and clear out the sensual haze, but he couldn't risk moving and giving the shooter another target.

"Will?"

"Hmm?"

"Thanks for the cover fire."

"Anytime," he replied.

A quiet giggle shook through her and into him. "It's fine with me if it's just this once."

"You've got a deal."

"From this side of the ridge, we should be able to get a lead on Lancaster's route."

"How do you figure?"

"He can't get due north without climbing gear. I didn't see any in Jeff or Bob's packs."

"Could be one person is carrying the load for all of them."

"Maybe so," she allowed.

"How will *we* get to the plane without climbing gear?"

"That depends."

He hesitated to ask. "On what?"

"What's in your pockets."

"Pardon?"

"If you have binoculars, I know of an overlook in that general direction that might allow us to get in front of Lancaster."

"How can you see anything up here?" So much of it looked the same to him. Vast and beautiful. Steep slopes of green and brown broken by sparkling water, outcrops of stone, even caps of snow up here in these higher elevations. Without a beacon or an overhead view, he couldn't fathom how she'd find a small downed aircraft. "This is the ski resort side of the range, right?"

"Yes. Why?"

"I was thinking about the plane's possible destination. Maybe somewhere nearby was a fueling stop or something."

"That could be any number of places along here, or well west. Are you thinking of contacting the local airfields?"

"Maybe. What if Lancaster tried to rent a helicopter before he came to you?"

"I can't image any pilot agreeing to search without a specific destination."

"True. But with the beacon, he could've given a decent search field."

"So if he gave a pilot general coordinates and still had to come to me…" Her voice trailed off, and her eyes scanned the little slice of sky they could see from their hiding place.

"You do know where he's headed. I knew you'd figure it out."

"I don't know precisely," she admitted, "but that does give me a better idea. There's a lot of treacherous ground to cover and at least five men determined to get there before you."

"One of them isn't walking well."

"Go team us," she mused.

But she didn't sound too enthused. He rubbed her knee. The risk to his sanity was worth it. "We'll get there first," he said, dragging his mind back to the problem instead of the woman.

"Don't get too confident," she warned.

"Why wouldn't I be confident? You're like an ace up my sleeve." Something about her gave him more than confidence. She gave him real hope.

# Chapter Twelve

Charly felt as though they'd been cramped for years in the tiny crevice rather than the hours it had taken for the sun to set. They'd listened to the chatter on the radio between Scott and Lancaster, debating who'd been with Charly and how to contain them. Lancaster had been furious at Scott's failure, but called them back to move on with their primary purpose.

Will had called her his secret ace, but she was thinking the reverse was true. He'd been right that this crew was more dangerous, more desperate than she'd first thought.

Charly didn't like moving at night, not on this side of the ridge, where any step could knock debris loose and give away their position. Or worse, send them tumbling down to rocks below. But they couldn't stay out here, exposed, with only her sleeping bag and each other as shelter against the elements.

Her brain stalled out, savoring the images that flooded her mind with that thought. Totally inappropriate thoughts, considering their life-and-death predicament. It smelled like snow and while she didn't expect a big accumulation this time of year, even a dusting could be enough to slow them down.

They had to get ahead of Lancaster and his crew.

They'd just escaped a barrage of bullets and yet part of her was consumed by the urge to get her hands on Will's rock-hard pecs and ripped abs. It was embarrassing. They needed to find a safe place to wait out the snowfall and regroup. Her distraction would mean an advantage for Lancaster if she didn't pull herself together.

"What do you think?"

She looked up at Will, standing by her side as she faced the vast emptiness just beyond their feet, where the mountain gave way to a steep, rugged canyon. His chiseled features were blurred by darkness, his eyes impossible to read.

"I think we need to take the chance." She reminded herself that he'd trusted her to deal with Jeff and Bob. It was time to trust him and his training.

Will took another step, peering over the edge. "Some chance."

She knew he was thinking about the stingy length of rope in her pack. Neither of them was geared up for real climbing. Under normal circumstances, she believed they were both smart enough to *not* do what she'd suggested. But they had to survive. The night, the weather, Lancaster.

"This cliff is riddled with caves. It's our best bet to get through the night."

He looked around, and she could practically feel the realization dawning. "Cliff. Caves. Under us, yes?"

"Yes." One wrong move and— She couldn't let her mind wander any closer to the negative. "I can get us there. We'll have shelter, a break from the wind and snow."

"They won't expect us to go over."

"And it should give us a safe vantage point when they set out in the morning," she added, keeping her voice low to match his. Having spent the day hiding, they didn't know how much progress Lancaster had made toward the beacon. In the dark, with no sign of a campfire, she and Will decided to go forward rather than search out their campsite.

"It'll work."

She wished she knew for sure, but as fat snowflakes began a slow descent, time for debate was over. If they waited any longer, she wouldn't be able to justify the risk. "This way." She checked the straps on her pack, tugged at Will's for good measure.

"It's not going anywhere," he assured her.

With a mental cross of fingers, she dropped to her butt at the cliff's edge and let her feet dangle in the wide abyss of dark. She supposed that was one small positive, not being able to see the distance from here to the bottom.

Will sat beside her and covered her hand with his. "Lead the way."

His absolute faith rattled her almost as much as it bolstered her confidence. This was the worst time to feel off balance, when she'd be scooting down a nearly invisible "stairway" with unyielding mountain on one side and nothing but air on the other.

"Okay. Down about six to eight feet," she began. "It's barely a ledge and I can't see the gaps well in the dark," she warned.

"Slow going. Got it."

She didn't give herself a chance to think about the benefit of anchors and ropes. Those things would only be a road map for Lancaster's crew in the morning.

Will tapped her on the shoulder, but she'd heard the same sound he had. Too big to be anything but one of

Lancaster's men. At this point she had no doubt whoever it was would shoot first and sleep well after.

As if answering her thoughts, a gunshot blasted out of the darkness.

Strange how her basic instinct to survive debated her lousy choices. Bullets or canyon floor? No time. She relegated the panic and defeatist thoughts to the back of her mind as she pushed herself over the edge and prayed her feet would find purchase on the narrow lip of rock that had been worn down by wind and rain.

Her mind whipped through the math as she slid, clinging to the mountain as it bit into her side. Only six to eight feet. *Only.* She should feel the ledge under her toes within a second or two.

She didn't.

Just their luck if she'd chosen to go over at a new gap in the ledge. But she knew this mountain. The ledge should be there. What was the worst that could happen? One of the scrappy trees would catch them.

Her fingers dug into loose rock and soil before her toes, straining for contact, found the narrow lip of solid rock. She nearly laughed aloud in pure relief. A moment later, Will landed beside her.

"Go, go, go," he urged, his hand on her pack, keeping her close to the cliff.

She glanced up and got a face full of dirt knocked loose by the men chasing them. Scrambling, belly pressed to the side of the cliff, she moved as fast as she dared. Faster, as shouts tumbled down from above.

The wind spun snow around her face, coming down heavy enough now to give her a pale outline of their immediate surroundings. She ducked under a scruffy tree, gave Will plenty of warning about the obstacle and kept going.

The wide beam of a flashlight speared through the dark, wrecking her night vision. She studied the terrain as the light swept back and forth, determined to make it to shelter before the men above them found their aim.

A strange crack and wail had her turning back, panicked that Will had slipped. The scruffy tree between them was bending under the weight of one of Lancaster's men. Rich, she remembered, as the flashlight illuminated his terrified face.

For a moment, she was frozen, a helpless bystander amid the swirling cries for help and the promises of death.

"Go!" Will shouted.

She couldn't. Wouldn't leave him to deal with this alone. Without her guidance Will couldn't get to safety, and waiting only gave Lancaster a better chance to shoot them. It was either help Rich or they all lose. The panicked man in the tree swore as the shallow roots jerked and gave.

"Give me your hand," she said to Rich with a calm she used for emergencies.

"Don't do it," Will shouted. "Let me. I'm stronger."

Someone on the cliff's edge held the flashlight steady, painting the horrible tabloid in a weak spotlight with snowflakes floating through like pale confetti.

"Kill them," Lancaster called, his voice colder than the bitter night air.

The man tested her humanity. She'd like to show Lancaster who had a clear shot in this instance—her—but Will was adamant about taking him in alive.

"Reach for me," Will ordered the man.

"Can't," Rich said, clinging to the tree.

"You can," she told him. If she could catch his jacket, she might be able to swing him to the ledge.

The tree lurched free of the mountain a bit more as Rich struggled. "Oh, God."

"Stretch!" Will barked.

To her horror, bullets chattered around them, followed by more dirt and debris from above. She heard shouts from the men fighting among themselves, but her eyes were locked on Will and Rich. She braced to help in any possible way.

Rich reached, his hand connecting with Will's. For a single heartbeat, she knew life would triumph. Then it changed.

Bullets marched through Rich and the snow, illuminated by the flashlight, turned into a red haze of blood. Will couldn't hold him, and the man and the scruffy tree tumbled away into the darkness.

"Move!" Will filled her vision, urging her along. She caught the muzzle flash of his gun as he fired off a few rounds to cover their retreat.

The light doused, by choice or bullet, she was blind, feeling her way with toes and fingers and memory. With a prayer, she scurried faster than was smart down the ledge, her slips and slides the only way to tell Will what was coming. Better to let the mountain take her than Lancaster.

She ducked into the shelter of the first cave and they sank back, waiting for any pursuit.

"They've given up for tonight," he said after a few minutes. "Can you keep going?"

It felt as if every cell in her body shivered. Wouldn't ever stop shivering. "Yes," she replied, victorious that she'd kept the word steady.

"I want more distance, if there's another safe place nearby."

"This side is full of caves. We can find another.

Just—" She paused, covered her eyes with her cold hands. "Just let my eyes recover a minute."

"Takes longer than a minute," he said.

"I know." She took a deep breath. "But humor me anyway."

"Sure."

Opening her eyes, she walked back to the cave entrance. With a big breath, she started out once more. Stupid or brave, didn't matter—they couldn't stay put—so she moved swiftly along to the next cave big enough for both of them. "Is this better?" she asked.

Will waited again, listening, before joining her and escaping the reach of the elements. Turning on his flashlight, he scanned the empty space. "Perfect." The light went out and his voice drifted over her. "You're amazing. Charly, that was… I just don't know what to say."

She grabbed the straps of his pack and pulled him close, until his lips landed on hers. The contact wasn't gentle. Nothing close to seductive. It was a raw celebration of survival. He wrapped his arms around her, pulling her against his solid body, chasing the chill from her blood.

She changed the angle, her lips parting, tongue seeking his taste and heat. Clutching his shoulders for balance, she let desire and lust burn away the grim reality of their narrow escape.

There was nothing for her outside of this moment. Nothing in her world but him. Them. Strong, steady and capable, Will became her gravity. She knew she'd float away without him.

She pushed at the straps of his pack, wanting to get her hands on all of him. Right *now*. Who knew how much time they had left? She wouldn't let this opportunity pass. Her palm slid across his chest, felt the heavy thud of his heart, and her pulse pounded an echo in her ears.

"I need you," she murmured against his lips while her fingers worked at his jacket. "Now."

"Hang on." Will leaned back from her sweet, soft mouth. Everything inside him wanted to seize what her body offered. Sure, there was plenty of mutual attraction on both sides, but he didn't want to be one more regret for her to deal with when the adrenaline faded.

He cradled her head to his shoulder and murmured some nonsense he hoped was soothing. "Let's just breathe a minute. We need to slow this down." That sounded pretty good. Almost reasonable.

"Sure." But she kept her hands fisted in the fabric of his jacket.

"We should start a fire."

"I've got plenty of fire for both of us." She pressed her lips together as she backed up a step, released him. "No fire. It could easily give away our position."

And he would've thought of that if she hadn't just fried his brain with that kiss. It was all he could do to stay sane enough to think past the desire.

She shrugged out of her pack and took her sleeping bag deeper into the dark cave. He heard the rustling as she rolled it out. "Warmer back here," she said.

"Good." He was hoping the cold air at the mouth of the cave would be as effective as a cold shower. "I'll take first watch."

"Get back here and get some rest," she suggested. "I'll wake up before dawn to watch for their movement."

"Charly."

"Worried I'll jump you?"

"The reverse, actually."

"If only," she said. "Flattering as that is, we're going to need each other—body heat—to get through the night without a fire."

He knew she was right even as he racked his brain for a suitable argument. He needed distance. Physically and emotionally. "Let's pretend it's another date. You owe me one anyway."

"I owe you a game of pool."

"And some conversation to go with it," he said. His feet felt like concrete blocks as he walked back to her. The date idea was solid. They'd talk and pretend to be anywhere but a dark, cold cave until she fell asleep.

He set aside his pack and sat down at the edge of her sleeping bag. Loosening the laces of his boots, he pulled them off and changed into dry socks before he leaned back against the wall of the cave.

"I'm not sure I'm good for conversation," she said. The zipper of the sleeping bag rasped as she spread it out. "Why don't you start? We've talked about my family, but not yours."

Good grief. How did he get through this minefield? His date idea had twisted back and bitten him on the ass. As much as he didn't want to discuss his broken family, it would at least serve as an effective mood killer. Being honest about his past would kill any chance he had with her if—*when*—they got out of this increasingly frustrating Lancaster situation.

"We need to figure out how to find the plane," he mumbled.

"Can't do anything until the morning," she replied. "You know I have two brothers," she said. "Do you have siblings?"

"That's first-date chatter."

"It's the best I've got right now."

Will reminded himself patience was his strong suit. Patience had carried him through hell week. Vast wells of patience had seen him through ops that went perfectly and those that had gone sideways.

Here, with Charly in the line of fire, his patience was tapped. He wanted nothing more than to put this deadly game of cat and mouse behind him. He wondered if he could find a way back up there and just take Lancaster and his crew out tonight.

And they both knew he'd dodged the more personal questions whenever they were together. He saw her moving—felt it, really, a more substantial form among the heavy shadows. He could chat. Keep it light and easy. An easy task when he wouldn't have to face her reactions.

His pulse kicked as she settled next to him, her hip pressed against his. She drew the sleeping bag up across their legs, casting her scent over him. Sunshine and moss. The strange combination was soothing. Between her body and the sleeping bag, he wanted to sink into the comfort.

He had enough decency, self-control and, yes, patience, to deal with it.

"I had a brother." And parents, too, until Jacob died. "Do you ever wish your brothers put as much into the business as you do?"

"Sure. But we're talking about you right now."

"We are?"

She linked her hand with his. "Yes."

He heard the edge in her voice and knew he was stuck. She wanted him to open up. It wasn't as if she didn't deserve a little honesty. He could do this. "My brother died."

"I'm sorry." For a long time, the only sound was her

soft breath. "I didn't realize how little I knew about you," she added. "Personally."

Well, crap. He couldn't help but wish for a rewind button. Only an idiot stopped a beautiful woman. Right about now they could be riding the crest of that adrenaline rush, the world's problems forgotten. If he hadn't put a halt to that kiss, she'd be naked under him now, incapable of forming words, much less giving voice to uncomfortable questions.

"Not much to know," he said, determined to keep it light. "All-American kid heads into the navy, gets cocky and somehow makes it through to become a SEAL."

"You never struck me as cocky."

"Huh." She had no idea how much he'd changed in recent years. "I'd better work on that."

"All right." Her soft laugh echoed through the cave. "New question. When was your first kiss?"

"Kindergarten," he confessed. "By the swings at the end of recess. She had blond pigtails and a frog on her shirt."

"Wow. Impressive memory."

"Some things you don't forget." And other things you couldn't forget no matter how much you wanted to. Jacob's face drifted through his mind.

"I bet you dated cheerleaders and homecoming queens."

Wary now, he hesitated. "Don't tell me guys weren't falling all over you growing up."

"Only in rugby."

"You played rugby?"

"Two seasons," she said with pride. "Keeping up with my brothers."

He'd pay good money to see those videos. "Bet you were good at it."

"I brought home my share of scrapes and bruises."

She didn't ask, but he heard himself answering. "My brother and I came up in soccer and eventually made the shift to baseball." He rubbed the scar on his chin. "Funny story. I got clipped by a bat in practice. My mom was scared of football…" His voice trailed off. She hadn't been big on sending her boys into the military, either, but he and his father had assured her all would be well. He remembered when she'd looked at him with pride shining in her eyes. But that sweet memory had been blotted out by the blame and sorrow overflowing her gaze from the other side of his brother's grave.

"My brother joined the marines," he heard himself whisper. Why didn't he just talk about something trivial, like taking the homecoming queen to the dance his senior year? "He told our parents he was inspired by me."

"Can you tell me what happened?"

He swallowed. "Worst-case scenario." It still sat like an elephant on his chest when he thought about it. Which was why he didn't think about it. "It was a training accident. He was the less than two percent of training casualties no one talks about. No one's fault, just…"

"The fluke that could've happened to anyone, but it happened to your family."

"Yeah." How was it she understood?

"I've seen my share of life, Will," she replied, making him wonder if he'd given voice to his question. "Up here you can do everything right and still get screwed over."

"My parents haven't spoken to me since the funeral."

She shifted, one hand stroking up and down his arm in a soothing touch. "You can't be serious."

He wished he wasn't. Wished he could shut up. "My

kind of work doesn't make it easy to stay in touch anyway," he said.

"You're stateside now," she pointed out briskly.

"True."

"Ah. They don't know. You haven't told them."

He didn't like how easily she figured him out. Smart or not, it wasn't something he wanted to discuss. "This is all a little heavy for a cave-date conversation."

She gave his shoulder a light thump. "Maybe it's time to stop running away."

She was right, but he didn't have to like it. "It was easier to work. I couldn't fix it, couldn't change what happened. Still can't."

"How long has it been?" She raised their joined hands and pressed a soft kiss to his scraped knuckles.

Her compassion, along with her courage, was a force he couldn't stand against. "Long enough to be a habit."

"Will."

The gentle censure tugged at the protective walls he'd built around his heart. If she brought them down, he had no idea what would happen. To him or her if he couldn't defend her. This was the worst time and place for an emotional breakdown. He searched for a way to get back to something lighthearted. "Enough about me. When was your first kiss?"

"Sophomore year."

"High school?" He turned toward her, though he couldn't get a read on her expression. "That's impossible."

"I'm sure it would've been sooner if I'd worn frog T-shirts."

He laughed and felt the heavy burden of grief easing inexplicably. "Hey, I'm a guy. We have standards."

"I noticed," she said, her voice full of appreciation. She cleared her throat. "First heartbreak?"

He wasn't sure anything could compete with the pain of losing his brother. They'd been so close, shared everything along the way. "Sally Bowman," he decided. Romantically, it was the closest he'd ever come to falling in love. "She ditched me at the homecoming dance to make out with the quarterback."

"Poor Will."

He didn't hear much sympathy in her tone. It made him smile. "And you?"

"I've had a few crushes along the way, but no one took enough interest to sweep me off my feet or break my heart."

The male population of Durango was stupid or blind. Maybe both. It sounded as though romantic neglect might qualify as a unique kind of heartbreak all on its own.

"Will?"

"Yeah?"

"If I told you I had a frog T-shirt with me, would you kiss me again?"

"Not tonight." It was too dangerous. Not mission danger—he was used to that. But he was far too vulnerable where she was concerned. Letting his desire get out of hand would erode his success on the mission.

"All right." She slipped away, burrowing under the sleeping bag and hunching her shoulders.

"Charly." He knew he should explain how much he wanted her. This just wasn't the right time to act on it. There had to be a way to assure her. He felt terrible that she would lump him into the category of the other guys who'd overlooked her.

"It was worth asking." She stretched her legs out

and then curled up once more. "Come here so we both stay warm tonight."

He stretched out beside her, his body curving around hers. It was almost too much as she pillowed her head on his biceps. He told himself the layers of clothing were a good thing as he breathed deep of the enticing mountain scents caught in her hair.

"Get some sleep." She reached back and patted his thigh. "I'll wake us up in plenty of time to get ahead of Lancaster."

# Chapter Thirteen

True to her word, Charly woke Will in plenty of time. Based on the lack of noise nearby, Lancaster's crew wasn't moving yet. Standing at the edge of the cave, Will gazed out across a bank of fog that looked thick enough to walk across. He pulled out the cell phone, waited for it to power up, only to confirm there was no signal. He turned it off and tucked it away, determined to try again later.

To the east, the sun teased the horizon, but it wouldn't be strong enough to burn through the low-lying cloud for hours. His binoculars were useless. The radio had been quiet all night. Will checked the battery, skimming through other channels, only to hear more silence.

"We should go," Charly said, hitching her pack onto her shoulders. "If we stay quiet we can get ahead of them."

"Go where? We can't see well enough to get out of here."

"Which means they can't see well enough to shoot at us."

"That didn't stop them last night."

"True." She planted her hands on her hips. "The climb down is tedious work."

"In moist conditions with no gloves, chalk or safety gear."

She cocked her head, squinting at him as though he was a newfound species. "I thought military types like you would see the fun in that kind of challenge."

Only if his life was the only one on the line. "It wouldn't be my first time saving a civilian from stupidity," he teased.

Her eyebrows shot up in mock horror and he relaxed, grateful they'd found their way back to a friendly rapport after last night's sharefest. "And here I was hoping for a chance to add 'saved a SEAL' to my résumé." She put it in air quotes, making him smile. "Seriously, there's an easier way around from this point."

"Around what?"

"The cliff."

"Did you call in a helicopter?"

"No good in that." Waving at the fog, she walked away from the mouth of the cave. "Come on. Trust me."

He did. Completely. Not the way he trusted his fellow SEAL team members, but in a way that went deeper. Deeper into territory he'd never explored with a woman.

Following her and the pale white beam of her flashlight into a narrow tunnel of rock barely wide enough for his shoulders, he was reminded of his brother.

Growing up they'd gone off without thinking about anything beyond the thrill of the moment, hell-bent on whatever adventure they'd cooked up. He trusted Charly that same way—on instinct. She hadn't steered him wrong or given him any cause to think she would.

The rock fell away in places, as though someone had carved out windows. He sucked in a breath at the views. The valley below still blurred by the fog, another mountain peak speared up, looking close enough to touch. He couldn't feel the breeze, but he got a sense of it as fog poured in between the peaks, filling the valley like a giant sink.

"My guess is the plane crashed into the side of that ridge. Across the valley."

"Why?"

"Pilot error, quirky thermals, you name it." She rolled her shoulders, fiddled with the straps. "I can't be sure, but based on what you've said and Lancaster's behavior with the beacon, it fits."

He pulled out his binoculars, searching the opposite peak for any hint of a crash. He couldn't see anything definitive. "Take a look," he said.

She raised the military-grade black lenses to her eyes, making a small humming sound as she adjusted and swept as much of the terrain as the weather allowed. Then she stepped out, swiveled the glasses back toward the cliff they'd slid down last night. "Vultures," she said, pointing. "Probably circling the man who fell last night."

He noticed she didn't use the name. He wasn't inclined to provide it. Everyone dealt with trauma and loss in their own way. If avoiding the name made it easier for her to deal with the shock and the brutal after effect, that was fine by him.

"Unless something like a deer or horse is also dead over there."

"Maybe the vultures will discourage Lancaster." But he doubted anything would keep the man from his revenge. "How many times have you been up here for pilots?" He wanted her thinking of other things, things that she had more power over. Things that might have happy endings.

"A few."

"Any of them crash into this side?"

"Not traveling westbound."

"Okay." So she was giving him a well-educated guess. Not that he expected anything less.

"Best route for us?"

She pointed. "This area is more like a serrated knife with ups and downs of varying degrees between these peaks. At the base of this cliff we can head upstream and cross the water where it's shallow. Then it's just a matter of finding something useful."

"Or we're back to tailing Lancaster." Come on, universe. Would it be so terrible to catch a little luck on this op? They were surviving, but only by small margins. He wanted to make some progress today.

"I hope it doesn't come to that," she muttered.

He agreed. So much cleaner to grab the Blackout Key and disappear, letting nature have its way with Lancaster and his mercenaries. Too bad Casey wanted the jerk alive. "Lancaster will head straight for the crash site. Any idea how he'll get down here?"

She snorted. "His men will be lucky if he doesn't test their ability to fly across." She cleared her throat. "The best way down is south of where we scaled the cliff last night." She paused again. "After losing a man that way, I can't imagine anyone else on his crew will be willing to go over the cliff face like we did. That delay alone should give us at least another hour's lead time to find the plane."

"All right. How do we get down there?"

A corner of her mouth tipped up. Tempting him to taste, to take. He'd missed a golden opportunity by halting things last night. He reminded himself where that kiss would've led, and how unfair that result would be to her. She deserved better than a guy who could only give her a moment's pleasure. She deserved a man who wasn't afraid of giving her everything. A man who had everything to give.

"We follow the stairs."

"Stairs?" he echoed.

"They aren't up to code and yes, they're bound to be slippery with this fog, but they are functional."

"Duly noted."

He shouldn't have been shocked that her description was spot-on. The mountainside gave way incrementally from their cave to the valley below. There were slips and some mighty big steps, but overall, their trek down was uneventful.

The fog still hadn't shifted and the visibility was terrible. Though the sun had to be working on it by now, he wasn't sure which would help them more. If they could see, Lancaster could see. The sense of solitude and security was deceptive and the vapor amplified some sounds and muted others.

Birds called and squirrels chattered, but they might have been at his shoulder or a mile away. Will pitched his voice low so it wouldn't carry. "How do you even know where you're going?"

"Compass for a heart," she said, smiling over her shoulder. "And technically I don't know more than our general direction."

A fat black squirrel scampered across a thick tree limb, watching them with obvious interest. "Are black squirrels common here?"

"More common than other places," she replied with a shrug. "Haven't you ever seen one before?"

"Sure." Probably. He didn't typically pay attention to wildlife on a mission. He kept his focus on his target and ignored the things—cover, animals or other people—who got in the way.

Charly crouched suddenly, pressing her fingertips to the soft, dark earth. She held up her other hand, signaling him to stop.

Obediently, he froze in place while she eased forward.

What the hell was she looking at? It couldn't be related to Lancaster and unless he'd lost all his field sense, they were nowhere near where Rich's body might have landed. They'd moved away from that deadly fall just by reaching the cave. Had some scavenger dragged the body this way? He wanted to ask, but refused to interrupt her.

She pressed a finger to her lips and motioned him closer. "Wolf." She pointed to the big paw print near her knee, then to the next one just out of her reach.

"They don't travel alone," he said, mostly to himself.

"No."

"What does that mean for us?"

She stood tall, her gaze tracking up into the trees, then back down. "Stay alert." She smoothed a stray lock of hair back behind her ear.

"You have a theory."

"What makes you say that?"

"I can practically hear the gears turning."

She smiled, but it wasn't an entirely happy expression. "The wolves might have come through, but they're not here right now."

"Please explain that," he said when she stopped.

"All the prey is too happy, too active. If a predator was nearby, the immediate area would be absolutely still, hunkered down and waiting it out."

"Okay, I'll buy that."

Now her grin was quick and sharp. "Remind me to send the government an invoice. Anyway," she continued, "I was really thinking that the wolves might have, um, found an easy meal if the plane went down nearby."

"Oh." Then the full meaning sank in. "Oh," he repeated, imagining a gruesome scenario.

"Apex predators don't turn down easy food if they can get it." She dusted her hands on her pants and set off again.

But now they were both thinking about Clint and how she'd protected his body from a similar fate.

"So the wolves must be somewhere else if the vultures are circling."

"It's a big mountain," she said. "How many on the plane?"

"No idea. I assume it was only the pilot."

"Well, let's get up there and find out." She moved with grace and speed, barely leaving a track along the way. He watched her deliberately choose one step over another without slowing, leaving the wolf prints intact.

"You'd be an excellent teacher," he said, thinking aloud.

"Because I can intimidate as well as track?"

"Something like that."

Her braid flowed down her back when she shook her head.

They stopped long enough to fill up their canteens with fresh water. He was fascinated as she pointed out the different tracks of animals who'd visited recently. "It's been years since I've given any thought to tracking down something other than people," he said.

A smirk curved her lips. "Nature was here first."

"I'm aware. Nature is often part of the briefing..."

"And what? You ignore it?"

"Not exactly. I listen. But it just…doesn't matter. The job has to get done no matter what else is out there." That was simply the way things went in the military. Especially on covert ops. Failure wasn't an option. Clichéd or not, it was a core principle of his service.

"Usually I give any threatening wildlife a wider berth," she said.

"But that's not a choice this time around," he finished for her. "I'll stay alert."

With a nod, she pushed to her feet, her gaze roaming across the cliff they'd just left.

The fog had thinned, but visibility remained limited. The disembodied voices of Lancaster and the mercenaries drifted through the air, accompanied by the occasional sound of an anchor biting into rock.

"I'll be damned," he said, catching a few words that confirmed the men were climbing nearby.

"They're following us straight down the cliff face," she whispered. "Fools."

"Either Lancaster's opposed to more detours, or the guy who fell had something they need."

Charly didn't seem to be listening. She stared into the water as she moved upstream. "Wait a second," she said.

He took a few long strides to catch up. "We have to reach the wreck ahead of them." Ideally, he'd get the key, set a trap for Lancaster, then haul ass off this mountain and let the authorities deal with the mercenaries.

She knelt by the water and swiped a hand across a wet stone, then brought it to her nose. When she turned and held up her fingers, her bright smile made up for the weak sunlight. "It's fuel." She stood, held her hand to his nose. "Take a whiff."

Whatever was on her hand smelled burned to him, as well. "Keep going."

The voices faded behind them, forgotten as they searched swiftly for any evidence of the downed plane. She watched the water; he kept checking the treetops. The damn thing should've left a mark somewhere out here.

He turned back, and his stomach clutched to see the brutal, rocky cliff they'd scaled last night. Intimidating didn't do it justice. Magnificent might've fit, if he hadn't been busy trying not to puke. Ledge or not, they never should've survived that climb in the darkness.

Blind luck? Grace of God? Mother Nature in a benevolent mood? Will gave a mental shout of gratitude to the universe in general.

Unfortunately they were losing the advantage of the fog and would have to take cover or take more fire from Lancaster's men.

"They'll spot us soon," he warned.

"This way," Charly said, pointing to the trees on the facing slope.

When they were safely out of sight, she asked for his binoculars again. He used them first, getting a fix on Lancaster's progress, then gave them to her.

"There." She pointed, held her arm steady while he took a look. "See it?"

Finally, he did. Through the lenses it didn't look like much more than a crumpled ball of paper caught in the rocks. "Could the wreck be downstream? In the water?" If so, Lancaster had regained the advantage.

"I doubt it. If the pilot lost control, that might be the first of a string of pieces that would lead to the crash site."

"Heading downstream."

"Cheer up," she said, with more cheer than the situation called for. "I've heard search and rescue pilots talk."

"So have I." He could imagine well enough a pilot coming over the ridge and cartwheeling out of control. If beacon and key were together, they'd lost any advantage.

"There's no sign of an explosion, so it didn't get blown this direction."

Her excitement, the renewed confidence gleaming in her eyes, roused his curiosity. "What are you getting at?"

"The small-aircraft pilots who fly up here," she explained, "talk about getting tossed and battered by the shifting winds and hard shear all the time."

"Which pushes pilots into this side."

"Yes." Her eyes were bright, eager. "I'm betting the wreck is near the upper tree line and only a bit farther downstream." She punched him lightly on the shoulder. "Lancaster isn't any closer than we are. In fact, we can move faster because it's just you and me. If he refuses to let them detour off the beacon's signal, it will take them longer because of the tougher terrain."

"This is easy terrain?"

"It's all relative," she said with a grin. "Besides, we're younger, more fit, and I'm the area expert. Come on."

Her fresh surge of energy boosted him, too. "Then let's get this done."

He thought she was part mountain goat the way she scrambled up the slope. His quads burned, and his lungs labored with the quick pace and thin air.

He didn't mind. It was all good and the effort felt like real progress. A couple hours later they hadn't reached the summit, but they had found another piece of the plane, this time part of the landing gear caught up high in a tree.

"That's more like it," he said.

"Yeah, we're getting close," Charly agreed. "And it's recent, so it's probably part of the plane you're after."

"Okay, the compass-for-a-heart thing I've seen first-hand. Last night proved well enough that you know every nook and cranny—literally—around here. But how can you tell how long ago that landed in the tree?"

"Easy. The cracked limbs would be brown and dead if it had hit more than a few days ago. It's still green."

"Of course." It made sense. Surely he would've come to the same conclusion. If he'd thought it mattered. "Have I mentioned lately I'm glad you're on my side?"

She pretended to check her watch. "Right on schedule." Her saucy grin faded. "But a plane could go for miles without that wheel."

He closed his eyes, imagining the rugged mountain trek ahead as miles of gentle, level ground. "In it to win it," he said, sweeping an arm out for her to lead the way.

He told himself he appreciated competent people in any situation. Charly was a friend and despite being attracted, he really should take a step back. For her sake and his.

When this was done, Casey could ship him off to a new assignment in another town. It was how a task force worked. The last thing Will wanted was one more tally in the loss column.

Fellow SEALs and his brother dead, his parents shutting him out—all of that was more than enough to manage. Which was why he didn't dwell on what he couldn't change. Being sad or pissed off didn't bring back the dead, and in his experience it didn't make coping any easier.

Work did that. Movement. Quantifiable progress in the form of successful ops or a cleared to-do list.

Leaving a woman as beautiful and interesting as

Charly? No. He had enough common sense to avoid that disaster. He wasn't ready for permanent and she deserved more than temporary.

A few paces ahead of him, he saw the misstep, could only watch as her foot slipped and she landed on her hip. She slid down the slope like a runner into third, using a tree trunk to stop herself.

"Safe," he teased, offering his hand to help her up. She put her hand in his, and he felt the jolt of awareness. Using him as anchor, she stood and suddenly their joined hands were trapped between their bodies.

Her face tipped up to his, her smiling lips so full and close. Another time, another place, he knew he wouldn't have hesitated. The devilish voice in his head urged him to go for it. "You all right?"

"Sure." Her gaze drifted to his mouth and then back to his eyes. "Slips happen."

Physically, yes. But a slip of the personal variety couldn't be allowed. He plucked a twig from her pack before it could tangle in her hair. "Better keep going."

"Right." She turned, resuming the steep hike with a little more caution.

It reminded him of the way she'd turned her back to him last night. For the first time since his brother's death he wished he wasn't so damned broken.

## Chapter Fourteen

Charly stayed on edge the rest of the day, ever alert for the potential danger from the mountain or Lancaster's advance. They'd stopped periodically to check the progress and as she'd anticipated, Lancaster's stubbornness had turned into an advantage for Will's cause.

As if that wasn't enough mental gymnastics, she couldn't keep her mind from wandering back to last night. Kissing Will, she'd felt something unlock. No one had ever made her feel that rush quite that way.

If he hadn't been sensible last night, there would've been no stopping her. She should be grateful. Instead, it was taking a great deal of her energy to stay sensible when she wanted to jump him, to get her hands under those dark clothes and explore every honed inch of him. At this point she didn't care if it ruined the friendship. She knew it would be worth it.

Except it wouldn't be. She respected him—more, she respected herself. He'd been right; they'd both been running on adrenaline and the thrill of survival. It was challenging enough to keep her mind on the various tasks ahead of her today and they'd only shared a kiss. Mind-blowing, but a kiss.

If they'd had sex, she'd probably be flitting about in a fog of her own making.

Her brain kept dancing through her every personal encounter with him. Hoping to put an end to the merry-go-round of it, she told herself she wouldn't let him talk his way out of another chance should it present itself.

She might not have as much experience as other women her age, but she wasn't an idiot. She knew Will was attracted to her. Knew he felt the chemistry simmering between them. A man just looking to add to his high score didn't take the time Will had taken with her. *Before* they'd hiked into this escalating situation.

"How are you doing?"

His voice lifted the hair at the back of her neck. "Fine." She carefully turned. "Do you need a break?"

Half a grin tilted his mouth up at one corner. "I'm good."

Yeah, she had to agree. With his jacket open and sweat dampening his shirt, molding the fabric to his muscled torso. She told herself the simmer of heat under her skin was an asset against the cooler temperature.

While he checked Lancaster's progress with the binoculars, she indulged in a long, cool drink from her canteen. "Hungry?"

He shrugged. "Sure." He accepted the beef jerky she offered. "Sounds like they've split up."

"What?"

"More radio chatter." He turned the dial and held it where she could hear it, too. "No need for radios if they're together."

"Damn it."

"You said it," he said. "Any ideas?"

Her thoughts scattered for a moment as he tipped his canteen back. A bead of sweat trickled down his neck. Why was that so sexy? Her body temperature climbed. "Keep moving. We have to be getting close."

He nodded as he capped his canteen. "I'll keep the radio on."

When they reached a place where they could walk side by side, she fought the reflex to take his hand. "What will you do when we get there?" she asked, desperate to keep her mind on the bigger issue.

"Assuming we get there first, I'll take control of the device."

"What does it look like?"

"I don't know."

Startled, she looked up at him, hoping he was kidding. The tension in his jaw, his gaze steady and aimed straight ahead, made her realize he was serious. "Great."

"It can't be too big, considering what it does."

"Why would it be on a plane? Seems easier to just have it shipped," she mused.

"Good question."

"Is there anyone with the answer?"

He chuckled, the sound low and deep. "The answer's irrelevant. However it happened, the thing is out here and it's up to me—to us, now—to find it before Lancaster does."

"You aren't curious about the how and why?"

"Only as it relates to my operational success."

"What does that mean?" It sounded irresponsible to her and nothing like the thoughtful, easygoing mailman he'd seemed to be back in Durango.

"Do you ask your customers why they want to take one excursion over another?"

"Sometimes, yes."

He reached down without missing a stride and plucked a fallen twig from the ground. "Bad example." He broke bits of dried bark from the twig as they walked on. "Remember when your parents would say, 'because I said so'?"

"Of course. It's a universal curse."

"Right. Well, there are times when military ops are simply a matter of pointing a team with a certain skill set at an objective. We take that objective because our commander said so."

"I guess I know that, logically. But it's a tough leap since I knew you first as my mailman."

He smiled down at her. "I know how to think for myself, but during an op what I think takes a backseat to what needs to get done." He flipped her braid. "For the record, I've never done anything on an op or been with a team that took action that I later thought was unnecessary or excessive."

Will watched her from the corner of his eye as she processed that information. A military mind-set didn't appeal to everyone. Not even everyone in the military. Why did he have such an issue with wanting her to understand him? It was dangerous, thinking of her as more than a civilian in harm's way.

Right now, in life-or-death circumstances, was the worst time to let things spiral out of control emotionally or physically. He was about to say as much when the radio crackled.

By tacit agreement, Charly and Will stopped to listen. The bickering was tense and ugly on both sides. Scott's injury was slowing them down and apparently the tracking device was giving them mixed signals.

"Echoes," she explained, then slapped a hand over her mouth as though Lancaster might hear her.

Will had to work hard not to laugh. At both her innocence and the target's unraveling. Impatient, Lancaster had sent Max and James to scout ahead and they'd only managed to get themselves lost.

"The plane's between us," she whispered.

"Or the beacon is."

She curled her lip, clearly unhappy with that reminder. "Let's hurry."

"Won't argue with that."

"We'll make better time if we hike up above the trees."

"But based on what we've found, the crash is down in here with us."

"And heading straight for the beacon is working so well for him."

She had a point. He looked around, as if the plane would suddenly materialize in front of them. "We could be sitting ducks up there," he said, thinking of the sniper they'd had to avoid yesterday.

She planted her hands on her hips. "Trust me?"

"Absolutely."

The word was barely past his lips before she was off like a shot, scrambling for the top of the ridge. Shaking his head, he went after her.

IN THE EVENING, Charly paused just long enough to appreciate a fiery sunset that deserved more than a few seconds of admiration. A day that had started in a soft blur of gray drifted to a close amid broad swipes of orange and purple across the endless sky. Another day, she told herself, with a tall cold beer in one hand, she and Will would have nothing to do but watch the sun kiss the sky good-night.

Tonight, they were racing against the encroaching darkness. If they stopped now and waited until morning, they'd lose the small advantage they'd gained today.

She wouldn't let it happen; for Will's op, Clint's honor and her own pride, she was determined to beat Lancaster.

At last they stumbled onto the track of the plane's fatal descent. Together they picked their way over downed limbs and broken trees until they reached the mangled rudder. A few yards ahead, she saw more of the tail and fuselage. Without a flashlight, she couldn't be sure about the wings or cockpit.

"Watch it." Will caught her arm, drew her around a twisted wheel and strut before she tripped. "Let's search what we can without the flashlights."

Through the radio, they'd been keeping tabs on Lancaster's progress. Max and James had been pointed in this direction, and odds were good they'd soon be dealing with unwelcome company.

She'd gotten into the habit of stroking the hilt of the knife sheathed at her hip as they'd hiked out today. Now, with both of them having gone silent, she drew it, mentally daring Max or James to make a move. She had no idea how Will intended to find anything in the dark. Then again, he'd made it clear this wasn't the time for questions—obvious or otherwise.

From down the hill, on the opposite side of the wreck, a beam of light sliced through the shadows and she stilled. Will tapped her shoulder. "Go."

She shook her head, not trusting her voice.

"Let me take this."

She shook her head again.

"Go back to the ridge. I'll find you."

The voices were clearer now, the excitement coming through. Max and James had made good time without the injured Scott and older Lancaster.

"Go."

It wasn't a suggestion—he expected her to follow it like an order. She took a step back as he moved forward. "I'll take your pack." If he was going two against one, or thought he was, he needed to be mobile.

With a frown, he shrugged out of the straps, dropping it silently at her feet.

She had the ridiculous urge to wish him luck, or even kiss him goodbye. Instead, seeing the light of a hunter in his eyes, she eased back into the shadows.

It was harder going with two packs, more of a challenge to move without making a sound, but she managed. Will didn't need to be worrying about her when he was up against two well-armed men who'd proven themselves ruthless.

Part of her wanted him to kill them both, while another part prayed they'd get out of here without being noticed at all.

When she was well back from the wreckage, but not anywhere near the ridge where he wanted her to hide, she looked for a good place to stow the packs. Somewhere they could find them if they had to make a run for it. Not if, *when*, she amended. Whether he took out both of them or not, with Lancaster nearby a hurried escape was inevitable.

Will could complain later, but she wasn't leaving him without some kind of backup. Knife in hand, she crept back down the slope.

Two beams of light roved over the plane and she knew Will was somewhere at the edge, waiting for his opening.

A loud snap of a boot on debris interrupted Max and James and the men aimed light into the surrounding forest.

If Will had done that it wasn't by mistake.

She tipped her head back and let loose a long wolf howl.

A moment later, a wolf answered her call. Max and James exchanged some harsh words, reaching for weapons or radios. The radio she and Will had taken when they'd left Jeff and Bob at the waterfall was still clipped to Will's belt. Had he remembered to turn it off? She moved closer, ready to leap into the fray if it gave away his position. But gunfire erupted from the trees—from Will—and James and Max hit the ground, searching for cover, too preoccupied to get off a call for help.

She used the commotion to race in behind the mercenaries. *Not the smartest move*, she thought, too late, as it put her on the wrong end of Will's gun, but she stayed put, ready to act.

More lights crisscrossed in the distance. They had only a few minutes before Lancaster and Scott arrived.

The options were too few. She felt around in the dark until she found a pinecone. Not a great weapon, but a decent distraction. She jumped up and hurled it at Max. It found its mark in the middle of his back. She crouched behind a tree as one of the men charged her direction. "Will, run!" she shouted. "The others are nearly here."

"You first," he called back.

Guns growled as bullets flew between Will and the one mercenary. She had to move or she'd be caught for sure on the wrong side of the crash site.

"Charly?" James was nearly on top of her, but he was looking high, instead of low. "Come on now. We can come to terms."

She knew his terms. Breath held, gauging her options and dwindling time, she listened, eyes closed.

*One more step. Come on, one more.*

Finally, he moved, and she drove her elbow into his knee, then jumped up and punched him square in the throat. Leaving him choking, she ran for her life to where she'd left the packs. It sounded like a war zone behind her. The only good news was that the chaos would keep any wildlife at bay for a while.

She hitched her pack on her shoulders, praying Will would show up. Hearing boots, she spun around, knife swinging.

"Easy." Will caught her arm with quiet authority. "It's me."

She flared her free hand, unwilling to drop the knife. He let her go in favor of picking up his pack. They moved farther into the trees before Will stopped her.

"Too close," she said.

"We won't stay long." He pulled her down beside him. "Are you hurt?"

"No. You?"

"I'm fine."

"Then let's move. They'll find us here."

Will shook his head. "They're too distracted." But the four men were already searching around the plane, trying to get organized.

She wanted more space. Now.

"Did you kill James?"

She shook her head, trying to slow the panicked beat of her heart.

"Oh. Here he comes."

She saw him stagger out, joining the others in a circle of gathered flashlights. The angry voices carried up to their position.

"Hunt them down!"

"You let them get away?"

That was probably Scott, but it was impossible to tell which man had shouted amid all the raised voices. Charly wanted to cover her ears, wanted to shut it all out. The tension rolled off the mercenaries in waves as the arguing and accusations were hurled back and forth.

Will's hand, warm on her shoulder, was the only thing keeping her from bolting. Irrational, but true—her flight reaction had her by the throat and wasn't letting go. Suddenly a gunshot rang out across the mountain, sending birds that had recently settled for the night into a swirl of panic and feathers flitting across the dark sky.

She, too, jerked in response, but Will had gathered her close. His strong arms were the only security, his embrace the beginning and end of her world. She clung to him, smothering her urge to scream against his warm chest. They were still too close. Any sound and they, too, would be dead tonight.

"You can't leave him there," Scott said.

"Watch me," Lancaster replied.

She couldn't look, but she heard the sounds, the smack and thud as punches were thrown. She hated the senseless killing and violence. Nothing was worth this. No one deserved Lancaster's blatant disregard for life. She wondered if she'd ever find her temper through the icy fist of dread clamped around her heart.

"It's too close to the wreck. The guide talked about predators."

"I don't give a damn. The pilot's dead. What's one more body? We'll be gone by first light."

"You're inviting trouble."

"You have your orders. Track them down."

"Impossible in the dark," Scott argued. "We'll camp here. Protect the site."

"Go find them!" Lancaster shouted. "Now."

Another hard smack, then someone was spitting, choking. "We can't track them in the dark. We don't know who's helping her, just that he has skills."

"I hired you for your skills! We aren't leaving witnesses."

"One thing we agree on," Scott declared with a threatening finality that chilled her. "I'll take care of it in the morning. We camp here. Get rid of the body."

"No." Lancaster sounded like a petulant child.

"You shot him, you get rid of him."

Will gave her a gentle squeeze. "Is there anywhere to hide up here?" he whispered against her ear.

With a nod, she pushed back. Moving carefully so they wouldn't draw Lancaster's attention, she led them back to the safety of the ridge.

# Chapter Fifteen

Will wasn't sure how she'd done it, but she'd gotten them away safely, unerringly finding their packs as they retreated from the crash site with no more than the moonlight to show the way. He had to admit her skills were more than a little eerie. She moved with absolute silence when she wanted to. He knew damn well if it hadn't been for her khaki pants he would've lost her.

"I've said it before, but I'm glad you're on my side," he said, walking deeper into the shelter. He dropped his pack against the back wall of the small cave she'd found.

"Same goes," she said, her voice catching.

He wanted to soothe, but exhaustion and adrenaline left him searching for the right words. "Thanks for not listening to me."

"Sure." She continued to stare into the dark, eyes wide, searching for Lancaster's next inevitable attack.

He put his arm around her, squeezed her shoulder. "You made those wolf calls, right?"

"One of them," she admitted, rubbing her hands over her arms. "The first one."

The woman he'd thought could never break was about to shatter. He had to do something. Anything. The world outside the cave started to come to life again.

Small things rustled. A sound similar to her wolf call rose into the sky.

"Is that one looking for you?"

"No. He knows a fraud when he hears it."

She'd sounded pretty genuine to him. A sudden screech split the air, making him jump. "Christ, that's loud."

"Screech owl," she whispered, hugging herself. "Worse when it bounces off the rocks."

He had to work, but he got her pack off her shoulders, set it beside his as the owl cried out again. "Will it go on all night?"

"So what if it does? It can't hurt you."

"It can sure as hell keep me awake."

"You sound like *My Cousin Vinnie*."

He turned. "What?"

"The movie? The city-boy lawyer trying to cope with the differences of a small town in the Deep South."

"I know the movie." She was starting to sound closer to normal, but she wasn't there quite yet. "I'll start a fire."

"That'll lead them right back to us."

"I don't think so." He patted his gun. "But they're welcome to try. We've got solid rock at our back, which leaves them only one approach. I guarantee I'll shoot first, and I don't miss."

"Fine."

He figured the chill gripping her from head to toe had more to do with her easy agreement than his weapons expertise.

When he had a small fire going, he came back for her. "See anything?"

"Not yet. What if they see the fire?"

"It'll be okay."

She turned, and his heart clutched at the pain in her midnight eyes. "He shot James. Because of me."

"No. James died because he signed on to work for a crazy man." He gathered her into his arms, helpless to do anything else. "It's not your fault." She didn't cry, but tremors ripped through her frame, pain and anxiety determined to find a way out. "Lancaster's gone off the edge."

"Not the right one," she said after a minute.

He choked back a laugh. "He won't get away with it, I promise." He ran his hand up and down her back.

"I believe you." Her breath quieted, and her heartbeat wasn't as wild against his chest. "I want to help you take him down."

"That's good. I'll need you."

She wriggled in his embrace, pressed a kiss to his cheek, then stepped back. "Okay. Let's make a plan."

"Sure." He was glad she'd turned the corner, but a manic rush of energy with no safe direction could be as problematic as the brittle shock. "But let's settle down for a minute first." He handed her a canteen.

She took a long drink, swiped her hand across her mouth. Then she shrugged out of her jacket. "I'm antsy."

"It happens."

She rooted through her pack, making a happy sound when she found some sort of wipes she used to clean away remnants of the day. "Want one?"

He accepted with a smile, started thinking about what they had left to eat. It was better than thinking about suffering another night alone with her in tight quarters. Another night when he couldn't touch her like he wanted to.

"Will?"

He turned, nearly bumping into her.

Charly looked up at him. She wanted to take a bite out of that square, beard-stubbled jaw more than she wanted another meal of granola bars and beef jerky. But it was clear he was expecting her to break apart at any moment. He was probably right. Part of her still felt shaky, but for increasingly different reasons than shock and death. She knew she should wait until they were done here. Until they had some time off the mountain to see how they felt about each other when life was normal again.

*Should* sucked.

But they shared the meal, and she gave a valiant effort to diverting her thoughts away from jumping Will's hard body. "We should talk," she said.

"About?"

"Anything."

He gave her a wary look over the top of the canteen. "Tell me about your first solo hike."

"No." She reached down and loosened her boot laces. "Something else."

He shifted his feet. "Okay." He pointed to his chin. "See this scar?"

"Mmm-hmm." She wanted to kiss it. Along with any others she could find.

"Happened when I was eight. Nine? No, eight, because—"

He went quiet when her hands gripped his hips. "Will?"

"Wh-what?"

"I'm done talking about the past."

"You are?"

She nodded. "Let's talk about right now." She trailed her fingers up over his chest. "I want you." She had to clear her throat, but she pressed on, determined to get the words out. "I want you to make love with me. Here. Tonight. Tomorrow doesn't matter. Might be too late."

"Charly, what you're feeling, it's just a basic reaction—"

"Stop. We both know this isn't 'just' anything." She pulled her braid over her shoulder, started combing it out with her fingers. "Do you want me, Will?"

His answer was to grab her with greedy hands, jerking her right up against his hard body. She had a split second to gasp before his mouth found hers. Claimed her. The heat of it rolled through her, sizzled and popped like sparklers.

She clutched his shoulders, straining for balance as his tongue swept into her mouth, one sensuous velvet stroke after another. Her body was primed and ready for him instantly. She felt as if she'd been ready for him her entire life. Pushing layers of fabric out of the way, she sighed in delight when her hands found warm skin at last.

He broke the kiss only long enough to strip off his jacket and shirt, then push away the barrier of hers. The firelight danced, highlighting acres of sculpted muscle. A better view than she'd imagined.

Amazed, hardly believing her eyes, she reached out, trailing her fingertips across his pecs, down the washboard abs. He was stunning and she was...

"Stunning."

She blinked. That had been her thought, but Will's voice. Aimed at her. She didn't want to call him a liar, but in her opinion the simple cotton bra—her entire body—was better defined as serviceable.

"Not too late for second thoughts." He tipped her chin up and she had to close her eyes or meet his gaze. "Do you want me to stop?"

No coward, she stared into his blue eyes, burning hot. For her. It was astounding. In all her fantasies, and her rare real encounters, no man had looked at her quite the way Will did now. "No second thoughts here."

His smile was a wicked flash before he leaned in and took her mouth once more. Kisses over her jaw, down her throat. The rough whiskers on his jaw scraped her skin as he nipped at the sensitive curve of her shoulder. She gasped as his hands cruised over her breasts, thumbs slipping behind the thin cotton to tease her nipples.

With a flick, her bra was undone and tossed aside. She couldn't find the energy to care as his mouth replaced his hands on first one breast and then the other. Running her fingers through his hair, arching into his lavish attention had her nearing a climax already.

She reached for his waistband, carefully opening the button fly around his erection. His breath shuddered across her skin when she closed her hand around him. She tingled, inside and out, as sensation layered over sensation while he learned what her body craved.

*Him.*

He laid her back on the sleeping bag as if she was the most exquisite treasure in his world.

And when he rose over her and drove into her with one swift thrust, she felt treasured, even as a sudden climax ripped through her. She reached for him, stroking everything she could reach. His broad back, his narrow hips, his biceps and shoulders strong as iron. Even that tiny scar he'd gotten when he was eight. Or nine. With her whole body she embraced him, drew him in and held as his rhythm seduced her, carried her up toward another peak.

Had anything ever felt as good?

Never. She wanted it to go on and on, felt as though it did as his body went taut on that final bolt of pleasure. Still intimately joined, he brushed her nose with his, then kissed her with such tenderness, she shivered beneath him.

He braced on one elbow. "Cold?"

"No. Probably never again." She kissed his chin.

"But you have goose bumps," he teased, his teeth scraping gently over her shoulder.

She caressed his calf with her toes. "Whose fault is that, I wonder."

He rolled to his side, tucking her close and wrapping himself around her. "Sleep. I'll take the first watch."

"All right." She smiled into the banked fire. If he felt half as good as she did right now they were most likely invincible.

# Chapter Sixteen

Will came awake suddenly, blinking to make sense of the near dark around him. He was alone under the sleeping bag and the sun wasn't more than a vague rumor in the sky beyond their shelter. That made two days running that Charly had managed to wake before him. How did she do that?

Though she moved silently, he knew her absence had been the distraction that pulled him from sleep. It wasn't the most comfortable self-realization. As a rule, he didn't actually sleep with the women who'd shared his bed. Or sleeping bag, as was the case here.

He sat up and smiled, watching her braid all of that silky midnight hair. Just hours ago he'd had all that in his hands. His body heated, recalling the feel of it sliding over his skin.

Their clothes were a mess and the closest thing they had to a shower was an ice-cold stream somewhere in the distance. Yet, wardrobe malfunctions aside, he wasn't sure he'd ever seen a woman as beautiful as Charly.

Knowing her had changed him. Made him want more than he could have. More than her body, he wanted to be the man she needed. However things went with

Lancaster today, he knew he wasn't the same man he'd been when he'd arrived in Durango.

"Going to laze around here all day?" She cast a look at him over her shoulder.

"I wish." His easy, instinctive answer surprised him. He decided to roll with it. They could get serious later. "When this is over, we need to come back up here."

She bowed her head a moment, then shifted around to face him. When she met his gaze, he noticed the sheen of tears in her eyes, but her voice was steady. "To banish this entire Lancaster debacle and reclaim this area as a more positive experience."

He nodded and reached for her hand, lacing their fingers. She had such strength in her hands. "Capturing Lancaster is step one, honoring Clint step two. But I don't want you standing at your shop and looking up here only to have that view haunted by dread or pain."

"I know bad things happen, no matter what or who caused them."

"You also know living is more than just surviving the bad things."

She blinked several times, and her eyes, clear now, locked with his. Leaning closer, she brushed her lips lightly across his cheek and then his mouth. "You are a thoughtful man, Will Chase."

She kissed him again and he let her, sinking into the kind, if overblown, compliment she offered. "It's a gift," he murmured against her warm skin, more than willing to change the subject.

"*You* are a gift," she corrected gently. "We should make time to visit the places that haunt you, too."

He froze, uncertain how to interpret that. Yes, he wanted her, but it was hard to believe she really wanted to be with him beyond this misadventure. No intelligent woman would. Not after the things he'd told her. The list was too long and, aside from his parents' home, the places that haunted him were on the other side of the world or locked in vaults in the dark corners of his mind.

"Strange as all this has been, we made some positive memories last night," she said.

"Agreed." He drew her close, wrapping her in his arms, trying to chase away the awkwardness he'd introduced. This perfect moment would be enough. For now, and for later when she came to her senses. If they didn't get another chance at this, he wanted her to know what he felt for her. He wanted her to know she was unique, precious, and any man would be lucky to have her.

It just couldn't be him. He didn't want to burden her with his baggage. When this was over, he'd explain that so she understood.

"It's three against two today."

"Almost seems unfair. To them," she said as she cinched her bootlaces.

She humbled him with her unwavering confidence. Knowing her skills and unflappable composure, it meant that much more.

He could almost hear the echo across the mountain as his heart dropped into her hands. Knowing men fell in love didn't mean he'd ever thought he'd be one of them. "Let's get back to the crash site," he said. Later was soon enough to deal with the emotions churning in his gut where Charly was concerned.

AN HOUR LATER, when they arrived at the crash site, he saw they were too late. Will reached for his knife as Scott, Max and Lancaster crawled through the wreckage, searching for Lancaster's life's work.

He wasn't surprised that the scene looked worse in daylight. The fuselage was cracked open like an egg. Sharp scents of fuel and oil spoiled the clear air. The wings were stubs, sheared by the trees, and the tail was absent, but Lancaster's presence was enough confirmation they were at the right site. Debris, like the first piece they'd found, was tangled randomly in the branches above and behind them. From above, Will imagined the crash site looked something like a poorly executed fire break. Will pulled out his phone and took pictures, wishing there was a cell tower to send them to Casey. If Lancaster had been able to get a helicopter up here, he would've gotten away with the Blackout Key too easily. Finally, a reason to appreciate high altitude and technology-free wilderness.

Despite their focus, by accident or design the men were positioned in a way that prevented a surprise attack. He couldn't take all three of them without a diversion. His best diversion was Charly, but using her as bait put a bad taste in his mouth.

"Some mess," he whispered to Charly.

"Where's a flare when you need one?" she murmured, her gaze on the scene, obviously not caring any more than he did about the fate of Lancaster and his two remaining mercenaries.

Will pictured his limited options. Action, reaction. Cause, effect.

"I can go in," Charly said.

"No." He didn't care that it was the right call.

"Bogus radio call?" She held up the radio.

He shook his head.

"Don't leave me out of it," she said through gritted teeth.

"Not that, either." He rubbed her shoulder, pressed

his lips to her temple. "First we need to know he found the key."

She nodded, making an okay sign with her fingers.

When Lancaster found the key, Will would be able to make a final decision about how to contain the men and the device.

He signaled to Charly and they retreated back into the thicker cover of the trees. "What's his best route out of here?"

"It's only a few hours on foot from here to another park access point by way of a cleared and well-marked trail."

"Then how much longer to Durango?"

"Not long at all if he has a car there."

"He won't go back over the mountain?"

"Would you want to go back the way we came?"

Will shook his head, suppressing his smile. "Just making sure there isn't a direct route."

"He'll make better time going down and taking the road."

"Does he know that?"

She grimaced. "I gave each of them standard trail guide maps for reference when we started out. But I'm not sure he knows where the trail is from here."

Will considered what they'd seen and heard. Lancaster had been furious about the shifting timeline and ongoing delays, natural and man-made, keeping him from the Blackout Key and his revenge. He was coming unhinged, had lost all but two men in the search. There had to be a way to turn that into an advantage.

A plan took shape in Will's mind. If—when—Lancaster found the damned key, this could all be over by the end of the day. He focused on that critical detail.

Yet Will knew that when Lancaster was in custody

and the key safely out of commission, he'd face a new crossroads with Charly. *One thing at a time*, he coached himself, hearing the team leader's voice from his first operation as a SEAL.

"What's wrong?" she asked, worry weighting her tone.

"Nothing. Unless the key isn't there."

"Right. But I can see the wheels turning," she said, repeating his words to her last night. "Tell me the plan."

"Our best option is to move around, cut off the logical egress from the crash site. He knows he needs to go downhill."

"All right," she said on a quiet chuckle. "Where do you want me?"

"Behind me," he said, ignoring the way her gaze narrowed. "After I send a specific emergency message over the radio."

"They could hear that."

"They don't know we have a working radio," he reminded her. "With the right phrase my message should bring reinforcements and not alert Lancaster." He hoped Casey had mobilized men into the Four Corners area after their last conversation—it would make the chain of custody cleaner. Either way, Lancaster was going down today.

"Do you want me to take Scott or Max?"

*Neither.* But that wasn't an answer she'd accept. "Max." The man who'd carried the tracking device from the start was tired, irritable and the closest to Charly's size. "Keep him alive if possible."

Her dark brows rose. "If?"

He nodded. "This is life or death. All three of those men are desperate. Hopefully it won't get that bad, but just in case, you're my priority."

"I am?"

He took a long breath. "I want you to live more than I want him alive to testify against Scott and Lancaster."

Her smile rivaled the sun. "Same goes." She pressed up on her toes and kissed him. "Assuming someone is smart enough to give you a medal or some kind of award for this, I want you to be alive to receive it."

"It's a deal."

They stayed low and moved quickly, both of them listening for any sounds of progress from Lancaster. The random shouts didn't sound good, and Will wasn't sure what that meant for his chance of success. He didn't see how it was possible that someone had found the crash site and robbed Lancaster of his prize.

But if the key had never been on the plane... He stopped that thought before it could gain momentum and cloud his analysis.

He paused when he got his first head-on look at the cockpit of the small aircraft. Burrowed into the scorched earth, sparkling as the sunlight danced on shattered glass, the pilot was slumped lifeless against the instrument panel.

Will halted when Lancaster's rambling suddenly ceased. Hearing the victorious shout, he knew he had to act. From here, the solution wasn't perfect, but all three men would be in front of him. Drawing his handgun, he stood tall and entered the clearing created by the downed plane.

With Charly at his back, he moved forward, confident he had the upper hand. "Arms up," he called. The three men stopped moving, but didn't comply. "Arms up," he repeated. "And drop the weapons. Reed Lancaster, your little field trip is over."

"Take them out," Lancaster ordered Scott and Max.

Will saw the hesitation in each man's face, knew they were weighing the odds. "Let Charly take your weapons." He gave her a nod, and she moved toward Max.

"You're outnumbered," Lancaster declared with absolute hatred in his eyes. "Do something," he barked at Scott. "Take them out!"

Will kept his gaze on Scott and Lancaster while Charly skirted the edge of his peripheral vision on her way to take care of Max. "Get real already," he said. "You can't win."

"Who the hell are you?"

Will kept his gun on Lancaster while he answered Scott. "Private contractor, just like you."

Scott vented his disbelief, and Lancaster bellowed as he raised his gun and fired.

The software genius had lousy aim. Will charged forward, furious and tired of this jackass. Two against one didn't bother him, not when he saw Charly holding her own against Max. He tackled Lancaster with all of his pent-up frustration, taking him down. The fumes from the crash rose up, choking him, but he ignored it.

Beneath him, Lancaster gagged, and Will knew that any second now Scott would land on him, or shoot him to protect his profit. He landed a solid punch and flipped Lancaster, using him as a shield against Scott. The older man landed a few punches with a force driven by madness, but Will fought back with knees, elbows and fists.

Until Lancaster was suddenly hauled off him and Charly's voice cut through the blood rushing through his head.

"I'm sorry," she said.

"Surrender or we shoot," Scott said.

Will looked up, blinking. Max and Scott had guns leveled on her. One at her head, one at her belly. He considered bluffing about backup, or that she didn't mean anything, but it was too late for that. He wasn't close enough for a rapid strike.

Defeated, he held up his hands. "You win."

CHARLY SCOLDED HERSELF. She'd disarmed Max, had him where she wanted him, and let herself get distracted when Lancaster took a shot at Will. That split second of panic and she'd lost her footing on the muddy ground surrounding the plane. Her mistake had distracted Will and now they were both propped against trees, hands cuffed at the wrist with zip ties, under the armed guard of Max and Scott.

"I have what I came for." Lancaster dropped to one knee too close to her face. He held up a black plastic box not much bigger than a deck of cards, then tucked it into his pocket.

"So take it and get off my mountain." She couldn't believe how much blood had been spilled for that unexceptional device.

"With pleasure," Lancaster said. With the unyielding tree at her back, there was no escaping his sour breath. She tried not to inhale. "If you get me off this damned mountain in one piece I might let you both live."

She had to give him points for the honest disclaimer. *Might* was a slim chance at life. And a slim chance was better than already dead. It felt like a lousy variation on the rock-paper-scissors game.

"I'll help you." She didn't look at Will. Couldn't risk taking her eyes off Lancaster. Right now Lancaster only knew they were working together. While he was obsessed with his device, she didn't want him to gain any advantage. If he recognized how far she'd go to protect Will, Lancaster would use her love as leverage.

*Love.* Charly closed her eyes as it washed over her. The feeling was impractical at best and the relationship—if running around a mountain counted as such—couldn't possibly survive. Still, if these were her final hours, she wouldn't live them in denial. Having seen Will in action, she knew the odds Lancaster found favorable—three armed men against a restrained man and woman—were only an illusion.

She opened her eyes. "Where do you want to go?"

"Durango."

"Do you realize what you're asking?"

Lancaster stared, his expression blank. "Enlighten me."

She suppressed the shiver as fear trickled down her spine. "You can't go back the way we came."

"Why not?"

She stared him right in the eye. "We've radioed park rangers and left a trail of bread crumbs." The lie, boosted with a grain of truth since they'd set up Jeff and Bob to be rescued, must have been convincing.

"You bitch." He backhanded her, bouncing her head off the tree. Her vision blurred until there were two of everything. She could only hope she was focusing on the real version of Lancaster.

"Tell me how to get off this mountain or you die right here."

"Fine." She tasted blood where her teeth had torn the inside of her cheek. "You're better off taking the cleared trail on this side of the mountain and hiring a car to get you out of Colorado." There wouldn't be any safe place for him, not anywhere in the world, with Will on his tail. With luck, they could gain the upper hand along the way to the trailhead.

Lancaster cut the straps holding her to the tree and

it shamed her when she slumped forward, still reeling from the blow. He hauled her to her feet by her bound hands. "Any tricks and I'll take my chances on my own."

"No tricks," she promised as they formed up. "But it's fine with me if you leave us here."

"Shut up and lead." Scott's rifle bit into her low back, pushing her forward.

"Just a second." She stumbled, heard Will's deep voice, but couldn't make out the words. Something was wrong, but the cause eluded her. "One second," she said again, from her knees. She peered out at the world, but it seemed as though she was watching the forest through a narrowing telescope. A flash of heat speared up to her head as a ring of darkness closed in. Her stomach twisted, and she battled the nausea. She was passing out. God knew what they'd do to her and Will if she couldn't function as a guide.

Deep male voices locked in a furious debate surrounded her, though the words were incomprehensible. It made the beckoning quiet all the more tempting. So tempting to give in, to be done with this entire problem.

Only the thought of Will's fate kept her from giving in. She thought of her grandmother's stories of ancient days. A time of honorable warriors and mystical shamans. She knew this land inside and out, body and soul.

"Water," she rasped, but no one seemed to hear.

She felt the cool, moist floor of the forest against her battered cheek. Her mind drifted like a feather on the wind, searching for a tether, a reason to land. *Will.* Will needed her. She sensed it and struggled against the pain reeling behind her eyes.

"Water," she said again, pushing herself upright, forcing her eyes open.

Someone echoed the command a moment before a canteen was placed to her lips. She sputtered and coughed, but it helped.

"More."

"No." Lancaster's denial didn't surprise her. "Can you see?"

"Well enough." Maybe. She didn't need to. This was the land of her ancestors. She could walk out of here blind if she had to. Though she hoped it didn't come to that. "One more sip. Please?"

"She'll lead us off a cliff," Max grumbled. "Give her the canteen."

The hard aluminum banged into her hands, and she managed to grip it before it fell to the ground. "Thank you," she said after another small drink. It helped to rinse the taste of blood from her mouth.

She closed her eyes, found her bearings and turned west. "This way."

"We should kill them and go," Scott said from a few paces behind her.

"Yeah, because that's worked so well," Max replied. "Four men are already dead because of this mountain."

"We can't let them live."

The announcement barely fazed her. Charly knew Scott was right. Witnesses were not part of the equation for the mercenaries. She wondered if Scott and Max realized Lancaster wouldn't leave them alive, either.

It wasn't her problem. At least not as long as she was breathing. She would lead and trust Will to figure a way out of his restraints as well as this nightmare.

# Chapter Seventeen

Will ambled on with the group, his hands tied behind his back, his weapons confiscated. Max had his knife and the radio; Scott had taken his handgun. Standard protocol and really, not problematic in the long run. He could take all three of these class-A jerks with his hands behind his back. And he would. Just as soon as Charly was clear.

It wasn't over, but getting captured wouldn't qualify this as his finest hour.

There was still a knot in his gut from Charly's collapse. Watching her, he knew she wasn't fully recovered—her left foot was dragging a bit, and no matter how they prodded her, she couldn't keep up a quick pace for more than a few minutes.

At this point, he wasn't sure she could even find the trail if it was lit with neon lights and a parade of forest animals waving signs. They hiked across relatively easy terrain under a heavy cloud of silence. He wouldn't make his move until he was sure she could get clear on her own. Or until they were out of time.

He had to believe his distress call had been heard by the tech-savvy specialists assigned to support this op by Director Casey. Regardless, he would be sure no one left this mountain with the Blackout Key. It was hard to comprehend how an unassuming black plastic block, small enough to fit into his palm, could be the nation's undoing.

The damned thing didn't look dangerous. He supposed it had been purposely designed to resemble a benign external hard drive.

"How does it work, anyway?" he asked as they crossed an open field. The grass was dormant now and small patches of crisp white snow dotted the area here and there. He imagined Charly had seen this field in every season, would know every plant, animal and stone. Remembering their earlier conversation, he decided he'd ask her about it when they were safe again. His mind played tricks on him, imagining what it would be like to kiss her here in each one of those seasons.

"Not your business," Max replied, pulling him back to the task at hand.

"Which means you don't know."

"I know you should shut up before I slap tape across your mouth."

"Seems like a lot of effort and a big waste of life to me." He wanted to provoke Lancaster. Casey wanted solid intel as to which pieces of Lancaster's grand scheme for revenge were already in place. "Now you can make your statement, is that it, Lancaster?"

"Shut him up," Scott grumbled.

"That little doohickey will show the billionaires who should be boss, right?" *Here we go*, Will thought as Lancaster abruptly turned on his heel and stalked back, a ferocious scowl on his face.

"This 'doohickey' can wipe your bank account in minutes. It will show the corporate mongers that they can't steal from the innovators." He shook the black square in Will's face. "My design, my creation will put the power where it belongs."

Power to the crazies. Not a great global policy.

"I was robbed," Lancaster continued in a calmer voice, "my career and reputation destroyed."

Will didn't see how kidnapping and murder would rectify anything, but he kept quiet.

"This device is literally the key to the kingdom that should have been mine a lifetime ago."

"You sure can hold a grudge."

"What I hold," he said, voice rising once more, "is justice. They will pay. One man, one program, one company at a time."

The man had mastered dramatic flair. Will might've laughed in his face, had Lancaster been less insane. "Were you ever in the theater? When you weren't working on the doohickey, that is."

"Imbecile." With that declaration, Lancaster left Will and Max to bring up the rear of the column as Charly guided them through a thick stand of trees. The trail couldn't be too far. When they got there, Lancaster wouldn't need hostages anymore.

"How much farther, Charly?"

"Don't answer that," Lancaster barked. "No more talking."

"You'll kill me anyway. I'll talk if I want to," Will muttered. "Hey, Charly, are there any snakes around here?"

"You're obnoxious," Max said, smacking the back of Will's head.

"It's a valid concern." He should have insisted the two of them create a code phrase, but he'd been distracted by the woman as much as by outliving Lancaster.

"Stick to the clear areas and it won't be a problem," she called over her shoulder, against Lancaster's wishes.

"Just shoot him now," Scott ordered. "Better to dump the body up here than closer to the trail."

Charly stopped and faced Lancaster. "You said you'd let us go."

"He's a problem."

"You're the problem," she snapped.

"That's hardly a rational argument," Lancaster replied. "I'm surrounded by idiots. Can you keep him quiet?"

Will met her pleading gaze, saw her shoulders go stiff. "Hush," she said without any heat.

"Last chance," Lancaster said to Will. To Charly, he gave a nod. "Go."

Scott jerked his chin at Max, and Will braced for the inevitable. With plenty of cover here for Charly to use for an escape, he decided to let them try and take him out.

Max kicked the back of Will's knees, sending him to the ground. Instead of sprawling, Will tucked and rolled, using the momentum to barrel into Scott. The mercenary leader went headlong into a tree trunk, knocking himself out.

Shouts and oaths bounced off the trees. Will scrambled for cover as Max started shooting.

"Will!"

"Run, Charly!" He caught the flash of color as Charly bolted out of sight. Smart. Let him handle this.

Max came at him, gun drawn. Will jumped to his feet, daring the mercenary to fire. Max bobbled the weapon, eyes going wide as Will charged him and the shot went high.

He planted a bone-crushing roundhouse kick into Max's ribs and the mercenary fell to his knees, wheezing.

A scream split the air, and Will jerked in that direction, praying Charly wasn't the source.

He quickly pinned Max to the ground, his boot on the man's throat. "Surrender or die."

Max spread his hands away from his body. Whatever words he was trying to utter around Will's boot sounded cooperative enough.

Will eased back, just enough so Max could catch his breath.

Looking around, he saw Scott still unconscious and no sign of Charly or Lancaster. He maneuvered until his hands were in front of him. "Cut me loose," he ordered. "Try anything and I'll kill you."

Max resembled a deer caught in the headlights of an oncoming truck.

"Use my knife. Slowly." When he was free, Will rubbed his wrists, then planted a knockout punch to Max's jaw. Dragging Max over to join Scott, he reclaimed his weapons and seized their packs and the weapons they'd brought in. Binding the men together back to back, he left them next to the tree.

"Charly?"

The complete lack of a reply turned the trickle of sweat between his shoulder blades to icy trepidation. Pausing every few steps to listen, he circled the area. No sign of her or Lancaster. Will resumed the route she'd been on, certain he'd find her right away.

He didn't.

Crap.

Lancaster wouldn't go down without a fight, but Charly was a scrapper fueled with determination to live. What did the persistent silence mean? It crawled under his skin, making him uneasy.

He looked up, watching the trees for the clues Charly had taught him. Nothing moved. Not a curious squirrel or scolding bird. Everything had taken cover, hiding from the loud humans. Everything.

Charly would've done the same. Moving with caution, ready and eager to combat any strike, he stepped, listened and stepped again. If Lancaster had found her or killed her, he'd be gloating or barreling down the mountain in an attempt to outrun Will.

And if Charly had subdued Lancaster, she wouldn't be hiding.

Damn it. If the roles were reversed, Charly would've spotted him by now. She'd be working her way around to help him out. He couldn't let his mind drift, couldn't afford the negativity of comparing his skills to hers. He might not know every inch of this particular landscape, but he knew his personal strengths.

He backtracked to where he'd left the gear he'd taken from Scott and Max. Picking up a radio, he double clicked twice, the signal he'd seen Scott use to get Lancaster's attention.

"Hold," came the whispered reply.

Will repeated the signal.

This time the single word, packed full of irritation, was accompanied by the hoot of an owl. He might not know exactly which type of owl she'd mimicked but he knew any owl worth the name was sound asleep this time of day.

Will smiled to himself and waited. She made the call once more and it was enough to give him a direction.

In a perfect world he'd pinch Lancaster between Charly and himself. He wasn't sure they had that much luck left. His knife in hand, the long blade back against his forearm, he advanced, using the trees as cover.

Finally, he caught a glimpse of Lancaster's sleeve. The man was crouched low behind a tree. Tired of playing cat and mouse with this jerk, Will was tempted to throw the knife and be done.

The required explanation and apology he'd owe Director Casey flitted through his mind. The nation supposedly needed the man alive. Resigned, Will ignored temptation and stuck with procedure, silently creeping closer to the target.

He recognized the jacket was a trap a moment too late—the blow landed hard across his shoulders. Lancaster followed up the surprise attack with a heavy branch he brandished like a baseball bat.

Dodging and ducking, Will's feet slipped on the forest floor as he blocked the vicious swings. He gripped the knife, but couldn't get close enough to use it. Couldn't get clear enough to throw it.

The radio at his belt crackled with voices, but the words were garbled, his mind fully occupied with his battle for survival. "Go for help," he hollered, not even knowing if Charly could hear him. He had to buy her enough time to escape. To live.

Will knew hand-to-hand combat. He faced Lancaster as he would an angry bear and stayed alert of his surroundings so he wouldn't run out of room. His fighting sense had been honed to a razor-sharp edge, and he knew how to learn from every engagement. There were solutions, even when fighting a man mad with desperation. Will's real disadvantage was keeping said madman alive.

On a pained shriek, Lancaster suddenly went down, his white-knuckled hands still locked around the branch.

He rolled to his side, and Will saw a knife, the hilt decorated with a mosaic turquoise feather, protruding from the man's calf. Over the fallen man, Will met Charly's enigmatic dark eyes. "Nice throw."

"You had him," she said. "I just got impatient."

He nodded, winked. "There are times when patience is overrated."

A smile bloomed across her face, and his heart tripped a little as it recovered from the fight.

"The owl call was a nice touch."

"I thought the same about the radio. He was almost on me at that point."

Will marched up to Lancaster and yanked the branch from his hands. "You are done."

"Who *are* you?"

"Just your average mailman," Will said, grinning at Charly. "You called in the troops, right?"

"Yes. But we're better off if we can meet them on the trail."

"Then that's what we'll do." He flipped Lancaster to his belly and secured the man's hands. A pat down for the Blackout Key came up empty. "Where's the key?"

"I lost it," Lancaster said.

"Not buying it." He tipped his head to Charly, and she went to search Lancaster's jacket. "Not here," she called, kicking around the debris at the base of the tree.

Will studied Lancaster for a long moment. The dirt-smeared face and cold eyes remained smug. Even now, the man thought he could win, thought he had some play left. Will reached for the ammo holder still clipped to Lancaster's belt. The older man grimaced and swore.

Opening the compartment, Will found the device. "Jackpot." He patted Lancaster's cheek. "Thanks."

Standing, he pocketed the device that had the attention of the nation's elite security agencies.

He pulled the knife from Lancaster's leg and cleaned the blade on his pants before handing it back to Charly.

"He can walk, but we should dress that before we move out," she said.

Will didn't want to do anything to assist Lancaster. The man had put them through a crucible on his selfish quest for vengeance. "Can you hold him while I go back for the other two and the packs?"

She tossed her knife from hand to hand, a wicked gleam in her midnight eyes. "No problem."

He jogged back to where he'd left Scott and Max. Taking only the weapons, he forced the other two to haul what remained of the packs. They wouldn't quite leave the forest as they'd found it, but it was as close as he could get.

"You're no private consultant," Scott griped as they set off.

"I'm a mailman," Will said, warming to the label. A mailman had routine in every day, and enjoyed a life beyond the job. A girlfriend or wife to take on dates. Hobbies. Family past and present to celebrate with on holidays.

He thought he could get used to that. Surprisingly, he wanted to try.

The men moved sluggishly, struggling with their injuries. Will thought it might be faster to just carry them to the trail, but squashed his impatience.

"Mailman." Scott snorted. "Right. You've cost me a major payday along with several good men."

"I didn't make you take the job," Will replied with no sympathy. "Who cares about the money? In prison I hear the currency is different."

Max groaned at that. "Damn you, Scott. I told you this sounded too good to be true."

"Is Lancaster dead?" Scott asked Will.

"Not for lack of trying to get me to kill him. Attacked me with a branch."

"Really?" Max tripped over a root and slammed into a tree. "More proof he's a lunatic. I'm not going down for a damned lunatic."

"You'll keep your mouth shut," Scott ordered.

"And let you get the better deal? No way."

"Quiet. Save it for someone who can do something with your statement," Will suggested, urging them along.

He didn't want to be away from Charly any longer than necessary. She could hold her own—and would—but he wanted this over immediately, if not sooner. He had a new life waiting for him in Durango and he wanted to get started on it. He hadn't fully appreciated the potential in this opportunity. Not until she'd opened his eyes and slipped under his well-fortified defenses.

As Charly and Lancaster came into view, Will felt himself grinning. Charly had propped Lancaster's feet up on a log, a minimal effort at first aid or comfort. Will laughed.

He tossed her the gauze and tape from the pack and kept Lancaster in line while she dressed the knife wound. "That should hold while we walk."

"I can't walk."

Will shrugged. "I'll drag you then." He reached for Lancaster's wrists and nodded for Charly to lead on. It took less than a minute for Lancaster to change his mind.

Along the way, Scott, Max and Lancaster groused and argued, exchanging insults and threats. Will looked to Charly and in her quiet smile he found an echo of his thoughts. They both wanted to be rid of these men. He checked his watch, finally noticing it had taken a direct hit. Ah, well. It was fitting. The watch had been a tool since his first SEAL operation and those days were now behind him.

"How much farther?" he asked Charly.

She looked up to the sky, then turned a full circle. "I'd guess just over an hour at this pace."

"Good." Just over an hour until they could hand over the prisoners. A few hours of questioning, then he could get cleaned up and start moving forward with his new life.

As they ambled on, he started considering and prioritizing the best tactical approach to keep her in it with him.

CHARLY FELT THE thudding of booted feet on the ground, heard the advance well before the team rounded the curve in the trail. Relief washed over her as a black-clad tactical team, alongside men and women in local police and park ranger uniforms, surrounded them.

Lancaster's device was quickly seized by the two members from the tactical unit. The three criminals were secured with metal cuffs at wrists and ankles and linked with belly chains and marched away.

Steve, her friend from the Durango police department, approached slowly, concern etched into his face. "Are you okay?"

"Yes," she replied, leaning her hands on her knees and gulping in air. "We're fine."

"Everyone in town's been going nuts since those other two were picked up."

She gave herself a mental high five that the ploy had worked in their favor.

"Did they talk?" Will asked, stroking her back.

"Not much beyond where they were staying and who hired them," Steve said. "You'll both need to come in and answer a few questions. It can wait until tomorrow if you need some time."

Charly stood tall and linked her hand with Will's. "Let's just get it over with."

They walked down to the blacktopped parking area choked with official vehicles from various agencies. If she'd had any lingering doubts that he was working on a major government operation, this sight dispelled them.

Will raised her hand to his lips. "You go on. I'll be right behind you."

She wanted to protest, suddenly afraid to be without him for even a moment. But that was clingy and weak. She was neither. If this was the end of her time with him, she'd manage.

Somehow.

"I'll be right behind you," Will repeated, giving her hand a squeeze.

She probably shouldn't believe him. He was an undercover agent, a former SEAL, and he'd accomplished his mission. But she hoped, wished, for more time as she followed his gaze toward an oversized dark SUV with blue lights flashing from the grille and above the rearview mirror. One man, aviator sunglasses blocking his eyes, sat in the driver's seat. The tinted windows could be hiding another person or a small committee.

She stuffed her hands into her pockets as he walked away, grateful for Steve's soft-spoken explanation of what she could expect when they reached the police station in Durango.

# *Chapter Eighteen*

His patience waning with the fading sunlight, Will waited on a bench across the street for Charly to exit the police station, heedless of the rain falling steadily as the day gave way to evening. The tidy brick building had felt small and insignificant after what they'd endured. Survived. He wanted nothing more than to take Charly home and start putting all of this behind them.

But there were details to manage when men died and his word—which should have been enough—wasn't. Evidence would be gathered. Reports filed, investigated and filed again. He reminded himself he had the utmost respect for law enforcement officials. As he felt the passing of each minute, counting them in his head, he knew it didn't take this damn long to give a statement. She shouldn't have to go through it alone, but he hadn't been allowed to join her.

He could hardly charge in there now. Lancaster was in custody, the Blackout Key had been turned over to Casey and he'd kept his promise to himself. Charly was safe.

So why weren't they done with her? He kept replaying that moment in the parking lot. He hadn't wanted to leave her, but she'd given him that look. The one that simultaneously reassured him she could manage and worried him that she didn't need him.

He made plans while he waited in the rain. He'd keep it simple, straightforward. She'd come to his apartment tonight, and he'd pour out a measure of tequila for both of them and just tell her all of it. At least the things she didn't already know.

Maybe they should stop and eat first. If they talked over dinner in a public place, he'd stay calm. The pub. That would work. He'd take her to dinner, answer any remaining questions she had for him, and then they would move forward. Together. Separately wasn't an option.

It calmed him to look at it like a mission: assess, plan and act.

Will saw Charly through the glass doors of the police station, watched her friend Steve wrap her in a gentle hug. It was nothing, Will told himself. He would comfort her from this point forward, on the rare occasions she wanted or needed comfort. Amazing and capable, that was his Charly.

The thought brought a smile to his face, and he came to his feet as she pushed the door open.

He waved, but she wasn't looking at him. Something inside caught her attention and she let the door close between them. After a short hesitation, she disappeared into the station under the arm of her cop friend.

She didn't look back.

His heart, the organ he'd thought only useful for pumping his blood, cracked. Bled. He sat down again, waiting. She would come back.

He'd believed her last night when she'd declared she wasn't done with him. If he'd misinterpreted, if she'd only meant she wasn't done with the sex, he'd count it a starting point. He'd never expected to meet a woman who wanted more than his body or money. He'd never gone looking for the kind of woman who'd encourage him to give more. But he'd damned well found her, hadn't he?

He pushed to his feet and stalked across the street, done with waiting.

"Charly left."

Will swiveled, glaring at the cop who'd spoken. "No, she didn't. I was waiting for her."

"Through the back." The cop jerked his thumb toward the back hall.

"She doesn't have her truck."

"Steve drove. She was upset."

"Naturally." Will had a plan to fix that.

A man with a singular focus, he searched the station.

"She's not here," the cop repeated when Will halted at the back door. "You should go on home."

*Impossible.* It was the only coherent word his mind could form. Impossible that she'd walk away without a word. He wanted to collapse. To rail. To demand an explanation. The tumultuous energy propelled him out of the station and down the street. It couldn't be over. It damn well *wasn't* over.

Will's determined stride gave way to a jog, then an all-out run as he aimed toward the Binali Backcountry store. She'd want to get her truck to go home. A slave to the emotions choking him, he ran right past her truck before he skidded to a stop. Her truck was parked on the street in front of the pub. The pub. Where he'd wanted to be anyway.

He swiped the rain from his hair and yanked open the heavy wooden door. His eyes on her, he quickly dealt with the customers who'd already heard the news of Lancaster's takedown. Shaking free of the gauntlet of congratulations, he walked straight up to where she sat perched on a stool at the end of the bar.

"What are you doing here?" he demanded roughly.

"You're wet."

"It's only water."

She turned away, asking the bartender for a towel.

His vision hazed. He couldn't take her back one more second. "Look at me." If he touched her, he'd likely toss her over his shoulder and haul her away to his apartment until they settled a few personal terms.

Barbaric, but it held a certain appeal. As plans went, sometimes improvisation was required. "You left me."

"No. I didn't. Let me explain."

"No." He crowded closer, pinning her lithe body between him and the bar.

"Will." Charly looked up into his face, feeling terrible, and terribly wanted at the same time. "I didn't leave you."

His lips, soft and hot on hers, smothered her explanation. She marveled that his clothes, rain soaked and plastered to his sculpted body, didn't just steam away from the intense heat between them. She pushed at his shoulders, for all the good it did. She might as well have been shoving at a mountain. "Will," she whispered when he eased back at last.

The hurt and confusion in his blue gaze, knowing she'd put it there, made her ache. "I didn't leave you." She got all the words out this time. "I wanted to surprise you. They said you'd gone home. I thought I'd bring a hot meal, cold beer and dessert to your place."

"Why?" His dark eyebrows slashed down into a frown she found more adorable than intimidating. He shook his head, scattering the droplets of rain clinging to his hair. "Doesn't matter. We need to talk."

"Yes." She bounced a little in her seat. She needed to tell him how she felt. Then maybe he could forgive her for what she'd just done on a wild impulse. "Yes, we do." Worried she'd overstepped, she knew she'd find a way to weather that storm if he got upset.

*If?* Upset was pretty much a guarantee. She stopped herself before that boulder could gather momentum.

As she'd been giving her statements, Will might as well have been in the room with her. She'd felt him that strongly. She'd given the facts, won the battle against the tears as she relived Clint's death, and managed not to do a happy dance while recounting burying her knife in Lancaster's leg.

When she thought of everything they'd overcome, she understood on a soul-deep level the motto "life is too short" that people often quoted so carelessly. She'd come down the mountain a changed woman and she'd taken the appropriate action in the aftermath.

Will needed his family—at the bare minimum he needed to give his parents a chance at reconciliation. A chance to get reacquainted with their remaining son. And she'd be there, helping him reconcile or helping him cut the ties.

Whatever life tossed at them next, they'd meet it head-on. As a team. He might not realize it yet, but she would soon make it clear he was no longer a one-man operation.

"I know that look."

"You just think you know that look." She patted the stool next to her. "The order's almost ready. Then we can go to my place and talk."

"I was going to take you to my place tonight."

She reached over and rubbed her hand across his thigh. His cargo pants were drenched, but she could feel the warmth of him under the fabric. "Maybe that is a better idea."

He could change into dry clothes and they could have a reasonable discussion before she stripped him naked and let him have his way with her. She felt her cheeks warm with anticipation.

He covered her hand with his. "So let's go. We're wasting time."

She felt the urgency nipping at her, but she needed to get the words out. "In a minute. We need food." She cleared her throat, cleared out the tension making her voice tight. "There's something I want to say first."

"I'm all ears." His thumb rubbed slow circles against her palm.

"Okay." She took a breath, considered ordering a shot to smooth out her jangling nerves. "I had Steve look up your parents." As she feared, he stopped moving, doing that turn-to-stone thing he'd done on the mountain just before he'd strike. "Hear me out," she said, chafing his hand between hers. "I want to meet your family."

"Charly."

The raw pain in his voice lanced through her heart. She barreled on. "Life's too short, Will. We can't live with regrets and questions that are too easily answered."

"Nothing's easy about my parents." He swiveled on the seat, the water from the knees of his rain-soaked pants seeping through her jeans. She felt him tremble and knew it wasn't just the cold.

"It might not be so bad," she said. "I talked to your mom."

The sound he made was some sad cross between a laugh and a snort.

"Your parents love you, I know it. They love you," she said again, "even if they were too hurt to show it the last time you talked."

"What did you tell them?"

"No revealing details, I swear. I thought about saying they'd won a trip from Binali Backcountry, but I didn't want them to blow that off. I wanted to be sure they came out. I told them you were working here, that we're friends."

He raised his eyes to hers, and that hot gaze lit up her whole system before he looked away.

"I wasn't going to tell them *that*." She cleared her throat. "Anyway. I asked them to come out and see you."

His silence unnerved her. Steve had warned her this was a mistake. He'd helped her find the right Mr. and Mrs. Chase of Illinois, but he'd warned her all the same.

Dread pooled just under her heart, threatening her resolve. She resisted the urge to backpedal. Will might not like her taking the initiative; he might not want to admit it, but he needed this. If only for closure, he needed this.

"They said yes."

"I see."

"Do you?" She dipped her head, but he was staring down at their joined hands. "Do you understand you don't have to meet them alone? I'll be with you. Right beside you." She wished like hell he'd look at her, say something. React. Good, bad or indifferent, any reaction was better than the silence. "If they're awful to you, if they don't want to try and be a family, you can tell me *I told you so* for the rest of my days. Right after I kick them to the curb."

She watched his throat work as he swallowed. Would

he ever find the words to reply? She could take it, whatever he wanted to say, she told herself.

His blue eyes moved like a caress from their joined hands up and over her face. When he met her gaze, the warm tenderness made her tremble. "I love you, Charly."

"What?" She couldn't have heard him right. Of all the responses she'd expected, that wasn't it. Wasn't even in the top ten. "What did you say?" she repeated dumbly.

"You heard me." He pushed on her chin until her mouth closed. "That's why I waited for you in the rain. That's what I needed to tell you. To show you."

A delicious shiver shot down her spine. "Will."

"Right here is where I need to be. Not just for the job. Here." He tapped her knee. "Out there," he said, tilting his head toward the door. "You've changed me and I didn't even know I needed it. You did that. Life is definitely too short to hold back the words. I love you."

She blinked away the sheen of tears blurring her vision and spied the laughter in the clear blue depths of his eyes. "Say it again."

He leaned in until they were nearly nose to nose. "Maybe later," he whispered. "After you say it back."

He meant it. The realization hit her heart with all the force of a bolt of lightning. This wasn't some ill-advised ploy to extend the connection they'd discovered on the mountain. It wasn't a tactic to keep her in his bed. Her imagination took a quick and happy detour thinking about making love with Will in the soft comfort of a real bed.

"Charly?"

She grinned at him, the happiness bubbling through

her system. Of course he meant it. Will didn't say things he didn't mean. After everything they'd encountered, he sat here surrounded by half the town speaking the most powerful words she'd ever heard.

He loved her. *Her.*

"Amazing." The word slipped past her lips, an absolute truth.

He cocked his head. "That might be close enough."

"No. Not even." She hopped off the stool, enjoyed the little wobble in her knees. She stepped in until her hips were surrounded by his strong thighs, until she could lean on the unfailing wall of his muscular chest. "I love you, too," she murmured against his lips.

She melted against him and a round of applause started, peppered with suggestions to get a room. Pulling back, peering at the onlookers, she soaked it all in. This was home, and as complete as she'd felt before Will, she felt a hundred times better now.

The bartender came out with the to-go bags, adding a bottle of champagne. "On the house for a couple of happy heroes."

"Thanks!" She reached for Will's hand, but he scooped her up into his arms. Her heart fluttered in her chest. "Seriously?"

"I'm sweeping you off your feet." He kissed her. "And I'll never break your heart."

"Same goes. You're my best fantasy come true."

"Tell me more." He winked. "I'll make them all come true. One by one."

Her pulse pounded as he swept her out of the pub to another round of cheers. She thought for sure he'd put her down once they were outside, but he carried her straight up the block to his apartment. She let her head drop to his shoulder with a happy sigh. Fantasies didn't come to life any better than her personal hero with a heart as big as the mountain.

# Epilogue

Thomas Casey updated his password for his online bank access, grateful it was still possible. He didn't like thinking about the setbacks they'd be facing now if the Blackout Key hadn't been recovered.

He'd been right about Will, despite their rocky start. The new mailman in Colorado meant Thomas was one step closer to completing the task force. One step closer to retirement.

As he clicked to open the next personnel file on his computer, he hoped he could make it three for three.

\* \* \* \* \*

# Sawyer winced slightly as Megan put some antiseptic on his arm.

"All right, I patched you up as well as my medical expertise will take us. But I take no responsibility for anything if you get gangrene and your arm falls off." Megan began to put away the first aid kit then stopped and just threw it on the counter. "This place is going to have to be burned to the ground anyway."

She turned away and looked back into the bedroom. Sawyer put his shirt back on.

"You can't stay here. Even after the police process it, it's not safe for you to stay here."

"I know." Megan's words were soft, her look lost.

Sawyer reached down and grabbed her hand, entwining their fingers together. "We'll make it through this together. But right now we need to get out of here in case our vicious friend decides to come back with friends of his own."

# COUNTERMEASURES

## BY
## JANIE CROUCH

MILLS & BOON

Published in Great Britain 2015
by Mills & Boon, an imprint of Harlequin (UK) Limited,
Eton House, 18-24 Paradise Road, Richmond, Surrey, TW9 1SR

© 2015 Janie Crouch

ISBN: 978-0-263-25295-8

46-0215

Harlequin (UK) Limited's policy is to use papers that are natural, renewable and recyclable products and made from wood grown in sustainable forests. The logging and manufacturing processes conform to the legal environmental regulations of the country of origin.

Printed and bound in Spain
by CPI, Barcelona

**Janie Crouch** has loved to read romance her whole life. She cut her teeth on Mills & Boon® novels as a pre-teen, then moved on to a passion for romantic suspense as an adult. Janie lives with her husband and four children in Virginia, where she teaches communication courses at a local college. Janie enjoys traveling, long-distance running, movie-watching, knitting and adventure/ obstacle racing. You can find out more about her at janiecrouch.com.

To my dear, sweet Megan. I count it as one of life's greatest blessings that you and I found each other again. You are a treasure. I promise to never leave you in another vat of ice for as long as I live. Here's to our adventures of the past, the present and the future.

# Chapter One

"Dude, I'm just saying, if you didn't want a terrible job assignment then you probably shouldn't have punched out your boss."

Sawyer Branson rolled his eyes and kept walking down the hall of the nondescript building that housed the offices of Omega Sector Headquarters. "C'mon, Evan," Sawyer told his fellow Omega agent. "I didn't punch him out. I tripped."

"Yeah, you *tripped* and your fist *accidentally* fell into Burgamy's jaw." Evan couldn't even say it without chuckling.

Hell, just about everyone at Omega couldn't say it without a chuckle now.

Sawyer stopped by his desk and began looking for a tie in the drawers. Okay, yeah, he had punched his boss two weeks ago, but only because it had been an emergency and his brother Cameron had been about to do much worse, like pull his gun on their boss.

So Sawyer had *tripped* and *accidentally* popped Dennis Burgamy—his supervisor here at Omega—right in the chin. But seriously, was it Sawyer's fault Burgamy had crumpled to the ground like a rag doll at the slightest tap?

Most importantly, though, due to the "accident" with Burgamy's chin, he and Cameron had saved Cameron's fiancée's life, arrested some very bad guys and pretty much saved the world.

Which had gotten Sawyer a two-week suspension without pay, thank you very much.

Sawyer rooted around in the drawer some more. Where was that damn tie? It was Sawyer's first day back and he wasn't about to walk into Burgamy's office without a tie, despite the fact that proper office dress was not high on the priority list at Omega Sector.

As a multiagency task force, Omega Sector had much more perilous concerns than whether or not the people who worked there—all handpicked and highly qualified—were dressed too casually. Sawyer, a five-year Omega veteran at thirty years old, especially did not worry about it. Usually.

Sawyer cursed under his breath as he continued his search for a tie, smashing a finger in one drawer while opening another. He heard a throat clear from behind his back and turned to find Evan swinging a tie from his finger.

"Thanks, man." Sawyer took the tie, figuring one with little golfers on it was better than no tie at all. "I'm just trying to do anything I can to get back toward Burgamy's good graces."

Evan gave a bark of laughter. "And also attempting to keep yourself from desk duty for the foreseeable future. Or the next twenty years if Burgamy has his way."

Sawyer rubbed a hand over his eyes at the thought of desk duty. The normal charm and charisma Sawyer counted on seemed to escape him—he had no idea what he was going to say to Burgamy in their meeting. Lord, Sawyer hoped it wouldn't come down to him being forced to a desk.

He was an agent. That was all Sawyer knew how to do. All he *wanted* to do.

And damn it, he was a *good* agent. Sawyer knew his strengths: he was likable and friendly. And people—witnesses, victims, hell, even perps a lot of times—had a way of opening up to Sawyer. Unlike his brothers, who tended to be the strong, sullen type, Sawyer was the strong, charming type. And people loved him for it.

He'd used his friendliness and charm to his advantage multiple times over the years. Sawyer just hoped he could figure out how to use them now when it mattered the most.

He gave another pull on the tie, straightening it at his collar. "Do I look okay?"

Evan gave the knot a mock straightening. "Yes, dear, you look as pretty as a princess."

Any other time Sawyer would've harassed Evan back, but he was too caught up in the thought of dreaded desk duty to bother. "Wish me luck, man."

Sawyer struggled not to compare the walk to Burgamy's office to a death march, but he had to admit he was distinctly nervous knocking on his boss's door. Not a feeling Sawyer was used to.

And damn his brother for all his falling-in-love stuff that had put Sawyer in this position in the first place. Sawyer would take his confirmed-bachelor existence any day.

Cameron entered the office at Burgamy's barked command.

Burgamy sat back in his office chair, dressed in impeccable officewear. His tie definitely had not come from a desk drawer, nor did it have little golfers on it. Burgamy obviously put a great deal of stock into the saying "Dress for the job you want, not the job you have."

Evidently the job Dennis Burgamy wanted was the director of the United States intelligence and/or fashion community.

Burgamy was always prepared in case he had to take an unexpected meeting with someone important. And often, Sawyer and his three siblings thought, went out of his way to make those meetings occur. Burgamy had butted heads with each of the Branson siblings, all of whom worked or had worked at Omega at one time or another. None of the Bransons liked Burgamy much. Although Sawyer was, to his knowledge, the only one of his family to have ever knocked his boss unconscious.

"Branson, come in and sit down," Burgamy told Sawyer without any pleasantries. Burgamy's nasally tone negated whatever credibility the man built with his impressive fashion sense.

Sawyer entered the room and sat at one of the chairs across from the desk.

"I want you to know that if it was up to me, you'd be fired right now," Burgamy began. Sawyer nodded; he didn't doubt it. "But since I'm the bigger man, and because your brother Cameron swears you actually tripped, I am willing to not push for your termination."

Sawyer didn't relax. Burgamy still had the authority to take Sawyer off active duty.

"Not to mention we have bigger problems than your lack of coordination or outright insubordination, or whatever you want to call it," Burgamy continued.

Sawyer nodded. "It won't happen again, sir. I can assure you of that."

Burgamy's eyes narrowed. "It best not, Branson. That little stunt you and your brother pulled? Well, you're damn lucky it all worked out the way it did or being fired right now—which you both would've been, believe me—would be the *least* of your problems."

Burgamy continued without even giving Sawyer the chance to speak. "The Ghost Shell technology in the wrong hands would be a disaster. Thousands of lives could be lost if terrorists got their hands on it."

Sawyer decided he better stick up for himself before Burgamy spun into a complete tizzy. "Absolutely, sir. But there was never any danger of the Ghost Shell technology falling back into DS-13's hands."

Sawyer didn't mention what an utter lie that was. Telling Burgamy that he and Cameron had basically delivered the encoding technology to the crime-syndicate group definitely wouldn't help Sawyer's case for non-desk-duty.

"Ghost Shell is in our custody, sir." Cameron continued with his most engaging smile. "So, all's well that ends well, as they say. And I really am sorry about the—" Sawyer made a popping sound with his tongue as he mimicked a punch to the chin.

Burgamy's eyes narrowed. "Well, Branson, I found out yesterday that all isn't as well as we think. You and your brother arrested Smith and some of the other key members of DS-13, but it looks like some others within the organization have taken Smith's place."

Sawyer wasn't surprised. In a crime organization the size and caliber of DS-13, removing one head usually just caused another, uglier one, to grow in its place. DS-13 was more than any one person; eliminating a single person— no matter how high up—would not bring the organization down.

"And we've found out that Fred McNeil, the FBI agent on DS-13's payroll, has gone completely off the grid," Burgamy continued.

"That's not surprising. McNeil had to know we'd be coming for him next. He's probably with DS-13 full-time now."

Burgamy nodded. "Intel confirms that he is. That's not the problem. Ghost Shell is the problem. We were able to trace Ghost Shell back to the company that made it." Burgamy slid a file across his desk to Sawyer. On the outside it was marked *Cyberdyne Technologies*.

Sawyer shook his head. "Cyberdyne. Can't say I've really heard of them."

"No reason you would have. They're a tech-development company based in North Carolina. Evidently, earlier this year one of their senior computer scientists got concerned about some software they were developing."

"Ghost Shell?"

"Yes. They were actually working on encoding technology for medical records and account-security type stuff. Then they realized Ghost Shell was something that could be used as a weapon if tweaked."

Sawyer nodded. He wasn't sure exactly how Ghost Shell worked, but he knew the results if it was used by a terrorist group: shutting down communication and computer systems within law enforcement and first-responder groups. Basically it turned the computers against themselves. If Ghost Shell was used in conjunction with a terrorist attack, the results would be devastating. Thousands of lives would be lost.

"One of Cyberdyne's computer scientists got concerned that something weird was going on at Cyberdyne. So, this—" Burgamy referred down to his notes. "Dr. Fuller contacted the FBI. Unfortunately the person put on the case was Fred McNeil."

"And Fred McNeil took the information given by said scientist and sent Ghost Shell straight to DS-13."

"Pretty much. Dr. Fuller had no idea Fred McNeil worked for DS-13. Of course, nobody did. Just bad luck all the way around."

Sawyer grimaced. The only bad luck was that Fred McNeil was still out there. Sawyer would like to take that treasonous bastard down. "But at least Cameron got Ghost Shell out of DS-13's hands before they could sell it to anyone."

Burgamy shook his head. "That's what we all thought. But we found out yesterday through a call to Cyberdyne that *two* versions of Ghost Shell were given to Fred McNeil."

Sawyer sat up straighter in his chair, his attention focused on Burgamy's words. "But we only recovered one."

"Exactly."

Sawyer clenched his jaw. "And McNeil still has it?"

"We've had no intel of him trying to sell it. Evidently even other members of DS-13 didn't know there was a second Ghost Shell. This second version wasn't entirely complete. McNeil needs somebody who can finish it for him."

Sawyer's thoughts spun. A not-working Ghost Shell was definitely better than the fully functional version; it gave them a little bit of time. But Omega Sector needed to begin active measures right away to keep Ghost Shell from becoming sellable by DS-13. An undercover operation would be the best solution, but difficult at this late a time. It had taken Sawyer's brother Cameron nearly a year of undercover work to truly infiltrate DS-13.

Omega didn't have that kind of time now.

"Okay, what's the plan?" Sawyer asked Burgamy. "I can try to set something up, call in a few favors to see if I can get in deep undercover with DS-13 quick. It's risky, but—"

"No, you won't be going undercover, Branson."

"Sir, I really think a quick, deep undercover mission is critical if we want to get Ghost Shell back."

"I agree that we're going to need to send someone in. But that someone will be Evan Karcz."

Sawyer knew his best friend, Evan, was highly qualified and even had an established cover that could probably work well in this situation. But Sawyer did not want to be left out of the action.

"I'll go in with him. He can use his buyer cover and I'll—"

"No."

Sawyer began to argue his case but then saw Burgamy's raised eyebrow and the way his boss sat back in his oversize office chair. The man wasn't interested in anything Sawyer had to say. Whatever was about to come next was Burgamy's retribution for Sawyer punching him two weeks ago.

Damn. Sawyer just hoped it wasn't a desk job at an out-post in Alaska.

"You will be heading to Swanannoa, North Carolina, for protective duty of Dr. Zane Fuller, the head of Research & Development at Cyberdyne Technologies."

Babysitting. Almost as bad as a desk job in Alaska.

Sawyer knew he had to make some sort of case against this assignment. "Sir, respectfully, I feel as if my talents may be better used somewhere else. Somewhere a little more…active." There was no way Sawyer wanted to spend the next couple of months babysitting some geriatric com-puter scientist. Not when there was real work that needed to be done.

"What's happening at Cyberdyne is active, Branson. Dr. Fuller at one time was working on a Ghost Shell counter-measure—a decryption system. That system being fin-ished will be key if DS-13 finishes and attempts to sell the new Ghost Shell."

Sawyer grimaced. "I understand that and agree, but I just think someone else might be better suited for this par-ticular job—"

"Someone who, say, isn't coming off unpaid leave for striking his superior officer?" There was the raised eye-brow again.

Sawyer shook his head and slumped back in his chair. All right, so Burgamy wasn't going to cut him any slack. Looking at his boss, Sawyer realized he wasn't getting out of this.

"All right, Cyberdyne it is." Sawyer spoke through his teeth with forced restraint.

"You'll be bringing Ghost Shell with you. Dr. Fuller needs it in order to complete the countermeasure system. Downright adamant about that. You'll have to explain what Fred McNeil did, and convince Dr. Fuller and the Cyber-dyne team to help us." Burgamy didn't even try to hide the delight on his face. The thought of Sawyer having to deal with a grumpy computer scientist for the next couple of months in the middle of Nowhere, North Carolina, made Burgamy practically gleeful.

Burgamy had chosen Sawyer's punishment well; he knew how much Sawyer would hate this.

Burgamy filled Sawyer in on a few more details—none of which made Sawyer any more excited about the operation ahead. But fine, Sawyer would pay his dues, protect some old head of computer-nerdom for a couple of months, then get back to Omega, where he could do some real good.

And he would damn well make sure he never punched his boss again.

# Chapter Two

Sawyer's arrival at the Cyberdyne Group Headquarters in Swanannoa, NC—more like Swananowhere, NC—the next afternoon did nothing to help reassure him that he would be doing any good in the fight against DS-13 while here. Sure, he could recognize the beauty of the Blue Ridge Mountains all around him. But he'd give it all up to be inside some sleazy warehouse somewhere, with no views but concrete and sewage, about to arrest some bad guys.

This place—no matter how beautiful the surrounding scenery—was a waste of his time.

Not that Cyberdyne and the work being done here was a waste of time, but as far as Sawyer could tell, Dr. Fuller and his cohorts were not in any danger. No attempts had been made on their lives, nothing out of the ordinary had been reported recently. Which was great. But it also meant that somebody with a little less experience in the field could be here completing this assignment rather than Sawyer.

Sawyer sighed and got out of his car. There was no point bemoaning this any longer. He cursed his brother Cameron once again on his way up the steps. This assignment from hell was all Cameron's fault for falling in love and trying to rescue the girl and save the world.

Sawyer rolled his eyes. Evidently Sawyer was a sucker

for a good love story. And this was what he got for it: Swananowhere.

Sawyer looked at the file again as he walked through the door. Cyberdyne Group had been around since 1983, a midsize company, mostly focused on conceptual and computer engineering. They'd done some contractual work for the US government over the years, but not as much as bigger corporations. Most companies similar to Cyberdyne in this area were located a couple of hours away in the Raleigh-Durham Research Triangle. But the original owner of Cyberdyne had loved the Blue Ridge Mountains so much he had built the Cyberdyne offices and labs just outside Asheville rather than Raleigh.

There wasn't a lot of information on Dr. Zane M. Fuller, the head of Research & Development at Cyberdyne—the person who had helped develop Ghost Shell and then turned it over to the FBI. Sawyer glanced at the file. Looked as if Dr. Fuller held *two* doctoral degrees from MIT—barrels of fun.

What the file didn't hold was any useful information about Dr. Fuller to help Sawyer plan out his protection detail. Was he married? Did he work fourteen hours a day? Did he have any bad habits that might get him into trouble?

Sawyer pictured a balding, cranky older guy with thick glasses and probably a bow tie. If that really was the case, Sawyer was going to take a selfie with Dr. Fuller and send it to Burgamy. His boss would probably cry tears of delight.

Sawyer might cry tears also, but they definitely wouldn't be of delight.

Sawyer made his way inside Cyberdyne, taking a few minutes to chat with the attractive and attentive receptionist at the front desk. Far be it for Sawyer to miss an opportunity to talk to a pretty lady, especially in a situation like this.

The receptionist called a security guard—not nearly as friendly or attractive—to escort Sawyer to the R & D wing. Sawyer gave the woman a wink as he walked away. Maybe a couple of months here wouldn't be so bad, after all.

The security guard led Sawyer down a series of hallways to a set of double doors. Sawyer watched as the man swiped a key-card through a scanner to unlock the door—adequate security, but not excellent and certainly not unbreakable—and opened it.

The Research & Development area was a much more open space than the hallway they had come through. It buzzed with activity, at least two dozen people working and talking at different stations and tables around the large room.

Another reception-type desk was near the door. The woman working here was not nearly as put-together as the graceful blonde at the Cyberdyne entrance. Here was a sort of mousy brunette with hair piled up in a messy bun at the top of her head and glasses perched on the edge of her nose. She didn't even acknowledge Sawyer and the guard as they entered the room—she was too busy rooting through a drawer.

Evidently she didn't find what she was looking for because she got up and walked over to a nearby filing cabinet and began searching through there.

Her gray pencil skirt and high-heeled black pumps with little bows made it difficult for Sawyer to stop staring at her legs. Wow. She might be mousy librarian on the top, but those legs… Sawyer noticed the security guard was also taking in the view.

When it became obvious the receptionist wasn't going to notice them, the security guard cleared his throat. "Excuse me, ma'am—"

The woman turned and took a few steps toward them. "Oh my goodness, I'm so sorry, Mark. You know me."

"It's no problem, ma'am." The guard's Southern accent was noticeable. He gestured toward Sawyer. "This is Agent Branson."

The receptionist glanced over at Sawyer, looking away before he could even smile at her. She turned back to the guard. "Thanks, Mark. We were expecting him. I'll take it from here."

The security guard smiled and nodded as he turned to leave—the man obviously had a little crush on the receptionist. Sawyer stepped forward to shake her hand and talk to her further, but she moved back.

"Can you give me a second? I'll be right with you." She didn't quite look him in the eye as she said it; her gaze never seemed to move past his chest.

Sawyer watched as the woman reopened the drawer in the filing cabinet and began rooting through it again. When the search proved fruitless, she moved to another drawer. She seemed to have forgotten Sawyer was even there. Sawyer just enjoyed the view of her legs until it seemed as if she might never come out.

"Did you lose something in there?" When the woman glanced up over her glasses, blinking at him with big round eyes, Sawyer offered her his most engaging smile.

She just continued to blink at him for a few moments, then shoved her head back into the search without saying a word.

Okay. Sawyer crossed his arms while watching her. He wasn't used to being ignored outright by women—especially cute little librarian ones with glasses, even though cute-librarian wasn't generally his type.

Of course, that didn't mean he couldn't still appreciate her. Sawyer could appreciate all women.

Eventually Cute Glasses found whatever it was she was looking for in the cavernous drawer—some sort of stain-remover stick or something. She gave a small sound of triumph and turned around. And seemed authentically surprised to see Sawyer standing there.

More blinks. "Um, yes. Agent Branson, right?"

Sawyer's eyebrows rose. "Forget I was here?" Sawyer shook his head with a half smile. She might be cute, but she was definitely the worst receptionist ever.

"I'm sorry, my mind tends to only focus on one thing at a time." She looked back up at him, again more at his general chest area than in the eyes. Meanwhile still blinking those big brown eyes of hers.

Maybe she was shy. Sawyer didn't mind shy and scatter-brained. Although the sophisticated beauty he met when he first entered the building was generally more his type, Sawyer certainly didn't mind spending a few minutes with shy, either. So he winked at her, when she finally peeked up at his eyes for a second, trying to put her at ease.

But that just seemed to throw her into more of a tizzy—she began reorganizing all the items on the desk—so Sawyer decided to just try to talk to her.

"So, I'm Sawyer Branson, the law-enforcement agent you were expecting. What's your name?"

"Megan." She was still clutching that stain-remover stick in one hand, moving office-supply products on the desk with the other.

"Have you worked here long?"

She looked at him oddly, then nodded. "About eight years."

Eight years? Wow, she must be somebody's relative or something if she was still this bad at her job after eight years. Sawyer smiled at her again—when he could catch her eye for a second—and leaned up against the desk. "That's great. Maybe if I have some questions about how things operate around here I can ask you about them."

Cute librarian Megan just nodded.

Sawyer looked around the open R & D area. People were

still working, although Sawyer noticed he and Megan had drawn some attention.

"I'm sure you know Dr. Fuller, right?" Sawyer asked in a conspiratorial tone. He might as well try to get as much information as he could before meeting the man.

That question certainly got Megan's attention—she finally looked him fully in the eye. "Oh." She said it with wonder as if some puzzle had just become clear to her. "You don't know who Dr. Fuller is." It wasn't a question.

"No, unfortunately, I was sent here without much information about him. Just that he needed protection while finishing a project for the government. As director of R & D, he would be your boss, right?"

Megan nodded. "Um, yes. Dr. Fuller is everyone's boss, I guess."

Sawyer smiled encouragingly; at least she was talking to him now. "Do you like him? Is he easy to get along with?"

Megan looked down and began moving items on the desk around again nervously. She obviously didn't want to answer his questions. That was fine. Sawyer didn't want to put her in a place where she had to speak badly about her boss. He decided to change the subject before Megan rearranged everything on her desk.

"Megan, do you think you could get me a cup of coffee somewhere or point me in the general direction of one? I'd just like to get some caffeine in my system before I meet Dr. Fuller."

Megan opened her mouth as if to answer him, but then just shut it again shaking her head. She seemed at an utter loss at what to say.

Cyberdyne really needed to look into replacing Megan as their R & D receptionist.

A man in a white lab coat, probably in his early forties, walked over to where Sawyer and Megan stood looking at each other. "Megan, is everything okay?" When Megan nodded, the man turned to Sawyer. "You must be Agent Branson. We were told you'd be arriving today. I'm Jonathan Bushman, Dr. Fuller's assistant."

Sawyer shook the man's outstretched hand. He decided not to mention the coffee; it had just been an attempt at changing the subject and he didn't want to get Megan in any sort of trouble.

"Great, Jonathan. I'm ready to meet Dr. Fuller whenever it's convenient."

Jonathan looked to Megan and then back to Sawyer, frowning. "But you already have." He gestured to Megan. "This is Dr. Zane Megan Fuller, lead conceptual and computer scientist for Cyberdyne."

OKAY, HAD THE federal agent just asked her to go get him some coffee? Megan had to admit he hadn't been obnoxious about it, but still…coffee? Of course, she couldn't really blame him. She had been puttering all around the desk, resorting back to her college behavior when she'd had no idea what to do when she was attracted to a member of the opposite gender—she'd practically lost her ability to speak for goodness' sake.

She had thought those days were long behind her, but evidently not when a man as gorgeous as Sawyer Branson talked to her. She could barely bring herself to meet his eyes for most of the conversation. He must have thought she was the worst secretary in the history of the world.

Megan had to remind herself that she was no longer that socially awkward, painfully shy sixteen-year-old girl she had been at MIT, intellectually ahead of all her classmates, but emotionally much less developed. Now Megan was twenty-nine years old, well respected and liked in her workplace and confident in her abilities and accolades.

If still a little shy socially.

Megan could see the wariness crossing Agent Branson's face as he realized his mistake. He probably wasn't too thrilled that he had asked her for a cup of coffee, either.

Megan stuck out her hand for him to shake. "Hi, I'm Dr. Fuller. Megan."

"Not the receptionist. I'm sorry about that." Megan could appreciate that Agent Branson had the good sense to at least look sheepish. His handshake was firm, and if Megan didn't know better she would almost swear she could feel his thumb caressing the back of her hand. That totally had to be her imagination. She pulled her hand back quickly.

"Yeah, there's not actually a receptionist for R & D, despite this desk. We just pretty much keep the desk as a catchall for office supplies and stuff." Megan held up the stain-remover stick. "I got a stain on my lab coat, so I was coming to see if I could use this to get it out."

Agent Branson nodded and gave her a half smile. "Well, a lab coat might have clued me in that you weren't a receptionist, but I definitely didn't know you were who I was here to see. My apologies."

Wow, if that was only a half smile, Megan didn't want to be around if he decided to turn his full charm on her. "I can still direct you to the coffee if you want it."

Agent Branson gave a bark of soft laughter. "Believe it or not, that was to make you feel more comfortable. You seemed to have lost the ability to speak for a while there."

Megan could feel a flush spilling over her. "Yeah, I definitely wouldn't have made a good receptionist. I'm more of a computer-person than a people-person."

Megan heard a throat clear from the other side of the desk. Jonathan. She had almost totally forgotten her assistant was there. Good Lord, she needed to focus. On the situation, not on Agent Branson.

"Jonathan, yes, okay. Um, Agent Branson, it sounds like you didn't know very much about me and we know even less about you. All we were told was that you would be 'a presence' here at Cyberdyne for a while. I don't really know why."

Agent Branson looked around. "Is there somewhere we could go to talk that isn't so open to everything?"

"Yes, of course. As you can see, we have an open work-space in general, but everyone also has offices. Mine is in the back." Megan began walking that way. "Should Jonathan join us?"

Agent Branson shook his head. "Right now, I'd just like it to be the two of us if that's okay. I'll need to talk with all of the R & D employees while I'm here, but I'd like to start with just you."

Megan could tell Jonathan didn't like that. But her assistant tended to be a little high-maintenance in that way. He always wanted to be involved with whatever was going on and tended to get a little churlish when he was left out. The behavior had been getting worse more recently. Megan tried to smile at Jonathan, but he had already turned away with a huff. Megan just shook her head and led Agent Branson back to her office, closing the door behind them.

Megan stood behind a chair at the table and gestured to another seat for Agent Branson. She couldn't help but admire the casual fluidness in how he filled the chair. As if he was a model.

If it wasn't for the scar on his chin and slightly crooked nose—it looked as though it had been broken at some point in his life—Agent Branson definitely could've made a living in front of the camera. Black hair, cut short and stylish, a perpetual five-o'clock shadow, gorgeous green eyes. Megan put a hand up to her chin just to make sure she wasn't accidentally drooling.

It was time to rein in all of this nonsense. Okay, yes, Agent Branson was attractive. Megan didn't know the specifics of exactly why he was here, but she did know that it wasn't for her ogling enjoyment. Megan took a deep breath in through her nose to focus herself, then released it gently through her mouth.

One of the advantages of being so intellectually advanced for her age when she was growing up—and always surrounded by older people —was that Megan had learned early how to act professionally even when she didn't feel that way. She wasn't going to let Agent Handsome discombobulate her any more than he already had today. She hoped they both would just totally forget the incident at the reception desk. That wasn't how she ran the R & D department—all flighty and unable to speak. She was a professional and she could handle this.

She could handle him.

Even though her lab coat had a small coffee stain on it, Megan grabbed it from where it hung on a hook on the back of her door and put it on. She immediately felt more secure with its familiar weight on her shoulders. She sat down and looked across the table.

"So, Agent Branson, how can we help you here at Cyberdyne?"

Evidently she had succeeded in adding the desired professionalism to her tone as she watched Agent Branson sit up a little straighter in his chair, his eyes narrowing slightly for just a moment. Obviously he was also expecting the nervous woman he had met earlier at the desk.

Well, she wasn't around anymore.

# Chapter Three

Sawyer watched pretty Megan transform into stuffy, prickly Dr. Zane Megan Fuller—just like her name tag said—as she pulled on that drab lab coat and buttoned it. The skirt underneath, and evidently the shy woman from the desk, disappeared. Sawyer could almost feel the temperature drop around him.

Okay, the asking her for coffee had been a bit of a misstep. Sawyer totally read that situation wrong—not something he was used to doing. He tried to think back to his conversation with Burgamy. Sawyer definitely would've remembered if his boss had said Dr. Fuller was an attractive young woman. Or if he had said *woman* at all.

What had Sawyer been expecting in Dr. Fuller again? Someone balding, with thick glasses and a bow tie? Sawyer could admit he'd let a stereotype get the better of him. It was his own fault and he knew better. But when he'd seen pretty little Megan fumbling around at the desk, blinking up at him with those big brown eyes and blushing for goodness' sake?

It had never even crossed Sawyer's mind that she would be the head computer scientist of a multimillion-dollar company. But the woman sitting across from him so coldly, lab coat around her like a suit of armor? He had no problem picturing her as Dr. Fuller, brilliant scientist.

"Yes, Dr. Fuller. I'm sorry for the confusion before." Reflexively Sawyer tried to smile at her, but he was met only with cold professionalism. "I've been sent here from the Bureau to discuss Ghost Shell."

Sawyer knew Megan would associate the word *bureau* with the FBI, but now wasn't the time to explain about Omega Sector. Omega was a task force made up of representatives from all different sorts of government agencies—FBI, CIA, Homeland Security, hell, even Interpol—who answered to bosses inside Omega. The task force was generally kept on a need-to-know basis. All Megan needed to know right now was that Sawyer was from federal law enforcement.

Megan nodded curtly. "I gave Ghost Shell to the FBI three months ago. Then I receive a follow-up call a few days ago with all sorts of questions you guys should already know the answer to."

Sawyer didn't respond to that directly. "I understand you've been working on a countermeasure to Ghost Shell."

That obviously wasn't the statement she was expecting. "Well, we were. But once I turned Ghost Shell over to the FBI, we put that on the back burner. Didn't seem important to work on the antidote for a poison we'd already gotten rid of."

"Unfortunately, it looks like the poison is back."

"What?" Her big brown eyes blinked at him again, but this time with confusion rather than shyness.

"Ghost Shell fell into the wrong hands not long ago."

*"What?"* Megan parroted herself. "I gave Ghost Shell to the FBI to keep that exact thing from happening."

Sawyer grimaced. "I understand your frustration."

Sawyer watched Megan's small fists ball on the table. He slid back a little in his chair, since it looked as if she might start swinging any moment. Not that he could blame her.

"My research team here at Cyberdyne put in hundreds

of man-hours on Ghost Shell! The work we did was brilliant and could've potentially made Cyberdyne millions of dollars. But I chose—my *team* chose—to stop our progress when we realized how easily Ghost Shell could become a weapon." One of her small fists came down forcefully on the table. "And now you're telling me some terrorist group has it anyway?"

"Well, yes and no."

One eyebrow rose. "I think perhaps you should just cut to the chase, Agent Branson."

Totally gone was the shy, stammering woman he had seen at the front desk. This woman in front of him—he definitely could not think of her as mousy in any way—was a force to be reckoned with.

"The agent in charge of the technology you gave the FBI—"

"Fred McNeil."

Sawyer shouldn't be surprised that Megan remembered the name of an agent she'd spoken to months before, given her reputation. "Yes, Fred McNeil. Ends up he was also working for a crime-syndicate group known as DS-13."

Megan closed her eyes and shook her head, her breath coming out in a hiss. "And is this DS-13 group terrorists?"

"No. But they would not hesitate to sell Ghost Shell to whatever terrorist faction was willing to pay the highest price."

"And now DS-13 has Ghost Shell."

"Again, yes and no." Sawyer held his hand out to stop the sound of exasperation he knew was coming. "In a mission two weeks ago, one version—the working version—of Ghost Shell was recovered. But until we contacted you just a couple of days ago, we had no idea a second version of Ghost Shell even existed."

"But you don't have the other version?"

"No, Fred McNeil is still at large with it."

Megan got up and began pacing around her office. "The other version, although not as dangerous as the first, is still definitely not benign. It's just as potentially dangerous."

"But it would take someone with a special set of skills to complete it, right?"

Megan shrugged a delicate shoulder. "My ego would like to think so. But really, anybody skilled in reverse engineering—taking something apart and figuring out what makes it work—and software development could probably do it. There's a dozen people at Cyberdyne alone."

"So the FBI should be acting on the assumption that Fred McNeil and DS-13 could have a working prototype at any time."

Megan took off her glasses and rubbed her eyes, leaning back against her desk. "Absolutely. With the right help, it won't take long."

"We're going to do everything we can to stop that from happening."

"No offense, Agent Branson, but my trusting the FBI is how this whole problem happened in the first place."

Sawyer grimaced. There really wasn't much argument around that one. "On behalf of the entire Bureau, I want to apologize for what happened. Nobody had any idea that Fred McNeil had flipped."

"Well, thanks for the apology, but that doesn't necessarily make me feel much better." The ice doctor was back in full force. "Did you work with Agent McNeil?"

"No. I'm in an entirely different...section of the Bureau. Never met the man."

"How do I know I can trust you?"

"Well, for one thing, I'm bringing Ghost Shell *back* to you, not the other way around. But also, there's a whole department involved this time. Not just one person. A lot more accountability that way."

Megan stared at him for a long moment. "I guess so. Fred

McNeil always seemed to want to keep things so quiet and just between us. Now I know why." Megan shuddered. "He was so smarmy. I should've known better."

"We're working around-the-clock to find McNeil and Ghost Shell before it can be developed more fully."

"What exactly do you want from us here at Cyberdyne?"

"We need you to finish the countermeasure decryption system you were working on before."

Megan shook her head and sat back down at the table. "I explained to whoever I talked to a couple of days ago that I can't do it without Ghost Shell. That's why I stopped working on it months ago."

"I have the first version of Ghost Shell with me. I know you will need this version to create the countermeasure so we can stop McNeil once he gets his version of Ghost Shell up and running."

*"You have Ghost Shell here, unguarded?"* Megan stood back up. "Then we need to get that drive into the vault right away. It's too valuable, too dangerous for you to just be casually carrying it around."

Sawyer tried not to be offended. "I think I'm capable of guarding a software system for a few hours, Dr. Fuller."

It looked as if Megan would argue the point further, but then decided to let it go. "Fine. But you'll have to excuse me for not having too much faith in FBI agents at the current moment. And, honestly, why shouldn't I just wash my hands of this entire thing? My team and I did our job right. It's you guys who messed things up."

Sawyer took a breath. He needed to convince Megan to help them. Because if she decided she'd already done her part, and that law enforcement were on their own, Omega's job was about to become a lot harder.

Sawyer looked at Megan, who was standing beside her desk, lips pressed into a white slash, posture rigid. He couldn't blame her for how she was feeling.

But they needed her help, and right now it didn't look as though she was very interested in giving it.

Sawyer knew his colleagues considered him to be the charming Branson brother; they teased him about it all the time back at Omega. People—and okay, he could admit it, women especially—responded to him. It was a gift, and Sawyer had used it to his advantage multiple times in different operations. It made undercover work a natural fit— who didn't want to like the guy with the easy smile and quick joke? But his easy smile didn't seem to be getting him anywhere in this conversation, not since the ice doctor had appeared.

It was amazing how different this controlled woman was from the pretty librarian-type he'd talked to at the desk. The woman at the desk Sawyer would've known how to reach, even with her shyness. Yet this woman didn't seem to see him as a man—hell, even as a person—at all. But he had to try to get her cooperation.

"You're right, the FBI has messed things up." Sawyer smiled and held a hand out to her in a gesture for her to sit back down. Standing up and towering over her wasn't the way to make her feel more comfortable. "And Fred McNeil fooled a lot of people, not just you."

Sawyer noticed Megan's posture slump slightly. Evidently McNeil's ability to fool her weighed more heavily on Megan than she wanted to admit.

Sawyer continued, "I don't have to tell you how important it is that Ghost Shell not fall into the hands of terrorists. *You're* the one who came to us with the problem because you could see the catastrophic damage Ghost Shell was capable of. Without you, law enforcement would have no idea of the potential threat they were up against."

He reached out and touched her hand that rested on the table. "Thank you for coming forward. I'm pretty sure nobody has said that to you, but somebody should have."

For a moment, looking into her big brown eyes, Sawyer saw Megan, not the cold Dr. Fuller. Sawyer realized maybe it had been *him* not seeing her as a person, not vice versa. Dr. Fuller and Megan were one and the same; he needed to remember that. Sawyer squeezed her hand in a friendly manner, then let her go.

"You're good at what you do," Megan said after a moment.

"And what's that?"

"Manipulating people."

Sawyer shook his head. "I know it seems that way, but I'm not trying to manipulate you, I promise. Everything I've said so far has been the absolute truth."

She looked at him with one eyebrow raised, but seemed to have lost a little of her coldness, so Sawyer continued, "But don't get me wrong, I'm definitely asking you for something. We need your help. We've got to have a way to stop Ghost Shell when DS-13 goes to sell their version on the black market. You are our best hope for that."

Megan sighed, resignation clear in her eyes. "All right, Agent Branson. Whether you're trying to deliberately manipulate me or not, I guess you're going to get what you want. I'll get the Ghost Shell countermeasure finished as soon as possible." Megan stood up again and wiped an imaginary piece of lint off her lab coat. "But I'm not doing it for you. I'm doing it because it's the right thing to do. I just hope you guys don't screw it up again."

"I'll make you a deal. You get the Ghost Shell countermeasure completed and I will personally make sure nobody on my end of things screws it up." Agent Branson had such utter confidence in his voice that Megan couldn't help but believe him.

Megan couldn't sit there and say she wasn't affected by Agent Branson. But it wasn't as if he was trying to talk her into going out with him; he was trying to get Megan to do something she was already willing to do.

Not that she wasn't willing to go out with him.

But not that he was asking.

Megan had to get herself under control. Him asking or not asking her out was not the issue here. Ghost Shell and saving the world was. *Focus. Be professional.*

"So should I announce the change in projects to everyone?"

Agent Branson shook his head. "No, we want to keep this to as few people as possible."

Megan nodded. That was probably best. Although she trusted everyone who worked in the R & D department, the fewer people who knew about all this, the better. "Okay, just my inner team then. That's seven people including me and Jonathan Bushman, my assistant, whom you met."

"That sounds good."

"Great. So I guess I'll call you in a couple of weeks when we have the countermeasure completed." Megan stuck out her hand to shake his. The sooner she got him out of her office, the sooner she could focus on other things. *Any* other thing besides his presence here.

"Actually, I'll be staying here for a while if that's okay."

"For the meeting with the team? That's probably a good idea." Her inner team rarely needed to be more focused than they already were, but Agent Branson could provide added motivation to get the Ghost Shell countermeasure completed faster.

"No. I'll be staying until you're finished."

"The whole time? You know, this isn't going to be done in a day. It's going to take a while. Plus, we are a secure facility, especially within the R & D vault. You can leave Ghost Shell here and come back in a couple of weeks. I promise it will be safe."

"Even so, I'll be staying."

This was not good. Having him here was going to wreak havoc on her concentration. "It'll be pretty boring. You understand that, right?"

Megan watched Sawyer's brows furrow as he nodded curtly, with no enthusiasm whatsoever. Evidently, he didn't really want to be here. Megan wasn't surprised; watching a group of scientists do conceptual engineering for days or weeks did not strike Megan as something a man like Sawyer would want to do on his own accord.

"Drew the short straw, huh?" she asked him.

Megan could tell she had surprised him. He laughed, then looked down at her with his megawatt smile. "Something like that," he finally said. "Maybe I'll tell you about it sometime while I'm here. You'll like that story."

Megan seemed to have forgotten how to breathe at his smile. She finally forced herself to look away and grabbed all the folders on her desk—most of them ones she didn't even need—and called her inner team to the conference room for a meeting.

This group of people had developed Ghost Shell at one stage or another and was well aware of its potentials and dangers. Without going into the details about what had happened with Fred McNeil and DS-13, Megan explained that developing the countermeasure to Ghost Shell had become a priority for them at Cyberdyne.

Sawyer's presence in the room couldn't be ignored, so Megan introduced him.

"This is Agent Sawyer Branson. He'll be here for the duration of the project. The fact that law enforcement feels his presence here is necessary should be a reminder of how crucial this project is."

Two of the women on the team—both in their midforties and both married with children—were all but ogling Sawyer. Megan resisted the urge to rap something against the conference table to get their attention.

Branson seemed to be taking it all in stride, smiling easily at the women. Of course, he smiled easily at the men, too. He just seemed to have a way that put everyone at ease.

Everyone except Megan.

Megan dismissed the meeting a little more curtly than she had planned, after they all agreed work would begin first thing in the morning. She left the conference room without waiting to see if Agent Branson was coming with her or not. If he wanted to flirt with everyone in the department, that was his business. As long as it didn't interfere with their work, Megan had absolutely no problem with it.

Good to see that the FBI had once again sent their very best.

Megan knew she was being unreasonable. What the heck was wrong with her? She sat down and rested for a minute. It had been a long day, made more stressful by the bad news Sawyer had delivered. She had been such an idiot to trust Fred McNeil. Even though Sawyer told her McNeil had fooled everyone, Megan knew she should've trusted her instincts with McNeil.

But Megan had never been good at trusting her instincts unless it came to science. Trusting her instincts with men had always brought her a heartache or headache.

Megan rubbed at a knot that was beginning to form in her neck. She took a deep breath and began reorganizing all the mostly unneeded files she had taken to the meeting back into their rightful places on her desk. Then she cleared off and straightened any other items that cluttered it or were out of place. She knew that a clean desk always made her feel better and would help her when she got to work tomorrow with a new, stressful agent on her hands.

*Project.* New, stressful *project* on her hands, damn it.

And speak of the devil... Agent Branson was making his way over to her office. He rapped on the outside of her office door, but entered without waiting for an invite.

"Get to meet everyone on the team?" It was the most neutral question Megan could think of.

"Yep. Seems like a pretty solid crew you have there." He looked around her office. "And looks like you've got that desk of yours about as pristine as they come."

Megan shrugged and smiled ruefully. "Having everything neat and organized helps me work. It'll help me focus when I get back to work in the morning. But right now I'm going to head home and have a nice glass of wine. How about you?"

Megan watched as Sawyer's head tilted to the side and he raised one eyebrow. "Sure. I mean, I don't know you very well, but I'd like to have a glass of wine at your house."

Megan could've bitten off her own tongue. He thought she was asking him out? No. He absolutely could not come over to her house for a glass of wine. She could barely form coherent sentences around him here. She definitely didn't want him in her home.

"No. I mean—I wasn't asking you over. I don't want you to come over to my house. I just meant—" Megan stopped herself—she was just making it worse.

"Oh, well, then, we could go out to a bar or restaurant or something." Sawyer's eyes were lit with amusement as he said it. "Just let me grab my stuff."

"No! I don't want to go out with you. I just want to go home by myself." It sounded rude even to her own ears.

Sawyer chuckled. "I know what you meant, Megan. I was just giving you a hard time."

Megan didn't know what to say. She just grabbed her purse from the back of the office door and left without another word. She was probably coming across as childish, but didn't care. His charming laughter followed her down the hall.

How was she ever going to make it through the next few weeks with Sawyer Branson around her all the time?

# Chapter Four

Arriving back at Megan's office at Cyberdyne first thing the next morning, Sawyer was determined not to tease her about the incident the night before. But he had to admit it was tempting. So tempting.

And icy Dr. Fuller was back in full force this morning. Sawyer could tell as soon as he walked in the door.

"Agent Branson," Megan said with a brief nod. "Good morning."

So they were back to Agent Branson. "And to you, Dr. Fuller," Sawyer responded in the same formal tone. Megan's eyes narrowed at that, as if she couldn't decide if he was mocking her or not. That was okay; Sawyer couldn't decide if he was mocking her, either.

"Is it all right if I put my things in here or would you prefer me somewhere else?" Sawyer asked her. He didn't have much—but he needed somewhere to set up his laptop and files. He didn't want to be totally useless while he was here; there were at least some things he could accomplish on the computer while babysitting.

Sawyer just hoped Megan's team would be able to construct the countermeasure quickly so he could get back to Omega as soon as possible.

"Here is fine. I'll just clear off the table for you." She

moved a few files from the table, then nodded curtly again. "There you go, Agent Branson."

"Megan, I thought that since you asked me out last night you could at least call me Sawyer." So much for his resolution not to tease her.

He could almost physically see the heat suffusing her face. "About that, um—" Megan wasn't looking in Sawyer's eyes, but he could tell she was at least forcing herself to hold still and not fidget. "I apologize. My words didn't come out correctly last night and then I didn't handle the situation well."

Now Sawyer felt bad. He had thought it was kind of cute the way she had gotten so discombobulated, but she obviously was berating herself for the behavior. "Megan, I was just kidding. Don't worry about it—"

"I behaved childishly."

"You didn't behave childishly. I deliberately misconstrued what you said and I shouldn't have. I knew the entire time you weren't asking me out. I should be the one apologizing, not you."

Megan finally looked up at him. "Fine. I accept your almost-apology, Agent Branson."

"Thank you, Dr. Fuller. But I do wish you'd call me Sawyer."

Sawyer wasn't sure if Megan was about to agree or argue the point when one of the lab technicians came flying into her office.

"Dr. Fuller, we have a huge problem in the vault. We need you to come right away."

A flash of relief crossed Megan's face before it was drowned out by concern. She turned and hurried out of her office without another word. Sawyer followed right behind her.

Obviously the lab tech's definition of *huge problem* and

Sawyer's differed greatly, Sawyer realized. There was no smoke here in the vault, no bullets, no blood.

The Cyberdyne R & D vault wasn't a vault like that of a bank. Instead it was just a secure area, with a further locked door and a higher security clearance needed to enter. No stranger could just wander around any part of Cyberdyne from off the street; everyone was escorted by someone. Beyond that, only certain people were cleared to enter the R & D department. From what Sawyer could tell, it looked as if everyone had their own key-card that tracked who came and left out of the general R & D department.

"The vault holds our more highly classified or secretive items," Megan explained as they entered the secure room. "But really, it's more of a safe place to store items than anything else."

"Who has access?"

"Me and select members of the R & D team. And security guards, I guess."

That was good. Limited access definitely made any area more secure. Sawyer made a mental note to get to know the head of Cyberdyne security.

"We don't really use the vault to keep out thieves or anything like that," Megan continued. "It's more to keep important items safe from a much more treacherous enemy—human error. When you've got multiple people walking around day in and day out you're bound to have spills, misplacements or other accidents. The vault is primarily to save important items from those sorts of problems."

Jonathan Bushman, Megan's assistant, was sitting with rigid posture in front of a computer station in the vault.

"What's going on, Jon?" Megan walked over to stand right beside him.

"It's the hard drive that housed the Ghost Shell countermeasure. It's critically damaged."

Megan pulled her glasses from the top of her head to get a better look at the drive. "What? It was fine the last time I accessed it."

Sawyer walked over closer to the two of them. "When was that?"

"I don't know, maybe eight weeks ago? We can check the logs to find out exactly." She said all this without looking at Sawyer. "Can you recover anything, Jon?"

"Nothing useful." Jon spoke with a heavy sigh.

Megan picked up the drive and held it in her hands like a wounded bird. Sawyer noticed some scratches on the outside of it.

"See those scratches? Do you think it was external damage that caused the problem? Or is it more internal issues?" Sawyer asked.

Jonathan just rolled his eyes and went back to scanning the screen looking for any recoverable data. Megan turned to Sawyer. "Something happening to it externally could certainly cause damage, if someone, say, stepped on the drive or put something heavy on top of it."

Sawyer nodded. "Could something internally have been done to it deliberately to make the data unrecoverable?"

Both Jonathan and Megan turned to look at Sawyer sharply. "Like some sort of sabotage?" Jonathan asked.

Sawyer shrugged. "It happens."

Jonathan was obviously about to take offense. Megan leaned back against the computer station so she was face-to-face with Sawyer. She put her hand on Jonathan's shoulder.

"I'm pretty sure we don't have anyone working here who would do anything like that. Especially not anyone who has access to the vault."

Jonathan nodded vigorously.

"But there's no way of telling when the damage was done?" Sawyer asked.

Megan shook her head. "No. It could've sat here damaged for weeks."

"Or it could've been damaged last night or this morning after you announced the team would begin working on the countermeasure."

Megan sighed. "Yes, Agent Branson. It is possible it happened within the last twenty-four hours. But I doubt it."

Sawyer decided not to push it since they had no way of knowing when the damage had occurred. "Do things get damaged in here often?"

"Not often, but it has happened. It happens more often out there." Megan gestured vaguely with a hand toward the general R & D area. Then she turned and refocused on the screen in front of Jonathan. Within moments they were in a deep discussion about what, if anything, could be salvaged. Neither looked very optimistic.

Sawyer stepped back and looked around the vault. There were cabinets and shelves of varying size. Everything seemed highly organized and labeled—via Megan's decree he was sure. Nothing lay around haphazardly or seemed to be damaged as far as Sawyer could tell. Like Megan had told him, the vault was equipped to protect its items from human accidents and mistakes. It seemed to do that very well.

Except for in this one case. Sawyer couldn't help but be suspicious of that.

His phone buzzed in his pocket. Evan Karcz. Good, maybe now Sawyer could get an update on what was happening back at Omega.

Sawyer walked out of the vault without saying anything to Megan and Jonathan. They were obviously deeply focused on the countermeasure salvage. Sawyer doubted they would miss him at all.

"Evan. How's it going in the real world?"

Evan chuckled a little at Sawyer's greeting. "I take it that means you're still less than thrilled with your Cyberdyne assignment?"

"Well, let's just say it hasn't been what I expected."

"Oh yeah? More interesting or less?"

Sawyer glanced over his shoulder at Megan before walking farther down the hall toward her office. "More interesting. Definitely more."

That got Evan's attention. "Is something happening there, Sawyer? Good news, I hope."

"Dr. Fuller thought it was going to take up to a few weeks to finish the Ghost Shell countermeasure, but we encountered a setback first thing this morning." Sawyer told Evan about the problem in the vault.

"Well, that's definitely not good. I hope they can recover something from the drive, because things are going to hell in a handbasket around here concerning DS-13 and Fred McNeil."

"Movement?" Sawyer proceeded all the way into Megan's office and closed the door.

"Word is, DS-13 is going to have some sort of infiltrative software system coming available in the next couple of weeks."

"That sounds exactly like Ghost Shell."

"I thought so, too."

"Dr. Fuller said there were a number of computer people who would be able to finish the work on their version of Ghost Shell. That it was only a matter of time."

"He was right, it looks like."

Sawyer decided to let the erroneous pronoun choice go for the time being. "So what's the plan?"

"I'm still going under. But as Bob Sinclair."

That stopped Sawyer in his tracks. "What?"

"I know, Sawyer, believe me, I know. But one of my

contacts who has direct ties with DS-13 reached out to me as Bob Sinclair about all this Ghost Shell mess."

"I thought you retired Bob Sinclair a year ago. After..." Sawyer couldn't even bring himself to say it.

Bob Sinclair was an undercover persona Evan had carefully developed as a high-end weapons buyer for terrorist groups. Juliet, Sawyer's sister, had gone undercover with him as Lisa Sinclair, Bob's wife. Until it had ended in tragedy.

"Sawyer, I know what you're thinking. And believe me, Juliet won't be involved this time."

"She better the hell not be, Evan. She's not ready."

"Nobody wants to protect Juliet more than me."

"Fine, just leave her out of it. And make sure Burgamy isn't putting any pressure on her to go back under, either." Sawyer didn't like being away from Omega where he could make sure for himself that his sister wasn't being pressured to go back undercover. But he trusted Evan.

"I just wanted you to know what was going on. Word is to expect a big sale coming up in the next couple of weeks. If that's Ghost Shell, we need to be ready with the countermeasure."

"Roger that. Dr. Fuller was pretty pissed off about what happened with Fred McNeil. Took a bit of convincing to get the team to trust that I wasn't going to do something similar and get working on the countermeasure."

Evan chuckled. "Dr. Fuller giving you hell? Even after only one day?"

"Yeah, she's something."

"She? I thought it was Dr. *Zane* Fuller?"

"Yeah, Dr. Zane *Megan* Fuller. Not sure if Burgamy left out the Megan part on accident or on purpose." Sawyer rolled his eyes.

"Well, I certainly imagined that wrong. I guess two degrees from MIT made me think middle-aged guy."

"You're not the only one. But try female in her late twenties."

Sawyer had to pull his phone back from his ear, Evan was laughing so hard. "Of course she is."

"Shut up, Evan."

"Look, I'll let you go play with your scientist, but tell her to hurry up with the countermeasure." Somberness crept back into Evan's tone. "It's going to be easy for this situation to get shot straight to hell very quickly."

"I know, man, you be careful. Your Bob Sinclair cover has some holes, especially without Juliet."

"Don't worry, I'll get it worked out. Looks like I might be coming down toward your current location. My contact is not far out of Asheville."

DS-13 with movement just outside Asheville? Another interesting coincidence Sawyer wasn't going to take at face value.

Sawyer saw Megan walking toward the office from the vault. "All right, man. Keep me posted if anything further develops. As soon as Cyberdyne has the countermeasure completed, you'll be my first call."

Megan tapped lightly on the door before walking in just as Sawyer was ending the call.

"How'd it go?" Sawyer asked her.

Megan threw the file she was carrying down on her desk. "I hope that whoever you were talking to had some good news for you. Because after a complete scan of the damaged hard drive, we discovered that almost nothing is recoverable. We're basically starting from scratch."

# Chapter Five

Four days later, Megan was considering killing herself and everyone around her. Absolutely nothing was going right with the Ghost Shell countermeasure. Everything she and the team did seemed to be one-step-forward and two-steps-back. First having to start from scratch after the drive was damaged, then errors both human and mechanical plagued them.

She was one mistake away from becoming a homicidal maniac.

Megan was used to working under pressure. Pressure was a challenge she generally enjoyed—it forced her brain to exert in ways not normally required of it. Thinking faster often produced new and exciting solutions that working a problem slowly often missed.

But right now thinking faster was just producing a bunch of junk.

Admittedly, the pressure Megan usually fell under wasn't the save-the-world variety. It tended to be more of the save money or time variety. Knowing that if they didn't get the countermeasure completed before Ghost Shell was sold on the black market by this DS-13 group then thousands of lives could be lost tended to put Megan a little on edge.

But really it was Sawyer Branson's constant presence

here that was damaging Megan's calm. Not that he was critical or did anything to deliberately make her uncomfortable, he was just always *there*. Observing, reporting, ready to help if there was anything he could do.

It was driving her absolutely nuts.

After yet another error in the computer coding had forced Megan's team to backtrack again this morning, Megan had decided to leave them to that part and take an early working lunch.

And yeah, Megan could admit she was hiding out a little from Sawyer here in the small break room of the R & D department.

She had brought with her the new drive she and the team had partially rebuilt over the past couple of days. Her lunch tote was stuffed with printouts concerning the source code and combinatorial algorithms needed for the project, as well as a ham-and-cheese sandwich. Megan hoped she could get some work done in here. Almost everybody used the larger companywide cafeteria to eat rather than this small break room. Blessed quiet reigned here.

Halfway through her sandwich and the printouts Megan heard the door open. She didn't look up from her work, hoping whoever entered either wasn't looking for her or would see she was busy and not disturb her. A few moments of silence reassured her.

"You're cute when you concentrate really hard like that."

Sawyer. Almost instantly the words Megan had been concentrating on became gibberish on the printout in front of her. She just couldn't think when he was around.

"I'm working." Megan knew she was being borderline rude, again, but couldn't help it. Acting cold around him was the only way not to become a babbling idiot like she had been on the first day.

"I see that. Mind if I hang out in here for a while? I'll be quiet, I promise."

Yes, Megan minded. His very presence in the room bothered her. Everything about him bothered her. "Fine."

True to his word Sawyer didn't say anything else, not even to point out how rude Megan was being, but it didn't seem to matter. Try as she might, Megan couldn't get any work done with Sawyer around. When she found herself reading the same page for the third time, she decided she'd had enough. She was going home.

Megan stood up and began cramming stuff into bags. She realized she had put the remaining part of her sandwich in her briefcase and the Ghost Shell drive in her lunch bag, but she didn't care.

Sawyer watched calmly from his table near the door. "Finished with lunch?"

"I can't work in here anymore. There's too much noise."

Sawyer looked around as if to discover what noise she referred to. Megan couldn't blame him. Except for the sound of Megan frantically stuffing papers into whatever bag happened to be closest, it was completely silent in the break room.

"I'm going home to work for the rest of the afternoon." Megan couldn't afford to lose another whole day, no matter what the reason. Especially because of her own ridiculousness. There was too much at stake.

Megan took her bags and marched out of the break room, without looking at or speaking to Sawyer, and headed toward her office. Jonathan and the rest of the team were sitting around one of the conference tables in the middle of the main R & D room looking much more relieved than when she had left them this morning. Jonathan stood when he saw Megan, a report in hand.

"Megan, it looks like we figured out the coding problem. Well, it was mostly Trish." Jonathan gestured to the woman next to him. "Now we just have to finish it."

"Great, you guys. I'm going to be working off-site this

afternoon, so I need you all to get this done so we can start fresh tomorrow. Hopefully, I'll have some of our other Ghost Shell problems worked out by then."

Megan encouraged everyone a bit more, then headed back to her office. Jonathan followed her, along with Trish, one of the newer Cyberdyne team members, who always seemed to be trying to get more face time with Megan.

"Where are you going to be this afternoon?" Jonathan asked Megan.

"Just off-site somewhere, probably at home. I need to get away from Cyberdyne for a little while so I can think clearly. Everything here is holding me back."

Megan noticed Jonathan's pinched features. Great, now she had hurt her assistant's pride. "Jon, you know how I am. Sometimes I just need to be away from everything to break through a problem." Megan turned to include Trish in the conversation. "If you two can get the coding finished, then tomorrow we can meet back here and really make some progress."

Jonathan finally nodded. "Okay, I guess you're right. Is Agent Branson going with you?"

Megan looked up and saw Sawyer walking toward them from the break room. "No, Agent Branson will definitely be staying here. Otherwise it will defeat the entire purpose."

Trish nodded as if she totally understood what Megan was saying. Megan just grimaced. Another woman under Sawyer's spell did not make Megan feel any better.

Jonathan gestured down to Megan's briefcase. "Do you have everything you need? Do you want anything we were working on this morning? I can get it for you."

"No, I think I'm okay. I've got the printouts and hard drive. That should be all I need. We're close, you guys, I can feel it."

Trish nodded. "I know. It feels good, doesn't it? To actually make forward progress? It seemed like the fates have conspired against us the last few days."

"Well, let's hope that's all behind us now."

Sawyer stopped outside her office and tapped on the door. "Can I speak to you for a minute, Megan?"

"Yes." Megan turned to Jonathan. "I'll see you tomorrow, Trish, Jon. Okay? Thanks for your help."

Both computer scientists nodded and left, already discussing the coding problem. Megan was thankful to have team members who were so dedicated to what they did.

"You're really going to work somewhere else today?"

Megan began unbuttoning her lab coat. "Yes. Believe it or not, it happens. Sometimes I need to be in a different element in order to break through a problem. It's just how my brain works." She turned her back to him to slip off the coat.

"I'll come with you."

"No!" Megan took a deep breath and then spun back slowly to face Sawyer. "I mean, that's not necessary. Thanks." Megan could tell Sawyer was about to argue, so she continued, "Sawyer, thank you for the offer, but I really just need to be alone. Otherwise I won't be able to get the work done."

"I'm not sure it's a good idea for you to be off on your own."

"I'm just going to my house, Sawyer. It's a chance for me to get in multiple uninterrupted hours of work. If I'm here, there's always someone who needs me for something or other distractions." Megan couldn't look at Sawyer's face as she finished the sentence, so she turned to her desk and began grabbing her bags.

"Fine." Megan was a little surprised to hear Sawyer say it. She thought she was going to have to present further arguments for why he couldn't come with her. And to be honest she wasn't sure what those arguments would be.

*Sorry, Sawyer, you can't come with me because when-*

*ever you're around I can't seem to focus on anything but how...*yummy *you look.*

Sawyer had been nothing but polite and friendly to Megan over the past few days—just like he had been to everyone. This craziness was all in Megan's head, not in his actions.

"Give me your phone," Sawyer told her. "So I can put my number in it."

Megan gave it to him and he continued, "If you have any issues, call me. Or if you decide to go anywhere but your house, let me know."

"Okay."

"I'm going to stay here because there are a couple of concerns I want to look into."

"About Ghost Shell?"

"Yes. But I'm not certain about anything yet, so don't worry about it now. We'll talk tomorrow when you get back. Right now the most important thing is that you get some real progress made with the countermeasure."

Megan agreed. "I know. I work best alone."

"That's the main reason I'm letting you go alone. I know you don't really like me around when you're working, Megan. I annoy you. That's fine." Sawyer smiled and winked. "My manly ego can take it, I think."

He thought she didn't want him around because she didn't like him? Obviously he couldn't see how her pulse started racing when he smiled at her. Better to keep it that way.

"Well, I'm sure you never lack for female company of those you don't annoy."

"I am highly suspicious of any woman who isn't annoyed by me." Sawyer winked at Megan.

She grabbed her stuff and headed toward the door without another word before she hyperventilated. She heard Sawyer chuckle as she brushed past him.

"See you tomorrow, Dr. Fuller," he called as she walked down the hall. Megan didn't respond. What could she say anyway?

Megan made her way down the hallway, reporting to Mark, the main security guard, that she was leaving for the day to work at home and would be back tomorrow.

When Mark smiled at her it didn't do anything to her stomach. She smiled back as he helped her with the front door.

The crisp winter air felt good against Megan's overheated skin. She walked slowly to her car enjoying—as always—the beauty of the Blue Ridge Mountains surrounding her. Here, outside and away from all the craziness inside Cyberdyne and her reaction to Sawyer, Megan realized she had made the right decision.

She already felt clearer, steadier. Ready to work. What she was doing was important and she was racing against a very real clock, but she was up for the challenge. Working at home would be just what she needed.

Megan opened her car door and threw her briefcase and lunch bag in the passenger seat beside her. Her house was only ten minutes away from Cyberdyne. She'd chosen it specifically for that reason. She cleared through the security gate and began her drive home.

As she stopped at an intersection about halfway between her house and Cyberdyne, an idea for solving one of the problems with the countermeasure became clear to Megan. She reached into her purse to grab her phone so she could make a voice recording, to remember it later.

A car behind her honked as Megan was getting her phone ready to record. The light had turned green. Megan waved to the car behind her and began to pull through the intersection.

Just as an SUV flew through the intersection in the other direction and T-boned into the passenger side of Megan's car.

# Chapter Six

The jar of the impact threw Megan's entire body into the driver's side door. Her head cracked against the window and she struggled to hold on to consciousness. Her car seemed to spin around in slow motion from the force of the SUV that hit it.

Megan sat dazed as the car stopped moving, trying to figure out what exactly had happened. Thinking was hard. Had the other car run the red light? Megan tried to test different parts of her body to make sure they were functional, thankful that everything seemed to move when her brain commanded it to.

Was everyone all right in the other car? Megan reached up to wipe the sweat trickling from her scalp, but when she brought her fingers down they were red. Blood, not sweat.

Megan tried to unfasten her seat belt, but it didn't seem to want to come loose. She glanced out the window and saw someone from the SUV that had hit her get out of the passenger side of their vehicle and begin walking toward her car. Thank goodness he seemed to be okay. Megan hoped the driver was, too.

And that they had insurance.

The man hurried up to Megan's car and leaned into the passenger-side window that had completely shattered.

"Oh my gosh." Megan's words came out in a rush. "Are

you guys okay? My seat belt seems to be stuck. And I think I'm bleeding. I might need an ambulance, but I think overall I'm okay."

The man didn't say anything, and Megan couldn't tell if he was injured or not. He was wearing a gray jersey jacket with a hood tied tightly around his face. And with the large, dark sunglasses he had on, Megan couldn't tell anything about him at all.

The hooded man reached down and grabbed Megan's briefcase that had slid to the floor during the impact. He stretched toward her and, in her dazed state, Megan thought he might try to help her with her seat belt. But then she realized he was trying to find her purse.

"Hey, what are you doing?" Was this man robbing her? The man didn't say anything, instead reached down to the floor where her purse had fallen. Megan pulled more frantically at the seat belt that wouldn't unlatch.

"Stop! Somebody help me!" Megan tried to grab her purse strap, to stop the man in any way she could, but he was too strong. And still Megan couldn't make out any of his features.

Once he had what he had come for, the man wasted no more time. He turned and jogged quickly back to the SUV. As soon as the man reached his vehicle, it began to pull away, the damage to it minimal because of the metal bars on the front grille.

Megan watched the vehicle go, trying to get the license plate as blood continued to drip down in her face.

A witness to the accident—some girl who couldn't be more than eighteen years old—ran up to her side of the car and knocked on the window. When Megan couldn't get it to lower, the girl opened the door.

"Oh my gosh, are you all right? I saw the whole thing. That car just plowed right into you, right? Ran a red light and everything. And then just left. That makes it a hit-and-run, right?"

Megan's head was beginning to throb. And still she couldn't get the seat belt to unfasten. Answering the teenager's questions seemed impossible, which was fine because she didn't actually seem to want any answers.

"I've already called the police. That was just so unbelievable. I've got to text my friends and tell them what happened. Oh man, you're bleeding. Are you okay?"

"I hit my head," Megan told her. "And I can't seem to get my seat belt to unfasten."

"Oh my gosh, let me try." The teenager did her best, but couldn't seem to get the belt to budge. "Oh, wait, I hear some sirens."

Moments later a barrage of first responders showed up. A fireman cut the seat belt so Megan could get out of the car and a paramedic helped her over to the ambulance. They offered her a stretcher, but Megan refused.

"You're going to need a few stitches on your scalp. We'll take you to the hospital."

"Fine," Megan told the paramedic. "But first I need to talk to the police. The people who hit me stole my purse and briefcase from my car."

The paramedic called the police officer over and Megan repeated her claim to him.

"Are you saying that because the items just aren't here? Are you sure you had your purse and briefcase in the car with you?"

"Absolutely. Right after the accident, I was sitting right here, and someone walked up, leaned through the window and took my belongings."

The police officer looked skeptical. "You hit your head pretty hard. Are you sure it was someone from the car that hit you that took your stuff?"

Megan's head was really beginning to ache and dealing

with a disbelieving police officer wasn't what she wanted to do.

"I'm telling you, I watched, trapped *right* here—" she gestured to the driver's side of her car "—as a man got out of the passenger-side door of the SUV that had just hit me and walked to my car. I thought he was coming to see if I was okay, but instead he reached into my car through the broken window, grabbed my briefcase and my purse, and then left. He didn't say a word."

The officer shook his head. "I'll put it in my report, but it just seems like a great deal of risk—hitting you with their own vehicle like that—just for a simple robbery. Did you have anything of great value in your purse or briefcase?"

"Less than a hundred dollars in my purse." Then her stomach dropped as she remembered where she had been going and what she had been carrying with her. "Oh no. Ghost Shell and the countermeasure."

"I'm sorry?"

"Stuff for work." Megan shook her head. The countermeasure hard drive had been in her briefcase, as well as all the printouts she was going to use to work from home. The printouts weren't a problem, but the countermeasure? Irreplaceable. This was going to set the Cyberdyne team back. Again. All the way to the beginning.

"Can you provide a description of the man who took your belongings?"

Megan rubbed the middle of her forehead with her fingers. It seemed as though everything in her body hurt. "No, I'm sorry. He wore a hooded sweatshirt that was wrapped tight around his face. And dark sunglasses. I can tell you that he's Caucasian, but that's about it."

"I'll need to get a list of everything that was taken. You'll want that filed for your insurance purposes." Megan could tell the police officer was still skeptical about her story of being robbed.

The medic helped Megan move up onto the gurney so she could be transported to the hospital. Megan felt nauseous and her head was throbbing. She knew she needed to call Sawyer and let him know about the robbery, in case he could possibly do something about it. But she dreaded telling him about losing the countermeasure.

"My phone wasn't in my purse," she told the medic. "Can someone check to see if it's in the car? I need to make some calls."

The medic nodded and went out to talk to the officers. Megan sat against the propped-up gurney. She chewed on her bottom lip, dreading the call to Sawyer. The medic rushed back, placing Megan's phone and lunch bag on her lap.

"Sorry, that's all there was," the woman told Megan.

Megan was placing the lunch bag to the side and picking up the phone when she remembered. She'd been so discombobulated in the break room when Sawyer came in that she had put the countermeasure drive and many of the papers in her lunch bag rather than her briefcase. She double-checked to be sure.

As the ambulance sped to the nearest hospital, Megan laughed out loud. She could tell the medic was concerned about head trauma, but she didn't care.

Megan laughed again. Whoever had just robbed her, hoping to get the Ghost Shell countermeasure, had actually stolen half of a ham-and-cheese sandwich.

SAWYER SCROLLED THROUGH the readout that Cyberdyne's security chief, Ted Cory, had provided. Sawyer's meeting with the man yesterday had been pretty tense. Sawyer pointed out potential security problems, Cory became defensive. Sawyer found that happened a lot when working with civilians. They took everything as a personal criticism.

But Cory had provided all the information concerning

the R & D doors and computer usage without complaint. The problem was that the info was massive. Every time someone accessed a door or a computer, it was logged into the security system. But given the number of R & D employees—even eliminating the ones who had nothing to do with Ghost Shell—the data was considerable.

But what really caught Sawyer's attention was a tiny bit of data that seemed to have been corrupted. It was barely noticeable—if Sawyer hadn't been looking for it, he wouldn't have noticed the discrepancy at all. But a small piece of manipulated data reinforced what Sawyer had been suspecting more and more each day he was at Cyberdyne.

Someone was deliberately sabotaging Megan's attempts to get the countermeasure built.

Certainly bad luck and human error happened, and most of the problems that had belabored Megan and her team could easily be attributed to either. But it was Sawyer's job to look past what could be considered accidental and see the pattern underneath. And now Sawyer was sure it was a pattern.

Sawyer looked at the readout for the vault's security door on the day he had arrived at Cyberdyne. The next morning Megan had discovered the original countermeasure had been damaged while in the vault. Sawyer, of course, had almost immediately accessed the data for who had been in the vault once Megan announced work would resume on the countermeasure. Unfortunately, almost every member of her team had accessed the vault that afternoon or early evening, providing nothing conclusive.

But now, looking at that report for earlier that same day, Sawyer found it: a manual override of the employee code for someone entering the vault the morning Sawyer arrived. Just the smallest of digital fingerprints that had been left behind by someone. No other manual overrides could be found anywhere in the system.

Someone who didn't want their employee ID number to be recognized had gone into the vault the morning Sawyer had arrived. And the very next day the countermeasure had been pronounced damaged beyond repair. It was too big a coincidence for Sawyer to ignore.

Trying to hide their ID number had been a mistake. One someone probably made in a panic when they found out Sawyer was coming and work would resume on the countermeasure. If they had just left the security info alone, it would've never caught Sawyer's attention and clued him in to the fact that someone in Cyberdyne was most likely on DS-13's payroll.

Sawyer pushed back from the computer screen, eyebrows drawing together. A traitor at Cyberdyne could explain many of the setbacks Megan and the team had faced over the past few days. And although Sawyer had no idea who the traitor was, knowing there was someone in their midst changed everything.

Sawyer's phone vibrated in his pocket. Megan. He hadn't expected to hear from her so soon.

Or at all, to be honest, the way she had admitted to not wanting to work around him.

He answered his phone. "Hey, you."

"Hi, Sawyer."

Sawyer could hear people talking and various noises all around her. "Sounds busy. Everything okay?"

"I need you to come pick me up, if you don't mind."

"Uh-oh, car break down?" Sawyer chuckled to himself. Things must be pretty bad if she was calling *him* to come give her a ride.

"Well, not exactly. I was in an accident."

"Are you okay? Where are you?"

Megan's voice dropped in volume a little. "Somebody ran into my car. I'm at the hospital, but—"

"I'll be right there."

Sawyer was already running down the hallway before she could begin her next sentence.

# Chapter Seven

Sawyer couldn't quite explain the tightness in his chest from the moment Megan had told him she'd been in an accident, but he couldn't ignore it, either. He'd broken multiple traffic laws on his way to the hospital, pressed by the need to see for himself that Megan was all right.

A flash of his law-enforcement credentials at the ER nursing station got him Megan's room number and silenced the questions about whether he was family and allowed back to see her. There was no way in hell he was going to be waiting out in the foyer.

He found the examination room quickly. She was perched on a table, clutching what looked to be an insulated lunch bag. Her gaze was unfocused across the room.

Sawyer knocked as he pushed his way through the door. Seeing that she was okay with his own eyes helped release the knot in his chest.

"Hey," he said softly, trying to get her attention without startling her.

Her gaze slowly moved toward him as he walked into the room.

"How are you doing?"

"I'm okay. I had to get four stitches in my head." She brought her hand gingerly toward her head. Her voice was soft. "I don't really like needles."

Sawyer walked the rest of the way over to the examination table, not stopping until he stood right in front of her. He was relieved when she didn't move away. "I don't blame you. I don't like them, either. Do you feel up to telling me what happened?"

"I was just driving home—I don't live very far from Cyberdyne. I went through an intersection and a car just came speeding through and rammed into me. Hit me on the passenger side."

Sawyer whistled through his teeth. Depending on the speed and size of the other vehicle, this could've easily been a life-threatening accident. Sawyer was just thankful the vehicle hadn't been coming from the other direction, hitting Megan on the driver's side.

"Was anybody from the other vehicle hurt?"

Megan shifted a little uncomfortably. "Sawyer, after the car hit me, someone got out of it, came up to my car and took my purse and briefcase."

*"What?"* Shock rolled through Sawyer.

"I was dazed. I'd hit my head on the window and was bleeding. I thought he was coming over to see if I was all right. But he just reached through the broken window and grabbed my stuff."

Sawyer immediately grasped what had happened. This hadn't been a random accident. Someone had deliberately hit Megan's car with the intent to steal from her. And after what he had discovered today at Cyberdyne, Sawyer knew whoever hit Megan wasn't after money. They were after the Ghost Shell countermeasure. Sawyer's curse echoed through the small room.

"You believe me?"

"Why would you make something like that up?" Sawyer turned more fully toward Megan.

She shrugged. "The police thought I might be."

"The police don't have all the facts in this situation."

Before Sawyer could help himself he reached up and touched Megan's cheek. "The most important thing is that you're okay. I'm sure DS-13 were the ones who hit your car and took the countermeasure. I know it's a setback—a big one—but you're still here. That's what matters."

Sawyer didn't tell Megan how lucky she was that she'd been dazed when that DS-13 member approached her car. If she'd tried to fight or keep the man from taking her briefcase, he might've just eliminated her right then and there. It wouldn't be the first time DS-13 had utilized such measures.

But as glad as Sawyer was that Megan was safe, losing what progress had been made on the countermeasure was devastating in a situation where time was already working against them.

"So, do you think you can provide me with a list of everything that was lost? Once I get you home, I'll go back to Cyberdyne and—" Sawyer didn't finish his own statement. What would he do back at Cyberdyne? He had no idea who he could trust.

Sawyer didn't have to finish his sentence anyway because the doctor came in. "Okay, Ms. Fuller, I've signed your release forms and you're free to go." The young doctor looked up from her chart and found Sawyer sitting next to Megan. "Oh, I'm sorry. I'll come back when you're ready."

"No, it's fine, Doctor. You can give any report in front of him."

"Well, you've got no signs of a concussion. That was my biggest concern. You're going to have some pretty big aches and pains for a few days, and your head will probably be very tender from the cut and stitches. But overall it could've been much worse, considering."

The doctor smiled at Megan and then turned and looked at Sawyer. Sawyer gave the pretty doctor his biggest grin, glad to hear Megan was going to be all right. The doctor smiled back.

"Here's a prescription for some pain medication, Megan. Don't be afraid to take it. Call my office if you need anything." She handed the prescription to Megan, and her card to Sawyer. "She probably shouldn't drive today," the doctor said to Sawyer. "Or really do much of anything, just to be sure." The doctor smiled once more at both of them and left.

Sawyer looked down at the doctor's card. Her cell-phone number was written on the back of it. Sawyer was glad Megan would be able to contact the doctor if needed. He reached back to put the card in his pocket when he noticed Megan's odd look.

"Are you okay? Does something hurt? Do you want me to get the doctor to come back?"

"I'm sure you'd be able to do that without any problem."

Of course he would. The doctor couldn't be very far; she'd just left. "Just hang on, I'll go get her."

Megan shook her head. "No, I'm fine. Don't worry about it." It seemed as if cold Dr. Fuller was back rather than the warm Megan he'd been talking to for the past few minutes.

Sawyer rubbed his eyebrows. Okay. "Are you sure?"

"You don't even see it, do you?" Megan asked, still shaking her head.

Sawyer grimaced. Maybe the doctor had been wrong and Megan did have a concussion or something. "See what?"

She seemed about to say something then stopped herself. "Nothing, never mind. You've got the doctor's card in case you want to call her, right?"

"Yeah, she left her cell-phone number on it, too. That was nice. It'll be easier for you to reach her if you happen to need something in the middle of the night."

Megan turned away from him. "Yeah, I'm sure that was her intent."

Wait, did Megan think the doctor had given *Sawyer* her

number? Was that why the temperature had dropped to below freezing in moments flat?

"Do you mind giving me a ride to a rental-car place? My car was completely totaled." Megan was already walking over to the chair where her jacket rested.

"Megan, don't be ridiculous. You heard the doctor. No driving today. I'll take you home. Plus, I need you to tell me everything you remember about the car and man in the accident. Also, a list of everything that was taken."

"That last part is easy."

Sawyer went over to help her put on her jacket, noticing the winces as she moved her arm and shoulder. "Oh yeah? Why is that?" he asked her.

She shrugged then winced again. "The only thing that was stolen was half a ham-and-cheese sandwich."

*"What?"* Now Sawyer was sure Megan had some sort of head trauma.

She looked up at him with her big brown eyes and smiled. "Um, yeah. I was in such a hurry today in the break room that I put the rest of my lunch in my briefcase and put the countermeasure drive in my lunch bag. The guy today took my briefcase and purse, but didn't even touch my lunch bag. Why would he?"

Sawyer couldn't help it. He reached down and picked Megan up off her feet in a hug, careful not to touch her injured areas. He quickly set her on the ground and watched as her mouth formed a little O. But at least she didn't slap him.

"So you still have everything to do with the countermeasure?" Sawyer didn't release her waist. He couldn't seem to help himself.

"Everything but some papers that are easily replaceable. Yep." Megan reached over and patted the lunch bag she'd set on the examination table. "Right here. I'll bet somebody was pretty pissed off when they saw what was in my briefcase."

Sawyer laughed out loud. He didn't doubt it. He wished he could've been a fly on a DS-13 wall for that discovery.

"Let's get you home so you can rest. No more nonsense talk about renting a car. I'll take you home and drive you wherever else you may need for a while."

"Fine. As long as you promise not to make fun of where I live."

One thing he had to give to Megan, she never said anything he expected her to. "Scout's honor, Dr. Fuller. Lead the way."

# Chapter Eight

Walking up to Megan's small house a little while later, Sawyer knew he wouldn't make fun of it; he wondered why she would think he would in the first place. She lived in what he would've expected—a nice neighborhood, with modern amenities and nondescript style. Not much character.

But hey, Sawyer didn't judge. Sawyer's town house outside DC was no prize. Of course, he was hardly ever there. As a matter of fact, there were probably some boxes still unpacked in his closet from when he'd moved in three years ago. Nobody could accuse him of being a homebody. Obviously, Megan was the same.

Sawyer helped Megan from his car and up to the door of her house. She seemed pretty steady on her feet, but his hand hovered at her elbow just in case.

But the inside of her house was the opposite of what Sawyer was expecting. It was the opposite of everything he knew about Dr. Fuller—head R & D computer scientist at a large technology development company.

The interior of her house was as warm and cozy and cluttered as the outside was sterile and modern. Sawyer stopped just inside the doorway, while Megan walked all the way in. She took off her jacket and hung it on what looked like a set of antique hooks attached to the wall. She then walked across the hall into the small kitchen.

"Are you coming in?" she called out as she put a kettle—a red one with white flowers decorating it—on the stove.

Sawyer slowly took his coat off and hung it on the hook next to Megan's. He leisurely wandered into the kitchen looking around.

Megan was watching him. "This is my house," she said, biting on her lower lip.

Sawyer smiled. "I see that. It wasn't what I was expecting."

"What were you expecting?"

"I guess something closer to what your office looks like. More—" Sawyer struggled to find the right words "—organized and contemporary."

"You mean cold?"

Sawyer shrugged. That was what he meant, but it seemed unkind to say it out loud.

"I know what people think of me at Cyberdyne." Megan's water was boiling, so she turned her back to him to pour it into two mugs with tea bags. "You probably think the same thing."

"Not necessarily. I think you have a hard job—made nearly impossible with all that's going down with Ghost Shell. You do what you have to do to get the job done. No fault in that."

She turned and leaned against the counter. "Maybe. I know I'm not everyone's favorite person. I definitely don't have a rapport with people like you do."

Sawyer could tell this weighed on her. He walked over and leaned against the sink so they were closer. "Well, I'm not able to use the words *symmetric key algorithms* in a coherent sentence like you do. So I guess we're even."

Finally a little smile. He didn't like the way her features were so pinched. She was probably in a lot of pain from the accident. "Why don't you go sit down on the couch? I'll finish the tea and get your pain meds ready. Time to stop thinking about work for a little while."

"But—"

"No buts." Sawyer wrapped his arm gently around her shoulder and urged her away from the counter toward the kitchen door. "You don't need to be Dr. Fuller right now. Just go relax."

Megan tilted her head sideways, looking at him oddly. Sawyer thought for a second she might argue, but instead she made her way into the living room. Good. She needed to just shut down for a little while.

Sawyer finished the tea and got out some of the pain medication she'd had filled at the hospital. He decided to make them something to eat, since he knew Megan had had only half a ham sandwich for lunch—the other half was with some pissed-off DS-13 employee right now. Sawyer's culinary skills were the opposite of legendary, but he was able to warm some soup and find some cheese and crackers for them both. He set it all on a tray he found on the kitchen table.

Megan seemed genuinely surprised when he brought in the food. "Wow, thanks."

She was cuddled deep into the oversize cushions on her couch, a blanket pulled up to her chin. She had kicked off her shoes and her legs were tucked underneath her. Her hair was down from the bun she so often kept it in, brown curls framing her face and shoulders. Her glasses were on the side table.

She barely looked old enough to have her own place, much less be the head computer scientist of anything.

And she was breathtakingly beautiful.

How had he missed that before? Maybe because the past few days he had gotten so used to seeing the prickly Dr. Fuller that he hadn't really noticed the woman underneath.

But here, surrounded by all the things that obviously made her feel at ease, Sawyer couldn't help but be drawn to her.

"My soup-warming skills are legendary, I have to warn you," Sawyer told her as he set down the tray beside her on the couch. "Many a gal has fallen prey to the chicken-noodle wonder."

She giggled. Dr. Fuller actually giggled. Sawyer knew he could easily become addicted to the sound of Megan's relaxed laughter.

"I'll bet. I'll try to control myself." She took a sip of the soup. "Mmm. But it may be hard."

Sawyer sat down on the other side of the couch and began eating his food. Yep, the soup was as bad as he suspected it would be.

"You know, without all your Dr. Fuller gear on—lab coat, glasses, hair pulled back—you don't really look old enough to be head of the R & D department for a company as large as Cyberdyne."

Megan shrugged. "I'm twenty-nine."

Sawyer did some quick math in his head. Her file had told him she had worked at Cyberdyne for eight years, had been head of R & D for five. He also knew she held two doctorates from MIT—but how was any of that possible when she was only twenty-nine years old?

Megan could obviously see his confusion. "Yeah, I went to college when I was fourteen, finished at sixteen. Went on to MIT for my graduate work and finished at twenty."

"Like a master's degree?"

"I got my master's then two PhDs in computer and conceptual engineering."

"While you were still a teenager?"

Megan took another spoonful of her soup. "Well, I was twenty by the time I finished."

Sawyer laughed. "Twenty? That late? What a slacker."

"Actually, one of my dissertation advisers alluded to that."

"That you were a slacker because you didn't finish two doctorates at MIT while you were a teenager?"

Megan shrugged. "Yeah."

"That's absurd."

"No, he was right. I was dragging my feet a little bit my last semester because I wasn't sure what I would do once I was finished with school. I was comfortable there."

"School had to be pretty different for you than for most people."

"Yeah, I was always the little freak."

"C'mon, now. I'm sure that wasn't true." But the way Megan said it, Sawyer knew she felt it was.

Megan reached over and put her empty soup bowl on the large trunk that served as a coffee table. "Nobody really knew what to do with me. I was the scary little kid who could do advanced math problems in her head, but never got any of the pop-culture references and turned a neon shade of pink if anyone used bad language."

"Weren't your parents around?"

"My parents divorced when I was young and I never really saw my dad. My mom remarried a great guy, but they had their own set of kids, twelve years younger than me. My mom couldn't exactly come live with me at MIT with two preschoolers in tow."

She tucked herself back under the blanket. "It wasn't too bad, really. Nobody was ever mean to me or anything. And the intellectual challenge of the doctoral program was exactly what my brain needed."

Sawyer honed in on what she *wasn't* saying. "Yeah, but it sounds like it was pretty lonely."

Megan looked at him with those big brown eyes, her

cheek resting against the soft cushioning of the couch. "It was an excellent opportunity for which I'm very thankful."

Sawyer put his own bowl and plate down and scooted a little closer to her on the couch. He noticed she didn't shift away at all—the total opposite of her actions at Cyberdyne for the past four days.

"It sounds like your college experience and mine are pretty similar," he told her.

That definitely got her attention. "Really?"

"Yeah, except nobody recognized my advanced intellectual giftings, so unfortunately they placed me in a fraternity. It forced me to get average grades and have great parties on the weekend."

Megan laughed. "Yep, sounds exactly the same."

He smiled. "It was definitely an excellent opportunity for which I'm very thankful."

"So how'd you end up going from fraternity to law enforcement?"

He reached over and tucked one of her curls behind her ear. Her eyes began to droop just a little. It had been a long and exhausting day for her.

"That's a long story for another time. Right now, I think we need to get you up to bed. Your body's had quite a shock today with the accident."

Megan shuddered. "I don't even want to think about it. I keep picturing that man with the hood coming toward my car. He was definitely after the countermeasure, Sawyer, I just know it."

Sawyer nodded. "I know you're right. But we'll talk about that tomorrow. Right now you need some sleep. I'm going to stay here and sleep on your couch. Just in case you need anything."

"Oh, okay." Megan stood, but tripped when the blanket she'd wrapped around herself caught her legs. Sawyer caught her just as she was about to stumble face-first onto the ground, a pile of limbs and blanket.

"Careful there."

Megan cringed, heat flooding her face. "Obviously my college awkwardness is not as far behind me as I would like."

Sawyer helped wrap the blanket around her in a more organized, safe-to-walk fashion. "I think anyone who gets T-boned and robbed in one day gets a free pass to be as clumsy as she wants to be."

"I wonder what excuse I'll use tomorrow," she said softly. Sawyer became aware of how close they were to each other.

"We'll just have to figure out tomorrow's problems tomorrow."

She leaned in just the slightest bit closer and Sawyer couldn't help it. He kissed her.

He half expected Megan to turn cold and step back from him unresponsive. But after a moment of surprised hesitation, she let go of her blanket and her arms slid up his chest to his shoulders. And Sawyer found it was him that was caught unprepared. Unprepared for the heat that flared up between them the instant his lips touched hers.

It was fair to say that Sawyer had kissed his share of women, but he couldn't ever remember feeling like this.

His hands slid to Megan's waist. A knot of need twisted in him as he pulled her closer. Had he really ever thought her cold? The very idea was absurd to him now.

Sawyer wasn't sure how long the kiss might have gone on if Megan hadn't made a small sound of pain when Sawyer wrapped his arms around her tighter.

Her head. Her injuries. How could he have forgotten?

Sawyer backed away from Megan just the slightest bit. "We should stop."

He loved the way her eyes opened and blinked up at him half-dazed. "Wh-what?"

Sawyer smiled down at her. "I think we better stop."

"Oh." Megan took a step back. Now her eyes were focused, but Sawyer didn't like what he saw in them. Confusion. Doubt. Embarrassment.

"Just to be clear." Sawyer grasped her waist tighter so she couldn't retreat any farther. "It's not that I want to stop. But you did have an accident today, remember? And you're on some pretty serious painkillers. How about if we try this again soon when those two factors aren't in play?"

Megan gave him a soft smile. "Okay."

THE NEXT MORNING when Megan awoke, she felt as if she had been hit by a truck. Which was pretty close to accurate. She lay in bed, keeping her body still to help with the aches and pains, but her thoughts were flying a million miles an hour.

A lot of them centered on her kiss with Sawyer last night. Megan replayed it in her head with a sigh, feeling like a giddy teenager. Sure, she'd been kissed before—she'd even had a couple of quasi-serious relationships. But those relationships had been with other computer specialists she'd met at different professional functions. The men at these functions, although polite and usually moderately attractive, tended to be relatively boring. Nerds, if she had to sum them up in one word.

They were not, by any stretch of the imagination, as handsome and confident and engaging and *hot* as the man who'd slept on her couch last night.

The man she'd kissed with pretty reckless abandon. And would've kept kissing—and more—if he hadn't stopped them.

Sawyer said he had stopped because he was worried about her injuries. And while Megan appreciated the consideration, she couldn't help but wonder if there was more of a reason why he'd stopped. After all, why would someone who looked like Sawyer Branson—six feet of lean, solid muscle, thick black hair and gorgeous green eyes, who was friendly and confident—be interested in Megan, who was, well, a nerd if she had to sum *herself* up in one word?

Yeah, it was probably good he'd stopped the kiss when he did. They'd both just gotten caught up in a moment. Megan decided she wouldn't bring it up or make a big deal about it. That would just make things awkward and uncomfortable with Sawyer.

Megan sighed. If there was one thing she was good at, it was awkward.

Megan forced herself out of bed, barely holding back a groan. Every muscle in her body hurt. She needed to get some food into her system and take one of the pain pills. Then she needed to get to Cyberdyne. Because besides the kiss with Sawyer, there was one other thing she hadn't been able to stop thinking about. The fact that in order for the SUV that hit her to have known she would be at *that* particular red light at *that* particular time yesterday, somebody at Cyberdyne had to have tipped them off.

There was a traitor working against them at Cyberdyne.

Megan had no idea who it was. She knew she needed to tell Sawyer, although she suspected he had already figured it out.

Megan showered to try to loosen some of the tightness in her muscles, then got dressed and made her way downstairs. Pastries and coffee from the coffeehouse down the street rested at her kitchen table. So did Sawyer, who was reading through the news on his tablet.

"Morning. How are you feeling?" he asked with a smile.

Seriously, could he be any sexier with his deep morning voice? And he brought coffee and food.

"Like I was in a car accident yesterday."

"Ah, yes, an unfortunate by-product of being in a car accident yesterday." Sawyer stood and held out the chair for her at the table. "Why don't you eat something. I'll get your medicine."

"Okay, thanks." Megan sat down as gingerly as she could and began pulling apart a blueberry muffin. "Thanks for staying last night."

Sawyer brought her medicine and a glass of water. "No problem at all. You feeling up to going to work today?"

"That's something I want to talk to you about. I think we've got a mole or a traitor or whatever you want to call it at Cyberdyne."

Sawyer sat back down at the table. "Why do you say that?"

"The people who hit me yesterday. They had to have been waiting for me, knowing when I'd be coming."

"And you think somebody from Cyberdyne tipped them off." It wasn't a question.

"Am I letting my imagination run away with me?" When she said it out loud, it sounded so cloak-and-dagger.

"No. I completely agree with you. As a matter of fact, before I went to pick you up yesterday I found evidence that someone—I couldn't tell who—had tampered with security log-ins for the vault."

Megan pushed her half-eaten muffin away, having no taste for it now. While formulating her theory that someone was a traitor at Cyberdyne, she hadn't considered it would be one of the people she worked closely with. But if someone who had access to the vault was the DS-13 collaborator, then it had to be someone pretty high up in the R & D department. Maybe even someone on her own team.

"What should we do? I can finish the countermeasure myself, but it will take a lot longer."

Sawyer pushed her plate of muffin back toward her. "Maybe not as long as you think, especially if all the problems you've run into over the last few days have really been sabotage attempts. Which would make sense."

Megan ate more of the muffin, running through scenarios in her head. Yes, she could finish the countermeasure herself, but it would mean stepping on quite a few toes. Yeah, there was a traitor, but there were a lot more innocent parties at Cyberdyne who had been working nonstop to get the countermeasure developed. They would not like the idea of being taken off the project.

"We wouldn't be able to tell my team why we're taking them off the project, would we?"

Sawyer shook his head. "No. We need to use this situation to figure out who the mole is at Cyberdyne. We'll have to think of something else to tell your team."

No matter what she told them, they weren't going to like it. Megan finished the last of the muffin.

"This isn't going to get any easier by waiting any longer. Let me go get ready."

Megan got up and was turning to leave the kitchen when Sawyer's arm snaked around her waist. He turned her back toward him gently.

"Because last night's kiss can't possibly be as good as I remember it."

Whatever Megan was about to respond was lost as Sawyer's lips came down on hers. Just like last night, thought of anything but the heat between them flew out of her mind. Megan reached up and wound her arms around Sawyer's neck, feeling him pull her closer with his hands at her waist.

When Sawyer pulled back, they were both out of breath. He rested his forehead against hers. "I guess my memory wasn't faulty at all."

Sawyer put his hands on her shoulders and spun her back around toward the doorway. "You go get ready. Tragically, I have to put saving the world above my own personal wants. But it's not easy."

# Chapter Nine

Knowing someone out there was working against them—
leaking information, and maybe a lot more, to a group of
criminals *intent* on causing harm to innocent people—
made just being at Cyberdyne more difficult for Megan.
All coworkers, people Megan would've deemed completely
trustworthy yesterday, were now cast in the light of suspicion.

Every shut door to an office made Megan wonder if
someone was selling secrets behind it. People who smiled
and waved seemed fake, those who didn't seemed secretive.

"I don't know how you live in the law-enforcement
world," Megan whispered to Sawyer. "I've been doing this
for all of thirty seconds and I'm already about to go crazy
trying to figure who the bad guy is."

Sawyer chuckled. "Don't overthink it. Just try to act as
normal as possible and let them make the mistakes."

Megan snickered. "Have you met me? Overthinking is
my middle name."

They entered Megan's office. "Just focus on getting your
team off the countermeasure project. Let me worry about
looking for suspicious behavior."

Easier said than done. Megan felt a little jumpy just
being here. She felt even worse knowing she would upset
her entire team by pulling them off the project. Megan took

off her jacket, which caused every ache she had from yesterday to announce itself. She winced.

"You okay?" Sawyer came over and helped her put on her lab coat.

"Yeah. Just—" Megan turned to him and smiled wryly. "I'm about to make most of my closest colleagues pretty angry. And I feel like hell. And now the pressure is all on me to get the countermeasure done. And I feel like bad guys are watching me from every corner."

Sawyer winked at her. "But besides that…"

Megan chuckled and walked out of her office, asking Jon Bushman to get the main team together in the conference room. Might as well get this over with.

Trish, the newest member of the team—a talented software developer—was the first to enter the conference room.

"Oh my goodness, Megan!" Trish rushed over and gave Megan a hug. "I am so sorry about your accident. I can't even believe you're back at work so soon. You should've stayed home longer."

The woman was much taller than Megan and her hug pressed right up against Megan's bruises. Megan grimaced in Trish's embrace.

Trish immediately let go. "Did I hurt you? I'm so sorry."

"No, it's fine. Don't worry about it," Megan assured her. The rest of the team filed in.

"And we heard you were *robbed*." Trish said. "That's just terrible. An accident and a robbery."

How had Trish known that? Megan certainly hadn't told anyone. She glanced over at Sawyer, who shrugged just slightly.

"Where did you hear that, Trish?"

"Oh, honey, are you kidding? Everyone is talking about how they took your purse and briefcase. The audacity of those thieves."

The rest of the team murmured their agreement. Evidently both the accident and the robbery were common knowledge. Everyone provided expressions of sympathy and support, many of them hugging her. Listening to them just made Megan feel worse.

Surely none of these people were the traitor. She'd worked with most of them for years. The thought of it being one of them was devastating to Megan.

"Thanks, everyone, for your concern. I'm feeling much better today." Not true, though it didn't really matter. "But it was pretty scary yesterday."

Megan tried to watch people while she said it, to see if anyone gave away any hint of guilt, but everyone just looked concerned. Megan knew Sawyer was in the corner watching also—maybe he would notice something. She didn't stop to look at him, but his very presence gave her a sense of strength.

"We're going to have to make some changes in what everyone is working on. As of right now, all work on the Ghost Shell countermeasure is to stop."

There were murmurs all around as her team tried to figure out why Megan would pull them off something that had been a top priority just yesterday.

Michael Younker, the oldest member of her team—and often the surliest—was first to speak up. "Megan, what's going on here? First we drop everything for this project, work frantically on it, and now a few days later you're telling us to completely stop." His lips were pinched together.

Megan could understand Michael's frustration. None of the team knew the details about why they had been working so hard on the countermeasure to begin with—the fact that Ghost Shell had been stolen and was about to be sold on the black market. To be jerked back off the project so abruptly was a professional slap in the face, not acceptable for people of the caliber and talent of Megan's team.

"Michael, I understand your frustration." Megan looked

around at her team. "I understand the frustration all of you must feel. But circumstances have changed, and I can't say much more than that. Everyone will need to go back to the projects they were working on last week before we changed focus to the countermeasure."

Michael stood. "Well, I'll be in my office working on older projects until you decide to reroute me on those, too." He stalked out of the room. The other members of the team left also, none of them as upset as Michael, but not happy, either.

Trish stopped to speak with Megan on her way out. "Don't worry about it, Megan. Michael just doesn't do well with abrupt change, you know that. He'll come around." She smiled and then headed out. Megan was preparing to go back to her office when Jonathan stopped her. He had the same pinched look as Michael.

Megan touched Jonathan on the arm. "Jon, I know these changes are a scheduling nightmare for you. Thanks for understanding."

Jon shook his head. "Well, I have to admit, I don't really understand all these abrupt changes. But you're the boss. Do you want me to put the countermeasure project items back into the vault?"

Megan hesitated, unsure of what to tell her assistant. She looked to see if Sawyer was still in the room, but he'd already left.

There was no point trying to hide the fact that she'd still be working on the countermeasure from Jonathan. He had eyes on everything in the lab; it wouldn't take him long to figure it out.

"No. Actually, I'm going to still be doing a little work on it. It's just not going to be a team effort."

"Then I'll help you!" Jonathan perked up quickly. "Two heads are almost always better than one."

Megan knew Jonathan was protective of everything she

worked on. She didn't want to hurt the man's feelings, but neither did she want to invite him in on the project. "I'll let you know if I need help, okay?"

Jonathan didn't say anything else, just nodded and walked away. But Megan could tell she had pricked his pride.

Sawyer caught up to her as she headed to her office. "You doing okay? Doesn't seem to be an angry mob after you."

Megan rolled her eyes. "It looks like I've only totally alienated two of my eight team members, so that's not too bad."

"That Michael Younker guy is no barrel of fun."

"Yeah, he's been like that ever since I arrived. He applied for the position I got. Wasn't too thrilled about it. We aren't ever going to be buddies, but I don't generally have problems with him."

There was a timid tap on Megan's office door.

"Hi, Megan, Sawyer." It was Trish. "Megan, I just wanted to tell you that I don't have many other projects on my plate right now. I know you said we won't be working on the countermeasure anymore as a team, but if you wanted me to work on it individually, I'd be glad to. I just mean I have time to, even if the team is off of it. In case it becomes important again."

Megan looked over at Sawyer, who stood behind Trish. His eyebrow was raised. Megan agreed with Sawyer's skepticism. Why would Trish volunteer for extra work?

"You know what, Trish, I'm not going to have anyone working on the countermeasure right now. But thanks for offering. I know Jon has some new projects that have come in recently. Let him know that you're able to take on a little more. I'm sure he'll appreciate it."

Trish smiled. "Sounds good. And really, I'm glad you're okay from yesterday's accident, Megan." The woman left.

"Her interest in the countermeasure was a little odd, right?" Sawyer asked Megan. "How long have you known her?"

"She's worked here for less than a year. As a matter of fact," Megan said as she looked through a scheduling file on her computer, "she started working here two weeks after I first got in touch with Fred McNeil at the FBI and told him about Ghost Shell."

"That a pretty interesting timeline."

"In her defense, Trish is definitely a go-getter. This isn't the first time she's asked for extra work. She's still trying to prove her value to the team, I think."

"I'm going to do a full work-up on her. On everybody who would've had access to the vault the day I arrived."

"Did you notice anything suspicious while I was talking to the team?"

Sawyer grimaced and shook his head. "No, but that doesn't mean anything. We just keep watching and you keep working."

He was right. Megan was going to have to stop worrying about who the traitor might or might not be and get to work on the countermeasure. That was the most important thing.

SAWYER WATCHED AS for nearly the entire next thirty-six hours Megan labored on the countermeasure. She locked herself in one of the smaller labs and worked constantly, only stopping when he brought her food and to lie down in the early-morning hours.

She was using one version of Ghost Shell—the version he and Cameron had seized from DS-13 a few weeks ago— to create a way to stop the second version still out in the open and dangerous with Fred McNeil. Sawyer didn't even pretend to understand the science behind engineering the countermeasure, but he had no doubt Megan could do it.

She wouldn't let him stay in the room with her, claiming

he ruined her focus. But Sawyer couldn't understand how *anything* could ruin her focus when she was like this. Her concentration was intense—like a professional athlete or a surgeon. Watching her work for the past day and a half, Sawyer had no doubt she was as brilliant as her reputation suggested.

She worked in a room in the line of sight from where Sawyer stayed in her office. He was able to run reports on all of the Cyberdyne employees and still keep an eye on Megan's room. As much as possible he tried to run interference for Megan—the fewer interruptions she had, the quicker the countermeasure would be finished.

The background checks Sawyer ran weren't uncovering anything of much interest or suspicion. It looked as if everyone on the R & D team pretty much lived within their means. No one had made any unusually large deposits or purchases over the past few months.

Trish Wilborne, the programmer who had joined Cyberdyne most recently, was admittedly the most suspicious. But not because of her actions, really just because of the timing of her employment. Sawyer would be keeping a close eye on her. He'd be keeping a close eye on a lot of people. All of whom seemed to be a little miffed that Megan took them off the countermeasure project then proceeded to ignore them all for two days.

They were all gone now; it was late in the evening and everyone had left for the day a few hours ago. It was only Sawyer and Megan. Sawyer enjoyed the quiet and relative darkness of the lab. He was able to not be quite so on guard. He took off his tie and threw it on the table next to his laptop. He stretched his legs out in front of him.

Sawyer was beat. And if he felt this tired, he could only imagine how tired Megan must be with her intense concentration over the past hours. Sawyer didn't know how long they were going to be here. It didn't seem as though

Megan was ever planning to come out of the intellectual cocoon she'd wrapped herself in.

The door to Megan's office burst open. "Okay, that's it. I've got to get out of here." Megan strolled in and began tossing an armful of items and files onto her desk.

Okay, evidently she was planning to come out.

"Everything okay?" Sawyer stood up, bracing himself for another set of technological terms from Megan that he wouldn't really understand about the latest problem with the countermeasure.

But instead, Megan turned and beamed at him. "Everything is fine. Absolutely fine. Hey, where is everybody?"

"Well, since it's nearly nine o'clock, everybody left hours ago."

"Nine o'clock? Wow. I thought it was about noon."

Sawyer shook his head, one eyebrow raised. "You've been in there a long time. I was about to come drag you out for dinner."

"I figured out the biggest part of the problem today, Sawyer." Megan's eyes all but sparkled.

"But I thought you were having trouble." Sawyer leaned on the desk, happy to see Megan so lighthearted. Despite the dark circles under her eyes, she was more relaxed than he'd ever seen her.

"I was. But everything just clicked for me today." She tapped on her temple with her finger. "Sometimes that just happens. It's awesome when it does." She walked unhurried to the door to hang up her lab coat. "Another day or two, Sawyer. That's all I'll need."

With a satisfied sigh Megan perched against the desk next to Sawyer, her shoulder brushing his. "The problem was the block cipher and the substitution-permutation network. Now I can see why we were missing it, since we're coming at it from reverse. We just needed a transposition cipher rather than a Feistel cipher."

Her voice bubbled with excitement, but damned if Sawyer had *any idea* of what she was talking about. If she was anyone else, he'd think she was being smug—using words no mere mortal could possibly understand. But looking at her smiling, upturned face, Sawyer knew she was just sharing her joy.

Sawyer gave a theatrical sigh. "I tried to tell you days ago the problem was the substi-permeated cipher. But nobody would listen."

She actually giggled. "Substitution-permutation network. That's when a network takes a block of the plaintext—"

Sawyer turned and kissed her. A light kiss, just to shut her up and share in her relaxed happiness. But when Megan sighed and melted against him, it turned into something more than light. Sawyer grabbed Megan by the waist and boosted her up onto the desk. A knot of need twisted in him as he grasped her hips and drew her closer. Her lips parted and her arms came up to wrap around his neck.

Sawyer's hands came up to cup Megan's cheeks and entwined into her hair. He tilted her head so he could have better access to her soft warm lips.

But then something made Sawyer tense. In some part of Sawyer's brain that wasn't kissing Megan—the part that had been trained years ago to always be on alert for danger—something registered. Sawyer wasn't quite sure if it was a sound or a motion that had subconsciously grabbed his attention, but something had.

He and Megan weren't alone.

Sawyer pulled his lips back from Megan's and he stepped away from her. Confusion clouded Megan's eyes as she opened them.

"There's somebody else here," Sawyer whispered.

Immediately tension racked Megan's body. "But I thought you said everyone had already left."

"They did. Maybe it's security." Sawyer walked to the office door and called out, "Hello?"

No answer.

Most of the lights throughout the R & D department were still off, casting an eerie shadow among the desks and tables. Sawyer waited a few more moments, then turned back to the office. Maybe his overtired brain was just being too cautious.

But then they both heard it. The clicking of the exit door on the other side of the department. Megan's gaze flew up to Sawyer's.

"Stay here," he told her as he turned and ran out the door.

"Oh heck no," she told him, following right on his heels. They ran to the exit and Sawyer used his security card to open it, looking out into the hallway. No one was there. Sawyer immediately got on his cell phone, calling the Cyberdyne security station.

"This is Agent Branson. I'm in R & D. I need to know the last person who exited the lab."

Sawyer looked at Megan while he waited for the security officer to get the information. Hopefully, this would be a big lead on whoever the mole was here at Cyberdyne.

"Yes, Agent Branson?" The security guard got back on the line. "According to the door security log, Dr. Fuller was the last person to exit the lab besides you."

Sawyer looked over at Megan. She didn't have her security badge around her neck the way she normally did.

"Okay. Thanks for your help." Sawyer hung up with the security guard. He deliberately did not tell the guard about Megan's missing badge.

"It was *my* badge used to open the door?" They began to walk back the way they had come, toward Megan's office. "I took it off earlier this morning when I was trying to catch a few minutes of sleep."

"Where did you leave it?"

"In the room where I was working. But I could've sworn it was there a couple of hours ago."

"You'll have to get a new one tomorrow." Arriving at her office, Sawyer walked in, but noticed Megan had stopped and was looking across the hall.

"What wrong?" he asked her.

"The door to the room I was working in is open," Megan whispered. "I know it was closed before, Sawyer. I *know* it."

Sawyer came out of Megan's office and crossed to the small conference room she had been working in for the past few days. Four different laptops were set up, as well as detailed specs about Ghost Shell and the countermeasure, a soldering iron, and various microprocessors and pieces of hardware. And that was just the stuff Sawyer recognized. It looked like a geek bomb had gone off.

"I don't think anything is missing," Megan told him, looking around more closely. "I brought the countermeasure and all my findings into my office with me a few minutes ago after I finally reached a point where I could break for the day. There wasn't anything valuable here."

"Did you bring your ID badge with you when you left this room?"

He watched as Megan looked around, obviously trying to remember the last place she'd seen her badge.

"No. I remember it was hanging off this chair." She pointed at one near the door. "I wanted to get it, but I had too much stuff in my hands."

That meant—

"Sawyer." Megan figured it out at the same time. "That means someone was in this room while you and I were just down the hall…distracted with each other." Heat flooded her face.

Sawyer half smiled at Megan's reaction and choice of words, but she was right. They had distracted each other and someone had used it to their advantage.

"Are you sure nothing's missing?"

Megan looked around again. "No, like I said, all the critical items I took with me. I was going to put them in the vault before I left. But, Sawyer, whoever came in here—if they were the least bit familiar with the countermeasure—would've been able to see what I've done, the breakthrough I made today."

It was obvious that leaving Megan's work here at Cyberdyne wasn't going to be an option. The traitor was able to get around too easily.

"I'll drive you home." Megan still didn't have a car and there was no way in hell he was going to let her drive herself home alone anyway. "Everything you thought was important enough to bring to your office a few minutes ago needs to go home with you. Cyberdyne isn't safe anymore."

# Chapter Ten

A little while later, in Sawyer's car, Megan fought to get all her rushing emotions under control. Elation from making such progress in the countermeasure, adrenaline from the incident in the lab with the spy or whatever, exhaustion from getting only two hours of sleep last night. She wasn't sure which one was taking precedence over the others.

Actually, that wasn't true. She knew exactly what thoughts dominated her head. No matter what thought flooded her mind, her attraction to Sawyer was always at the forefront.

She couldn't stop thinking about Sawyer Branson.

She'd managed to block him out of her mind over the past couple of days as she worked, but it hadn't been easy. She'd done it because it had to be done. And the results had been the much-needed breakthrough in the countermeasure.

But sitting next to Sawyer in this car, she didn't think she'd get him out of her head anytime soon. Not that she really wanted to. As a matter of fact, she'd like to get closer to him. And if the way he'd just grasped her hand was any indication, it seemed as if he'd like to get closer, too.

But he was temporary. Megan couldn't let herself lose sight of that. Sawyer Branson may be interested in her, and they could probably have a wonderful time together, but it would definitely be temporary. When this case was over Sawyer would leave.

Her heart would do well to remember that.

Megan leaned her head back against the headrest and closed her eyes.

"You have to be tired."

Megan nodded. "Yeah. It's been a crazy day."

"I thought we'd go get a bite to eat, but if you're too tired, I can take you straight home."

Before Megan could reply, her stomach grumbled loudly, answering for her. They both laughed. "I guess food is a good idea."

Sawyer pulled over at a local restaurant and they were quickly seated due to the late hour. Megan glanced through the menu—since she was so hungry, everything looked good. She gave her order to the waiter almost at random the first time he came by their table.

The waiter looked at Sawyer. "Just repeat her order for me."

Megan noticed Sawyer's odd look as she handed over her menu. "What?" she asked.

"You." Sawyer half smiled while shaking his head. "You read the entire menu and picked out what you wanted in about eight seconds. I wasn't even through reading the appetizers yet."

Megan shrugged and began to play with a little bit of straw wrapper. "Yeah, I can process information pretty quickly. Do you want to call the waiter back and get the menu again?"

"No. It was just pretty impressive."

"My brain sees information and processes it as a whole sometimes, rather than me having to read individual words. Plus, I was hungry and in a hurry."

"I could tell by the amount of food you ordered. It's nice

to be out with someone who isn't afraid to eat. Although it's hard to believe you can fit that much in your tiny body."

Megan hadn't really thought about how much food she was ordering—but really an appetizer, salad and entrée all for one person was probably a lot. Sawyer was probably used to going out with a different type of woman than Megan. Probably someone much more sophisticated, who actually considered the fact that ordering enough food for a small country might be a little off-putting.

"Yeah, I probably went a little overboard." Megan tried for light laughter, but her laugh sounded uncomfortable even to her.

Sawyer reached over and took her hand from where she was tugging on her bottom lip. "No. Whatever you're thinking in that giant brain of yours…just, no. You knew what you wanted and you got it. Not a thing in the world wrong with that."

Megan gave a wry smile. "And I missed dinner."

"We both did. So thank God for your ability to make a decision and not waste time."

Megan was glad that he really didn't seem to care. She was just so bad at dating. And had no frame of reference at all in going out with someone like Sawyer.

Not that this was really a date. But she had to admit, he hadn't let go of her hand since he took it a minute ago.

"So on your first day you promised to tell me the story of how you ended up here in Swannanoa, even though you didn't really want to be."

Sawyer grinned at her from across the table. He didn't let go of her hand. "Ah, yes, well, I accidentally punched my boss in the jaw and knocked him unconscious."

"How do you *accidentally* punch somebody?"

"I tripped."

"Is that so?"

"Well, let's just say my boss—not the most likable guy

in the world—was sure to say no to an extremely important question my brother was about to ask him. But I'm a clumsy idiot and I fell right into my boss, clocked him in the jaw and basically took my boss out of the equation. Terrible accident."

Megan did not believe for one second that someone with as much masculine grace and control over his own body as Sawyer could have possibly stumbled to such a degree. And she was sure his boss—as soon as he regained consciousness—figured out the same thing.

"So as punishment for your clumsy idiocy you were assigned to us here at Cyberdyne."

"Yeah." Sawyer cleared his throat, looking sheepish. "At the time I thought it was a pretty bad assignment. But I was wrong."

Megan felt his thumb stroking over her knuckles. She looked at their hands—hers was so much smaller than his big, capable ones.

"So your brother works for the FBI, too?"

"Why do you ask that?"

"Just figured he wouldn't be asking your boss an important question unless he also worked with you."

"Yeah, Cameron's in law enforcement, too."

"But not the FBI?"

Sawyer shifted his weight so he was leaning his elbows on the table. He let go of her hand. "Actually, Megan, I can't go into too many details, but no, my siblings don't technically work for the FBI. Really, neither do I."

Megan straightened in her chair. "I don't understand."

The waiter chose that time to bring their food—all of it. Megan had to wait while the plates were set on the table and general pleasantries exchanged before she could get her answer.

"So?" she asked as soon as the waiter was gone. She took a bite of salad while she waited for Sawyer's response.

"Like I said, I can't go into a lot of specific details, but my brother and I work for an interagency task force known as Omega Sector."

"I've never heard of it."

"Well, it's not top secret, but it's also not advertised. The people involved are handpicked."

Megan understood. A best of the best type thing. Megan wasn't surprised Sawyer had been chosen. And since Fred McNeil had been an FBI agent when he stole Ghost Shell, it stood to reason that another agency would be used to clean up the mess he'd left.

"So your brother is part of Omega Sector, too?"

"Yeah, actually, my sister, Juliet is, too. Although she's not an active agent like Cameron and I. At least not anymore."

Megan wanted to ask more about that, but decided not to. She didn't want to put Sawyer in a position of not being able to talk about something. She took more bites of her food.

"So you've got one brother and one sister?"

"And one more brother. He lives in Virginia, runs a charter airplane business."

"Four Branson siblings altogether?"

"Yep, I'm the youngest. And of course, the most charming, best-looking and smartest."

"And don't forget modest."

Sawyer smiled. "That's right. They remind me of that every chance they get."

Megan envied Sawyer his close relationship with his siblings. Megan's brothers were too young for her to be close with, although they were fun little kids.

They ate in companionable silence for a while, both of them starving.

"Any of your siblings married?" Megan asked as she was finishing up her food.

Sawyer shook his head, taking a drink of his water.

"My oldest brother, Dylan, was but…that didn't work out." Megan noticed the slight pause, but didn't push.

"My sister—" Megan could see Sawyer clench his jaw. He cleared his throat and started again. "My sister, Juliet, is…working through some stuff. She's not involved with anybody right now." Obviously whatever stuff his sister was working through was upsetting to Sawyer. Megan reached over and grabbed his hand. She didn't know what to say, but she at least wanted him to know he wasn't alone.

Sawyer ate a few more bites and seemed to collect himself. "Cameron, my middle brother, just got engaged. It's pretty sickening how in love the two of them are." Sawyer gave a dramatic sigh and rolled his eyes. Megan giggled.

They spent the rest of the meal with Sawyer telling stories from his childhood. Growing up with him and his siblings each being less than two years apart meant they had been tight—and had gotten into lots of trouble together. Some stories had Megan laughing so hard it was making her head and side ache all over again.

Sawyer saw her wince. "Come on. Let's get you home." He paid for the food and they headed out to the car.

The drive to her house wasn't long. Sawyer was still entertaining her with stories of childhood antics when they pulled up to her driveway.

"I know you'll be glad to sleep in your own bed tonight rather than the couch at the office. I know I'm looking forward to not sleeping in an office chair."

"First night it was my couch, and last night it was a chair. It hasn't been a great couple of nights for you."

Sawyer winked at her. "Don't you worry about me, sugar. I can handle it."

"Well, I've got a new plan." The words were out of Megan's mouth before she even realized what she was saying. "Why don't you try my bed tonight?"

# Chapter Eleven

Sawyer put the car in Park and all but ripped the keys out of the ignition.

Megan's bed was possibly the best plan he had heard in his entire life. Sawyer hadn't wanted to rush things, had recognized that Megan was different from the women he normally dated. She was special. And he was pretty darn sure she didn't take sex casually.

Which, okay, he could admit scared him just a little bit. But heck, everything he felt about Megan scared him. And none of it seemed casual.

Those big brown eyes of hers were looking at him right now, a little in shock at her own words.

"Megan…" There were so many things Sawyer wanted to say. *Yes, please* being the primary one. But he also didn't want her to rush anything. It had been a crazy couple of days. She was tired, had been in an accident, plus what had happened with the unknown intruder in the lab.

Sawyer just wanted Megan to be sure. But couldn't find the right words to say it exactly.

Then Sawyer saw hesitation—the fear of rejection—steal over her face. "It's okay. I understand—" she began softly. She thought he didn't want her.

To hell with that.

Sawyer got out of the car before Megan could finish

her sentence. He strode around it quickly and purposefully, keeping eye contact with Megan through the windshield the entire time. He reached down and opened the passenger-side door.

Megan was still looking at him with those big brown eyes when Sawyer reached down and unlatched her seat belt. He helped her out the door, then promptly picked her up and set her on the hood of the car. He grasped each of her legs just under the knees and slid her all the way to the edge of the hood, hooking her legs on either side of his hips. He stepped forward so they were completely pressed against each other.

"Get one thing straight in that giant brain of yours—I have wanted you from the moment I first thought you were a receptionist and asked you to get me some coffee."

Sawyer grasped either side of her face and tilted her chin up with his thumbs. He brought his lips down very gently to hers, savoring the feel of them.

"And I've wanted you more every day since." He punctuated each word with a brief kiss.

Sawyer slanted her head to the side so he could take advantage of her lips, her closeness. To sink into that soft, wet mouth. He could feel Megan melt against him—both of them wanting to get closer than their current location would allow.

"Let's go inside," Sawyer said to her softly. Both of their breathing was ragged.

Megan nodded. Sawyer reached back inside the car to get the countermeasure items they'd brought home with them—not wanting to leave that out in an unmanned vehicle. Megan got her purse and took out her house keys.

Her eyes were sparkling; no doubt clouded them now. Sawyer reached up and trailed his finger down her cheek. "You're beautiful."

Megan gave a wry grin. "I get lots of compliments, but that's not the usual one."

Sawyer tucked his arm around her as they walked up the stairs to her door. "Oh yeah, what's the usual compliment?"

"Something about my brain. Never about my looks."

"Well, then, you should consider not hanging around with so many visually impaired people."

Megan giggled again—a sound Sawyer was coming to love. Serious Dr. Fuller didn't do enough of it.

Sawyer took her key from her and opened the door, ushering her inside. He closed the door behind them, locking it.

"Saw—Sawyer?"

Sawyer could hear the terror in Megan's voice. He instantly drew his weapon and spun her around so she was behind him.

Her house had been totally ransacked.

Furniture laid overturned and viciously ripped apart, pictures and knickknacks thrown to the ground and broken without care. Someone had definitely searched this place, inflicting the most damage possible while doing so.

If Sawyer had to guess, he would say this was payback for the countermeasure not being in Megan's briefcase when they had attempted to steal it the other day.

Megan whimpered behind him and he wrapped an arm around her, pulling her up to his back, but didn't turn around. Whoever did this could still be in the house.

"Megan, I want you to stay here by the door. I'm going to check things out." When Megan didn't answer right away, Sawyer glanced at her. She was looking around at the ruins of her home, eyes unblinking, obviously in some sort of shock.

Sawyer knew he couldn't comfort her right now. He needed to check the rest of the house, make sure no one was still inside. Sawyer quickly turned all the way around so he could look Megan in the eye, wanting to make sure she understood. "Megan, I'm going upstairs. Somebody could still be here, okay? I want you to stay right by the door. I'll be back in just a second." He handed her the counter-measure drive.

Megan took it, nodding blankly, her eyes still on her destroyed living room. Sawyer wasn't sure she even heard him.

Sawyer walked farther into the living room and kitchen. Both looked clear so he headed up the stairs. Megan's bedroom had not escaped the rampage. Every item of clothing she owned had been dumped out of the drawers and shredded, her pillows, blankets destroyed. He definitely did not want Megan coming up here to see this.

"Just stay down there, okay, honey?"

Sawyer didn't wait for her response. He glanced in the bathroom, then crossed over to the second bedroom Megan used as a home office. This room hadn't been spared, either; papers were spread over the floor and it looked as if part of Megan's computer—the part that wasn't in pieces—might have been taken.

Sawyer was reaching for the closet door when it burst open. Sawyer's weapon was knocked out of his hand as a large man tackled him. Sawyer rolled to the side, but not before he felt the sting of a blade cut into his arm.

The man—in a hoodie, similar to what Megan had described with her car accident—quickly scrambled away from Sawyer and began moving toward the door. Sawyer flipped his leg out, catching the man across the ankles, causing him to stumble, but not fall all the way to the ground.

Both men raced to get to their feet. It was obvious that Hoodie didn't want to stay and fight; he just wanted to get away. Sawyer didn't plan on allowing that to happen.

Ignoring the pain in his arm, Sawyer ran to get his weapon. Hoodie took off in the opposite direction down the stairs. Sawyer was just moments behind him, weapon in hand.

"Stop. You're under arrest," Sawyer called out as the man reached the bottom of the stairs. "Don't force me to use my weapon."

When Sawyer reached the bottom of the stairs, he saw that the man had stopped, but now he was using Megan as a shield. Megan had obviously left her place by the door to come see what the commotion was upstairs and walked right into Hoodie's path. His knife was pointed at her throat.

Sawyer looked Megan in the eyes; she seemed frightened, but not injured. He tried to reassure her with a glance and saw her slide the countermeasure drive into the inside of her jacket. That was his girl—using that giant brain of hers. Hoodie had no idea how close the item he'd been looking for actually was. Sawyer gave his full attention back to the man.

Caucasian. Six feet tall. Close to a hundred and eighty pounds, but light on his feet. Well-balanced.

And a knife at Megan's throat.

The man slowly backed his way toward the door, bringing Megan with him. The perp didn't say anything, but kept himself well hidden behind his human shield. There was no way Sawyer could get off a clean shot.

With each step the hooded man took backward, Sawyer took one forward, weapon still raised and ready to fire. When they reached the front door, Hoodie opened it with one hand, the knife at Megan's throat still in the other.

Sawyer knew the man was going to have to turn and run in just a moment. Sawyer was ready for the chase, knowing he wouldn't be able to use his weapon. He couldn't just shoot a perpetrator in the back as he was running down the sidewalk. This wasn't an action movie. Sawyer had laws he had to obey.

But instead of turning to run, Hoodie took a step forward. The next thing Sawyer knew, Megan was flying toward him—shoved by the assailant with enough force to knock Sawyer down as he attempted to catch her. Hoodie took advantage of their predicament, darting outside.

Sawyer got back on his feet and out the door just in time to see the other man get into his vehicle parked down the street and drive away. Sawyer slammed the side of his fist on the door frame.

"He's gone. There's no way I can catch him now." Sawyer turned back to Megan. She was still on the floor, having scooted so her back was against the wall. Her arms were wrapped around her knees. Sawyer crouched down next to her, running a hand over her hair.

"Are you okay, sweetheart? Did he hurt you?"

Megan unwrapped her arms from her legs and sat up, leaning her head against the wall. "I'm okay. He just scared me out of my mind. I know you said there might be someone still here, but I didn't really think there was. Then I heard the noise upstairs…" Sawyer saw a tear escape one of her eyes.

Sawyer sat all the way down next to her, picked her up and deposited her in his lap. "I'm sorry he got past me. But I'm glad you're okay."

"Does the rest of the house look like it does in here?" Megan gestured to the living room with one hand.

Sawyer hesitated, but there was no point beating around the bush. "Yes. I'm sorry, Megan. It looks like he destroyed pretty much everything."

Sawyer thought Megan might lose it over that news, but she held it together. She wrapped an arm around him and squeezed, then stood up. He knew exactly when she noticed his arm.

"Oh my gosh, you're bleeding, Sawyer. Why didn't you tell me you were hurt? Here I am talking about all my stuff and you're hurt!"

"It's not bad, promise. He came out of the closet cutting at me, but I had on my jacket and shirt, so it's not very deep."

"Do you need stitches?"

"No, definitely not. Maybe just a bandage if you have some upstairs."

"Yes, come up. I'll wrap it for you."

"Megan, you should know, it's not pretty up there."

Megan took a deep breath. "It's just stuff, I know. I keep telling myself it's just stuff. But it's still pretty hard."

"I know it must be." He began walking up the stairs.

"This is tied in to whoever was in the office earlier tonight, isn't it? The one who overheard us talking about the countermeasure breakthrough."

"Without a doubt. The assailant who broke in here obviously thought you'd be here alone with the countermeasure." Sawyer didn't even want to think about that. "You weren't here, so he thought he'd check to make sure you hadn't left it lying around."

They entered Megan's bedroom, where all her clothing lay in shambles. All the color left Megan's face as she realized the extent of the damage. Almost everything she owned had been damaged or destroyed.

"He definitely wasn't subtle about it," Sawyer continued. "And it looks like he just got angrier as he kept searching."

Megan reached down and began to pick up the clothes on the floor, but Sawyer stopped her.

"I know it's hard, but just leave it. I'll have Omega send a local law-enforcement team over here to process this as a crime scene."

Megan dropped the piece of clothing back onto the ground. "My first-aid kit is in the bathroom."

While Megan was getting out the bandage for his arm, Sawyer removed his jacket and shirt, then called Evan

Karcz at Omega. He put the phone on speaker so he could talk while Megan was bandaging his upper arm.

"Evan, it's Sawyer."

"Hey, Sawyer, how's it going with your hot little scientist?"

Megan raised one eyebrow and Sawyer gave her a wry grin. "You mean Dr. Fuller, who is standing right here with me while you're on speaker?"

"Um, yes, well. What I meant was—"

"Save it, Evan." Sawyer could hear the other man's audible sigh of relief in having gotten out of that one. "There's been a break-in at Megan's house."

"DS-13 related?"

"Definitely." Sawyer winced slightly as Megan put some antiseptic on his arm. "It's been totally ransacked. They were looking for the countermeasure. Thankfully, they didn't get their hands on that or the second version of Ghost Shell, or DS-13 would be unstoppable. We had some suspicious activity at Cyberdyne a couple of hours ago, as well." Sawyer explained the incident with the unknown person in the lab.

"So what's the plan?" Evan asked.

"I'm going to have Omega send some locals out here to process Megan's place."

"It sounds like both her work and home have been compromised."

Sawyer shifted so Megan could wrap his arm with a bandage. "When I call in, I'm going to get a local safe house where we can lie low for a few days. But I wanted you to be aware that DS-13 is getting more aggressive. First the car accident, now this."

"There's definite movement in DS-13 with whatever version of Ghost Shell they have. And interestingly enough, whatever is happening is in Old Fort, North Carolina. I'm heading there right now. That's relatively close to you, isn't it?"

Sawyer looked at Megan and she nodded. "Thirty minutes," she told them.

"DS-13 has put word out again that they'll have something to sell—something of great interest—*soon*. A lot of big-name buyers are coming in."

"Including Bob Sinclair?" Sawyer still didn't like this plan of Evan's. There were too many ways Sawyer's sister, Juliet, could get drawn in.

"Yeah, but just Bob. No partner this time." Evan was trying to reassure him, Sawyer knew. "But whatever you guys are doing, Sawyer? Do it soon, man. Things are starting to get hinky out here."

"All right. Be careful, Evan. I guess we both might be out of touch for a while."

"Will do," Evan responded. "You, too."

Sawyer ended the call.

"All right, I patched you up as well as my medical expertise would allow. But I take no responsibility for anything if you get gangrene and your arm falls off." Megan began putting away the first-aid kit, then stopped and just threw it on the counter. "This place is going to have to be burned to the ground anyway."

She turned away and looked back into the bedroom. Sawyer put his shirt back on.

"You can't stay here. Even after the police process it, it's not safe for you to stay here."

"I know." Megan's words were soft, her look lost.

Sawyer reached down and grabbed her hand, twining their fingers together. "We'll make it through this together. But right now we need to get out of here in case our vicious friend decides to come back with friends of his own."

## Chapter Twelve

They found a pair of pants and a sweater that hadn't been destroyed and gathered whatever toiletries could be salvaged before heading back to Sawyer's car. Megan took a last look into her house as she was closing the door and about to lock it. What was the point in locking it? If somebody broke in now, they'd probably just run out screaming the way they'd come.

The place she had carved out for herself, her haven, was destroyed. Sure, a lot of it could be replaced: furniture, appliances, clothing. Megan held ample insurance to cover it. But she knew she'd never sit in that house again and feel the same safe, secure level of comfort she had for the past few years.

Megan forced the thought of her house and all her belongings from her mind as she got into Sawyer's car. If she thought about them too much right now, she'd be a basket case. She turned and laid her cheek against the cold glass of the passenger-side window.

"I'm going to take you to my hotel for now. I've got to call all of this in, and you need a few hours' rest."

Megan was too exhausted to argue even if she wanted to. But she didn't want to.

"This is only for a few hours," Sawyer continued. "DS-13 has been putting forth quite a bit of effort to halt the development of the countermeasure. And if what Evan said is accurate, we don't have a lot of time before DS-13 is ready to sell their version of Ghost Shell."

Megan nodded wearily. "I can get started on it again at Cyberdyne first thing tomorrow."

Sawyer shook his head. "I don't think that's going to work. Cyberdyne is too dangerous. Whoever is working for DS-13 on the inside? We don't know who that is or what that person is prepared to do."

Trish Wilborne, the programmer, came to mind at Sawyer's words. Was she the traitor? Time-wise it would make sense. But Megan didn't know if her exhausted brain could be trusted, so she didn't say anything to Sawyer about it.

"I have the critical elements of the countermeasure, but I still need some items from Cyberdyne if I'm going to work on it somewhere else."

"Like what?"

Megan closed her eyes, her face still against the window. "Well, in a perfect world I would need a clean room where I could control environmental pollutants, my electron microscope, a randomizer, EEPROM programmer, a particular digital signal processing chip and programmer, power supplies, capacitors, a breadboard—"

Megan would've continued, but Sawyer reached over and touched her gently on the arm.

"All right, I get it, although I didn't understand half those words. I'll talk to Omega about getting us a safe house where you can work, hopefully some sort of lab, but it probably won't have all of that."

"I could still do it without all of that, but it wouldn't be optimal."

"Well, be thinking about the bare minimum you need, just in case."

Megan nodded, closing her eyes and laying her head back against the headrest. She would think about what items she really needed, but not right now. She was just too tired.

They pulled up at the hotel where Sawyer had been staying when he wasn't sleeping at her office or on her couch. Megan could barely force her muscles to move from the car. She opened the door, but couldn't muster the strength to get out.

Sawyer came around and crouched down next to her open door.

"Hey." His friendly smile was ridiculously sexy. He probably had no idea. Or maybe he did. Megan could only stare at him. "You doing okay?"

"I think I might be broken. I can't seem to get out of the car."

Sawyer reached over and tucked a strand of hair behind her ear and trailed his fingers along her cheek. It was all Megan could do not to lean into his hand. "You've been through quite a lot in the last thirty-six hours. Not much sleep, and then periods of intense adrenaline."

"And a knife at my throat."

"That, too, definitely. It's enough to make anyone's body shut down."

Sawyer stood, reaching into the car to help her out. Megan was glad to find her legs could support her own weight.

"Do I need to carry you?"

"That would be mighty conspicuous, wouldn't it? You carrying me through the lobby and hallway?" Megan giggled.

Sawyer gave her that smile again. "Probably. But no more conspicuous than you keeling over in the middle of the lobby."

"I'll be all right. I'm feeling better."

"You look better." He ran a finger down her cheek. "At least you have a little bit of your color back—you looked pretty traumatized there for a while." Sawyer grabbed the small bag they had packed from her house, slipped his arm around her waist and led them inside and up to his room.

Sawyer only turned on one small light in his room and led Megan directly to one of the beds, pulling the blankets back.

"In you go. You've got to get some rest. We need to go back to Cyberdyne in a few hours for the items you need before anybody shows up there for work."

Megan didn't argue with him, just slipped off her jacket and shoes and lay down in the bed. "What time is it right now?"

"Almost midnight. Get some sleep, sweetheart."

"Don't you need to sleep, too?" The words came out slurred. Now that Megan was lying down, she could barely force herself to stay awake.

"I will. I need to make some phone calls to Omega. But you get the rest you need. I'll be fine."

It was the last thing she heard before sleep claimed her.

SAWYER WATCHED MEGAN fall asleep right in the middle of their conversation. That was fine; her body and mind were obviously exhausted. Sawyer tucked the sheet and comforter around her more securely. He wished he could erase that traumatized look she'd had at her house. How the hell were things snowballing out of control so fast?

Sawyer moved to the table on the opposite side of the room so he was less likely to disturb Megan, although he doubted anything would wake her up right now. He dialed in to Omega, wishing his sister, Juliet, was at the office. She worked an odd mixture of desk jobs at Omega—part analyst, part handler. She was too good to really be either, but that was what she wanted right now, and Sawyer and his brothers supported her.

But it was midnight, so Juliet probably wouldn't be in

the office when Sawyer called in requesting the specialized safe house he and Megan needed so she could get the countermeasure work finished. He'd just be talking to a random handler. Not how Sawyer preferred it, but right now his only option.

Sawyer made the call, first providing his credential and identification codes. He then gave the handler the information about the break-in at Megan's home and their need for a specific type of safe house. Sawyer felt better after the call was completed. Although Sawyer didn't know the handler personally, he seemed competent and ready to find Sawyer what he needed. Sawyer knew local law enforcement would be called out to Megan's house and the scene processed. If anything of any value showed up, Sawyer would be notified immediately.

Knowing that was taken care of, Sawyer felt more relaxed. It was now nearly one o'clock in the morning. Sawyer knew he needed sleep himself. Sawyer looked at Megan's sleeping form in the bed. She had held up so well over the past couple of days, but he was afraid things were only going to get more difficult. If what Evan said was true and DS-13 was really close to having their version of Ghost Shell ready, he and Megan had to work even more quickly than Sawyer had originally thought.

DS-13 calling buyers to an area so close to them here in Asheville really caught Sawyer's attention in the same way it had caught Evan's. Had DS-13 gotten someone from Cyberdyne to help them finish their Ghost Shell? Was it the same person who had been sabotaging the countermeasure work?

That would make a lot of sense.

Sawyer knew Megan had a hard time thinking of one of her team in the R & D department being the culprit, but it had to be. He and Megan needed to get to Cyberdyne, retrieve the necessary items and get out before that person came in to work tomorrow. Sawyer would then take Megan to a secure location so she could finish her countermeasure magic.

Sawyer kicked off his shoes and lay down in the bed next to Megan. The thought of sleeping in the other bed—even for the few short hours they had—wasn't even an option. In his mind, Sawyer kept seeing that knife pointed at Megan's throat. It was a picture he'd take with him to the grave.

Megan was lying on her side, facing away from him. Sawyer slid one arm under her shoulder, wrapping it around her, hooked his other arm around her hips and slid her back against him. Megan murmured sleepily for just a moment, then relaxed in his embrace.

As tired as he was, Sawyer wanted to enjoy a few moments of just holding her. It was an unusual feeling for Sawyer—he didn't tend to be a cuddling type of guy. But something about Megan brought out his protective instincts. Maybe it was her savvy brilliance layered with shy beauty. An odd mixture, unique to Megan.

Megan was unique and appealing to Sawyer in ways he never thought possible.

Sawyer pushed those thoughts out of his mind. He was here to protect her and to do whatever needed to be done to get the countermeasure complete. And although she was an itch he definitely hoped to scratch at some point, there was no need to get caught up with flowery emotions.

He liked her. He was sexually attracted to her and was sure she was attracted to him, too. But she was the job. He'd do well not to forget that.

Sawyer fell asleep pulling *the job* closer to him.

MEGAN AWOKE TO Sawyer gently squeezing her shoulder. He was standing right beside her, freshly showered and ready to go.

"Good morning." He smiled at her, but it wasn't the same

relaxed grin he'd had last night. "I know you must still be tired, but we need to get to Cyberdyne before anyone else arrives there."

Megan sat up. "What time is it?"

"Almost 4:30. You need more rest, I know, but like I said—"

"No, it's okay." Megan swung her legs over the side of the bed. "Just let me take a quick shower and we can be on our way."

"Sure." Sawyer had already sat down, typing something into his phone, not really paying her much attention.

Megan wasn't sure what she had expected—a good-morning kiss? More of his sexy smiles? She couldn't put her finger on what the problem was, but it seemed as if last night's quiet intimacy—at the restaurant, before the traumatic break-in and even afterward when they'd arrived here at the hotel—was now gone.

But Megan could've sworn in the middle of the night, when she'd barely woken up for just a moment, that she'd been lying in Sawyer's arms. Maybe her unconscious mind had imagined it just to soothe her.

Megan glanced over at Sawyer again. He was still messing with his phone. Megan began to speak to him, but then decided to leave it alone. She walked to the shower instead.

The shower helped her feel better, washing away some of the feeling of violation that had come from seeing everything she owned in shambles. The hot water and few hours' sleep fortified her; she felt stronger, not so overwhelmed. Ready to get the countermeasure finished.

And Sawyer had a lot on his mind. There was no reason to assume he was creating distance between the two of them on purpose. He was stressed trying to figure out who the traitor was at Cyberdyne, keep Megan safe, get ahead of DS-13. It was a lot. And she'd only talked to him for two minutes, and not her most alert two minutes at that. No need to borrow trouble.

Megan changed into her recovered outfit and put on what makeup she had. She quickly braided her hair so that it fell neatly down her back.

Coming out of the bathroom, Megan heard Sawyer on the phone. Whoever he was talking to, Sawyer wasn't happy with the conversation.

"We knew there was a probable security breach, Mr. Cory. That's why I was sent here in the first place."

Ah, he was talking to Cyberdyne's head of security, Ted Cory. Sawyer gave Megan a curt nod of acknowledgment.

"Dr. Fuller needs to finish the project she's working on. I'm not exaggerating when I say it's of national-security importance that she finish it."

More talk from the other side. Sawyer stood up in disgust.

"We've already established that the Cyberdyne labs have been compromised, Cory. She can't work there safely. The Cyberdyne board of directors isn't taking into account—"

Megan watched as Sawyer's grip on the phone became white-knuckled.

"No, the FBI doesn't have a subpoena for the equipment. So, yes, it is still Cyberdyne's property." Sawyer shook his head. "Then I guess she'll have to work on it at the lab. But I want it on record that I don't think this is the best solution. Dr. Fuller is sleeping right now, so tell the lab not to expect her until midday. She'll bring the countermeasure with her when she comes in."

Sawyer listened, rubbing his eyes.

"When are you meeting with the security team to let them know? Fine. If it's okay, I'll sit in on the meeting in case I can be of any assistance to you or answer any questions."

Sawyer disconnected the call and all but threw his phone down on the table in disgust.

"So, that didn't sound very promising."

"I called the head of security to bring him up to speed. I was about to let him know your badge had been stolen and that we were coming in to get the equipment you need in just a few minutes. Then he informed me that Cyberdyne is basically on lockdown in terms of equipment."

"What? They've never done anything like that. I've always been able to take work home with me as long as I clear it through the right channels."

"Evidently there was a meeting with the president and board of directors sometime yesterday with concerns about what is happening security-wise. Nothing—equipment, technology—is supposed to leave Cyberdyne. You're required to return Ghost Shell and the countermeasure immediately. Cory's holding a meeting to notify the entire security team of the new policy at seven o'clock."

"So I'll have to work at Cyberdyne." Megan didn't like the idea, but didn't see any way around it.

For the first time Sawyer really looked at her. The hardness in his eyes softened and he crossed the room to sit next to her at the foot of the bed. "Megan, if you do that, we'll be playing directly into DS-13's hands. They want us trapped there at Cyberdyne, where you're always being watched and they can keep trying to do damage."

"You believe DS-13 is behind the lockdown at Cyberdyne? Do you think Cory is in on it?"

"DS-13 behind the lockdown wouldn't surprise me. Omega recently found out that DS-13 is more far-reaching and powerful than we thought. But I doubt Cory is actually working for them. The pressure on the chief of security for the lockdown at Cyberdyne is coming from the board of directors. It would've been very easy for DS-13 to just put a bug in the ear of one of the board members about security. Then sit back and watch it domino. Cory is just a pawn."

Megan took a deep breath and blew it out, shrugging.

"Regardless of who put pressure on whom or why, the outcome is still the same. They're not going to let us take anything out."

"That's right. Once Cory has the meeting at seven o'clock with the security team, nothing's getting out. Furthermore, they're expecting you to be in around noon and to turn over all Cyberdyne property you have in your possession."

Sawyer was looking at her intensely. The way he emphasized his words were odd. Then it clicked for Megan—Sawyer wasn't telling her these details because he had accepted them as their circumstances. He was telling her so she also could see the tiny hole they were about to try to fit through.

"But I'm not going to be there at noon, am I?" Megan asked him. "We're still going right now to get everything out before security learns about the new policy."

Sawyer nodded and took her hand. "That was my thinking. But you have to be sure, Megan. You and I know how important the countermeasure is, but Cyberdyne probably is not going to see it that way—at least not for a while, if ever."

Megan looked down to where Sawyer had linked his hand with hers. Gone was the coldness and distance she had felt between them earlier. "I know," she whispered.

"Omega will do its best to explain to Cyberdyne why you did this, and why it was important and necessary, but it won't make a difference for a while. You'll basically be cut off from Cyberdyne."

Megan didn't want to waste any more precious time arguing about this. Losing her job was nothing compared to the cost of a terrorist group having access to the damaging capacities of Ghost Shell with nothing in place to stop the damage. It would basically turn the government's own communication equipment against itself—crippling law-enforcement agencies and first responders. It would leave the country wide-open and vulnerable for an attack.

Thinking about it that way, Megan didn't even have a choice. She had to get the countermeasure completed and in place as soon as possible. No matter what it cost her.

Megan stood. "Let's go. We don't have any time to waste if we want to get in and out before the security briefing."

Sawyer stood up and drew her into his arms for a tight hug. Megan leaned in to him, trying to draw some of his strength. "You're amazing," he whispered. They pulled apart, gathered their stuff and headed out the door.

Megan couldn't help but think she'd already lost her car and her home in an attempt to complete this project. Plus now it looked as though she was about to lose her job.

Megan glanced at Sawyer walking beside her in the hallway. He reached over and put an arm around her, pulling her to his side as they walked. He looked down at her— warm, sexy smile back in place.

Megan just hoped by the time it was all over she wouldn't also lose her heart.

## Chapter Thirteen

When Sawyer had awakened that morning—his internal clock making an alarm unnecessary—Megan had still been wrapped in his arms. Except to turn to face each other, he didn't think either of them moved from the embrace the entire time they had slept. Staring into her face—her features so relaxed and young-looking in sleep—Sawyer knew the best thing he could do was put some distance between them. Before things became any more complicated than they already were.

He could tell that Megan picked up on it right away. Her giant brain had been working at full capacity from the moment she opened those brown eyes. She hadn't said anything, but he'd recognized the slight confusion over his withdrawal.

Of course, that decision to withdraw had been shot to hell when Sawyer saw—once again—Megan's strength and determination. Her willingness to sacrifice her job, although hopefully it wouldn't come down to that in the long run, and do what had to be done with the countermeasure spoke volumes about her. Sawyer found he wasn't able, and sure as hell wasn't willing, to try to keep the distance between them when she was willing to put so much of herself on the line.

He'd just have to deal with the tomorrows as they came.

Right now, he wanted to keep Megan as close as possible. He glanced over at her in the passenger side of the car to make sure she was okay. Her eyes were worried, but she gave him one of her shy smiles.

Sawyer had been smiled at by many women over the years, but none of them took his breath away the way Megan did.

Sawyer's phone buzzed, catching his attention. It was Omega, with a secure code, letting Sawyer know they had received his update about the circumstances at Cyberdyne changing and his plan to remove the equipment needed to finish the countermeasure. An appropriate safe-house address would be delivered soon.

That was the great thing about working for an elite task force like Omega: the ends justifying the means was regular practice. Bending some rules when necessary, such as removing needed items from a company, even though said company had forbidden it, wasn't even frowned upon in Omega. Omega always kept the big picture as the priority. And the big picture now was getting that countermeasure finished.

Sawyer was glad they would have the safe house ready soon—once he and Megan left Cyberdyne with the stolen equipment, there would be no coming back. They were pulling through the outer gate of Cyberdyne security now. Sawyer showed the guard both his temporary Cyberdyne badge and his law-enforcement credentials and the guard waved them through.

Sawyer relaxed just the slightest bit. The guard hadn't asked to see Megan's security badge, nor had he seemed to recognize who she was, so obviously the security team wasn't on high alert yet. Which was good, because Megan didn't have a badge to show him.

Sawyer parked the car in the closest spot to the front door, not difficult since the lot was nearly empty. He backed the car in so it faced forward out of the parking spot. It might save them precious seconds if they were leaving in a hurry. But Sawyer hoped it wouldn't come down to that.

Sawyer turned to look at Megan. "All right, sweetheart, are you ready? Remember, we can't take the flux capacitor and everything else you listed last night." Megan's eyes narrowed at the '80s movie reference, but he didn't stop to explain it to her. "Only the most essential items. And only what we can carry out in a backpack, very low-key."

Megan nodded. "I know what I need. But I should warn you, if I get bored and want to build a DeLorean time-travel machine, that's going to be difficult without a flux capacitor."

Sawyer reached over and kissed her. He couldn't help it. "Then by all means, grab the first flux capacitor you see."

They got out of the car, the brisk winter air surrounding them, the sun having not even risen yet. "Okay, just try to act as natural and relaxed as possible. There should only be security guards around at this time. Just talk to those you normally would, and keep it as brief as possible." Sawyer ushered her in the door. They needed to get a move on; it was already nearly 6:00 a.m.

Sawyer used his badge, which almost had the same clearance as hers anyway, to get them in the main Cyberdyne doors. The overnight guard working the front desk seemed a little surprised to see anyone coming through the door at this hour, but not suspicious. Sawyer saw the guard slide a magazine of dubious type to the side and under some papers.

Good, let the guard be more worried about getting caught looking through his dirty magazines while on the job than wondering why he and Megan were here at such an early hour. Or worse, wanting to see Megan's badge.

"I've met a lot of the security team, but not you. I'm

Agent Branson. Dr. Fuller and I are getting an early start on the day."

The man swallowed hard. He knew he'd been caught doing something worth reprimand. "Uh, yes, sir."

Before the man could flounder any more, Sawyer cut him off. "I understand you have a full security team briefing at 0700? I'll be there for that." The man nodded. "Until then, I trust that this front door is being watched more by security than it was when I entered?" The man nodded again, wide-eyed.

"Um, yes, sir. Sorry, sir."

Sawyer just turned and led Megan down the hall.

"Wow, pretty impressive, Agent Branson," Megan said once they were out of earshot. "I didn't think you had that in you."

Sawyer winked at her. "Well, sometimes boyishly charming is not the way you want to go. Now that guy will be worried that I'm going to bring up at the security meeting the reading of certain types of magazines at the front desk while on duty. He won't be thinking about what we're doing at all."

"Who has a giant brain now?" Megan asked him.

Sawyer smiled and used his badge to let them into the R & D lab. "Okay, get what you need and let's get out. Is there anything I can help you find?"

"No, I know what I need and where to find it, but it will take a while. Some of it has to be separated from the main system and programmed to be available for use elsewhere. That means I'll need to…" Megan was already walking toward what she needed as she spoke, her voice trailing off.

Sawyer kept an eye on the door as Megan moved frantically around the lab. Every once in a while he could hear her talking, but knew she wasn't speaking to him. She was having arguments with herself, so he left her alone.

Sawyer logged in to the security system so he could see who was coming into the building. A few early birds, mostly sales or office managers had logged in, but no one from R & D yet, thankfully.

"How's it going?" Sawyer called out.

"I'm almost done. Five minutes. I just need to bypass this system." Sawyer could hear her fingers clicking on the keyboard.

Five minutes was okay. That should give them enough time to get out before Ted Cory got there for the seven-o'clock meeting. If he saw Megan here, after Sawyer told him she wouldn't be in until midday, they were sunk.

But then the screen flashed an ID badge Sawyer was definitely not expecting.

Megan's. Damn.

Whoever had stolen Megan's badge yesterday was back. Even worse, this meant as soon as Cory arrived, he would be alerted that Megan was in the building.

Sawyer watched the screen as Megan's assistant, Jon Bushman, and Trish Wilborne also logged in through the front door at the same time. They were obviously coming in together. Megan's theory of Trish being the mole was looking more conceivable.

Things were going to hell quickly.

"Megan, time to go," Sawyer called out. "Right now. We've got all sorts of problems."

Megan rushed over to the desk with the backpack full of the items she needed. "Okay, I've got it all. What's going on?"

"Well, *you* just logged through the main door."

"The person who stole my ID badge?"

"Yep." Sawyer cursed under his breath when he saw the next entry in the front door. Ted Cory, head of Cyber-dyne security.

"All right, we've got to get out of here. Everybody and their brother has decided to show up early."

"Who?"

"Both Jon Bushman and Trish Wilborne showed up together, not long after your badge was swiped through the door."

"Trish Wilborne? I really think she's the mole, Sawyer. It makes more sense than anybody else."

"I'm beginning to agree with you. But we've got another problem now, too. Ted Cory just logged in. Damn it, we've got to get out of here."

Megan handed Sawyer the bag full of equipment. "Here, you take the stuff and go. Get it out of the building. That's the most important thing. I'll say my hellos, act like everything is normal and get out as soon as I can."

Sawyer didn't like the thought of splitting up, but didn't see any way around it. Jon and Trish were going to be here any moment. And Ted Cory would check the log first thing and find out Megan was in the building. Once he did that, neither she nor Sawyer would be able to leave with any items.

But Sawyer was afraid Cory might not let Megan leave at all.

"Okay, we'll split up. I'm going directly to the car. You get out of here as soon as you can behind me. Don't let Ted Cory corner you. You won't have a bag, so that's not quite so suspicious, but he can demand that you return Ghost Shell and the countermeasure, and if you don't he could have you arrested."

Megan nodded.

"Don't let anybody get you alone. We don't know who we can trust, so we can't trust anyone," Sawyer continued. Megan nodded again. Sawyer could hear Jonathan and Trish talking as they entered in the door to the R & D lab.

Sawyer bent down and kissed Megan hard, briefly. "I'm going to stay out of sight until I can get past those two. Hurry," he told her and strode out one of the side doors, so no one could see him. He didn't like this at all, but he didn't see any other choice.

MEGAN WATCHED SAWYER disappear around the corner just as Jon and Trish walked in. Megan clutched her hands in front of her. What was she going to say to them?

*Just act normal.*

That probably included not jumping on Trish and punching the other woman until she admitted she was the traitor. And it was barely six o'clock in the morning. What were they doing here so early?

And why were they here together at this hour? The pair hadn't noticed Megan yet and she watched as Trish brushed up against Jonathan and he smiled down at her.

How long had this been going on? Had Trish seduced Jonathan? Was she trying to get close to him to get information? Or maybe access to something he had that she didn't? It would make sense. Jonathan looked completely enamored with Trish.

How had Megan never noticed this before? Jonathan was always so tense and uptight around the office. Megan had never actually thought about his personal life outside Cyberdyne.

But evidently he had one. And evidently Trish was part of it. For how long Megan didn't know.

Megan was supposed to act normal around them. But what was normal? Normal for not suspecting one of them was a lying traitor was different than the normal reaction for the boss finding out two underlings were sleeping together.

Both of which were a different normal from having to get the hell out of there as quickly as possible to avoid arrest.

"Oh my gosh, Megan!" Trish finally noticed her. Trish

and Jonathan all but leaped apart. "What are you doing here so early?"

Megan had to hand it to Trish, she didn't look panicked at seeing Megan here at Cyberdyne, just embarrassed at being caught in an illicit situation. "Maybe I should be asking you guys the same thing," she told them, one eyebrow raised.

Trish and Jonathan looked at each other briefly, then back at Megan.

"Actually," Jonathan spoke up, not quite meeting Megan's eyes, "we thought we would get here early and get our work out of the way, then try to talk you into letting us help with the countermeasure when you got in. But you're already here."

Megan wanted to stay and ask more questions—see if she could get any information out of Trish in particular—but knew she needed to get going. Once Ted Cory knew she was in the building, getting out would be much more difficult.

Plus, it wouldn't take Trish or Jonathan long to figure out items were missing if they got back in the lab and started looking around.

"Actually, I've been here all night." Megan ran a hand over her face in mock exhaustion, hoping they wouldn't notice she was in different clothes. She decided not to bring up the obvious relationship between Trish and Jonathan. She didn't have time, and compared to everything else that was going on, it really didn't matter. "I'm about to go get some breakfast at the cafeteria and head outside for a few minutes to get some air."

Megan began walking to the door, but realized she didn't have her badge. The badge was needed to get in or out of the R & D lab.

"Hey, Jon, do you mind scanning the door for me? I left my badge in my office. I just want to grab something to eat super quick." Megan spoke to Jonathan, but looked right at Trish, searching for any changes in her expression that might give the other woman away. But there was nothing. As a matter of fact, Trish was just staring at Jonathan, looking gooey.

But the question seemed to catch Jonathan off guard. "Um, what? Well, sure, that's no problem, I guess." He walked over, scanned his badge and opened the door.

"Okay, thanks. I'll see you guys in a few minutes."

"Should we get started on anything?" Trish called out to Megan just as she was turning away. "I know you said you didn't want anybody else working on the countermeasure, but Jon and I were talking about it and we really think we could help."

Yeah, Megan just bet Trish thought she could help. Jonathan shot an irritated look at Trish, then smiled sheepishly at Megan. "Whatever, boss. Just wanted you to know we were ready to help if you need it."

Megan glanced down the hallway; the way she needed to go was all clear. But when she looked the other way, a door was opening. Ted Cory stepped out into Megan's line of sight.

She needed to leave. Right now.

"Thanks, Jon. We'll talk about it when I get back from breakfast, okay? I'm famished."

Jon was about to respond, but Megan turned and began walking down the hallway.

"Megan, how are you going to get back in the lab without your badge?" Jon walked out after her.

Megan turned, but kept taking steps in the direction of the exit. "I'll just have security let me in. No problem." She could see Ted Cory making his way toward them. He would see her any second.

"Well, just hang on, I'll run and get the badge for you, so you can have it."

Megan did her best to keep Jonathan between her and the director of security so he wouldn't be able to see her, but that wouldn't work for long. She stopped her backward walk so she could get rid of Jonathan. She didn't want him trying to come with her all the way to the cafeteria, where he thought she was going.

"That would be great, Jon. Thanks so much."

Jonathan nodded and turned back toward the R & D lab. As soon as his back was to her, Megan began walking briskly down the hall. She glanced over her shoulder and saw Ted Cory talking to Jonathan. Evidently he asked Jonathan where Megan was, because Jon was pointing right at her. Ted turned and began moving in her direction.

Megan walked as fast as she could without outright running. She didn't want anyone to put the building on lock-down because of suspicious behavior on her part. Then she'd never get out. Megan wasn't far from the main doors.

She didn't know why Ted Cory wasn't calling after her. Maybe Jonathan had told him she was going to the cafeteria and he planned to follow her there to talk to her.

Megan made it to the main foyer. If she turned to the left she would only have a little bit to go to get to the main doors, but knew she wouldn't have enough time to make it to them if Cory radioed for the locks to be set. So instead she turned to the right as if she was going to the cafeteria.

Halfway down that much shorter hall she looked over her shoulder. It looked as if Ted Cory wasn't following her anymore, or if he was he had paused for a moment. Megan ducked inside the women's bathroom.

Megan waited, ear pressed against the door, hoping to hear the security chief pass her. She prayed he would think she had gone the few more yards to the cafeteria. Although all he really had to do was stay at the security desk near the front door. She wouldn't be able to get past him.

After just a few moments she could hear someone talking as they went down the hallway. It was definitely Ted Cory, sounding as though he was talking to another one of the guards.

"I want you to keep an eye on her while we have the all-hands meeting. She is not to leave this building under any circumstances until I have a chance to interrogate her."

Megan didn't like the sound of the word *interrogate*.

Their voices became softer as they passed by the restroom door and continued toward the cafeteria. As silently as she could, Megan opened the door and began walking back toward the main door, praying Cory hadn't said anything to whoever was working the front desk.

She forced herself not to look back as she quickly covered the ground to the main door. She smiled at the security guard at the desk—he smiled back, so evidently Cory hadn't talked to him about her yet—and continued casually toward the door.

"Going outside?" the guard asked.

"Yeah, just need some fresh air." Megan smiled again, but kept walking.

Damn. Megan realized she didn't have her badge. She couldn't get through the door at this hour without it and definitely didn't want to ask the security guard to help.

Megan pretended to crouch down and tie her shoe while she got out her phone and sent a text to Sawyer to meet her at the door. She knew the car wasn't very far; he could be here in just a few moments if she could just stall.

Megan tied the other shoe while she was down there and pretended to dust something off her foot. There, that should be enough time for Sawyer to be at the door once she crossed the lobby. Megan stood, ready to move.

She was startled by a hand grasping her shoulder and spinning her around. Ted Cory stood glaring at her.

"I got a message earlier that you would be here this morning earlier than I had been told. Going somewhere, Dr. Fuller?"

## Chapter Fourteen

Megan kept her expression neutral and her posture relaxed as she faced the director of security, hardly listening to what he was saying. She thought fast.

"Hi, Mr. Cory. Just thought I'd step outside for a few moments to get a little fresh air. It's been a long couple of days—I've put in a bunch of hours. I'm feeling pretty stiff."

As if to demonstrate, Megan reached her arms over her head and linked her hands, stretching her back and torso. She glanced over and saw Sawyer walking up to the glass Cyberdyne doors. Megan shifted to the side so Mr. Cory would be less likely to see Sawyer's approach.

She was going to have to make a run for it. Megan hoped Sawyer would be ready. Once she began running, he would only have a few short moments to get the door open before a member of security remotely overrode the locks. The chances of Megan getting out were slim. At best.

"You don't have any items belonging to Cyberdyne on your person, do you, Dr. Fuller? You may or may not have heard, but due to recent security issues we are initiating a mandatory lockdown policy. No items are to be taken from the building."

Megan patted down her thin sweater. "Nothing on me, Mr. Cory. And I think the lockdown is an excellent idea. It's important for Cyberdyne items to be safe."

Mr. Cory still looked at her sternly, standing between her and the door.

"The policy also means you'll need to return any items you've taken out of Cyberdyne. Even if it was acceptable in the past for you to remove them, it no longer is."

"Absolutely." Megan nodded enthusiastically. "I brought everything in with me this morning. They're all in the R & D vault. Would you like to come down with me and see?"

Cory relaxed minutely. Obviously he felt if Megan was willing to escort him to the R & D vault she really had returned the items she'd taken yesterday. Either that or Cory knew he'd have Megan in his office for interrogation if she hadn't. Either way, Cory felt he had Megan where he wanted her.

This was Megan's best chance to escape, while Cory was slightly more relaxed. "Dang it, this shoe just won't stay tied." While bending down to tie her shoe again, Megan glanced out the door. Sawyer was there. Ready.

Megan threw herself upright, grasping her arm with the other hand and jabbing her elbow as forcefully as she could into Ted Cory's stomach.

Not expecting the blow, the man doubled over. Megan began running for the door as fast as she could. Behind her just moments later she could hear the commotion as the other security guards struggled to figure out what was going on.

Megan saw Sawyer use his badge to open the sliding doors. They slid all the way open, but almost immediately began closing again. One of the guards was manually overriding the door.

Megan ran faster. There were only a few yards to go, but she wasn't going to make it.

Then Sawyer moved forward and wedged himself in the closing door, his back against one edge, foot and hands against the other. Megan knew he wouldn't be able to hold it for long, and once it shut she wouldn't be able to get out.

"C'mon, baby, you can make it," Sawyer called to her, teeth gritted, body straining.

In a final burst of speed, Megan scampered through the door opening, under Sawyer's leg where he was holding it with all his strength. As soon as she was through, Sawyer dived out of the door and it slid shut. Sawyer helped Megan up from the concrete and they ran to the car.

The closed door now worked in their favor as the security guards were locked inside the building as they tried to reset the override. Sawyer started the car and they pulled speeding from the parking spot.

Fortunately, the security gate held no barriers besides a mechanical arm. It was lowered to stop traffic, but Sawyer didn't even slow down as he drove straight through it, splintering it into multiple pieces.

Megan looked out the back window and saw the security guard run out of the gatehouse, but there was nothing he could do about the damage now.

"I told them they needed stronger security at the gatehouse," Sawyer muttered, then turned and winked at Megan. "I'll bet they'll listen to me now."

Megan's heart was pounding. "That was really close."

Sawyer reached over and grabbed her hand. "I know. You did great."

"I wasn't sure you'd know when to open the door."

"Well, thankfully, all the men's attention was focused on you—as usual—not on me standing right outside the door. Although I was pretending to be on a phone call in case anyone looked."

Megan ignored the "as usual" part. She had found that men's attention was very rarely directed at her. Well, maybe it had been a few moments ago, since she was putting on the this-is-how-you-become-a-fugitive show, but not normally.

"And that is quite a sucker punch you have there, Dr. Fuller. If you ever want to try a different profession, you might want to look into MMA."

"MMA?"

"Mixed martial arts. You could be in the Ultimate Fighting Championship in no time, if this morning is any indication."

Megan knew Sawyer was trying to make her feel better, but the gravity of what she had just done wasn't lost on her. She had probably just thrown eight years of her professional life away. There was no way she'd be able to go back to Cyberdyne like it was before, no matter how important the countermeasure project was or how many lives she saved. She was a security risk now. And that was something that would follow her even if she moved to a different company.

Her field was a rather close-knit group. Highly competitive with each other, sure, but also chatty. What Megan had just done—stealing company property, assaulting the head of security, tearing through the guard gate as if she was in some sort of *Dukes of Hazzard* episode—would be all over the computer R & D community by the day's end.

Maybe Megan *should* look into a job as an MMA fighter. Because she wasn't going to be working in the computer R & D field anytime soon.

"Are the police going to be after us?"

"Probably. But not right away."

Megan looked over at Sawyer. "Are you going to get in trouble for what just happened?"

Sawyer shrugged, but definitely didn't look overly concerned. "Omega won't like that little stunt with the gate." He cringed a little at that. "But given what happened at your house, your car accident and the evidence of a traitor inside Cyberdyne? No, I'm definitely not going to be in any trouble."

"So what's the plan?"

"First, back to the hotel, where we can pick up everything. Then on to the safe house."

"Do you know where that is yet?"

Sawyer scowled just a bit. "It's not anything close to a lab, like I was requesting. But I guess that's to be expected on such short notice."

"All right, well, a lab isn't critical. I just need somewhere where I can spread out and not have anybody try to kill or arrest me for a while."

Sawyer chucked softly. "Roger that."

Halfway back to the hotel, Sawyer's phone vibrated in the console between them. Sawyer glanced down at the text when they stopped at a red light.

"Okay, slight change of plans," he announced, returning the phone to its place.

"Bad or good?"

"Evidently Omega found us a new safe house. It's farther out of town, but the remote location gives us more room like you wanted and Omega feels it's more secure." Sawyer frowned when he said it.

"But you don't agree?"

"No, they're probably right. Less traffic is probably better. But it won't be ready for a few hours."

There was something else Sawyer wanted to say, it seemed like, but he wasn't talking. Megan knew she shouldn't borrow Sawyer's trouble, too; she had enough to worry about. If there was something that concerned him enough, he would share it.

But Megan couldn't ignore the little nagging pulse in the back of her mind. She'd had it before, usually when she was in the middle of a development project, frustrated because she and the team couldn't get something right.

The certainty that she was missing something. Something important.

Megan could swear that was the case now, but for the life of her couldn't figure out what it was.

She just hoped she figured it out before it was too late.

THAT HAD BEEN too damn close. Now that they were safely in the car and no one was coming after them—that bit he'd told Megan about the cops not coming after them was somewhat of a stretch—Sawyer could relax a little.

When Sawyer saw Ted Cory catch up to Megan, he had thought it was all over. She had handled herself like a champ—more than Sawyer would've expected from almost anybody, even a seasoned agent. The lady definitely had a giant brain, but she wasn't afraid of action. Otherwise, she'd be locked in Cory's office right now threatened with arrest if she didn't provide the countermeasure and Ghost Shell.

It would've set them back from finishing for at least two or three days, possibly much longer. Exactly what DS-13 needed in order to be able to sell their version of Ghost Shell as soon as possible.

Sawyer definitely hadn't counted on Ted Cory being at the office so early and immediately searching for Megan. But Megan had made it out and that was what mattered.

Sawyer needed to call in to Omega and let them know what had happened. He'd told the truth when he'd assured Megan he wouldn't be reprimanded for getting her out; Megan finishing the countermeasure was more important that the security director's rules at a private corporation.

Although Omega definitely wouldn't like the ramming-the-gate thing. Sawyer snickered a little. He'd like to be a fly on the wall when his boss, Dennis Burgamy, got that news.

Sawyer just wanted to get Megan to the safe house so she could finish the countermeasure. This new safe house sounded as if it better suited their needs, which made it fine by Sawyer, although he wished Omega would just pick one place and stick with it. Sawyer didn't like changes when his and other's lives were at stake.

They arrived at the hotel. Sawyer parked around back and they quickly made their way to his room. Where Sawyer stayed wasn't public knowledge, but there weren't many hotels in the small town of Swannanoa and the local police would certainly be patrolling around here before long.

Megan was looking a little shell-shocked. Sawyer led her over to the bed and encouraged her to sit down.

"You okay?" he asked.

"Yes. I just don't know how you do this all the time—the lying and narrowly escaping and running crazy."

Sawyer kissed her forehead. "Believe it or not, my job is not always like that. Or at least the craziness is a little more spread out."

Megan shook her head and sat back. "If you say so."

Sawyer gathered all his items and packed them quickly. It wasn't long before they were leaving, heading out the back just so no one in the lobby would happen to remember seeing them.

Sawyer drove them out of town, the opposite way from where the safe house was located. They needed to get some food, and Sawyer needed to check in. But just in case someone remembered seeing them and were questioned, Sawyer didn't want to be anywhere near where he and Megan would be going.

Sawyer found a diner of the twenty-four-hour variety not too far south of town. He pulled in, keeping an alert eye for anything—or anyone—that might be out of place. But nothing drew his attention. He got Megan into a booth, they both ordered and then Sawyer stepped outside to call in to Omega. He made sure to stay where he could see the booth from the window.

Sawyer dialed the number for Omega, then entered his

personal security code. He waited to be connected to a handler so he could make his report.

"Blowing up a security gate, baby brother? Seriously?"

Sawyer felt himself relax. It wasn't often Juliet ended up as his handler, but since he wasn't technically undercover right now, he didn't have one specific person he was reporting to. She must have seen his code and decided she wanted to take the call.

"Blowing through, sis, blowing *through*."

Juliet laughed. "Either way, I'm sure Burgamy is not going to be thrilled when he gets the report."

Sawyer smirked at the thought of his boss hearing about it. "I guess that will teach him to send me on a babysitting job."

"You always seem to find trouble, Sawyer, no matter what you do or where you go."

"It's a gift." Sawyer chuckled. "How did Omega hear about the gate already?"

"Cyberdyne's head of security called and reported your rogue activity."

"And what was he told?"

"The usual—that you were working on orders that were above his security clearance and that sometimes desperate measures are required to complete those orders."

Sawyer was glad Omega had his back. At least he wouldn't have to worry about the local police coming after them. "I hope that's enough to keep Ted Cory from doing something stupid on his own."

"Me, too," Juliet told him. "How is everything going with Dr. Fuller? I heard she ended up being…not what you expected."

Sawyer could hear the smile in his sister's voice. "Where'd you hear that from?" he asked her.

"A little birdie."

"Yeah, well, I imagine that little birdie is about six foot

two with brown hair?" Sawyer had no doubt that Evan was the one telling his secrets. Especially if it was to Juliet. "I thought you didn't talk to Evan very often."

"I don't usually. But he had info about you, so…we talked for a while."

Sawyer didn't want to bring up Evan or any subject that would cause Juliet more pain. She'd been through enough.

Sawyer changed the topic. "I guess this report-in was almost unnecessary since Ted Cory did a lot of it for me. The important thing is I've got Dr. Fuller in pocket and we've got everything she needs to finish the countermeasure on her own."

Sawyer looked into the diner and saw that their food was being delivered. He gestured for Megan to go ahead and eat. "I'll be taking Dr. Fuller to the updated safe house soon."

"How long does she think it will take to complete the countermeasure?" Juliet asked.

"I'm not sure. Less than twenty-four hours, I hope."

"Evan's concerned."

Sawyer nodded. "I know. The timing is going to be pretty tight on this. As soon as the safe house is ready, I'll take Megan there immediately."

"Megan?"

"Dr. Fuller. Don't you give me a hard time about her, too." Sawyer grimaced. "She needs a few hours of sleep, which unfortunately is going to have to happen in the car, I guess. She's been under a lot of stress the last couple of days." Sawyer explained about the accident and break-in at her house. "Plus what happened at her job today."

"You might as well let her sleep, especially if the safe house isn't ready. She'll be able to work much more efficiently if she's firing on all cylinders."

"You're probably right. Thanks, sis."

"Be careful out there, Sawyer. She's not a trained agent."

Sawyer wasn't sure if Juliet was warning him off Megan

on a personal level or just reminding him of the obvious: this entire situation was much harder on Megan than it was on him. Megan didn't have any training or expertise on how to deal with this type of stress. Either way, Sawyer knew he should listen to his sister.

"I hear you, Jules. I'm on a twelve-hour report-in schedule right now, so I'll be calling back in this evening."

"Be safe."

Sawyer hung up and walked back into the diner. Sawyer knew he would do anything necessary to keep Megan safe from DS-13. The question was, who would keep her safe from him?

# Chapter Fifteen

A few hours later Sawyer sat in the backseat of his car, his back resting against the door, an exhausted Megan sleeping up against his chest. They had finished their meal and left the diner. With still a couple of hours before the safe house would be ready for them, and Megan close to a breakdown, Sawyer had found a park for them to stop at.

A full stomach made them both feel better, but Sawyer could tell that exhaustion was pulling at Megan. She had been quiet through most of their meal, unfocused, drifting. Sawyer had never seen Megan like that. It looked as if Juliet had been right; the pressure—the entire situation—was proving too much for Megan's system to handle.

Sawyer couldn't do much about the pressure, but he could give her a couple hours' rest so she could hopefully reset. He had no doubt she could get the job done if she could just rest for a while. Even giant brains had to shut down sometime.

When they'd stopped at the park, it had taken Megan long moments to even realize they weren't moving anymore. She turned and looked blankly over at Sawyer.

"Hey, sweetheart. We're going to stop here for a while and let you rest."

"Where are we?"

"A park. But a good one where we can be partially hidden and I can see if anyone is coming."

"Is it safe for us to sleep?"

"You're going to sleep. I'm going to be watching out while you do."

"But are you okay? Don't you need sleep, too?"

Even after all she had been through, exhaustion clear in her features, she was still concerned about him. Sawyer shook his head and ran a finger down her cheek. "I'm fine, hon. It's time for you to rest now."

Megan had gotten into the backseat and stretched out, almost instantly falling asleep. Sawyer had remained in the front. Even in her sleep, Megan couldn't get comfortable, shifting around back and forth. Sawyer realized she was shivering. The temperature outside the car was dropping and sitting here in a running car would be pretty conspicuous.

Sawyer didn't have a blanket, but he definitely had his own body heat. He could be on guard just as easily from the backseat as the front. Removing his Sig from his shoulder holster, he kept it in his hand as he got out of the car and slid into the backseat.

Megan hadn't even awakened when he shifted her slight weight so she was sleeping up against him. But she had cuddled into his warmth. Sawyer had circled her with one arm and kept a watchful eye out for any enemies who might approach, although he doubted DS-13 would be looking for them in a park.

He hadn't minded holding Megan against him for those hours while she slept, keeping her safe. Of course, having her snuggle and rub up against him constantly was pretty much torture. But Sawyer found he didn't care if it meant Megan could get what she needed.

A first for him, he could admit. Sawyer loved women.

Loved their softness and their idiosyncrasies and their beauty that came in all shapes and sizes.

But Sawyer wasn't a man who just tended to hold one while she slept when there were other things—and in this case, he could think of quite a few detailed other things—he'd rather be doing with her. But right now he was content to just hold Megan against him and listen to the adorable little snore that escaped her tiny frame every once in a while.

It must be this case that was causing Sawyer to act so out of character. The case had almost killed both his brothers last month. So solving it was obviously of abounding importance to Sawyer's subconscious.

Yeah. He'd just keep clinging to that thought and not the thought that he couldn't get this tiny, giant-brained woman out of his mind.

As if on cue, her brown eyes fluttered open. She smiled sleepily at him and stretched. Sawyer grimaced as the entire length of her body was pressed against his.

Then her brain caught up to her body and she stiffened. Obviously, she had just realized that she was all but lying on top of him.

"Feel better after your nap?" Sawyer asked, turning her a little so she was more firmly resting against his chest.

"I can't believe how much better I feel. Although, um, wasn't I back here by myself when I first went to sleep?"

"You were shivering and couldn't get comfortable, so I got back here with you."

"Oh." Megan looked up at him and smiled softly. "Thank you. How long have I been out?"

"About four hours."

"Oh, wow. You know in nap cycles, sleeping ninety to one hundred twenty minutes allows for all the sleep cycles to be completed including REM and deep slow-wave sleep. This allows your mind to return to a state of *replenishment*..."

Sawyer listened, smiling and shaking his head, until she

finished her thoughts about naps, then kissed her. Because unlike sleep cycles and brain activity, kissing her had been on his mind for the past four hours.

Every time he kissed her he figured that it couldn't be as good as he remembered it. And every time he was wrong. It was always this good.

Megan sighed and snuggled closer to him. Sawyer placed his Sig on the floor and reached down, grabbing Megan's hips and pulling her closer. Her head slanted to the side and her lips opened, giving Sawyer fuller access. Her tongue dueled with his, hesitantly at first, then with more boldness. Sawyer felt Megan's hands slide up into his hair, gripping hard. He pulled her closer.

And cursed the fact that they were in the backseat of a car, in an open area. And that just because DS-13 hadn't found them yet didn't mean they weren't searching.

And that this was a park, for God's sake. If they didn't stop they might scar some poor little kid for life.

But despite all that, Sawyer didn't want to stop. He definitely didn't want to.

"Megan…" he murmured against her lips.

"I know. I know. We have to stop."

"Believe me, I don't want to. But it's not safe and damn it, I don't want our first time to be in the back of a car like a couple of teenagers."

Megan giggled slightly at that.

Sawyer kissed her lightly again. "But I want you to understand something, Dr. Fuller. Soon. Very, very soon—" he rested his forehead against hers "—we are going to finish what we started here. And when we do, there won't be any break-ins or parks or anything else in the way. It will be in a bed where there is no one around but you and me."

A COUPLE OF hours later, stopped again for a meal, Megan felt much better. She was ready to get on to the safe house and finish the countermeasure. After everything DS-13 had cost her—her home, her vehicle, her possessions, her job—it was time to make them pay for a change. Finishing the countermeasure would do that.

She looked across the booth at Sawyer. She also wanted to get to the safe house so she could finish what she had started with him.

Megan barely refrained from licking her lips thinking about it. And the glances she caught Sawyer giving her every once in a while weren't helping. As if he was considering crawling over the table to get to her.

It made Megan giddy. And she loved it. But at the same time she was well aware that this was Sawyer's MO. He was probably always this focused on women he was attracted to. She'd do well not to read anything more into it than what it meant: a good time for however long he was here.

Hey, she'd take it. If there was one thing all the craziness of the past couple of days had taught her, it was not to waste time worrying so much over the future that you were completely blind to the present sitting right across from you smiling.

But now that her brain wasn't so exhausted, that little nagging bit of her subconscious was back. Nothing about Sawyer. She knew it wasn't about him. But Megan couldn't shake the feeling she was missing something and it was starting to make her twitchy.

"What's wrong?" Sawyer asked her.

"What?"

"You've got that look. Your I'm-using-my-giant-brain-to-figure-out-something-important look."

Megan laughed a little at that. "My subconscious is tugging at me. I've missed something, somewhere, but I don't know what it is."

"About the countermeasure?"

"No, not really. At least, I don't think so." Megan took another bite of her food. "But it's something important."

"Okay. What can I do to help?"

Megan shrugged one shoulder. "I don't know that you can do anything. I've learned to just leave it alone—the harder I try to figure it out, the more elusive it seems to become. It'll come to me."

Megan just hoped it wouldn't come to her too late to be of any use.

They finished eating and headed back out to the car. Megan was ready to get to the safe house and get started. Sawyer was tense in the car, constantly looking in the rear-view mirror.

"Is somebody following us?"

"No." Sawyer shook his head, but didn't look over at her. "I just want to make sure. In such a remote area, it's critical that no one be following us when we reach the safe house."

Twice Sawyer turned off the main road in a direction opposite from where they were trying to go. He drove for just a few moments, then turned and went back the other way. Anyone following them would've been obvious. Megan mentioned that to Sawyer.

Sawyer shook his head. "They're only obvious if they are the only car following us. If I was DS-13 trying to follow our car, I'd have more than one vehicle. Tag-teaming makes a tail much less noticeable."

That made sense to Megan. Still, she didn't see how anybody could follow them, and not be obvious, the way Sawyer drove.

Eventually, after at least thirty minutes out of their way and back, Sawyer felt secure no one was following them. Megan could see him relax, which made her feel better.

He reached over and plucked her hand out of her lap and brought it to his lips, kissing the back of her palm. "Sorry. I don't mean to be fanatic. I just don't want to take a chance with your safety."

Megan smiled. "I understand and appreciate it. Of course, I have no idea where we are."

"Don't worry, I have the address encrypted on my phone. I got a message earlier this morning with the info from Omega."

Something in how Sawyer said the words jarred loose what her subconscious had been trying to get at: *I got a message earlier.*

"Sawyer, stop the car," Megan told him. "I remember. What I couldn't figure out before, I remember."

To his credit, Sawyer didn't hesitate or brush her off. He immediately pulled the car over at a nearby gas station, but parked far away from the building and pumps.

"What?" Sawyer asked her. "Is it something bad?"

"It was something Ted Cory said this morning. Everything happened so fast when he grabbed me that I didn't really put it together it until now."

"What did he say?"

"When you talked to him on the phone while we were in the hotel this morning, you told him I wasn't coming in until the afternoon, right?"

"Yeah. I tried to buy us some extra time."

"But then you reported in to Omega that we were going in this morning to retrieve the needed items, right? Omega and you and I were the only ones who knew we would be there early this morning, right?"

Sawyer nodded. "Yes, but I don't understand what you're getting at."

Megan turned and faced Sawyer fully. "The very first thing Ted Cory said to me as I was trying to get out the door at Cyberdyne was, 'I got a message that you would be here this morning.'"

Sawyer leaned his head back against the seat, obviously

processing what Megan was telling him. "You're sure he said 'I got a message' not 'I thought you'd probably be here' or something like that?"

"I'm positive. I can recall the entire conversation word for word if you want." Megan tapped her finger against her temple. It was the truth. She could recall probably the past one hundred conversations she'd had almost word for word. It had just taken her subconscious a little time to put together that Ted Cory's words were important in an unusual way.

"No need. I believe you." Sawyer ran a hand over his eyes.

"Does this mean what I think it means?"

Sawyer clenched his jaw visibly. "It means everything is blown to hell, that's what it means."

# Chapter Sixteen

Damn it, Sawyer wanted to punch something. He had thought there might be someone involved from Omega, but hadn't wanted to believe it. Now the truth was too obvious to ignore.

Somebody had contacted Ted Cory and warned him that Megan would be coming in this morning, despite what Sawyer had told Cory. That was why he had been there so early. It was probably why Trish Wilborne—if she was the Cyberdyne traitor—was there so early, also. It made sense.

It also meant nothing involving Omega was trustworthy anymore. Including the safe house.

Or the car they were driving. Or the phone Sawyer had.

Sawyer immediately opened the car door.

"Where are we going?" Megan asked.

"Hang on just a second," he told her.

Sawyer stayed seated, but set his phone on the ground outside the car, then shut the door again.

"To answer your earlier question, yes, it does mean what you think it means. Someone inside Omega is working against us, too."

"And you put your phone outside because you think they're using it to track us."

Sawyer grimaced. "If it's someone using Omega's resources, they're almost definitely using it to track us. I put it outside because a smartphone can also be used as a transmitting device with the right technology."

"Should you destroy it?" Megan was starting to get that pinched look again. Sawyer hated that, but couldn't blame her.

"I might. But not until we come up with a plan." Sawyer hit the steering wheel with the bottom of his fist. "No wonder they weren't tailing us. They didn't need to. They knew where we were going."

"Do you think they planned to wait until we got to the safe house, then ambush us?"

Sawyer ran tense fingers through his hair. "Definitely, if not worse."

"What are we going to do?"

That was the million-dollar question. Sawyer still needed to get Megan to a safe location so she could finish the countermeasure. But with the resources Omega had, staying hidden from the mole would be difficult, if not impossible.

Omega would be able to trace any car he and Megan tried to rent. If Sawyer stole one, Omega would be able to access traffic and security cameras from all around. They also had local law enforcement on their side.

When Omega wanted to hunt someone down, especially when they knew the general location and description of that someone, it was damn near impossible to get away.

The first thing Sawyer knew he needed to do was get some reinforcements on his side. He needed to call Juliet and let her know what was going on. The only way he could do that safely would be on a pay phone.

"Okay, I'm going to open the car door and get my phone and leave it in the car as we get out. Don't say anything until we are both outside of the car and the phone is inside," he told Megan.

"They can hear us even with it powered down?"

"It's my Omega phone. A mole there could've had access and modified it to transmit."

"Kind of like some new technology that's being used by people who think their spouses might be having an affair."

Sawyer nodded. "In essence."

Megan shook her head. "Do you have a plan?"

"I'm going to call someone in Omega I know I can trust, my sister, Juliet. She'll have access to information we need."

They both were silent as they got out of the car and Sawyer put the phone inside. Then they walked over to a pay phone on the side of the gas station. Sawyer dialed Juliet's number. When she picked up, he didn't let her get many words out. "Hey, sis. Our stepmom just called and told me there's a huge sale down at the local coffeehouse."

There was a short pause. "Really? That's awesome."

"Yeah, she said you might want to bring your computer so you can research which coffee to buy."

"Alrighty, then. I'll go check it out and call you back."

They both hung up. Megan was looking at him as if he'd lost his mind.

"Do I even want to know?" she asked him. "Please tell me that was some kind of code."

Sawyer smiled. "We don't have a stepmom. Our parents are still happily married and live in Virginia. *Stepmom* is kind of a family code for 'get someplace where you can talk privately.'"

It wasn't long before Juliet was calling him back. "What's up, Sawyer? This better be worth me going outside in this weather. It's cold."

"Are you somewhere that you can talk without anyone from Omega overhearing?"

"Yeah. I'm totally out of the building."

"We've got a big problem, Juliet. Megan figured out that someone at Omega is working against us."

"Damn it, I knew it!"

That wasn't the response Sawyer was expecting from his sister at all.

"You did? Why the hell didn't you tell me, then?"

Juliet backtracked. "Well, I didn't know for sure. But I was looking up the info on the safe house you're going to—Evan wanted to know where you'd be exactly."

Sawyer didn't mind Evan Karcz knowing the safe-house location. Evan wasn't actual family, but he was close enough. Although, if Sawyer had to guess, Evan had only asked about the safe house in order to get Juliet to talk to him, not just because he wanted to be aware of Sawyer's location.

"Evan's questions made you think there was someone working against us?"

"No. I went into the system to get him the address. Found it no problem."

Sawyer rubbed his face with this hand. "Juliet, I don't get what you're talking about."

"I was prepared to filter through addresses because you had mentioned being given a second address. But there was only one in the system."

"Okay. But that still doesn't necessarily mean—"

"Sawyer, there was no record *anywhere* of a first address. The second—the more remote location—was the only one attached to your case. If you hadn't mentioned you'd been given a second, different safe-house location, I wouldn't have looked twice at the file."

"Is it possible it was a clerical error?"

"No. Once I went back and found your call-in record from last night, I was able to trace the original safe house assigned to you. Someone deliberately went in and deleted all record of that assignment, so it looked like the second safe house was the one originally assigned."

Sawyer was silent. He didn't want to let his imagination get the better of him, but the only reasons he could think of for someone to make it look as if the second house had been originally assigned was for some definite nefarious purposes. "That's bad."

"It's very bad, Sawyer. It looks like someone is preemptively covering their tracks. The only reason I can think that someone would do that—"

"Is if they were going to take Megan and me out of the picture entirely, then make it look like an accident or attack from DS-13 or something." Sawyer finished Juliet's idea for her. He heard a slight gasp from Megan and turned to look at her. Her eyes were giant as she looked at him.

"You can't go to that safe house, Sawyer."

"I know, sis, but neither can we run if someone's got Omega's resources to use when looking for us. We won't get far."

"I assume you don't have your phone within earshot. Remember, it can be used not only to track you, but for remote listening."

"No, it's sitting inside the car. I didn't want to destroy it, hoping we'll be able to use their own system against them. Feed them false info while they're listening in."

"Okay, but don't say anything around it you don't want overheard. Even if it's off," Juliet continued.

"Okay, got it." Sawyer told her.

"Do you want me to take the information I have to Burgamy, or even higher up?"

"No, we don't know who the traitor is. I don't want to take a chance on notifying the wrong person." Sawyer looked down at Megan, who was standing next to Sawyer so she could hear as much as possible. Sawyer hated the thought that someone in law enforcement had lied and put her in jeopardy *again*. He grabbed her hands, which were clenched tightly in front of her, gently running his finger over her knuckles.

"Sawyer." Juliet spoke and got his attention again. "I think I'm coming up with a plan."

If there was one thing his sister was known for, it was strategic planning.

"Megan needs time and a quiet place to work, right?"

"Yes, and the sooner the better."

"Evan is out in that area. You call in to Omega and let them know you can't get to the safe house right away for some reason. I'll have Evan check out the safe house, see if there's anything interesting to be found. Meanwhile I'll keep poking around here."

"And then what?"

"Well, if we find what I think we might find, it's going to prove that DS-13, and whoever is helping them at Omega, have decided if they can't keep you in-pocket then dead is an acceptable alternative."

If possible, Megan turned even paler at Juliet's words. "What exactly are we going to do about that, Jules?" Sawyer asked his sister.

"Give them what they want."

A FEW HOURS later they got the confirmation Sawyer had been dreading. A text came in on Megan's phone, telling them to call Aunt Susie when they got a chance. Since Megan didn't have an Aunt Susie, they figured out Juliet had news for them.

They had spent the past few hours driving around. Sawyer had made two calls in to Omega. The first, immediately after the conversation with Juliet, to tell them he thought they were being followed and therefore wouldn't be going to the safe house. The other about an hour ago to say they were stopping at a supercenter for some items Megan needed due to the break-in. Which was true—they had stopped to get a few things.

Most important, clean, untraceable phones that could

be used once Sawyer stopped using his current one to feed false info to Omega.

But generally they were just stalling and it would become obvious soon, so Sawyer was thankful to see his sister's text.

But he definitely wasn't thankful for the news.

"Evan found explosives, Sawyer," Juliet told him when they stopped at a payphone and called a few minutes later. "He's on the other line with us."

"Somebody's definitely trying to take you out," Evan stated, seriousness evident in his tone. "But all home-baked stuff, nothing that would raise red flags in an arson investigation. Given the location—a remote building, non-residential neighborhood—it looks like someone might be trying to make it look like an accident." Evan explained a few more details.

The expletive that came out of Sawyer's mouth was not one he would normally use around his sister, or any woman. "If DS-13 is willing to kill Megan, then things have just gone from bad to hell-in-a-handbasket. Especially if they've got Omega's resources at their disposal."

Sawyer wrapped an arm around Megan, pulling her closer to him. He needed to get them off the street as soon as possible. But they wouldn't be able to hide for long.

"I think your plan is the best one, Juliet," he told his sister.

"What plan?" Evan asked.

"Megan and I are going to give them what they want. We'll go to the safe house and make them think we're staying. But we'll get out immediately. They'll blow it up like they planned and will think we're dead. But we'll be gone."

Evan chuckled wryly. "Juliet, your plans get more crazy each time."

"Hey, my crazy plans have saved your life more than once, Evan."

"I'm going to need you to have a car waiting for us there, Evan," Sawyer interrupted. "And once we leave the not-safe safe house, we'll need a hotel in Asheville."

"This won't hold them off forever, Sawyer," Juliet told him. "It won't take long for the official arson report to read that no bodies were present. I can probably stall the report, but not for long. This whole stunt will only buy you forty-eight hours, tops."

Sawyer looked down questioningly at Megan, who was standing close enough to listen to the conversation. She nodded.

"Forty-eight hours will be enough. It has to be."

# *Chapter Seventeen*

Megan felt as though the world was spinning at a pace out of her control. Having someone after the countermeasure, even wrecking her car and breaking in to her house felt like a game compared to this.

DS-13 was trying to kill them.

Megan had sat mostly silent for the past few hours as Sawyer had fed misinformation to his workplace and formulated plans with his team. Plans to escape, evade, misdirect. But most importantly, survive.

On one hand, Megan could appreciate the logistical nature of what they were doing—the elaborate planning going into all of it. It wasn't unlike the projects she worked on and developed for Cyberdyne. It all had to fit together perfectly to work. The planning appealed to her giant brain, as Sawyer so loved to call it.

But on the other hand, Megan was just downright frightened. She hadn't said much of anything today because of Sawyer's phone possibly being used to transmit data. What if Megan accidentally said something that gave away important information about the plan? What if she blurted out something about traitors?

Better to keep as quiet as possible.

Megan wrapped her arms around her midsection, not sure if she might fly apart any second.

She was outside, sitting on the trunk of the car. Sawyer's phone was inside, so there was no need to monitor their statements for the moment.

Sawyer had removed all the countermeasure equipment from the backseat and was carefully packing it in two backpacks. They'd need to travel a couple of miles carrying the equipment, to get to the vehicle Evan had left for them.

"Once we get inside the house, you need to immediately announce you want to sleep," Sawyer told her, not looking up from his careful packing. He was in full mission mode. "I'll say that I'm going to unwind for a couple of hours and unpack, and mention that we won't plan on leaving the safe house for multiple days."

Megan nodded.

"Once we get the house dark, we'll immediately want to leave. I don't know when they'll trigger the explosives. Evan says it's on a remote detonator, so it can be detonated from anywhere."

"Sawyer." Megan hardly recognized her own voice. "How do we know they won't set off the explosives as soon as we walk into the house?"

Sawyer stopped packing and stood, walking over to Megan and standing right in front of her. "That is a possibility." He unwrapped her arms from around her stomach and put them on his shoulders instead. "But it is far more likely that they will wait until we are more settled in for the night. Especially if they're trying to make it look like an accident. Plus, if the mole doesn't want to blow his own cover, it will be much less suspicious if the building doesn't blow up ten seconds after we walk in."

He kissed her briefly, gently.

Megan could agree with the logic of his statement, and the odds. But she was still not thrilled about the thought of them walking into a building—even just for a few minutes—designed to kill them. But it didn't look as if there were many other options.

Sawyer kissed her again and went back to packing. Once the backpacks were ready, he placed them in paper grocery bags. He noticed Megan's raised eyebrow.

"To make it look like we're planning to stay in the house for a while, in case someone's watching. Got to have groceries."

"Oh, right." There was so much Sawyer thought of that hadn't even crossed her mind. Megan was obviously not cut out for subterfuge.

Sawyer placed the grocery bags in the backseat, then helped Megan down from her perch. He walked her around to the passenger-side door, opening it for her and helping her inside. Megan couldn't help but smile, although she knew it was tense.

"Are we on a date?"

Sawyer winked at her. "Not yet, but soon. Believe me, you'll know when I have you out for a date."

Despite all the tension, Megan's heart gave a little jump.

Sawyer walked around to the driver's side and grabbed his phone. He texted Omega, letting them know he and Megan were heading to the safe house. The sun was setting, providing them the darkness they would use to sneak out before the bomb went off.

They hoped.

Megan wrapped her arms around herself again, stomach twisted even tighter. A lot could go wrong in the next couple of hours. All of which would have the same result: Sawyer's and Megan's deaths.

Sawyer put the phone down, his message sent. This was it, the plan was in place whether Megan was ready or not.

Sawyer glanced over at her, concerned. Given the way Megan was manually attempting to keep her body functioning, she couldn't blame him for his concern.

"Okay, this is it. You ready?"

"No offense intended, but I don't really have much of a choice, do I?" Megan tried to force herself to relax, but couldn't.

Sawyer shook his head. "No, neither of us has much of a choice. Let's get to the safe house so you can get a little rest then get started."

Megan remembered someone was listening, so she went back to being silent. It wasn't long before they reached their destination.

The building itself wasn't what Megan was expecting, although if she was honest, she couldn't pinpoint exactly what she had been expecting. A haunted mansion, perhaps? Complete with gargoyles?

It was just a small garage/workshop that looked as if it had some sort of living quarters on the top. It backed up against a body of water—maybe a small lake? Megan couldn't be sure in the darkness. Trees and bushes surrounded it, but no other houses or buildings.

That was good—at least nobody would be hurt by the explosion. Megan hoped the same would be true for her and Sawyer.

"Okay, this is it. I'm going to open that garage door so we can park inside."

Sawyer had to manually open the garage door, an old-fashioned kind that swung out like a traditional door, instead of up. He pulled the car in and closed the door behind them.

As she watched the door close, Megan fought to keep her panic in check. The walls seemed to be closing in around her. She could only think, *Are we about to die any second*?

Megan jumped when Sawyer opened the backseat door to remove the "grocery" bags. He raised an eyebrow at her, then gestured with a circular motion of his hand for her to breathe. Megan closed her eyes and took a deep breath letting it out slowly.

She had to keep it together. If she started sobbing right now, the whole ruse would be up, not to mention might cause whoever was listening to trigger the bomb.

Megan forced herself to get out of the car and she and Sawyer walked up the stairs into the living quarters together.

"This isn't as bad as I thought it might be, although a few windows might be nice." Megan stood right in the middle of the small living room, unsure where to go.

"Glad it meets your approval, because we're going to be here awhile."

Megan didn't want to draw out the conversation in case someone was trigger-happy. "I'm really tired. I'd like to sleep for a while before I start work on the countermeasure."

It was almost word for word what Sawyer had told her to say. Megan wasn't much of an actress.

"That's fine." Sawyer nodded. "I'm going to unpack this stuff and just hang out."

Megan went into the bedroom and turned on the light, walked around a little, went into the bathroom for a while, then came back out and turned off the light. Following the script Sawyer had provided almost down to the letter. Megan heard the TV come on and knew he was doing the same.

Megan lay down on top of the bed. After long moments, Sawyer came into the room, keeping to the shadows, both backpacks in hand.

"Are you ready?" he asked her in a voice barely over a whisper.

Megan nodded.

"My phone is by the television speaker, so I doubt anyone can hear us now," Sawyer continued. "We're going to need to go back down the stairs and out the garage door.

This place, with hardly any usable windows and only one door, has got to be a fire hazard. Somebody picked it well, if they were trying to trap us."

"I didn't even see a window."

"It's downstairs and pretty small. I'm not surprised you didn't notice it. I don't know if anyone is actually watching the house or not, but we've got to keep low. Even once we're outside, try to blend in to the trees as much as possible."

"Okay," Megan whispered.

They each slipped on their backpacks and made it to the bottom of the stairs. Once back in the garage, Sawyer motioned for her to stop.

"I just want to see these explosives for myself." He walked over to a corner, shifted a few boxes and lifted a blanket.

If that was the bomb, it wasn't like anything Megan had seen in the movies. It just looked like a couple of fertilizer bags stacked on top of each other, with some cans around it. The only thing even mildly suspicious about it was the really old notebook computer sitting on top of it.

"Ammonium nitrate. Surrounded by paint thinner and gas. All stuff you'd expect at a place this old and remote. Suggesting it was an accident wouldn't be far-fetched."

"What is that computer?"

"The timing mechanism. Most of it will get burned away, but if any of it is found, nobody will think much of it."

The screen of the old laptop booted on, startling them both.

Sawyer muttered an expletive, then grabbed Megan's shoulders and pushed her forward in front of him, toward the large garage door. "Go, go!"

Megan got to the door and began to push it. It wouldn't budge.

"Sawyer, I can't get it to move."

Without a word Sawyer came around in front of her

and put his shoulder to the door. She heard his curse when he couldn't get it to move, either. It was completely stuck.

Sawyer grabbed Megan's hand and ran to the window in the back of the garage. He used a hammer to break the glass and used the side of it to clear the glass from the sill, and ripped off both their backpacks.

"That laptop screen coming on means that something has happened with the remote trigger. It could go off any second." Sawyer was already hoisting Megan through the window as he said it.

Now that Megan understood, she didn't waste time asking questions. She scrambled through the window, falling the few feet to the ground on the other side.

She immediately got back up, catching the backpacks as Sawyer threw them out in front of him. The brisk air surrounded her, time moving in slow motion, as Sawyer deftly began to make his own way through the window.

Until he got stuck. Megan watched as his large shoulders were jammed in the sill.

"Megan, I need you to run." He said it to her as he attempted to back out and resituate himself.

"No. I can help you."

"Megan, just go now. Take the equipment with you. If this building goes up, then what you've done with countermeasure has to make it out of here."

She ran over to him and tried to help as Sawyer struggled to fit through the window. "It's not more important than your life."

"Megan, look at me." Megan stopped her frantic pulling at his shoulders. "No offense, but the countermeasure is more important than either of our lives. Please go."

Megan felt tears streaming down her face, but she understood what Sawyer was saying. If the bomb went off right now, both of them would die and the countermeasure would be totally destroyed.

Megan grabbed both backpacks and began running. She looked back at Sawyer, but he had disappeared back inside the window.

Damn it, she was not leaving him to die some fiery death; she didn't care what he said about the importance of the countermeasure. She dropped the bags far enough away that they would be safe, then circled back to the house. The window was too small; she'd never be able to help him out of that.

But something was blocking the garage door in front. Maybe she could get it out of the way.

She ran around to the front of the building knowing that if someone was watching them, it was going to ruin Juliet's brilliant plan of faking their deaths. Of course, if she and Sawyer both died, the plan was also ruined. She hoped that whoever had blocked the door was gone, although she kept to the shadows on the off chance that it would help.

A crowbar had been lodged in the double-door handles— a simple but effective means of trapping people inside. And an explosion would certainly knock the doors off their hinges or burn them completely—still making an accident look feasible.

Megan slid the heavy door open just a tiny bit and stuck her head inside.

"Sawyer!"

He was over by the pile of ammonium nitrate.

"Megan? What the hell are you doing here?"

"I've got the door unblocked. Just come on."

Sawyer ran as fast as he could toward her. "I was trying to defuse this, but couldn't. The computer is counting down. We've only got a few seconds."

He grabbed her hand as they rushed out the door, sprinting for the trees. Megan could hear a loud sizzling noise behind her, but didn't look back.

Even knowing the explosion was coming, the force of

it surprised her. There was a bright light before heat and pressure threw her to the ground. She felt Sawyer slide his body over to protect hers from any debris. Twigs and branches flew everywhere.

Once it seemed safe, they both turned from where they lay and looked back at the damage. Megan gasped. Flames shot high in the building, the garage already completely collapsed. No one in that building would've survived.

Sawyer dragged her into his arms. "Your brain has been officially demoted to huge rather than giant after that stunt. You could've been killed."

"Whatever. Like you wouldn't have done the same thing."

Sawyer chuckled at that. "Let's get out of here."

# *Chapter Eighteen*

They circled around to the backpacks, then hiked to the car Evan had left for them. Sawyer was still pretty mad at Megan for risking her life like that, but had to admit she had saved his, so he couldn't be too angry.

At this point Sawyer wasn't sure if their plan to fake their deaths had worked or not. Someone had obviously been at the house, as evidenced by the crowbar wedged in the garage door. Whether that person had stuck around and was able to see them coming out or had left to avoid the first responders who had arrived not long after the explosion, Sawyer didn't know.

Regardless, it didn't change their plans. Everything that tied him to Omega—car, cell phone, even his clothes—had been left in that burning building. There was no way anyone could track them using those items now. Sawyer used the new phones he had bought at the supercenter yesterday to text Juliet and let her know that they'd made it out.

Sawyer drove around for a while to try to make sure no one was following them, then headed to the prearranged and prepaid motel. Evan and Juliet had picked a good one for them, on the other side of Asheville. Sawyer could park directly in front of the door, just steps away from their room if they needed to leave in a hurry.

It was an end unit, so no one would be passing his and

Megan's room to get to their own. There should be no one around at all. Just the way they needed it to be.

Sawyer backed the nondescript car into the parking spot outside their room. He grabbed the backpacks out of the backseat and handed them to Megan, then grabbed the bags of supplies—real food and clothes—Evan had left for them. Sawyer took one last look around as he shut the car door. There seemed to be nothing around them in the darkness, except the Blue Ridge Mountains looming nearby. He led Megan to the room and opened it with the key Evan had left for them.

Sawyer put down the bags and immediately looked around the room. It was actually two adjoining rooms; Megan would need all of one room to finish her work. The motel was definitely older, as evidenced by the actual metal key Sawyer had just used to get in, but clean and adequate for their needs. Plus there was a window in the back that could be used for emergency escape.

Not that Sawyer really wanted to be trying to fit through any windows again.

Sawyer pulled the blinds completely closed in both rooms, and locked and bolted both doors after placing the do-not-disturb sign on both doorknobs. This was it, their home for the next few days.

Sawyer turned and found Megan standing exactly where he'd left her just inside the door. She still cradled both backpacks in her arms.

She looked exhausted. She stood there, covered in dirt from their most recent brush with death, gazing at the motel room without really seeing it. Given everything that had happened to her over the past few days, Sawyer was amazed she had remained upright and functional this long.

Sawyer walked over and took the bags from Megan's unresisting arms and laid them down on the table.

"Hey," he whispered to her. "How about a hot shower?"

Get some of this grunge washed off you." Sawyer led her to the bed and sat her down, then went and turned on the hot water in the shower. When he came out of the bathroom, she still sat exactly where he had left her.

Concern flooded Sawyer. What Megan had been through over the past few days would be physically exhausting and emotionally draining for even the most seasoned agent. For a civilian with no experience in this sort of work at all? Sawyer could barely imagine the toll it was taking.

And then to ask her to tackle the countermeasure development on top of all that had happened? Sawyer wasn't even sure it was possible for her, but he had to try.

He crouched beside where she sat on the bed. "Megan, let's get you in the shower, okay? It will help you feel better."

Megan turned to look at him, but seemed uncomprehending of what he wanted. "Shower," he told her again slowly.

"Sawyer, I don't think I know where I am." The confusion in her voice tore at his heart.

"You're at a motel, sweetheart. Don't worry about that right now. Let's just get you into the shower, okay?"

Megan nodded and Sawyer helped her stand and walk into the bathroom.

"Can you get undressed?" Megan nodded again, but then just stood there staring blankly at the wall.

Okay, time to take matters into his own hands. She obviously wasn't able to even complete simple tasks on her own in her current state of mind.

Sawyer reached over and began unbuttoning Megan's shirt. She looked at him as he did it, but made no move to stop him. He peeled the shirt off her shoulders and dropped it onto the sink, then unhooked her bra and removed it. Sawyer did his damn personal best not to stare at her firm, beautiful breasts.

He knelt down, picking up one of her feet at a time to remove her shoes and socks. She began to lose her balance and grasped his shoulders to keep from toppling over.

Sawyer looked up at her through the steam that was now filling the bathroom. "Just hold on to me."

She nodded once again, but at least there was a little bit of awareness in her eyes now, rather than the scary blankness.

Sawyer swallowed hard as his hands moved to the button and zipper of her jeans. He undid both, then slid them down her legs. Her lacy underwear followed suit and he helped her step out of them.

Sawyer cleared his throat, his breath just shy of ragged. "Okay, into the shower you go." He tested the water and adjusted it so it wouldn't scald her, scooped the shower curtain aside and helped her in.

He heard her sigh when the water hit her and closed the curtain around her oh-so-naked form. He had tried to keep his eyes focused above her neckline as much as possible. But Lord, he was only human.

He had to admit this was the first time he had ever gotten a woman he wanted *this* much naked and then just left her alone.

Yeah, he definitely wanted Megan, but not when she was so traumatized she could barely function.

Hopefully, the shower would help perk her up a little. Help her refocus. "Megan, I'll be right outside the door. If you need anything, just call for me. Okay?"

He heard a murmur of agreement, then headed into the motel room, leaving the door cracked open so he could hear her if she called out.

Sawyer took a couple of breaths. Deep breaths. He needed a cold shower. He sat down on the end of the bed and threw himself backward. It was going to be a long night.

THE SHOWER BROUGHT life back into Megan's veins. Slowly she began to feel again. First the heat from the water spraying down on her, then the realization that she was filthy—small twigs and grass were matted into her hair. She began to work her fingers through her locks to get the mess out.

It felt as if her brain was waking up from hibernation. She remembered the explosion, although she didn't allow herself to dwell on Sawyer almost getting trapped in that building. But then everything after that was a blur. They obviously must have made it to the car, and here she was in a shower in a motel room, so that must have gone as planned, also.

She could even vaguely remember Sawyer helping her take off her clothes, which should embarrass her, but she didn't have the energy for it.

Megan stood in the shower for long minutes. She finally opened the shampoo and washed her hair fully. At least she wasn't quite as zombielike as she was before, although she was still exhausted. After washing the rest of her body and rinsing, she shut the water off.

"Doing okay in there?" she heard Sawyer call out from the room.

"Yes, much better. Thanks." She opened the shower curtain and found the door to the bedroom still open. In the mirror she could see Sawyer lying on the bed, propped up on his elbows. His eyes met hers. Megan almost snatched the shower curtain over to cover herself, but figured Sawyer had already seen her naked, so there wasn't much point in it now. She watched as his eyes slid down her body and back up.

The exhaustion that filled her body moments before now vanished. All of her senses seemed heightened.

Sawyer stood up from the bed, keeping eye contact with her. He grabbed a T-shirt—one of his—and threw it over his shoulder, walking to the bathroom. He offered her his hand and she stepped out of the tub onto the mat. Sawyer took a towel from the wall hook and shook it out, then wrapped it around her like a cape, keeping hold of the edges.

Megan said nothing, just continued to stare at Sawyer. He took the edges of the towel and gently dried her face and the excess water from her hair. Then he began to wrap the edges of the towel around his fists, pulling her closer. He didn't stop until she was fully pressed up against him.

"I'm wet," Megan whispered.

"I don't care," Sawyer responded before bringing his lips down to hers.

Sawyer had kissed her before, but this was different. Megan had no doubt how this kiss was going to end. Her bones felt as though they were melting. Everything about this felt right.

After a few minutes, both of them breathing hard, Sawyer released her lips. He used the towel to dry the rest of her body, kneeling in front of her and kissing various areas as he went along. A sigh escaped Megan as his lips made their way across her belly and dipped lower to the outside of her hips.

But then Sawyer stood up and pulled the T-shirt off his shoulder and began to put it on her.

"Um, Sawyer? I think this," she whispered as she gestured to the shirt he was pulling over her head, "is not going in the correct direction."

Sawyer's voice was more husky than usual when he responded, "Believe me, there is nothing I want to do more than take you to that bed. Right now. But fifteen minutes ago you couldn't even remember how you got here."

"But—"

Sawyer put a finger up to her lips. "Later. I promise. Later. But right now, you need to rest. Plus, I'm filthy."

He pulled the shirt over her head and she put her arms through. The shirt swallowed her, falling to midthigh.

"I'm pretty damn sure I never looked that good in that shirt."

Megan smiled and followed as he led her to the room. He pulled back the covers of the bed and she scooted in. "Sleep. I'm going to take a shower, then I'll be sleeping right next to you."

He turned and walked back into the bathroom. And didn't even look back once.

Megan lay on the bed for a long time, but sleep was a million miles away. She knew her body needed sleep, but she needed Sawyer more. At one time she would've let Sawyer's choice to shower fill her with doubts: maybe he didn't really want her, maybe he didn't feel this same attraction the way she did.

But she wasn't going to let that happen right now. She had seen the way Sawyer looked at her. He wanted her, too. And the fact that he was gentleman enough not to want to take any sort of advantage of her because she'd had a rough few days? Honestly, that just made her want him more.

Sawyer had almost died tonight in that building. Megan still felt a tightness in her chest when she pictured the moment he realized he couldn't get through that window.

So, yes, Megan could admit she was exhausted and definitely wasn't used to the level of…excitement the past few days had provided. But she wasn't going to waste any more time with Sawyer.

Sleep could damn well wait. She wanted him now.

Megan had never been particularly forward in her love life, but she wasn't going to let that stop her now, either. She climbed out of bed, pulled his shirt over her head and dropped it. Then walked into the bathroom.

She paused for just a moment, then slid the shower curtain open. Sawyer was facing the showerhead, facedown, arms braced on the wall in front of him. Megan's breath hitched as she watched as the water poured down his muscled back—and beyond.

Finally she reached out and touched him gently on his back, but then snatched her hand away. The water was so cold.

At her touch he turned sharply to look at her. She hadn't meant to startle him.

"Sawyer, I didn't mean to use up all the hot water. I'm so sorry." Megan was distressed at the thought that he'd had to take a cold shower because of her inconsideration.

But Sawyer gave her that half smile that made her insides melt. He reached out with one arm and put her hand on his chest, using his other hand to fiddle with the water controls. Immediately hotter water began pouring down his body and her hand.

"Cold shower by choice," Sawyer said to her, his voice husky. "It was the only way I was going to be able to get into that bed next to you, knowing you weren't wearing anything but my T-shirt."

He looked down her naked body, one eyebrow raised. "Although you seem to have misplaced that."

Megan laughed softly as Sawyer turned off the shower. "I did. I can be pretty absentminded sometimes."

"Fortunately for you I have a particular soft spot for absentminded scientists who end up naked in my bathroom."

Megan walked the few steps to take a clean towel from the rack. "That happens a lot to you, does it?"

"All the time. But usually they're old, gray-haired guys and I tell them to go put their clothes back on."

Megan laughed, but it faded quickly as Sawyer stepped out of the shower, gloriously unconcerned about his nakedness. Megan still had the towel clutched in her hands. She thought about handing it to Sawyer, but instead opened it and took the few steps that separated them. She began drying his chest.

"Megan, I just want you to be sure about this," Sawyer whispered, his face only a few inches from hers as she slowly rubbed the towel across his chest and stomach. "Just because we're here together doesn't mean this has to happen."

"I know." Megan nodded, unable to take her eyes away from his body.

Sawyer reached down and put a finger under Megan's chin so she was forced to look in his eyes. "Are you sure?"

"I don't know that I've ever been so sure of anything." She meant it.

Sawyer snatched the towel out of her hands and quickly dried his back and legs, but didn't do a very good job of it.

"I think you're still pretty wet," Megan whispered huskily, watching him.

"I don't care." Sawyer echoed his words from earlier.

He threw the towel to the ground and pulled her to him. They both let out a sigh as their naked bodies touched each other. Finally.

"Damn, you're beautiful." Sawyer muttered.

Megan reached up and wound her arms around Sawyer's neck, pulling his lips down to hers for a kiss. She couldn't be without him for one more second. This time she was the aggressor, her tongue invading his mouth, teasing him.

Sawyer moaned. He reached down and grabbed her by the back of the thighs and hiked her legs around his waist, wrapping his arms under her hips. Megan snaked her arms more securely around his neck. They both moaned as the contact brought her breasts against his chest.

Sawyer walked—Megan draped around him—to the bed, their mouths never separating from their kiss. Then

Megan lost herself in the passion as Sawyer laid her down on the bed and reminded them both of why they were so lucky to be alive.

## Chapter Nineteen

The next morning Sawyer stretched out in the bed. Alone. That wasn't how he really wanted it, but he could see Megan through the door of the adjoining room already hard at work on the countermeasure. She was humming as she moved back and forth around the table he had pulled to the middle of the room. Sawyer smiled. Humming had to be a good sign.

It was all he could do to keep from humming himself. Last night had been nothing short of incredible. When Megan had shown up in that bathroom, all of Sawyer's good intentions about letting her rest had completely flown out the window.

And thank heavens for that.

Sawyer was no monk. He'd certainly enjoyed the company of women throughout the years, although not nearly as many as his confirmed-bachelor reputation might suggest. But there was something about that tiny scientist with her giant brain—it had been reinstated from huge back to giant, since she had the good sense to come back into the shower last night—working so steadily in the next room that had Sawyer feeling things he never had before.

Which scared the hell out of him and felt absolutely perfect at the same time.

Sawyer threw the covers off, since he was so warm. The

heater in Megan's workroom must've been on full blast. Of course, she was keeping it that warm so she could work in just his T-shirt.

And that thought—despite the fact that she hadn't been out of his arms all night long, and that neither of them had gotten much sleep—almost had him in the workroom dragging her back to the bed.

But Sawyer knew Megan needed to work. What she was doing now was more important than Sawyer's personal desires.

But he was still tempted. Even knowing she would immediately delve into phrases like *symmetric ciphers* and *source codes* and a bunch of other stuff he didn't understand. Sawyer shook his head, grinning.

Sawyer swung his legs over the side of the bed and got up. He put on his clothes, then made coffee and ate a breakfast of fruit and cereal from the groceries Evan had left. He knew how Megan took her coffee after all these days of working with her, and brought it, along with some food, to the other room. She didn't even look up when he walked through the door.

He set the coffee cup on the table next to her and stood there. Still nothing. It was almost a blow to his ego until he realized she wasn't ignoring him. There could probably be a nuclear holocaust around her and she wouldn't notice.

"Hi," he finally said. Nothing. Her glasses were perched on her nose; she was holding some sort of hand scanner over a circuit board with one arm and typing one-handed into a keyboard with the other. Still humming.

Sawyer finally reached down and cupped her chin, forcing her to look up toward him. He could actually see the exact moment she recognized it was him touching her. Annoyance in her brown eyes melted away to something much more soft. And beautiful.

"Hi," Sawyer said again. "I brought you some coffee and breakfast."

"Thanks," she murmured, taking her glasses off. "I was working."

"I noticed." Sawyer reached down and kissed her. "I don't want to interrupt you, but I wanted to make sure you had something eat."

"Yeah, I sometimes forget when I'm in the middle of a project."

Sawyer looked around. Items were meticulously laid out all over the mattress, where Megan had torn off all the blankets and sheets. Sawyer had no doubt Megan knew the exact location of every item in this room, could find each element blindfolded if she had to.

"You eat this, and get back to it. I'm going to check in with Juliet." He bent down and kissed her, but pulled away before temptation to deepen the kiss could overwhelm either of them. "Nice work outfit by the way. You should try wearing that to the office sometime."

Sawyer laughed as color flooded Megan's cheeks. He kissed the top of her head, then walked into the other room, still chuckling.

Sawyer found one of the cheap no-plan mobile phones he and Megan had bought at the supercenter the day before. Since Sawyer's regular phone had disintegrated along with everything else in the explosion yesterday, he needed something that could keep him in basic communication with Juliet and Evan. He'd gotten a phone for him and one for Megan.

Sawyer dialed a prearranged number. It was neither Juliet's nor Evan's cell phones, just in case someone was listening in on their ends.

"Damn it, Sawyer, you should've checked in last night." Sawyer rolled his eyes at the lack of traditional greeting from his sister.

"I sent the text saying we were out."

"A one-word text lets me know you're alive and is completely acceptable under many circumstances. But you've now been at that motel for more than eight hours."

"Aw, c'mon, Jules—"

"If I pulled something like that, you'd throw a fit. You know it. So don't try your charming act on me."

His sister was right. If she had checked in with only one word, Sawyer would've been worried. But that was because of what happened to her the last time she was in the field. Sawyer didn't want to bring that up.

"You're right, sis. I'm sorry. I should've provided an update once we were secure in the motel."

"Fine. Don't do it again."

"So what's happening at Omega? Anything suspicious?"

"Sawyer, it's the craziest thing. I'm filtering through every system I can, trying to see who might be logging in any suspicious activity. But I'm not finding anything."

"What about me reporting in, then the building blowing up? Does everyone believe I'm dead?"

"Well, that's the thing. When I looked up the handler's computer file for your case, the *original* safe-house location was back in the system. And the last transmission logged is from you, notification that you had made it to the safe house and were planning to stay there for the next few days."

"That's what I said. But I was referring to the second safe house, the one that is now mostly a pile of ash."

"I know. But according to the log-in report, there was never a second safe house mentioned."

"So if our bodies had shown up dead at the second safe house?"

"Nobody at Omega would've had any idea how you got there." They both paused. "It gets worse, Sawyer."

Sawyer rubbed a hand over his face. "Great."

"I've only got reasonable computer-hacking skills, and

whoever is changing all this in the Omega system is way out of my league."

"Does that mean the mole is some computer nerd within Omega?"

"I think it might not be a mole inside Omega at all, Sawyer."

"What?" Sawyer definitely wasn't expecting that.

"Based on how the IP addresses are being bounced around and log-ins are being used, I think it may be someone *outside* Omega completely. Someone hacking a limited part of our system."

"Why would someone just hack a limited part of the system?"

"Anything going too deep would set off all sorts of alarms and red flags. But just getting in, making some small changes and getting back out? If I hadn't been specifically looking for it, I never would've seen it."

"Damn it, Jules. What the hell does this mean?"

There was a pause on the other end. "Sawyer, I have to ask you some questions about Megan. Questions you might not like. Can she hear you?"

Sawyer looked into the other room, where Megan was once again bent over the desk hard at work on the countermeasure.

"She's working in the adjoining room. Not listening to me at all."

"No offense, Sawyer, but are you sure? She's *Dr.* Zane Megan Fuller. Two degrees from MIT. Her IQ is twice ours. Is it possible that she's doing one thing, but also aware of your conversation?"

Sawyer shook his head. He did not like the direction this conversation was going. Especially not after last night. "Just hang on a second," he told Juliet.

Sawyer walked over to the doorway between the two

rooms. He noticed that Megan still hadn't eaten her breakfast, although the coffee was already finished.

"Hey, I'm going to close this door. I'm talking with Juliet and don't want to disturb you."

Megan held up a hand in acknowledgment, but didn't look up from what she was doing or actually respond. But honestly, Sawyer hadn't expected her to. He closed the door between them, grabbed the phone from the bed, then walked into the bathroom and shut that door for good measure.

"All right, Juliet, now I'm sure Megan can't hear me. What the hell are you trying to imply?"

"Look, all I'm asking is for you to keep an open mind."

"Spit it out, Jules."

"I know what changes have been made to the system, so I know what I'm looking for. Some of the suspicious changes are coming from an untraceable IP address, which is to be expected."

"But?" Sawyer prompted.

"But some of the changes are coming from *your* Omega log-in ID, Sawyer, from *your* phone. For anyone who searches deep enough, it looks like you are the one who made the changes in the system."

"But I didn't do anything like that. I'm not even sure I would know how to."

"I know that, baby brother. But there has been someone with you this whole time who very definitely does know how to."

*Megan.*

"It's not her, Jules. I'm positive about that. It's someone else—whoever the mole is at Cyberdyne."

"I know you don't want to believe it, Sawyer, and I don't blame you. But the last change in the system, erasing the second safe house and reentering the first? That came from your phone's log-in ID. *After* you and Megan had broken out of Cyberdyne."

Sawyer muttered a foul expletive under his breath. It was one thing for his phone to be used while they were still at Cyberdyne. Sawyer didn't want to think it had been taken from him without his knowledge, but it was possible.

But since they'd left Cyberdyne? No one had been in possession of his phone except him. Although Sawyer had to admit there had been minutes where Megan would've had unrestricted access, also. And if the Omega system changes had come from his phone...

Sawyer slammed a fist against the wall. Damn it, had Megan been completely fooling him this entire time? Had last night just been part of the plan to get closer to him?

If so, she'd certainly done that.

"Sawyer..." It was Juliet. Sawyer had completely forgotten he was on the line with her.

"I'll call you back." He hung up without saying anything further.

Sawyer walked out of the bathroom and opened the adjoining door to the rooms and stood in the doorway. As usual, Megan didn't even look up from where she was working and paid no attention to Sawyer whatsoever.

Sawyer tried to relax the tension flowing through his jaw and shoulders. Megan wasn't doing anything suspicious. The opposite, in fact. Hard at work—as she had been for hours—on what he had asked her to do: finish the countermeasure.

As she leaned over the table to reach for something she needed, Sawyer watched as the hem of his T-shirt slid up, giving him a tantalizing glimpse of her upper thigh and the rounded curve of her buttock.

His body instantly responded, memories of last night flooding through him. Evidently his body didn't care if Megan was guilty or not. But damn it, Sawyer refused to believe she was guilty. The hours he had spent with her had shown him who she was. She was brilliant, quirky and often awkward. But she was also kind and patient when others couldn't keep up with what she was saying—which was a lot of the time.

Sawyer had seen her face when her apartment had been robbed and last night when she was so exhausted she didn't even know where she was—nobody outside Broadway was that good of an actress.

And damn it, she came back for him last night in that building. There was no way she could've known how close that bomb was to detonating. Not to mention, if her entire MO had been to kill him, then that would've been the easiest place to do it.

No, his gut—and he'd been trusting it too long to stop now—told him Megan was innocent. Whatever the circumstances were regarding the hacks at Omega, Megan wasn't the one doing it. There had to be some other explanation.

Sawyer couldn't be without her a second longer. He strode over to the table, took what was in her hand and laid it down as gently as he could. He scooped her off her feet, noticing the surprised look on her face as he kissed her almost brutally. He carried her into the bedroom, removing clothes from both of them as he went.

His lovemaking, unlike last night, was unceremonious and almost desperate. Sawyer used it as a weapon to cut away at the accusation that Megan was the traitor.

Because that would mean Sawyer had already lost her forever. A panic unlike any he'd ever known crawled through his gut at the thought. Sawyer pushed those overwhelming feelings away and concentrated on losing himself inside the sweet softness of Megan.

# Chapter Twenty

Megan lay sprawled on the bed, unable to will any of her muscles to move. What exactly had that been about? She would've thought that after last night they had gotten all of that lovemaking stuff out of their system.

Evidently not.

But this had been something different. And while Megan had enjoyed every second of it, it was almost as though it had been tinged with desperation. And of all the adjectives she'd use to describe Sawyer—sexy, charming, personable—*desperate* did not make it anywhere on that list.

"This sort of behavior," Megan said, waving her arm around at the bed from where she lay on the pillow next to Sawyer, "is not helping me get the countermeasure completed."

Megan expected some lighthearted or even sarcastic remark from Sawyer. But instead he rolled over so he was lying completely on top of her, face just inches from hers, his weight propped on his elbows.

"You are trying your best to complete the counter-measure, right, Megan?"

Megan wasn't really sure what he meant by the question. Was he making some sort of joke she didn't understand? She wasn't particularly skilled at bedroom talk. "Well, not right at this second I'm not." She smiled at Sawyer, but it faded as he continued to just stare at her intensely.

"Sawyer, what's going on?"

Megan could see Sawyer clench and unclench his jaw, and he seemed to struggle for words. She reached her hands up from between them and cupped his cheeks. "Just tell me. Has something else bad happened?"

Megan didn't think there was anything bad left to happen.

Sawyer still hesitated. "Megan," he finally said. "I need you to be totally honest with me. I will do everything I can to help you, but you've got to be honest with me."

Megan had no idea what he was talking about. "Honest about what?"

"Since we left Cyberdyne, and even before, have you used my phone?"

"The one that you left in the safe house that blew up?"

"Yes? Did you use it at all?"

"No." Megan frowned. His questions did not clarify the matter at all. "I had my own phone. Why would I use yours? Plus we thought someone might be using yours to spy on us. Double reason not to use it."

Sawyer's brows were furrowed together. "For texts, Megan? To send any information? To log in to any systems that my phone would have access to?"

And there it was, the real question he had wanted to ask. *Had she used his phone to log in somewhere she shouldn't have been?*

Megan had always considered her intellect a blessing and a privilege. Her ability to look at random pieces of a problem—even with some pieces missing—and figure out how they worked together as a whole was her gift.

But she very much wished she didn't have that ability right now. She was able to understand what Sawyer was hinting at without him having to say the words outright.

Sawyer thought she was the traitor. That she had used his phone to access Omega's system and plant false info.

"Get off me. Right now." Megan said it softly, slowly.

"Meg—"

"Right now!" This time her voice was much louder, barely lower than a yell.

Sawyer rolled to the side and Megan flew off the bed, bringing the sheet with her and wrapping it around herself.

"You think *I'm* the traitor?" Megan whispered, backing away from the bed.

"Megan—"

"And you just did *that*—" she gestured to the bed "—with me, thinking I was a traitor?"

"No." Sawyer shook his head, sliding toward her. Megan took a step back. If he touched her now she would shatter into a million pieces. "No, I knew you weren't. Megan, I knew you weren't. That's why I made love with you again."

Megan just clutched the sheet tighter to herself. "Then why would you ask me those questions, Sawyer?"

Sawyer reached over and pulled on his jeans. He sat on the edge of the bed and put his head in his hands. Megan felt as if cold was permeating her entire body.

"Megan, Juliet told me that there's not a mole inside Omega at all. The system has been hacked and that's how the information was given to me about the false safe house. And it looks like my phone has been used to access info in the Omega system since you and I broke out of Cyberdyne."

"And you and I were the only ones to have access to your phone during that time." Megan whispered the obvious statement.

"Yes." Sawyer looked up from his hands and stood up. Megan took another step backward.

"But even when Juliet told me that," Sawyer continued, "I knew it wasn't you. I knew there had to be something else. Some other way my phone was being used."

"Then why ask me that, Sawyer? Why?" Her voice broke on the last word.

"Megan, you're so much smarter than me. Than all of us. If you had done something stupid, or under duress, or because you were scared, I just wanted to give you the chance to tell me. To let you know that I would help you, protect you in any way I could."

The tears Megan couldn't keep back finally fell. He hadn't really believed she was innocent. He had made love to her thinking she was a liar and a traitor.

"Megan." Sawyer took another step toward her, but stopped when she held out an arm in front of her. "I handled it wrong. I'm sorry. I should've told you what Juliet said about the phone and together we would have figured out how it could've happened and what it all meant."

Megan nodded, but didn't say anything. Yes, that was how he should've handled it.

She needed to be away from him. She felt as if her heart was breaking, which was silly because they'd only spent one night together. But she needed to be alone where she wouldn't feel so exposed and vulnerable.

Megan knew she really couldn't blame Sawyer for reacting to the news about the phone hack like a cop. That was what he was. The same way she tended to overanalyze everything because she was a scientist. That was what she was.

But right now she was simply a woman who had been accused of something terrible by the man she had just given herself to so completely mere hours—*minutes*—before.

So, yes, her brain could understand Sawyer's questions and his need for them. But her heart was having a much more difficult time.

SAWYER WOULD GIVE everything he owned to never see that look on Megan's face again. She had been so strong through everything—harm to her body, seeing her posses-sions destroyed, losing her job—and now Sawyer's heart broke as he watched the tears flood out of her eyes and onto her cheeks. She looked at him as if he had just killed something precious.

And Sawyer was desperately afraid he had.

"I'm going to get dressed and get back to work," Megan whispered.

"Megan—" Sawyer reached for her wanting to do some-thing, *anything*, to take away that look in her eyes.

"No," she told him, taking another step away. "You're law enforcement. I get it. But right now, I just need you not to touch me." She turned and fled into the bathroom. Mo-ments later Sawyer heard the shower running.

Sawyer sat back down on the bed. How had he screwed this up to such a monumental degree? His gut had told him Megan didn't do this. He should've just trusted that and left it alone. Or talked to her about all the possibilities. God knew with her giant brain she could come up with some ideas about what could have happened that he'd never even considered.

Instead he had taken her to bed and then promptly ac-cused her of treason. Just what a woman always wanted.

Sawyer got dressed. He should be thankful Megan hadn't told him to go to hell and stormed out of here re-fusing to finish the countermeasure after the way he had just behaved.

But she didn't. And she was going back to work on it. Because that was just the type of person she was.

Sawyer grimaced. He had to make this right with her. But damned if he knew how.

He decided to call Juliet back while Megan was in the shower.

"As of right now, we work based on the assumption that Megan Fuller did not use my phone and log-in ID to make any of the hacks at Omega," Sawyer told Juliet without greeting.

"Sawyer—"

"No, Juliet. She didn't do it. It happened some other way. We have to figure out what that is."

"Okay."

"Okay?" Sawyer hadn't thought it would be that easy to convince his sister.

"Sawyer, you're there with her. I'm not. If you say you know she didn't do it, then I believe you. I'll start running other possibilities."

"Thanks, Jules."

"I'll take care of things on this end. You guys just get the countermeasure finished."

"We will."

"And, Sawyer, you two be careful. There are still too many unknowns in this situation for my peace of mind."

Megan was coming out of the shower as Sawyer hung up with Juliet. She was wrapped in a towel.

"I need my clothes." Megan grabbed her bag and went back into the bathroom without another word. When she exited a few minutes later, she was fully dressed in her own clothes.

Sawyer guessed she probably wouldn't be wearing just his shirt anytime soon.

"Megan, I'm sorry—"

"Look, Sawyer, like I said, I can't blame you for assuming the worst. That's your job, I guess." She threw the bag down and crossed to the doorway of the other room. "But right now, I don't want to talk about it. I don't know if I'm ever going to want to talk about."

Every word was a dagger to Sawyer's heart. But he couldn't blame her.

"Right now," she continued, "I just want to work. That's what I'm best at and probably what I should stick to." She walked into the other room, turned down the blasting heat and began working.

There were so many things Sawyer wanted to say to Megan, but he didn't allow himself to do so. Because ultimately she was right: their personal problems were secondary to getting the countermeasure finished. That had to take priority.

Sawyer hoped he would have a chance to apologize—and that she would listen—once the mission was completed.

# *Chapter Twenty-One*

Sawyer watched Megan work tirelessly for the next day and a half. She ate only when Sawyer reminded her to, and slept only once, at her desk. Sawyer tried to carry her to the bed when she slept, but she immediately awoke and wanted to get back to work.

She didn't talk to him at all, except to politely thank him for any food or assistance he brought her. She just worked. And worked and worked.

Her ability to concentrate and figure out all the complex parts of the countermeasure would've been quite impressive to Sawyer if he could get over the heavy feeling in the pit of his stomach. He had screwed up so badly. The more he thought about it, the more he realized how much he had hurt Megan by his accusation. Especially the timing of it.

If he could reach his own ass, he would kick it. Multiple times.

There was nothing he could do now but not interrupt her and allow her to finish the countermeasure. Then he'd get it to Omega and spend however long it took to make Megan accept his apology. But until then all he could do was sit here and wish he had handled the whole situation better. Him, the person Omega sent in when they needed someone with finesse with people. Well, finesse had been nowhere to be seen this time.

Sawyer stood up from the table where he'd sat for the past few hours. It was dinnertime and he was tired of eating microwaved junk. They needed some real, fresh food. And Sawyer needed a chance to get out of this room where he was constantly surrounded by his mistakes. Not to mention Sawyer wanted to call Juliet again—totally out of Megan's earshot—to see if any progress had been made.

Sawyer walked into the other room, where Megan worked. He could see exhaustion in her features and marveled at how she just pushed it aside. He walked over to stand behind her and gently began rubbing her shoulders.

For just a moment Megan sighed and relaxed into his hands. She tilted her head so her cheek rested against one of his hands that massaged her. But then Sawyer felt awareness—and tension—creep back into her form. Soon she was totally stiff, so Sawyer stopped and removed his hands.

"Thank you," she said in that polite tone he was coming to detest.

"How are things going here? Is there anything I can do to help?" Sawyer had made the offer more than once over the past few hours. He maybe didn't have a giant brain, but he had a pretty steady pair of hands.

"I'm close, Sawyer. Just a couple more hours, I think. But fatigue is pulling at me. Making me slower."

"Why don't you lie down for a few minutes?" He saw Megan's panicked glance at the bed and sighed. "Not with me. I'm going out to get us some fresh food. You can rest, refresh your brain, for just a few minutes while I'm gone."

Megan rubbed a weary hand over her face, removing her glasses. "That's probably a good idea."

Sawyer walked with her over to the bed. She lay down and he pulled the covers over her. He got the second phone they had picked up at the store and placed it on the nightstand next to her.

"If you need anything, use this phone, not the motel phone. Speed dial one is my phone, two is my sister, Juliet. But I should be back in just a few minutes. I'll leave you the car in case you need it."

Megan nodded, her big brown eyes looking up at him. Sawyer couldn't help it—he had to touch her. He brushed some of Megan's unruly hair out of her face. She didn't flinch away. That was at least a start.

He reached down and kissed her, but pulled back before either of them had to choose whether to really engage in the kiss or not. But she didn't turn away from him. Another start.

"Sawyer..." Megan whispered hesitantly.

Sawyer wasn't sure if she was going to say something good or bad. Either way it didn't need to be said now.

"Sleep," he told her. "We can talk later."

She brought her hand out from under the covers and grabbed his as he was standing. "Be careful. Hurry back."

Sawyer nodded and Megan let his hand go, snuggling herself back into the blankets. Sawyer wished he could be the one there keeping her warm. But at least she was talking to him. It was a start.

SAWYER WAS WALKING back from the deli where he'd bought sandwiches and salads thirty minutes later when he realized he was being followed. He'd almost missed it, but someone had turned a little too sharply away from Sawyer when he'd left the deli. That small movement had caught his attention.

Sawyer kept walking, at a faster-than-casual pace. But he had circled around so he was leading them away from the motel. Sawyer glanced around as he walked. As far as he could tell, there were three people following him. Make that four.

Sawyer didn't know how DS-13 had found them—something he'd missed at the safe house?—but at this moment he didn't care. The most important thing right now was to keep them away from Megan. Obviously, DS-13 didn't know about the motel or they would've been there already.

Sawyer tried cutting down a different road, speeding up as he turned a corner, attempting to lose his followers. But with four of them there wasn't much use. Realizing Sawyer knew they were following him, and therefore wasn't unwittingly going to lead them to Megan and the countermeasure, they had dropped all pretense of secrecy.

Now they just wanted to capture Sawyer.

Sawyer ducked inside a small restaurant, a mom-and-pop place busy with Asheville locals coming out for a meal. Sawyer scanned the room as he walked seemingly casually through the restaurant. An older couple, just removing their jackets and sitting down at a table, provided him with what he was looking for.

Sawyer set the deli bags down on a recently vacated table and grabbed a glass of water. He made his way toward the older couple. As he neared them, he tripped, spilling the water on their table.

"Oh my goodness, I'm so sorry," Sawyer gushed to them. "I'm so clumsy." He grabbed paper napkins from the dispenser on the table and began wiping up the mess.

"It's only water, young man," the older woman told him. "Don't you worry about it."

Sawyer slid closer to the man and continued to mop up the water. "It's my first day working here. Why don't you move to this table right over here and I'll get this table cleaned up?"

Sawyer removed the couple's jackets from their chairs—slipping the man's car keys out of the pocket while he did so—and moved them to a new table. He apologized for the spill again and then quickly made his way toward the back of the restaurant.

Reaching the couple's car would be his best chance to

get away from the DS-13 men following him. There was no way Sawyer could escape them on foot.

Sawyer went out the back kitchen door, ignoring startled looks from employees, and circled back to the parking lot. He pushed the lock button on the vehicle's keyless-entry remote, knowing the sound would draw attention, but it was the only way to know which car was the couple's.

He heard the honk and made his way toward the area, ducking between other cars as he saw two of the DS-13 men come out the kitchen door of the restaurant. Sawyer had no idea where the other two men were, but they were around here somewhere.

This was going to be close.

Sawyer beeped the horn again. There. A silver Toyota just a few yards away. Perfect. Sawyer made a dash for it, looking over his shoulder. The two by the back door saw him and were running, but as long as they were planning to take him alive, they would be too far away to catch him.

Sawyer unlocked the car as he ran to it. He threw the driver's side door open and dived in, glancing out the passenger side at the two men running toward him. Sawyer was starting the ignition and attempting to lock the door when the driver's side door opened and a gun was pressed to his temple.

"I'm going to need you to step out of your car, Agent Branson."

Damn it, the other two men had circled around the other way. Sawyer hadn't seen them, but they had obviously seen him. And now they had him. Sawyer turned off the car.

"Slowly," the man with the gun told Sawyer. "And just in case you're thinking of making any big scene, we will kill any bystander who comes over here to see what is going on."

Sawyer stepped out of the car and got a good look at the assailant. This was the same hooded guy who had broken into Megan's apartment and put a knife to her throat and sliced Sawyer's arm.

"You look a little more proper without the hoodie," Sawyer told the man as Hoodie reached over and pulled Sawyer's sidearm out of the holster inside his jacket.

Hoodie nodded and smirked at him. "How's the arm?"

Sawyer walked, flanked by the four men, farther back behind the restaurant, down an alley near a Dumpster. He didn't make any attempt to get away. Sawyer couldn't risk it; he had to take them at their word that they would kill bystanders.

As soon as they were out of direct vision of other people, they stopped. Two of the men grabbed Sawyer by each arm in case he was inclined to run.

"We're going to need you to tell us where Dr. Fuller and the stuff she took from Cyberdyne are," Hoodie, obviously the leader of this group by the way they kept looking to him for instruction, said.

"She took the stuff and split, man. I haven't seen her in days." Sawyer gave him a friendly grin.

Hoodie nodded to one of the other men holding Sawyer's arm. Before Sawyer could even brace for it, he punched Sawyer in the gut.

Sawyer doubled over, coughing, only part of it for show. But the longer he could stretch things out here, the safer Megan would be.

"Want to try that again, Agent Branson? We know you made it out of the safe house with her, but then we lost you. Where is she?"

"Look, take it easy. I'm not trying to piss you off, but she's gone, man. Once we figured out the safe house was a trap, the FBI took her into protective custody." Sawyer damn well wished that really *was* what had happened right now.

"You better hope that's not the case, Agent Branson, or

you won't be much use to my boss. That probably won't bode well for you."

Sawyer would take his chances with the DS-13 boss. He shrugged. "It is what it is, man. She's gone."

That got him another punch, this time in the face. Sawyer spit out blood from where his cheek had ground into his teeth.

"Then why are you still here, smart guy? Where is Dr. Fuller?" Another punch in the face.

Sawyer was momentarily saved when Hoodie received a phone call. He turned away—obviously to speak to someone important. Sawyer knew this would be his only chance. If he didn't get out now, torture and death at the hands of DS-13 most certainly would be his fate.

Not to mention leaving Megan unprotected and exposed.

Sawyer kept his body slumped over for a moment—not difficult considering the punches he'd already taken. But then he burst forward into action, jerking the gun away from one of the men holding him. Elbowing the other man, the one who had hit him, in the jaw on the way to standing fully upright was Sawyer's pleasure.

Their skirmish drew the attention of the fourth man, the lookout a few feet away. He rushed over, giving Sawyer three men to deal with. Sawyer punched the first man in the jaw, then sent him flying with a kick. But the other two were already on him. One grabbed Sawyer in a bear hug, forcing Sawyer to head-butt him to get free. Sawyer heard the man howl in pain and figured he'd just broken his nose.

Sawyer turned to face the third man. He didn't want to waste time fighting him, just wanted to get past him so he could escape while the other two were still on the ground and the leader was occupied on the phone.

But then everything turned gray as a blow came to the back of his head. Sawyer fought to hold on to consciousness as he fell to his knees. "My men are idiots, Agent Branson."

The leader was bouncing his pistol casually in his hand—obviously what he had just used to hit Sawyer with. "I'd like to get rid of you right now, but evidently we're going to need your cooperation to get Dr. Fuller and the counter-measure she's working on."

Then he punched Sawyer in the jaw, and holding on to consciousness wasn't an option.

# Chapter Twenty-Two

Sawyer woke up tied to a chair. Without giving away that he was conscious, he tried to take stock of the situation. Six men in the room, four he recognized from the alley. One behind him that he couldn't really see. But the last one…

Fred McNeil. The crooked FBI agent. The one who had given DS-13 Ghost Shell in the first place and had almost killed his brother a few weeks ago. And based on listening to their conversations for a few minutes, it looked as though McNeil was in charge.

The building itself seemed to be some sort of trailer. Glancing as inconspicuously as possible out the window, it looked as if they were in a junkyard. That did not bode well. Too many places where a body could be dumped and never found.

Sawyer had no idea how long he'd been out or how far they were from the motel.

"Looks like Sleeping Beauty is finally waking up." It was McNeil. "Agent Branson, we haven't had the pleasure of meeting, although I did meet your brother."

"Yeah, McNeil. I know who you are." Sawyer had to spit some blood out of his mouth so he could continue. "I can't say it's a pleasure, though."

McNeil chuckled in a way that made Sawyer's skin crawl. "You look like your brother. Cam Cameron. God,

I should've known something wasn't right when they told me that was his name. No real person would have a name like Cam Cameron. It had to be someone working under-cover." McNeil shook his head. "Your brother certainly took down a large chunk of DS-13. And cost me a lot of money."

"Cameron's been a problem child since birth." Sawyer shifted in the chair, testing the bonds on his wrists tied be-hind him. Unfortunately, there wasn't any give in the thin cords. "I'd be happy to deliver him to you if you want to let me go."

McNeil came over and stood right in front of Sawyer. "Tempting, but I think not. You all actually did me a favor when you got rid of Mr. Smith. One less person taking a chunk of the money."

Somehow Sawyer didn't think the former head of DS-13 would agree, but didn't mention it.

"But you also took Ghost Shell. Frustrating." McNeil sighed dramatically. "But at least I had the other Ghost Shell version, although it wasn't quite as operational. Fortu-nately, we got someone to help us overcome that problem."

"Oh yeah, who's that?"

"I wanted the best to help us, and believe me, I scoped out Dr. Fuller for that role. But she wasn't interested. Cold fish, that one."

Sawyer barely refrained from smirking. He thought of his night spent with Megan. To call her a cold fish was ri-diculous. She just had the good sense not to get involved with the likes of Fred McNeil. Sawyer shrugged. No point antagonizing someone who already had you tied to a chair and planned to do you bodily harm. "Women. Whatcha gonna do?"

"See, I already like you better than your brother. So much more reasonable. But I found someone better than Megan, actually months ago when I first was at Cyberdyne. Someone able to complete our version of Ghost Shell and who has excellent hacking skills—with cloned phones." McNeil crouched down in front of Sawyer. "Very helpful for when we needed to know where you were."

There it was, verbal proof that Megan wasn't the traitor.

Sawyer thought he might feel some tiny measure of relief upon hearing the news, convincing that last little part of him of her innocence. But no, in his heart he had already been 100 percent convinced. He didn't need any jackass like McNeil announcing Megan's innocence to know it was true.

"So we got the next best thing. You remember Jonathan Bushman, Dr. Fuller's assistant?"

Bushman stepped up from behind Sawyer. "You." Sawyer all but spat the word. "She trusted you."

Jonathan scoffed, "The esteemed Dr. Fuller didn't trust me. She always thought I wasn't smart enough to work with her on the truly important projects. She's been that way for years. Always wanting to work alone because she thinks she's so ridiculously brilliant."

How could Sawyer have missed the disdain Jonathan had for Megan? Sawyer had been too busy looking for the traitor in the faces of other Cyberdyne employees and missed what was right under his nose.

"It was you, not Trish," Sawyer said.

Bushman rolled his eyes. "Trish was a pawn to divert your attention from me. She doesn't know anything about this. Sorry you were too stupid to figure that out."

Sawyer wished that for just ten seconds his hands could be untied so he could punch Jonathan in his whiny face.

"And now Megan's going to get what's coming to her," Bushman continued. "Because after the stunt she pulled at Cyberdyne, nobody's ever going to hire her in the computer R & D field again. I'll finally get my shot at being director."

Sawyer shook his head. If DS-13 had their way, Megan wouldn't work again in the R & D field because she'd be dead. They weren't going to let her—or Sawyer—out of here alive once they had what they wanted.

"Plus, I'll have a little lucrative work on the side, provided by McNeil," Jonathan continued. "Best of both worlds, and no Megan around to lord her brilliance over all of us."

Sawyer shook his head as Jonathan walked away. If that was what Jonathan really thought of Megan, then he was obviously delusional. Arguing with him wouldn't help.

"So with the help of Mr. Bushman here, we have the new Ghost Shell ready to be sold," McNeil continued. "But unfortunately, word of the countermeasure Dr. Fuller is working on has already leaked out. That news is making Ghost Shell less potentially profitable than I had hoped. So I'm going to need the countermeasure."

"Yeah." Sawyer dragged the word out. "I don't have it."

"I'm aware of that, Branson. But Dr. Fuller does. Where is she?"

"In protective custody, probably somewhere in Virginia. Or maybe Oklahoma."

Sawyer wasn't prepared for the fist that hit him on the jaw. His head flew to the side. He couldn't keep from groaning and had to spit blood again.

McNeil stood up, rubbing his fist. "I hope that's not the case, for your sake." He held out his hand and Hoodie brought over a phone.

Sawyer's phone.

"You really should be more careful with your phones, Agent Branson. First you allowed your Omega phone to be cloned by Jonathan. Then he could access Omega's system—limited access, but enough to do harm. And now you've lost this one."

McNeil came and stood in front of Sawyer again. "Looks like a pretty cheap phone. You probably won't be too sad to lose this one. Only a couple of numbers stored. Let's try them."

Sawyer struggled against the ties that bound him, but could not get loose in any way.

McNeil laughed. "Oh, so now I seem to have your attention. Care to revise your statement about the location of Dr. Fuller?"

"Screw you, McNeil. She's somewhere you're never going to be able to get to her."

"Why don't we test that theory, Branson? Let's give the lovely Dr. Fuller a call, shall we? We'll put it on speaker to make it more fun."

Sawyer watched helplessly as McNeil began to dial the number to Megan's phone.

AFTER SAWYER LEFT, Megan had lain in the bed expecting sleep to overtake her, but it hadn't. She just couldn't get her brain to shut down. Too much thinking about the countermeasure and, if she was honest, about Sawyer.

Megan was still hurt that he would accuse her of being a traitor while lying next to her naked in the bed. But when she thought through the actual conversation they'd had, Megan realized Sawyer had been stretching himself far outside his law-enforcement comfort zone.

He had thought there was a possibility she had gotten herself in trouble and had been offering to help.

Okay, yeah, he'd had terrible timing in the offering of his assistance, but at least he'd been willing to listen to her side of the story, rather than just assume the worst. For a man who fought for justice so unflinchingly, that had to mean something.

So when she really thought about it, Megan realized Sawyer was trying to show he cared.

Megan still wasn't ready to just forgive and forget, but neither was she going to continue to consider it the crime of the century. Sawyer was a man. He'd said something stupid at the wrong time. He wasn't the first or the last man to do so.

Plus, now that Megan was almost finished with the countermeasure, they had only a few days left before Sawyer headed back to Omega Sector headquarters. Megan didn't want to spend that time fighting. She'd have plenty of time to be alone when she was attempting to put her life—in all of its many broken pieces—back together after Sawyer was gone.

And Sawyer would be gone; Megan was sure of that. He was not the serious-commitment type of guy. She had known that going into all of this, so she wasn't going to regret it now.

Megan got out of the bed. Sleep was nowhere to be found, so she may as well keep working. She didn't know how long Sawyer would be gone.

She was so lost in her work a little while later that it took three or four rings for Megan to realize the phone Sawyer had bought for her was ringing. She stood and rushed to the table to get it. It must be Sawyer; he was the only one with the number.

"Good to finally hear from you, stranger." Megan laughed into the phone, hoping her joking tone would help Sawyer know she wasn't so mad anymore.

But silence met her.

"Sawyer?" Megan was much more hesitant. Was he mad at her now?

"Megan, don't listen to them—" Sawyer's words were cut off in a whoosh of breath.

"Sawyer?" What was happening? "Are you all right? Sawyer?" Megan was panicked when he didn't respond.

Then a much louder voice came on the line. "Hello, Dr. Fuller. It's Fred McNeil. Do you remember me?"

Fred McNeil. Yes, Megan definitely remembered him,

and not in any sort of good way. She shuddered just thinking about him. "What do you want?"

"We want you to deliver the countermeasure you've been
working on to us."

"Megan, no—" She heard Sawyer call out again before
his words were cut off, by a blow, Megan was sure. She
flinched.

Megan didn't know what to do. Did she bluff and pretend like she didn't have the countermeasure? Would they
kill Sawyer if she told them that?

Chances were they would kill them both if she just
handed the countermeasure over to them.

"I don't have it anymore." Megan prayed she was saying the right thing. "I handed it over to the FBI. The *real*
FBI this time, McNeil. I can't get it."

"Hmm. That's unfortunate for Agent Branson, Megan.
Let's talk to him about that for a moment."

There was silence for several moments before Megan
heard the sickening crunch of a human bone being broken. She heard Sawyer's deep moan of pain before he silenced himself.

"Sawyer!" Megan sobbed, bile pooling in her stomach.

"Megan, no." Sawyer said it through deep gasps of
breath.

"Now, that's a shame. It looks like Agent Branson's arm
is pretty broken. But don't worry, he still has his other one.
And his legs, and all his fingers and toes. Lots of unbro-
ken bones still left."

Tears poured down Megan's cheeks. What was she supposed to do?

"Fine, McNeil. Just stop, please. I'll bring you the
countermeasure."

"I thought you said the real FBI already has it."

"No, they don't. I have it. I'm in a safe house."

"Megan—" They cut him off again with another blow. Megan couldn't stop the sob that escaped her.

She knew what Sawyer was trying to tell her. McNeil would kill both of them once he had the countermeasure. Sawyer didn't want her to give up her life. But neither was Megan going to allow them to torture Sawyer to death.

"You need to bring me the countermeasure." McNeil provided her with an address just outside Asheville. "Right now."

"Fine, McNeil, but I'm in Charlotte. Omega didn't think the Asheville area was a good place for me to stay after DS-13 blew up the safe house." Megan closed her eyes and prayed this bluff would work. It was the only shot. "It's going to take me a couple of hours to get to you."

"Fine. Two hours. After that, I will break one of Agent Branson's bones per minute."

Megan bit back her sob. "I'll be there."

"And if there is any sign of police or anyone else, I will kill handsome Sawyer here in the most painful way possible."

Megan heard another thud and groan. She thought she might vomit.

"Clock's ticking, Dr. Fuller."

Megan stared at the silent phone in her hand. Her mind kept replaying the sickening crunch of Sawyer's arm breaking.

Megan wasn't sure what to do, but she knew she couldn't do anything alone. Sawyer was right: if she showed up and just turned over the countermeasure, there was nothing to stop McNeil and DS-13 from just killing them outright.

Megan punched the button for the other number stored in her phone: Sawyer's sister, Juliet. But it was a man who answered.

"Sawyer?" the man asked.

"Who is this?" Megan asked. "Where's Juliet?"

"Is this Dr. Fuller? I'm Evan Karcz. We talked briefly on the phone a few days ago. You might remember my foot being firmly planted in my mouth during that conversation."

Yes, Megan did remember Sawyer's friend Evan. "I thought this number was for Juliet."

"She's inside Omega right now, so she had calls from this number forwarded to me. Where's Sawyer?"

Megan felt the sobs bubbling out of her. "They have him."

An ugly expletive burst from Evan. "What? Who?"

"Fred McNeil." Another expletive from Evan upon hearing that news. "Sawyer went out to get us some dinner, but then I got a call from McNeil saying to bring the countermeasure." She gave Evan the address. "I only have two hours."

"Why did they give you that long?"

"I told them I was in Charlotte and couldn't get there before then."

"Smart, Dr. Fuller. You probably just saved Sawyer's life with that bit of quick thinking."

Something tight inside Megan loosened just a little, until she remembered… "Oh, God, Evan, they hurt Sawyer. Broke his arm while I was on the phone with them. Said they would break the rest of his bones—"

"Megan." Evan didn't let her continue. "We're going to get him out."

"How?"

"I'm nearby and you're nearby. McNeil doesn't know that and we're going to use it to our advantage."

"Okay." A plan. Megan knew she needed to focus on a plan in order to keep from panicking. "How?"

"Do you have enough stuff to build something that looks like a fake countermeasure device?"

Megan looked around. She didn't have much. "Maybe. I could probably fool the average person."

"Can you fool McNeil?"

"I think so, yes. But only for a little while."

"Okay, build something quickly, make it seem as legitimate as possible. But, Megan, you need to leave the real countermeasure at the hotel. If something goes wrong, we can't take a chance on McNeil and DS-13 having both Ghost Shell and the countermeasure."

"But—"

"Megan, Sawyer would want it that way. You know that."

Megan sighed. She did know that. But she didn't like it.

"I'm going to get a couple of local law enforcement I know I can trust and head over there. I'm looking up the address McNeil gave you, and it seems like it's a junkyard, which is both good and bad. I will try to get Sawyer out before you even arrive, but if you don't hear from me, go in at the scheduled time."

"And do what?"

"Show them the fake countermeasure. Stall as long as possible. Don't get yourself killed and be ready to run at any moment."

All that sounded a lot easier said than done. "You know I'm not an agent, right, Evan?"

"After all the great things Sawyer's said about you, I have no doubt you'll do fine."

Megan hoped so; all their lives depended on it.

# Chapter Twenty-Three

Despite the cold weather, sweat pooled on Sawyer's fore-head as he sat in the room. Everything in his body hurt, but his broken arm, now retied to the chair, was the worst.

No, knowing Megan was on her way here to face down McNeil and his cronies, and not being able to get out of this damn chair, was the worst.

The sun had set not long ago and Sawyer knew time was running out. He wasn't sure where McNeil and Bushman were, but they weren't in this room. Only one guy, look-ing bored and mad not to be part of the action, stood guard here with Sawyer. Which just served to frustrate Sawyer more. He was one measly guard away from being able to save Megan.

Sawyer knew he had only one option, but it was going to hurt. He took a deep breath and began rocking until he tipped over his chair.

Even landing on his uninjured arm, the pain was excru-ciating, rocketing through his entire body. Sawyer fought to hold on to consciousness.

"What happened? Did you pass out?"

As Sawyer had hoped, the guard came over to see what the commotion was about. Sawyer pretended to be uncon-scious, then kicked out the guard's knees when he was close enough, causing the man to crumple to the floor. Sawyer then spun—gritting his teeth from the agony in his arm—and kicked the guy as hard as he could in the chin. The guard fell back, unmoving. Sawyer scooted around until he was able to grab his gun.

Sawyer used all his strength to shift his weight, cursing violently as he was able to break off part of the chair. His hands weren't completely free, but at least now he was able to move. Sweat poured down his face as Sawyer took unsteady steps toward the door.

He saw the doorknob turn and jumped to the side, hugging the wall. Sawyer couldn't get a good grip on the gun with his functional arm because of the pieces of the chair he was still tied to. He placed the gun in the hand of his broken arm, praying his fingers would work when he needed to pull the trigger.

The door opened too slowly to be a member of DS-13. Sawyer didn't let his guard down, but didn't attack, either. A man he didn't recognize, dressed in black, entered the room, weapon raised. Sawyer put his gun against the man's temple.

"I really don't want to have to kill you. And my fingers may be a little trigger-happy, so you should definitely not make any sudden movements."

"Agent Branson?"

"Who are you?"

"I'm with Agent Evan Karcz. We're here to help get you out."

A voice came from behind the man. "Sawyer, if you're done messing around, there are some bad guys to get rid of."

Sawyer lowered his weapon. Only Evan would say something that asinine.

The other man with Evan moved into the room to secure the unconscious guard. Evan helped Sawyer get loose from the rest of the chair. "Damn, Sawyer. You look like hell."

"Yeah, thanks." Sawyer grimaced as Evan helped him splint his agonizing arm against his chest. Then Sawyer pushed the pain aside. "Evan, talk to me. Is Megan okay? Please tell me she's not coming here."

"I couldn't stop her, man. It was our best possibility of getting you out. By now, she's already here. I had her leave the countermeasure at the motel and piece together a fake. She felt pretty confident that she'd be able to fool McNeil and buy us some time."

Sawyer cursed under his breath. "It's not just McNeil she has to fool. It's her assistant, Jonathan Bushman. He's the mole who has been working for McNeil and DS-13. She won't be able to trick Bushman for long. Where are they?"

"It looked like McNeil and his men are camped near the main fence. It's a good vantage point for them, junk piles on three sides. No easy way in or out. I left one man there covering everything with a rifle, but he won't be able to take out everyone…"

Before Megan got killed. Evan didn't say it, but Sawyer knew it was the truth. If bullets started flying, Megan would be in the middle of it.

Time to change the plan.

"Evan, grab another chair and tie me to it—they won't recognize it's a different one in the dark. And get rid of the guard. McNeil's men will be coming for me. He'll want me down there to keep her in line. They'll have to untie me and won't be expecting me to have a weapon."

"Sawyer, no offense, man, but are you sure you can even fire a weapon right now? You look like you might keel over any second."

"You guys just get over to where Megan is meeting McNeil. I'll make it. Be ready to move, and take out all of McNeil's men, on my signal."

Sawyer tucked the guard's gun into the waistband of his jeans, under his shirt. Then Evan helped take the splint off

Sawyer's arm and tied him back to the chair. Sawyer took deep breaths to try to keep the pain in check.

"Hang in there, man," Evan told him on the way out the door.

"Evan, Megan's the most important thing. She makes it out of here alive, no matter what. You make sure your men know that."

"Roger that." Evan disappeared into the night.

They were almost too late. Just a few minutes later one of McNeil's men—Hoodie, just Sawyer's luck—stormed into the trailer. He looked around for a moment. "Where the hell is Edwards?"

Sawyer didn't respond, so the man walked over and kicked Sawyer's chair, sending pain radiating throughout his body. His moan of pain didn't have to be faked. "Hey, where is Edwards? The guard."

"I don't know." Sawyer mumbled the words.

"That screwup never knows when to stay put." Hoodie was still cursing as he untied Sawyer and began pulling him out of the trailer. Just as Sawyer suspected, the man didn't retie Sawyer's hands and definitely didn't think to check him for weapons. Given how swollen Sawyer's broken arm was, Sawyer didn't blame him.

But that didn't mean Sawyer wouldn't use the underestimation to his advantage.

MEGAN'S HEART POUNDED as if she was running a sprint. She was driving into this junkyard by herself, taking the word of a man she'd never met—just because he was Sawyer's best friend—that he would protect her somehow.

She was bringing in a useless piece of hardware to pass off as a sophisticated anti-encoding hard drive. A technically savvy ten-year-old would be able to see through it in moments.

The real countermeasure was supposed to be back at the

motel, but it wasn't. It was under the passenger seat. The
longer she had waited for Evan's call, the more frantic she
had become. When she couldn't wait any longer, and had
to leave immediately in order to make it to the junkyard
in time, she had made a decision: she would bring the real
countermeasure. If the countermeasure could possibly save
Sawyer's life, then she was damn sure going to have it as an
option. Omega Sector would just have to find some other
way of getting it back.

Megan could feel her heart beating again and wondered
vaguely if she would have a heart attack and all of this
would be for naught anyway. She took some deep breaths
to try to get herself under control.

Evan Karcz had told her to stall if she got to this point
without word from him. Megan tried not to imagine all the
things that could've gone wrong that would've led to him
*not* calling. Those thoughts would just get her pulse up in
the stratosphere again.

Megan pulled up to where Fred McNeil stood, along
with a bunch of his gang, or whatever they were called,
and got out of the car.

*Stall*.

"Dr. Fuller, so nice to see you again," McNeil said.

"Sorry, I can't say the same thing, Mr. McNeil." Megan
looked around. "Where's Sawyer?"

Fred McNeil laughed curtly. "Always so abrupt. He's
coming. Where is the countermeasure?"

"Right here." Megan held up the fake device. "But you
should know that unless I enter a certain code, this device will transmit its blueprints to every law-enforcement
agency in the state. New countermeasures can be made
within a day."

Megan almost scoffed at the size of her own lie, but
managed to refrain.

"She's lying. There's no way it could do that."

Megan's head spun around at the sound. She could not believe what she was hearing. "Jonathan? *You're* the one working for them? Why?"

Jonathan rolled his eyes. "I actually found some people who appreciated my abilities. You certainly never did."

Megan shook her head. "I don't understand. I always appreciated your work."

"Yeah, I could tell that by how you always wanted to work alone. Always thought you were better than everyone else."

"Enough," McNeil called out. "Look, here's Agent Branson joining us right now. A little worse for wear. Sorry about that."

Megan's throat dried up at the sight of Sawyer. His arm—obviously the broken one—was held at a terrible angle against his chest. His face was battered and swollen. Megan couldn't believe he was even able to walk on his own—not that he really was walking; he was almost being dragged by the man with him. The man Megan recognized from the attack at her house.

McNeil grabbed Sawyer and threw him toward Megan. Megan cried out and caught Sawyer the best she could as he stumbled, moaning. He seemed barely conscious. "See? Sawyer is alive. Now give us the countermeasure."

Megan couldn't even figure out how to possibly stall any longer. Evan Karcz better make his move soon.

"Here." Megan held up the fake countermeasure, her other arm around Sawyer. But she knew it wouldn't fool Jonathan, not even for a moment.

"Bushman, check it out."

Jonathan took the drive from Megan, but didn't even make it over to his laptop resting on a car hood. "This isn't it, Mr. McNeil."

"How do you know?"

"I worked on the countermeasure long enough to know this isn't it. She's trying to pass off a fake."

McNeil pulled out a gun and pointed it right at Sawyer. "I sure hope you have something more than that to offer us, Megan. Or a broken bone isn't going to be the worst of Agent Branson's problems today."

"Wait, wait! I have the real one. It's in the car."

She heard Sawyer's curse from his hunched-over form. But Sawyer was already hurt enough; she couldn't let him be shot if there was any way she could stop it. Megan backed up toward the car, her arm still protectively around Sawyer as if she could ward off the gun McNeil was pointing at him.

Megan opened the door of her car and reached under the seat to get the countermeasure. She then held it out to Jonathan. "Here. You know this is it, but you can test it anyway."

"See, now, that wasn't so difficult, was it?" McNeil asked. He put his gun back into his holster and gave his attention to Jonathan.

Megan noticed Sawyer was now standing right in front of her and was pushing her back toward the car, since the door was open.

"Get in and stay down," Sawyer whispered to her.

"What?" Megan said to him just as softly. Had she heard him right? How was Sawyer even capable of talking at all?

"Just do it, baby. Now!"

Megan dived into the car and Sawyer shut the door. She watched as Sawyer straightened and pulled a gun from the waistband of his jeans. None of McNeil's men were expecting such an abrupt, strong move from the man who had been barely conscious just a few moments before.

Especially not McNeil. Sawyer was able to get a shot off at McNeil first, who died with a surprised look on his face without even getting his gun back out.

Sawyer emptied the entire clip of his weapon, trying

to clear out anybody who might fire in their direction. He got help from somewhere up in the mountains of junk. Megan couldn't see them, but Evan and his men were covering Sawyer.

It didn't take long. In less than a minute all of McNeil's men were either dead or wounded. Nobody had suspected Sawyer capable of the move he had made.

Heck, Megan had been standing right next to him and hadn't expected him to be capable of that. She opened the car door and scrambled out and over to Sawyer. She wanted to put her arms around him, but there didn't seem to be anywhere on his body that wasn't injured.

"Sawyer, oh my gosh, are you okay? I thought you were nearly dead."

Sawyer crumpled down onto his knees. Megan looked down at his shoulder and realized blood was pouring from a wound.

Sawyer had been shot.

Megan grabbed Sawyer in her arms and helped him lie down on the ground, putting pressure on the wound to stop the bleeding. Sawyer was unconscious and losing blood fast.

Evan and his men came down from their vantage points at the top of the junk heaps. They checked the status of the DS-13 men. Most of them were dead; they secured any who weren't. Jonathan Bushman, who had hidden by a car when the bullets started flying, was led away in handcuffs by one of Evan's men, an unbelieving look on his face. Megan barely spared him a glance. He deserved whatever he had coming to him.

"Evan, we need an ambulance here. Right now!" Megan held Sawyer's head in one hand and kept pressure on the bleeding wound with the other. Sawyer wasn't stirring at all now and his color was a sickly gray.

An ambulance, this far out of town, would be too late.

Evan scrambled over to them, looking at the damage to Sawyer's body. "Damn it," Evan muttered. "Sawyer, you stay with us," he yelled down at Sawyer's unconscious form.

"An ambulance is not going to get here in time, Evan." Tears rolled down Megan's cheeks.

"We don't have to wait for an ambulance. We have something better coming—thanks to Juliet. Listen, there it is."

At first Megan couldn't hear anything over the panic roaring in her own ears. But then she did: a helicopter.

Megan's terror subsided just the tiniest bit. "Hang in there, sweetheart," she whispered in Sawyer's ear. "I've still got a lot more yelling to do before you go."

# *Chapter Twenty-Four*

It was a tough climb out of the hospital for Sawyer. Even with the helicopter transferring him to the trauma center as fast as possible, he was in critical condition for days. It was not just because of the bullet wound, but the internal injuries and bleeding he'd suffered at the hands of McNeil's men.

Much of the early hospital stay was a blur for Sawyer. He could remember his family being there—his brothers and sister, even his parents. But all he had wanted was Megan. Once he knew she was there with him, he had felt as if he could rest. She was safe, she was next to him, it would all be okay.

When Sawyer had become more coherent, Evan had assured him that *both* copies of Ghost Shell and the countermeasure were safely in Omega's keeping. All of McNeil's men were either arrested, including Jonathan Bushman, or dead. They'd taken another huge chunk out of DS-13 and didn't expect to be having to deal with that crime syndicate group again anytime soon.

Sawyer was glad, but he was more concerned about the situation with Megan. Every time he had awakened those first few days, she had been right beside him. Sometimes holding his hand, sometimes asleep on the chair, but always there.

Surely that meant that she cared, right? That she had forgiven him for his ridiculous words? That she was willing to give their relationship a try?

Because one thing was absolutely clear to Sawyer after what had happened at the junkyard: he could not live without Megan. That tiny little scientist with her giant brain had lodged herself permanently in his heart.

All he needed was a chance to do the same to her heart. Turnabout was fair play.

But the past couple of days in the hospital, Megan hadn't been around. Sawyer had been up, walking, recovering nicely, surrounded by all his loved ones offering their support and encouragement.

All his loved ones except the most important one.

By the end of the third day without Megan, Sawyer was such a bear that his own family had threatened to disown him. The medical staff stayed as far from him as possible, only entering his room when it was necessary and leaving as quickly as possible.

It was Evan who finally addressed the issue.

"Dude, you're starting to make us all wish that bullet had hit you a few inches to the left."

"Where the hell is Megan, Evan?"

"You heard Juliet tell you she'd gotten a new job somewhere outside this area. So my guess is she's busy packing. Getting ready to leave."

If Sawyer could've reached Evan, he would've slugged him for his nonchalant attitude about Megan walking out of Sawyer's life. But Evan had known Sawyer too long and made sure he stayed out of arm's reach.

"Damn it, Evan, she can't leave me, go take another job, meet other people. I love her." Sawyer sounded like a crazy person, even to his own ears.

"Have you let her know that?"

"No. She hasn't been here in three days!"

"Well, I guess you better get to her, then, moron."

So here Sawyer was at Megan's house. Sawyer still wasn't at full speed, and the doctors had some concerns about the possibility of continued internal bleeding. But Sawyer had turned on all the charm, promised extended rest at home and had gotten released from the hospital.

And promptly drove to Megan's house.

Megan was in the process of cleaning up the mess that had been made by DS-13 and packing anything salvageable. To his surprise, Sawyer found his mother and Juliet helping her. When they saw him, his mom and Juliet discreetly made their way outside, giving Sawyer and Megan privacy.

"Hi."

Megan stopped packing the box she was working on at his greeting. "Are you supposed to be out of the hospital?"

"Well, you disappeared, so I got them to release me."

"I'm sorry, I wasn't trying to abandon you. You had your entire family there, and I have so much to do with the packing..." Megan gestured around the room with her arm.

Sawyer, known for keeping a cool head no matter what the circumstances, felt panic bubble up inside him. "No."

"No, what?" Megan's expression seemed genuinely puzzled.

"No, you can't take a new job wherever it is and leave me, and we never see each other again."

Megan looked a little concerned. "Sawyer, are you on medication that makes you loopy? Do you need to sit down or something? You're acting a little strange."

"No, I'm not on any damned medication like that, and I don't need to sit down!" Sawyer fought a losing battle with the panic. She was leaving him, for God's sake. How could she be so calm and collected? Didn't he mean anything to her at all?

Sawyer stormed over and grabbed her by one shoulder with his good hand. "I'm sorry, okay. I'm so sorry I said all that stupid stuff. I never thought you were the traitor, really. Don't leave me, Megan. Please. I love you."

"Sawyer—"

No, he couldn't let her continue. He had to make her give him a chance. "I know we haven't known each other that long, and that saying I love you is crazy. But it's true. I don't want you to move far away. I want us to be where we can see each other." A brilliant idea occurred to Sawyer. "We should get married."

Megan shook her head. "What? Sawyer, stop."

"It's okay. You can take the new job far away. I'll quit Omega and move with you and work at an FBI field office somewhere." The idea seemed brilliant to Sawyer. "Just as long as we can be together."

"Sawyer. Just listen to me—"

Sawyer didn't want to listen. He didn't want to hear all the reasons why Megan thought their relationship wouldn't work. How he had ruined it by not trusting her completely. So Sawyer did the only thing he could think of.

He kissed her.

He expected Megan to pull away, but she didn't. She stepped closer so their bodies were pressed together. Her lips were as hungry for the kiss as his were.

Eventually, Megan eased back from their kiss. Sawyer didn't want to let her go, but knew it had to happen.

"Sawyer—"

Sawyer put his forehead against hers. "Whatever you're about to say, I just want you to know I love you."

"Man, let the woman talk," Juliet said it from the doorway. "If you would shut up for just one minute, I think you might get your happily-ever-after." She grabbed a box and walked with his mom into the kitchen, leaving them alone.

"What the hell is she talking about?"

Megan smiled. "Well, if you'd stop acting like such a

crazy person and listen I would tell you that yes, I took a new job."

"I know. You're moving."

"I took a job at Omega, Sawyer. At the main headquarters, in the cyberterrorism department. I believe that's just a few floors from your office, if I'm not mistaken. I might be asking you to bring *me* coffee." Megan's smile was the most beautiful thing Sawyer had ever seen.

Sawyer wrapped his arm around Megan, pulling her against him, relief almost taking his breath away. She wasn't leaving him. He had all the time he needed to convince her how perfect they were for each other.

"And just so you know," Megan said, peeking up at him from where she was tucked against his chest, "I love you, too, Agent Branson."

Looked as if she didn't need to be convinced, after all. He always knew she had a giant brain.

\* \* \* \* \*

*Look for more books in Janie Crouch's*
OMEGA SECTOR *miniseries later in 2015.*

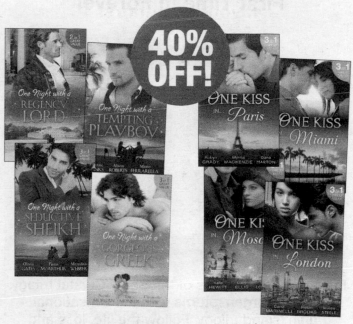

# MILLS & BOON®

## Why not subscribe?
Never miss a title and save money too!

Here's what's available to you if you join the exclusive **Mills & Boon Book Club** today:

- ✦ *Titles up to a month ahead of the shops*
- ✦ *Amazing discounts*
- ✦ *Free P&P*
- ✦ *Earn Bonus Book points that can be redeemed against other titles and gifts*
- ✦ *Choose from monthly or pre-paid plans*

### Still want more?
Well, if you join today we'll even give you
***50% OFF your first parcel!***

So visit **www.millsandboon.co.uk/subs**
**or call Customer Relations on 020 8288 2888**
to be a part of this exclusive Book Club!